Main Liners VI:

Visions

Barbara K. Clement

W & B Publishers
USA

W & B Publishers

For information:
W & B Publishers
9001 Ridge Hill Street
Kernersville, NC 27284

www.a-argusbooks.com

ISBN: 9781635543582

Book Cover designed by Dubya

Printed in the United States of America

Prologue

Philip Rawlins' extraordinary exit from Patricia Granville Barker's residence would have astonished anyone who had witnessed it. Without bothering to close the front door of the 1920s stone Normandy Tudor mansion, he darted into the Porte-Cochère, his leather soled shoes skidding and slipping with each step along the slick Belgian block pavement, until finally he reached the black BMW 8. Its lock clicked at his presence, allowing him to escape inside.

"God," he gasped aloud, using his left hand to wipe a smear of brilliant red color from his lips, while ramming the key-less ignition button with his thumb to start the engine. A dense film of sleet covered the windshield and rear window. He turned the windshield wipers to high and the defroster to maximum. Seconds later, a small jagged patch of ice caught the wiper blade, crashing on to the hood and opening a small sight line for the driver. Philip Rawlins pushed heavily on the accelerator; with tires spinning across the drive, he exited through the estate's massive wrought iron gate, making a fast turn to the left on to Ithan Avenue.

Had he stopped before exiting, he'd have spotted the 15 foot box truck that now hurled itself into the BMW's driver side door, launching the car into a roll that crossed the thoroughfare, missing a Ford Focus by mere feet, then skidding on its roof dangerously close to an ancient Pontiac Firebird, before finally settling on the icy athletic field of the Agnes Irwin School.

Philip Rawlins lay quite still; his body trapped between two pressurized safety air bags. Blood oozed from his nose and mouth. His eyes stared straight ahead.

Chapter 1

It's a fact: traffic congestion on the Schuylkill Expressway any day of the week conjures up visions of driving through circle nine, the lowest level of Hell. This late October afternoon was no exception as Main Liners, working in Philadelphia's Center City headed back to their suburban homes some fifteen miles away. Add to that, an icy sleet that had begun to fall earlier in the day, autumnal darkness and windshield wipers that had seen better days and you have Jessica Rawlins whose patience was close to cracking when she finally arrived in the Warden lobby of Bryn Mawr Hospital and staggered through the corridors to the main elevator bank.

Caroline Rawlins was not only her best friend but her cousin-in-law which is the only reason Jessica would have flown out the door of her office at regional CIA headquarters on Market Street in Philadelphia to respond to Caroline's urgent text message: *"Philip in ER at BM Hospital after car accident. Come quickly!"* The message had been sent almost two hours earlier and now Philip was no longer in ER but somewhere in the hospital undergoing surgery. Bryn Mawr Hospital's lobby receptionist had left the premises hours earlier; ER's volunteer staff knew nothing but read a note on Philip's chart indicating he was in surgery; but where in surgery? Several years earlier, when visiting a patient, Jessica had found an informed volunteer in the Green Room, a waiting area on the third floor, where most surgeries took place. If Philip was still in surgery, the Green Room volunteer probably would know where he was and hopefully that is where she could find Caroline.

Jessica's impatience was noticeable as she pushed the elevator button for the third time.

"That won't make it come any faster, dearie." A pink smocked hospital volunteer scrutinized the sopping woman, a steady stream of water trickling to the floor from her soaked umbrella and raincoat. "Pretty nasty out there tonight, isn't it? Looks like you've had to walk a distance, too. No room in our garage again? Ever since they've started blocking off areas because of the construction, there is never a spot for visitors to park."

She moved closer to Jessica trying to elicit a response. Jessica merely glanced her way and nodded but said nothing. As the elevator doors slid open, three staff members exited.

"What floor you going to?"

"Three," Jessica responded.

"Oh, I'll bet you're here to see about someone in surgery? If you're going to the Green Room to wait, it's closed for the day. The volunteer who sits at the reception desk usually leaves about 5 o'clock. She'll sometime stay a little later; but not to worry, there's another smaller waiting area directly across from the Green Room."

Jessica's attitude softened as a ping announced the elevator's arrival. "Thank you, I'll go there. I'm looking for someone."

"Well, let me show you the way; I'm going in that direction myself. My name is Letty Fox, I'm a volunteer. Usually, I'm assigned to the reception desk in the Warden lobby and leave about 5 p.m. too, but I was asked to stay a little later tonight to help out up here if needed. Apparently, there's been a bad accident over on Ithan Avenue."

Jessica followed Letty through a darkened corridor to a dimly lit room where alone, in a back corner, Caroline waited.

"Oh Jess," she sobbed as Jessica came toward her. "Thank you for coming. He might die, they said. Philip might die! How can this be happening to us?"

"Exactly what did happen?" Jessica placed her umbrella on the floor and picked up a box of tissues from a side table, offering it to the distraught woman who grabbed several to wipe her eyes and nose.

"How could he have been so.... so damned stupid? It's just too horrible to even imagine. His car, the police said, was hit broadside by one of those big delivery trucks as he was leaving the Granville Barker estate. I heard one of the witnesses telling the police that Philip just tore out of the drive like a bat out of Hell, without stopping. You know how bad the traffic on Ithan Avenue can be. With the freezing rain, it was crazy! He didn't have a chance! Oh. Damn, damn, damn....." Jessica put her arm around the hysterical woman, trying to comfort her as she continued to weep.

"Mrs. Rawlins?" a physician still in surgical scrubs stood just inside the small doorway of the waiting room.

"Yes," both women answered.

"Mrs. Philip Rawlins?"

"Yes, I'm Philip's wife. How is he?" Caroline moved hesitantly to meet the doctor with Jessica following closely behind.

"I'm Dr. Harry Caldwell, an Orthopedic Surgeon; I was in ER when your husband arrived. He's not very well, I'm afraid. He wasn't wearing a seat belt and his car rolled over twice before landing right side up. He had to be cut out of what's left of the car. He sustained some serious neck, spine and head injuries. He's out of surgery and in recovery; we'll be bringing him to his room in a couple of minutes"

"Is he awake? May I see him?" Caroline interrupted.

"He'll be in the Intensive Care Unit, Mrs. Rawlins. He has not regained consciousness..." Jessica noted the surgeon's eyes glance downward to the floor as he reported the last bit of information.

"Yes, but can I see him?" Her voice was imploring.

"Of course, I'll take you to ICU, but preferably you will stay for only a few minutes. He'll be undergoing more tests this evening. Waiting around here would do neither of you any good. I suggest you go home and get some rest and come back in the morning.

"Dr. Caldwell, may I have a moment?" Letty Fox stood several feet outside the doorway, signaling the surgeon with her tousled, grey- haired head to come out into the corridor... alone.

"What up, Letty?"

"It's the Radnor police; they say they must speak to Mrs. Philip Rawlins. What should I tell them?

Harry Caldwell glanced back into the waiting room to see the two women huddled together. "Tell them to come back here in about ten minutes after she sees her husband. If they want to speak privately, you can close the door."

"I'll tell them!" Letty strode back to the elevators where two uniformed Radnor Police officers stood waiting.

"Ten minutes," she announced. "Dr. Caldwell says ten minutes."

Chapter 2

Vatican City, the Papal apartment

The sound had been excruciating, a piercing howl that seemed to emanate from beyond the physical body—a soulless sound that echoed through the heavy door leading to the Pope's bedroom. Several members of the Memores Domini peered cautiously through the partially open door of the private ten room apartment. Father Malcolm De Laurencin had scurried past them, through the chilly corridors of this 17th century papal residence on the top floor of the Apostolic Palace; flashlight in hand, trembling slightly as he neared the bedroom door of the sleeping pontiff. As Regent of the Pontifical Household, Fr. Malcolm essentially acted as chief of staff and confident for the Holy Father whom he had known since seminary days.

"Holy Father, Holy Father wake up, you are having a dream," he called out in a calm but insistent voice, as he unlocked the massive oak door of the simply furnished bedroom. The elderly priest stepped slowly into the room until he was beside the narrow, wood frame bed where Pope Leo XIV lay on his left side, facing away from him. The Ppe's breathing was deep and heavy; he appeared to have lapsed into a deep sleep again. Father De Laurencin waited several seconds then turned away. As he approached the door, a fragile voice called out, "Father Malcolm, Malcolm is it you? Is there a fire?"

Dressed in a white cotton smock, the elderly Pope had used his elbow to force himself to a semi sitting position to see his visitor. The only illumination came from a full moon which shone through two immense windows of the corner apartment that over looked St. Peter's square, three stories below. The clerestory panel of one window had been opened fully, filling the bedroom with a moist chill. With eyes closed, Leo inhaled deeply. The fear which had engulfed his sleeping body appeared to be receding, lingering only in the form of a feverish flush. Malcolm could not help but notice Leo's body dripping with perspiration despite the chill that permeated the ancient walls of the apartment.

"Holy Father, you've been...shouting, screaming. It's the third time this week. It's 3:20 a.m. We all are concerned; I had to come and check on you! Perhaps I should call a doctor!"

"No, no, Malcolm, no doctor; I'll be fine. What can I say? I'm sorry to be such trouble to all of you. Please, thank everyone and tell them not to worry about me. Now, go back to bed."

De Laurencin crossed himself and said goodnight, closing the door to the Holy Father's bedroom but not locking it.

A small lamp lay on the table next to Leo's bed. He flicked it on. He was exhausted but petrified of what might happen should he fall asleep again. He pushed his aged body into a sitting position and rose unsteadily to his feet.

How he loved this room: his bed lay in full light of the moon and the windows opened to allow calming fresh air. It was comforting. He straightened the crumpled linen top sheet and woolen blanket, fluffed the two goose-down pillows, then turned off the lamp and dropped on to the mattress. As he turned to lie on one side, his arm positioned comfortably beneath a pillow, he felt it, a cold, tacky wetness. Turning on the lamp again, he pulled back the covers. A deep scarlet stain had settled into the bottom sheet of his bed. He lifted his left arm to find it smeared with color and then he saw it, the back of his smock was soaked not with perspiration but with a substance that could only be blood.

A rush of nausea overcame the Pope who stumbled toward the small lavatory located at one end of bedroom. As he steadied himself against the sink, he reached for a phone which hung from a wall next to the toilet. "Damn, the hour," he said aloud.

"Malcolm, I need you to get in touch with someone. Write this down, I want to speak to the Prior Provincial of the Edmundites. Yes, the Order of the Edmundites. They are located in Pennsylvania next to their University. Yes, it is on the Main Line. You know the Main Line, outside of Philadelphia, don't you? I want to speak to their Prior Provincial first and no I do not know his name. After that, I want you to call an old friend, the Rev. Sean O'Reilly, O.S.E. at St. Edmund University, a celebrated forensic archaeologist. Yes, of course I mean right now. Why do you think I'm calling you?"

Chapter 3

Caroline spent less than five minutes at the bedside of her husband in Intensive Care. Jessica waited just outside the door, where she could see the battered Philip on a respirator, his head encased in a halo of metal, his eyes closed, swollen and blackened.

Tubing hung from several large IV bags of saline solution with drugs in smaller pouches attached to a vein near Philip's right shoulder. In the near darkness of the room, he appeared to be deeply sedated. Caroline grasped his left hand and kissed his cheek. Her face was taut as she turned away from him, nodding to his nurse to follow her outside the tiny room.

"Dr. Caldwell, the ER doctor we spoke to just before we came here, told me Philip would undergo several tests sometime this evening. What are they?" she whispered.

"Let's see, Mr. Rawlins is scheduled for another CT scan of the head and brain as well as a PET/CT and MRI of his body. His doctors are trying to assess exactly where and to what degree of trauma, he suffered in the crash." She continued to key information into the computer just outside Philip's unit. "… and, I can also tell you that his orthopedic surgeon, who is Dr. Caldwell, also will be asking for additional scans of those areas where bone damage is evident and excessive." She did not continue, noticing in an instant that Caroline had grown quite pale and looked at a point of collapsing.

"Mrs. Rawlins, may I get you some water? Perhaps you'd better sit down over here for a moment." Jessica guided the shaken woman to an aluminum office chair that stood immediately outside the ICU and accepted a paper cup filled with cold water for her to sip.

"Thanks, I'd never have recognized him, Jess. He's so… so hurt!" She whimpered as she sipped the water and drew a tissue from the box presented to her by the ICU Nurse. "Thank you, I'm fine now. If he awakens, please let him know that I was here?"

Five minutes later, Caroline and Jessica entered the waiting room where Letty Fox waited with two Radnor Police officers, Jeff Burns and Larry Hawkins

"All I can tell you is that I had just turned into our driveway, about 6:20 p.m., I think, when Philip came flying around the bend in his new BMW 8. I said something to him like 'Philip, watch where you're going! You almost sideswiped me!' Because, his car had stopped only inches away." She gestured with her fingers, exaggerating the closeness of the encounter. "He was very sweet and said something like 'Sorry, dear, but Poulette called a few minutes ago, very upset, saying something about her jewelry box and Lydia Sindona coming into her room in the middle of the night trying to get hold of it.'"

"Stop there, Mrs. Rawlins," Officer Hawkins interrupted, checking his notebook"... you said he was going to see Poulette? Is that what I heard you say? 'Poulette had called him?'"

"Yes, everyone around here knows her as Poulette; actually her name is Patricia Granville Barker. She is a very attractive and gracious widow who lives in the big Tudor estate on Ithan called Edencroft. You may have seen the Granville Barker name scrolled on the big iron gates at the entrance?"

Lt. Jeff Burns looked up, "I know where it is; that's where your husband was coming from when the accident occurred. Have you any idea why he went to see her?"

"Well, yes; not long ago Poulette called Philip about possibly putting her house on the market. Philip is in real estate and has had quite a lot of success selling estates on the Main Line. I think that was back in May. Then, a few weeks ago, he was called to her house ostensibly for tea and as he described the situation: he was ushered into a very cozy room, a fire lit library where she sat serenely on her favorite settee near the fireplace. In front of her on a table, there was a heavy antique silver tea service." Caroline gave a slightly embarrassed giggle as she continued "Everyone who knows Poulette remarks that she is quite beautiful and looks far younger than her years. She's trim, with lovely skin and champagne blond hair. I'd say she has to be in her seventies, maybe even her early 80s. At any rate, she has quite a reputation for having a multitude of male friends, and an appetite specifically for men many years her junior. I've never picked up on it but Philip told me she has a coy way of flirting. For example, he said, after asking him to sit next to her, she leaned in quite close and in an almost inaudible voice asked, '...Now, I've forgotten, Philip, do you take crème with your tea or a slice of lemon? Or perhaps you'd like something else,' at which point he admitted to me that he could be totally enthralled and charmed by her. He kept his senses though, or at least he said he did when he replied 'Just sugar... one cube please, Poulette,' Although knowing Philip, he might have answered with a voice that was as intimate and alluring as that of his hostess. After that, she got down to business, tucking her trousered legs beneath her and sinking deeper into the feather-tucked, toile cushions of the small love seat. He told me that she said, 'You must be wondering why I really asked you here, Philip. I'm taking Edencroft off the market as of today. Biscuit?' Poulette offered with a delicate wave of her wrist, indicating a plate brimming with paper thin sugar cookies. 'No, no thank you, Poulette. May I ask why?' The question was more rhetorical than anything else. In truth, Philip told me he was not surprised. Working as he did, on a regular basis with older clients, especially those deeply rooted in Main Line culture and society, he had learned that it was not unusual for them to change their minds from one day to the next.

"It's my late husband's son, Marcus. He has been living in Canada for the last ten years and recently decided to come back to the United States and to Villanova. Edencroft was always meant to be his, that is, after I was gone. But now, it seems only right that he should have it now, if only for tax reasons. I already have a lovely suite on the third floor. It was once a servant's apartment. It's quite comfortable with an elevator, fireplace and a small kitchen; enough for me to make a pot of tea or heat a muffin. He intends to keep our cook and the rest of the staff. So, as you can see, I can be quite comfortable up there. I'm sorry Philip; I know how hard you have been working these last few weeks with the stager and photo-graphers. You really have done a splendid job, you know but.... family comes first." Poulette raised her left eyebrow and took another sip of tea from a porcelain cup that Philip noted closely matched the blue and pale yellow print of the love seat. But typical of Poulette, her hospitality was measured by certain efficiency. Once she had delivered her message, her lack of a need for Philip's company and conversation became very meager and it was more than obvious that it was time for her guest to depart. Philip, being the perfect gentleman told me, he said, 'Please know, that I am always at your service, Poulette. And please, give my regards to Marcus. It's been too long since we've seen each other.' 'I'll do that, Philip,' Poulette answered smiling sweetly. In the late afternoon light of the foyer, Philip said he could swear she looked 25 years younger than her age. Her smile, he noted, always held a certain promise that he felt both flattering and disconcerting."

Sergeant Larry Hawkins' radio interrupted the interview and he stepped outside the waiting room.

"I think that will be about all for this evening, Mrs. Rawlins. We may need time with you in the coming days. This Lydia Sindona, you mentioned. We'll speak about who she is at that time. How can I reach you?" Lt. Burns rose from the chair next to the sofa where Caroline and Jessica had seated themselves. Caroline handed him a business card. "This has my cell and home phone numbers on it."

"Fine, uhhh, Mrs. Rawlins... I wonder if I might speak to you alone for a moment?" His tone was solemn.

" I'll wait for you in the corridor." Jessica walked slowly hoping to catch something of the conversation between the two.

"No, absolutely not! What are you saying? That's impossible... I mean he wouldn't!" Caroline darted out, passing Jessica and Officer Hawkins stopping when she reached the elevator. She pounded the down button, crying uncontrollably, before Letty Fox and a nurse settled her down in a small office next to a nurses' station. Jessica followed quickly behind them. Lt. Burns was nowhere in sight.

"Please, let me talk to her for a moment," Jessica begged as Letty and the nurse stepped aside.

"What did he say to you, Caroline?"

"He said, he said that... that there was bright red lipstick on Philip's shirt and face, not blood but lipstick. He wanted to know if Philip was having an affair... an affair with Poulette and now Poulette is missing!"

Chapter 4

"...also, a pound of the homemade chicken salad, the one with tarragon in it... and that should do it!" Jessica Rawlins watched as the container was weighed and added it to two other containers already in her cart. This would be a Whole Foods dinner night... green bean salad with pimentos and fresh almonds, carrot slices with dill and lemon, all served with a generous handful of crispy plantain chips. Frieda Rolvaag their longtime cook and house-keeper was away visiting family, which left Jessica and Alex some well needed time to catch up and enjoy their privacy. The latter had just returned from a three week trip to the Middle East and probably would be suffering from jet lag.

After pulling herself together at the hospital, Caroline decided she needed a quiet evening at home, with a cold glass of Chardonnay and a hot bath more than she needed the company of Jessica and Alex.

"You promise you'll call if anything comes up," Jessica had urged; Caroline only nodded. Both of them knew she would use this alone time to center herself before falling into what undoubtedly would be a fitful sleep.

As their automatic garage door opened, Jessica pulled her apple red Jeep into its parking place. Through the rain splattered car windows, she spotted Alex' immense black umbrella drying at the entrance to the mudroom. He must have just arrived and would have no way of knowing about Philip, his first cousin and closest friend. She grabbed the fabric grocery bag containing their dinner, took a deep breath and pushed the door open.

***

Jessica continued to tear the freshly washed Romaine lettuce and place it in a wooden salad bowl. "... and that is all I know at this point. But honestly, Alex, the entire idea of anything even remotely improper going on between Philip and Poulette Granville Barker is ridiculous, isn't it?" Jessica shook several fresh leaves from the colander and placed them on a paper towel to be patted dry.

Alex was unusually quiet, not commenting at all about Philip, his accident or his condition. Jessica turned her gaze to the outside where only a cold and damp darkness loomed on a moonless night.

"Dinner ready soon?" he called to her as he displayed a very special bottle of wine. "It's a Brunello from Boompa's wine cellar. As you can see from the label, he got a case of it from Cornelius Granville Barker back in the early '70s. When you mentioned Poulette, I remembered we had something down there with the Granville Barker label on it. See here, at the bottom on the label, is his name and family coat of arms." He held up the bottle proudly for Jessica to see.

Jessica wrinkled her nose. "First off, have you heard a word I've been saying about Philip and Poulette, his terrible accident and secondly, we're having chicken salad... and I thought a nice cold white wine might be better suited and finally, if this Brunello is that old, it's probably turned to vinegar. Here, give it to me and I'll use it in my salad dressing."

"Not this bottle, my love. This one is definitely for drinking. It's a 1979 vintage which in Italy is about as good as it gets; an excellent year for Brunello. Good vintage years can be stored for as many as 40 years. As for your chicken salad, this wine will go with anything, believe me."

"Speaking of Granville Barker, Alex, I have .... "

"Stop, right there, Jess" Alex huffed as he continued to pull the ancient but still moist cork from the wine bottle.

"Now, we'll let this breathe for about 15 minutes and then see how a really good vintage wine tastes."

"Do you remember Marcus, Poulette's step-son, who's been living somewhere in Canada all these years? Well, he's supposedly moving back and into the old family house. Poulette has told several people on the Main Line that the reason she will not be selling Edencroft is because she is planning on taking over the top floor as her private apartment. Apparently, the house has an elevator and she claims the area is quite attractive and livable."

Jessica looked up from her salad preparation to see Alex standing at a distance from her with a framed photo in his hand.

"Hey Jess, isn't Marcus, Caroline's old lover, the one...?" Alex didn't finish his sentence. Jessica's cell phone interrupted them. It was Caroline; the hospital had called to tell her that Philip had lapsed into a coma.

***

St Edmund's Friary, Villanova, PA

Just after 8 a.m., only hours after Father Malcolm De Laurencin, the Regent of the Pontifical Household placed a call to Father Austin Cheney, Prior Provincial of the Edmundites, an order of friars following the ancient rule of St. Edmund. Father Sean O'Reilly arrived in the Prior Provincial's office where he now found himself paging through an old copy of National Geographic magazine and sipping coffee from a paper cup.

For Father Austin Cheney, the Prior Provincial and for Sr. Elisabeth "Beth" Castelli, the Provincial's long time secretary, a meeting called for "first thing in the morning" meant immediately after Mass, which the Order's remaining three Sisters of St. Edmond celebrated at 6:30 a.m. at the nearby St. Katherine of Sienna Church in Wayne. When Father O'Reilly arrived, Sr. Beth already had him scheduled for the first meeting of the day and was on the telephone scheduling the Prior Provincial's busy agenda for the rest of the business day.

Motioning to the Mr. Coffee maker, set on a small filing cabinet near the outer door, she invited him to pour himself a cup and wait to be called into his superior's office.

The minutes dragged. Father Sean put down the National Geographic and walked to the file cabinet to pour a second cup of the strong brew. Sister Beth paid no attention as she continued to sort through the morning mail and answer an occasional telephone call.

Just as he was about to sit down again, the door to the inner office opened. Father Austin Cheney invited his guest inside to an informal conversation area at one end of the office.

"Sean, I see you already have coffee. Sister Beth sprang for some Blueberry muffins from Hope's cookies this morning; right from the oven, she promises."

Father O'Reilly selected one from the plate with an overabundance of blueberries oozing from the top.

"Now, Austin, what all of this is about? What's going on?"

"I don't know, Sean; I honestly don't know!" Beads of perspiration formed on the Prior Provincial's forehead.

"I received call a little before midnight from the Apostolic Palace, from Pope Leo's right hand man, Father Malcolm De Laurencin. The Pope had an "episode" as Father Malcolm described it. It was the second or the third time in just this week he has experienced these, how did he describe them, these nightmares?"

"Austin," Father Sean interrupted, "did Malcolm describe these nightmares the Pope is having to you?"

Father Cheney picked up his paper coffee cup from the table next to the sofa and cradled it with both hands before taking a sip. "Yes, I took some notes, thank God. It sounded very strange and it was late and frankly I was tired. I wanted to make sure I was getting everything right. He said the Holy Father described them as visions. He told Malcolm that in the dream or vision, it is always late at night. He knows this because it is very dark and he is in a city that he is not familiar with; there seem to be no people anywhere." Fr. Austin Cheney paged through his small notebook and then continued.

"Father Malcolm went on to say that the Holy Father's definition of 'not familiar' in the dream was that he seemed to know the city he was in and where he was going but…. Now, Sean, this is a direct quote … The Holy Father said, 'let me explain it this way: I, am not the subject of the dream. I have another identity … but I don't know who that "I" is. I … I am running along what seems to be a river bank. I know that I am being chased. I can feel my lungs giving out. I trip and fall over something and as I look up, I see them coming after me in the distance… I get up and begin to run again. I can see the bridge in front of me; I head for it and…."

"And what?" Father Sean O'Reilly urges.

"And…"

Father Cheney turned the page of the small notebook, "The Holy Father said, 'I don't know what or I don't remember whatever it is. In the dream, all I know is that I am terrified. I can't escape... that I realize." Father Cheney gulped what was left of the now cold coffee and placed the empty container on the table.

"Did he mention whether this dream is always the same?" Cheney considered the question for a brief moment, not wanting to let any detail slip away.

"No, no, Sean, Malcolm said it isn't. In the first dream, the Pope recalled that he was not frightened; he was merely walking, not running and then as the recurring dreams continued, it seems that he was being pursued and the pursuit became more frightening. I...," Father Cheney hesitated.

"Please go on, Father," Sean O'Reilly coaxed.

"Malcolm said, the Holy Father felt that he was being led to his death; that his pursuers ultimately would catch him and he'd ... he'd be killed."

"But there's more, Sean, The Holy Father claimed that there was blood and a lot of it in his bed when he rose from this last dream or vision. But Malcolm told me that there appeared to be nothing on his sheets and no abrasions or wounds on his back or body. No wounds of any sort that he could see."

The priest waited for a reaction from O'Reilly.

"Austin, I know this may be a strange question, but is there any way to find out from Malcolm whether Pope Leo might be involved in any .... What shall I say... any ritualistic penitence such as flagellation?"

"I couldn't ask that... It, it would be outrageous! No, no of course not; nothing like that, I'm sure ... ever!" Father Cheney seemed taken aback by the suggestion.

Father Sean O'Reilly finished the last of his muffin and gulped down the rest of the coffee in his cup. "Austin, why did you call me?" he finally asked." I'm certain it wasn't to discuss the nightmares of the Pope and eat muffins."

"I called you because I was asked to by the Holy Father via Malcolm. Pope Leo says he knows you; you were in seminary together. Do you remember him?"

"I do; we were not on the best of terms." Sean O'Reilly answered.

"Well, you obviously made an impression on him and he has followed your scholarly work in the field of forensic archaeology. After the paper you did on the Scavi and discovery of St. Peter's final resting place, he has kept up with everything you have been doing. Now, he wants your help. He wants you to come to the Vatican for several months. This is why he called me. I've already given my permission. Sister Beth has your airline reservations for tonight's flight to Rome. Good luck and keep in touch!"

Father Austin Cheney stood up and put out his hand.

Sean O'Reilly was almost too amazed to rise from the cushioned chair where he had been comfortably seated.

"But, Austin, why does he want me? I'm an archaeologist, not a...a psychiatrist. "

"He wants you, Sean, for whatever reason. Besides, could I possibly go back to Malcolm and say, "Tell the Holy Father, Sean O'Reilly says, no, he doesn't want to come?""

O'Reilly put out his hand and shook his head. "I think this is a big mistake," he said softly. "...but obedience is my middle name."

Chapter 5

More than two days had passed since Philip's near fatal accident and his equally dramatic lapse into a coma. Caroline had remained at his side in the Intensive Care Unit nearly all of that time, even sleeping on a pullout sofa to be near him should he awake. On the third day, late into the morning, he opened his eyes and tried to raise his right arm.

"Philip, Philip, it's me; can you hear me?" Caroline had joined his ICU nurse who already was checking his vital signs.

"Can you speak, Mr. Rawlins?" the nurse asked several times as Philip continued to move his eyes from side to side but said nothing.

"Philip, please say something. You've been asleep after a terrible car accident. Do you remember?" Philip stared past her face to some point on the opposite wall.

"I don't think he sees or hears me;" she muttered. "... Philip, please, darling, squeeze my hand if you can't speak but recognize me." Philip's hand remained motionless.

"Mrs. Rawlins, if you would step outside, his doctors want to examine him."

Caroline walked unsteadily to the medical station some feet away, trying to grasp what was happening to Philip. A privacy curtain across the entrance to his bed prevented her from hearing anything meaningful. Then, from behind her, she heard, "Mrs. Rawlins? I'm Dr. Jacob Hoffert, your husband's neurologist."

"Oh, Dr. Hoffert, you startled me. What's happening? Is Philip awake? Does this mean he's going to be all right?"

"Let's sit down over her for a moment," Dr. Hoffert led the way to a private office several feet from the ICU with a desk and two comfortable chairs. He closed the office door.

"Please come in and take a seat. As you know, your husband was not wearing a seat belt at the time of the accident. When his car rolled over, his head hit the hard roof of the car several times resulting in a traumatic brain injury. It is the kind of injury that could have killed him; but it did not. Since the accident, he has been in what we call a state of altered consciousness."

"You mean, a coma," Caroline interjected. "But, he looks as if he is coming out of it."

"There are different states of altered consciousness. He might have transitioned into what we call a minimally conscious state where he has some awareness of where he is and who he is or, he could be in a vegetative state."

"Stop, please not a vegetative state. That would be horrible. He'd just lie there for the rest of his life not knowing what...."

"Mrs. Rawlins, please, don't jump to conclusions. There are opportunities for him to progress; it is not uncommon for someone with his injuries to transition to a state of greater recovery."

"You mean he could come out of this and be back to normal; that is what you're saying, isn't it?"

"I'm saying that this process takes time, a lot of it. What we would like to propose to you is that we move Philip out of ICU today to another part of the hospital where we can observe him for the next several days. The kind of evaluation we need to do will take time. When that is completed, we propose sending him to Bryn Mawr Rehabilitation Hospital which has a specialized program, inpatient in Philip's case, to aid in his recovery."

"Well, how long would it take and ... will it really help?" Caroline looked to be on the verge of tears. She reached for a fresh tissue in her handbag to dab tear-filled eyes.

"The average stay is 28 days but additional care could be recommended either as an outpatient, commuting from your home several times a week or he could continue as an inpatient if that is preferable. Of course, nothing, as I said earlier can be guaranteed." Hoffert stood up making it obvious their meeting was at an end.

"Well, thank you, Dr. Hoffert. When will Philip be moved?"

"Sometime later today; actually when we can find a bed for him. May I suggest you go home and get some rest? By the time you come back, let's say about 6 p.m., he should be in that room...all right?"

"Yes, all right!" Jacob Hoffert opened the door for Caroline who glanced back at the ICU only a few feet away. The curtain around Philip's bed was still closed. He was undergoing what would be the beginning of a myriad of tests. "Thank you, again," she uttered walking quickly toward the elevator. As she pushed the down button, the doors of an elevator some twenty five feet down the corridor marked "staff" opened; two women and three men emerged. "Marcus?" she said softly. "Marcus Granville Barker?"

***

Alex Rawlins was heading to the showers next to the squash courts at the Main Line Cricket Club when he encountered an old acquaintance. "Hey, I don't believe it. We were just talking about you the other night, Marcus. How in the Hell are you? Rumor has it you are back here for a while." The six-foot two inch Granville Barker had aged well, Rawlins noted. His body was athletic; his face remarkably unlined and his hair, tinged with only a slight bit of gray and intact.

"Well, yeah, I arrived a few days ago and since I still hold membership here, thought I'd drop by and see if I could find a squash partner; Iggy Carlson turned up at about the same time and he needed a partner, too."

"Well, we'll have to have a drink when you have some time," Alex replied nonchalantly heading to the showers.

"How about today?" Granville Barker's voice was high and his expression almost suppliant "I have to pick up some things at Joseph Banks in Haverford right now and have a couple of other errands nearby. But, I really need some... some advice from you, if you can spare the time. How about meeting me in the bar in about.... let's say... ninety minutes?"

Alex was certain what he saw in Marcus' face, could only be interpreted as apprehension. He checked his watch. "Sure, Marcus, see you in the bar in 90 minutes."

***

Alex pulled the cork from a fine Morey St.-Denis 2010, just as Jessica opened the door to the mudroom. "Perfect timing, my good wife. Caroline is already testing Trader Joe's latest frozen canapés which I found in the freezer and she popped in the oven and I'm about to let you taste this fine Burgundy, a gift from your boss, Jed Watkins."

There was a pop as the cork slid out of the bottle top and Alex bent low to smell it.

"The cork smells fine; but what would you have done if it turned out to be vinegar?" Jessica grinned as she removed her muffler and tossed it over a chair.

"I'd open another bottle, of course, and send Jed a thank you note for his wine." Alex could see Jessica's grin widen as she picked up a goblet from the bar and held it out for a sample.

"It really should breathe for a while, you know," she pronounced as he began to pour a sample into her glass.

"Yes, well, we'll break the rules tonight. I have something to tell you."

"I take it, whatever it is; is it good news?"

Alex swirled a small amount of the Burgundy in his wine goblet. Then, took a sniff, examined the color and sipped. "Excellent! We won't have to lie to Jed about the quality of this bottle. It is absolutely wonderful."

Caroline's champagne flute was nearly empty. "What about me?" she called out, smiling at her host who stood with the champagne bottle in hand and a white towel folded around his arm emulating a restaurant sommelier.

"Madame, a new bottle; it seems there is nothing left in the last."

"Thank you, Alex … and now will you please tell us the news!" Caroline leaned forward in her chair.

"All right, all right; I've been waiting for Jess to get home; I knew she'd want to hear this, too. I ran into your old friend Marcus at the Cricket Club, Caroline; he had just finished playing squash and he asked me to meet him later for a drink in the bar. "

"… and what did you boys talk about?" Jessica's tone was more than a little curious.

"Not what you might think, Jess. Did you know Caroline... or did either of you know that Marcus is an Edmundite priest?"

The silent shaking of their heads led Alex to continue. "...and, he is a psychiatrist, too. After getting his B.S. from Princeton, he went on to the Harvard Medical School for his M.D. and then did his residency in psychiatry at the University of Pennsyl-vania. So Marcus can now be called Dr. Father Marcus

Granville Barker." Alex stopped momentarily both for a reaction and a sip of the Burgundy.

"What's he doing back here?" Jess asked, noting that Caroline was sitting back silently listening.

"That's the part that is disturbing." Caroline leaned forward and was thoughtfully silent for a moment.

"It's about Poulette...."

"What about her?" Caroline's voice had a note of concern. "I saw her just three weeks ago at an Acorn Club fall luncheon. She seemed fine. She certainly didn't look ill. You are talking about illness, aren't you Alex?"

"Poulette is in Bryn Mawr Hospital for a few days; in fact the rumor that she had disappeared after Philip's accident was incorrect. She was in the hospital that day and has been ever since under observation because she has a brain tumor; an inoperable brain tumor. It showed up recently when she had an MRI because of recurring headaches. Her neurologist, Jacob Hoffert was a classmate of Marcus at Harvard and thought it appropriate and important for Marcus to know about the situation. That's why he has come back to the Main Line and also why she stopped the sale of the house."

"Oh my, Dr. Hoffert is Philip's neurologist, too. I just talked to him about Philip's condition earlier today. Did Marcus say how long Poulette might have?" Caroline's expression was one of sincere compassion. "I take it she isn't aware that Marcus has come back to take care of her until...." She stopped abruptly.

"As for how long... Marcus didn't say and I certainly would not ask such a question. Unfortunately, that is not the reason why he has come back; not exactly the reason anyway. Marcus has been called to Rome and has to leave here in a few days. It's not an assignment he can turn down because the request comes directly from the Pope." Alex paused again, this time to stand up and pour himself another dram from the wine bottle on the bar.

"But, he can't just leave her alone to... you know... and he certainly doesn't intend to tell her, does he?" Jessica pondered the news, as shocked as the others. Poulette had never been a friend nor even a favorite acquaintance. Her flirtatious behavior over the past years had led to numerous indiscreet liaisons, none more scandalous than a very public affair with Dr. Lucas Sindona, the very married and extraordinarily attractive surgeon whose only patients were alleged members of the Mafia.

"No, Marcus doesn't intend to leave her alone. Do you remember Lydia Sindona? She was in my dancing school class at the Cricket Club. Not a raving beauty, but she was very smart. Well, she went off to Smith and then Harvard Medical School, soon after Marcus finished there and is now, with an M.D. and a Ph.D. she is doing neurological research at the University of Pennsylvania. She's still single and living in an apartment with a month to month lease, in Wayne. Marcus talked to her about Poulette's condition and decided to hire her to live in the house with Poulette; you know, to keep an eye on her and report back to him about any changes in her condition."

"She's not a member of the Sindona family who ..." Jessica began.

"Jess, Jess, that was years ago. Forget it! Yes, Lucas Sindona was her father but he has been dead for years now. She's a lovely girl and from what Marcus said a very astute and talented neurologist. Having her live with Poulette can relieve a lot of the guilt Marcus feels about leaving his stepmother alone and she is qualified to give him a medical opinion about Poulette's health."

"Does Poulette know about this arrangement?" Caroline asked, scooping up the last of the hot canapés which had grown quite cold.

"No, Marcus was on his way back to the hospital to tell her."

"She'll probably take the news very well," Alex added. "Poulette is one of the most practical women I know. She loves Marcus and will understand that having someone pleasant as a housemate, like Lydia will mean companionship and be good as a safety measure too."

Jessica grasped her wine goblet. She knew nothing of Lydia Sindona except her heritage; even her surname made her cringe. Poulette might not be as happy with the arrangement as Marcus hoped. Then, what would he do?

Chapter 6

"I don't know what I feel, Jess. Philip either lied to me or, he was seeing someone he didn't want me to know about. Poulette was in the hospital when he told me he was meeting her at her house. "But Jess, who was he meeting if not Poulette? I just can't get it out of my mind. I can't ask him, not while he is in this condition. I feel just terrible... guilty for doubting him, yet suspicious, too."

"You certainly shouldn't feel guilty, Caroline. You've literally been living at the hospital and now Bryn Mawr Rehab? Philip will get better and he'll have an answer for you, one of these days. Until then, he also would want you to get out and see other people. You deserve an evening with family. Besides, we've missed you!" Jessica gave Caroline's goblet a slight clink as she raised her glass in a toast and took a sip of the cool Chardonnay. As usual, they had been waiting in the bar at Rosalie for their reservation to be called for well over 30 minutes.

"Reservation for Rawlins: Please follow me. Your table is right over here," Todd, the Captain at the chic eatery in the Wayne Hotel, led the party of three to a well-placed table --- with a view.

"You do see who's seated right across from us, don't you?" Caroline muttered using her head to designate a table for two not more than ten feet from theirs.

"Isn't that Lydia Sindona?" Jessica whispered back."... An improved version, I'd say; she looks fantastic; and who is she with?"

"And here we are," Todd pulled out a chair presumably for Jessica, who in turn smiled but moved to the other side of the table where she could better observe without too much notice. "Geoffrey, your waiter will be with you in a moment."

"What exactly is going on?" Alex helped move Jessica's chair closer to the table.

"Don't look now but Lydia Sindona, the woman we were talking about the other night, is seated right across from me. You know the daughter of the mobster surgeon. Caroline and I are wondering who she's with. He's quite good looking."

"Oh, that's Lombroso," Alex's voice was much too strident considering the topic. "I can't remember his first name, at the moment, but he's a big league investor from Canada. The Wall Street Journal wrote a front page feature on top tier international investment bankers last week and he was one of them. He's got at least ten billion in big bills. His picture ran with the story. Interesting, I wonder what he's doing here."

"Well, I'm impressed, Alex." Jessica tried again to lower the volume of the commentary. "... not only that you know who he is, but that Lydia appears to have more than a casual relationship with him. If I am not mistaken, he has his hand over hers and is squeezing it."

"Enough, ladies, here are the menus and let's hear what Geoffrey has to say about today's specials."

"To begin with, our chef is offering a..."

Geoffrey did not have a chance to complete the thought when a server, coming through the swinging doors from the kitchen, tripped, sending a tray laden with hot food flying over the heads of diners, to land on the table where Lombroso and Lydia Sindona were seated. Pan roasted duck breast in a cherry gastrique, drizzled down the front of Lydia's bronze beaded cashmere sweater. She sat motionless for several seconds, too stunned to say or do anything. Alex reacted immediately handing their napkins to the still stunned woman and her equally horrified partner.

"Oh, Madame, are you all right?" Todd shouted as he pushed through what had in an instant become a crowd of on lookers, the majority of whom were rushing in from the adjoining bar area to witness the incident.

Jessica, having joined Alex, was now hovering beside Lydia, offering the startled woman her napkin which was accepted gratefully.

"Thank you, everyone, but I'm not hurt," Lydia finally responded. "But, if you'll excuse me, I'll try to get myself in order and get some of this...."

"Please Madame, let us help you," Todd was gesturing to a staff member who appeared from the kitchen with a freshly pressed chef's jacket in a small size. "Perhaps you would like to change into this and we'll make certain your beautiful sweater is properly cleaned and returned to you. Again, we are so sorry!"

"I'll come with you," Jessica suggested helping the startled woman to her feet while picking up her handbag which also was sticky and stained with the wine-colored gastrique. Todd cleared a pathway through the now crowded dining room and out into the lobby where Jessica and Lydia disappeared into the powder room.

"I'm Jessica Rawlins; you probably don't remember …." She stopped mid-sentence.

"Oh, but I do, Jessica," Lydia commented dryly as she wiped her throat with a damp towel to clear away the sauce stain. "I must admit those memories are not very pleasant."

Jessica handed her another damp towel from several she was now holding. She had noted Lydia's voice carried a slight accent. "It has been a long time, Lydia; I'm sorry if I offended you in some way in the past."

"You're quite right; it has been a long time, Jessica. I've been living and working abroad for more than a decade, but I'm back now and planning to stay for a while." Lydia tossed the used towel into a basket and picked up the chef's jacket which lay on a small bench. As she walked into a stall, she continued. "I've been selected to head a research project at the University of Pennsylvania Medical School."

"Oh, in what field?" Jessica recalled that Alex had earlier mentioned something about neurology.

"I'm a research neurologist," Lydia tossed the stained sweater over the door of the stall where it nearly landed on the floor and a minute later emerged looking remarkably chic in the crisp white chef jacket.

"What kind of a project will you be working on?" Jessica, who was now folding the stained sweater, gestured to a vanity table where the jewel clasped but stained evening bag lay. Lydia opened it to withdraw a hair brush, lipstick and gold compact while wiping away, with another moist towel, what she could of the red sauce that clung to its surface.

"Can't tell you that," Lydia muttered as she stared into the mirror and ran the brush through her brown highlighted chin length coiffure.

"I suppose you'll be living in the city, close to your work." Jessica had also remembered something from the conversation with Alex about Lydia moving in with Poulette while her stepson Marcus was abroad.

"No, no I'll be living here on the Main Line." Lydia snapped the purse closed and grabbed the stained top from Jessica.

"Thank you, Jessica for your help. Now, if you'll excuse me, I'll get my coat and get out of here!'

There was no mistaking Lydia's tone. It was clipped and hostile. As they emerged into the hotel lobby, they caught sight of Roberto Lombroso standing with the Captain holding Lydia's coat, ready for her to slip into.

"Todd will take your sweater, my dear and have it delivered to you when it returns from the cleaners....and thank you, Miss," he hesitated for a moment "... for coming to Lydia's aid." He smiled, oblivious of the grimace Lydia's face displayed.

"I'm Jessica Rawlins and I'm only glad I could be of assistance. It was nice seeing you, Lydia. Perhaps we'll run into one another, again."

Roberto Lombroso smiled, placing his arm around Lydia Sindona's shoulder while escorting her though the crowded lobby of onlookers and out into the parking lot.

"How did it go? " Alex watched the couple depart.

"Not very well, I'm afraid. I'll tell you all about it later. Right now, I'm starved; let's go back and order."

It was a long drawn out dinner with Caroline begging to know every detail of the very clipped conversation Jessica had with Lydia in the ladies room. By the time Todd brought the party a complimentary after dinner cognac, Alex had pronounced the topic closed. However, he appeared to be the only one with no desire to speculate about Lydia Sindona's future or that of her billionaire boyfriend, Roberto Lombroso.

***

Poulette's mood was gloomy; she had little to say as she watched Marcus tightly fold the last few pieces of clothing that lay on the bed and place them into his single piece of luggage. She had not slept well since returning home from her visit to Bryn Mawr Hospital's neurology wing; unable, now to fully comprehend why Marcus had to leave immediately for the Vatican and why he thought she needed someone she'd never met to stay with her. She was perfectly recovered from whatever had caused her to collapse. In fact, she felt so well, she could scarcely remember the incident at all.

Besides, she already had Bernadette Perkins, perhaps the best, most experienced full-time housekeeper on the Main Line, who also filled in as a cook; and there was Bertrand Fox, a man of a certain age, a modern day butler, who could act as her driver until she felt ready to drive again.

But, Marcus had made it perfectly clear. "Dr. Sindona is an old school friend. She is moving to this area to do research at the University of Pennsylvania and it would suit both our purposes for her to have a nice place to come home to at the end of the day. She also is someone I could count on in case of an emergency; someone, who could make certain you were all right and well taken care of."

"She'll be staying in your room?" Poulette had asked.

"Well, I thought that might be the most convenient place; but, if you have any other ideas, just let me know."

Marcus had looked into the eyes of his stepmother where he could read her fear and concern.

"Something is happening to me, Marcus," she finally blurted out.

"Can you describe it?" he had asked.

"No, it's just...." and she stopped unable to define exactly what she had in mind.

"Don't worry, Poulette, I'll be back before you know it and we'll resume what we had planned." Marcus zipped up the black nylon bag and kissed Poulette's forehead as he passed her chair.

"Lydia will probably be arriving sometime later today. I asked her to call you before she left Philadelphia to let you know she would be on her way." And then he was gone.

The minutes and hours vanished without so much as a thought by Poulette. She hadn't been asleep, but sitting, silently in the same chair where Marcus had left her. Only now, as a cell phone continued to ring, on the table next to her, did she realize that nearly five hours had passed. Outside, the sun had nearly vanished and a light snow was beginning to fall. Poulette grabbed for the phone instinctively.

"Yes, oh yes, Dr. Sindona, I've been expecting your call," she lied. "That would be lovely. I'll have Mrs. Perkins set an extra plate for dinner. We'll eat in my apartment, if that suits you? Good, see you soon." Still dazed, Poulette put down the cell phone and pushed an intercom button on the desk near the window. "Mrs. Perkins, there will be two of us for dinner in my apartment this evening. Yes, if you could bring up something to munch on with our drinks that would be lovely. Our guest will be staying in Marcus' room for a while."

Poulette realized that Mrs. Perkins had answered her but she couldn't understand what she was saying. It was a fog that was setting in, a dreadful engulfing fog that just would not clear away.

***

Roberto Lombroso's cell phone rang just as his Gulfstream 550 touched down at Toronto's Pearson International Airport. "Monsignor Rosario, I've been expecting your call; where are you? Good, then you can join me for dinner tonight? Let's say, eight o'clock at Scaramouche. I take it everything is going well at the Institute for the Works of Religion? Yes, as always, I look forward to seeing you."

Lombroso tucked the IPhone inside the pocket of his jacket and proceeded to unbuckle his seat belt as the plane rolled along the bumpy tarmac.

"Paolo," he called to his assistant seated forward in the craft. "Get me reservations for three at Scaramouche for this evening and tell them I want table number 24. Make certain it is 24."

"Yes, sir," Paolo D'LaSerna called back, having heard the same request numerous times in weeks gone by.

For the recent Harvard MBA graduate, this was a dream job. In addition to travelling the world with a billionaire investment banker who reputedly made his fortune the 'old fashioned way' by hard work and clever hedge fund investing, Roberto Lombroso was among the most admired men for his efforts in helping to advance education and promote healthcare in some of the poorest regions of the world. One recent article in the Financial Times actually referred to him as St. Roberto while reporting on the launch of an elementary school in Scampia, a seedy district in northern Naples.

Having visited the area with Vatican officials on several occasions, Lombroso wrote a check for the entire cost of a school, which would be designed by celebrated Italian architect Lucius Sulla and would house the most advanced classroom technical equipment, an athletic pavilion and a chapel dedicated to St. Januarius or St. Gennaro, the patron saint of Naples. The only stipulation Lombroso made was that the school be run by the Piarist Fathers, an ancient order of priests dedicated to educating the poor. For that good deed, which cost Lombroso close to $700 million, the Pope awarded him the Grand Cross and Star of the Papal Order of St. Gregory, one of five pontifical orders bestowed on Roman Catholic men and women for unusual service to the Holy See. This, the highest rank of the Grand Cross, had only been awarded to eight Americans in the last thirty years. There was little doubt Lombroso was proud of the honor. Whenever a church occasion called for it, he would proudly don the elaborate dark green wool uniform trimmed with silver braid, a black beaver-felt hat decorated with black silk ribbons and white ostrich plumes, several yellow and red rosettes for his lapel, white leather gloves and a short sword with a handle made of mother of pearl that was embellished with a medallion of the order.

Of course, he wore his red sash and star quite proudly on the left side of his breast, as only members of this ultimate order are entitled to do.

"Shall I send a car for Dr. Sindona?" Paolo called out as Lombroso descended the plane and walked to a waiting black Mercedes.

"No, Paolo, she'll not be with us this trip," Lombroso called back, slamming the door to the car as it sped off.

Chapter 7

Vatican City – The Papal Apartment

"But it's well after 8 o'clock; why hasn't the Holy Father eaten?" Father Malcolm De Laurencin's angry tone masked the fear he felt as he observed Pope Leo XIV in his private quarters, kneeling before a crucifix and praying incoherently and stridently.

Giovanna Rossini, the Pope's cook and a member of the Memores Domini, a lay association of dedicated individuals who preside over the Holy Father's personal care shook her head and covered her mouth.

"He's been this way since he returned from his walk about 4:30 today. Sometimes he cries out in the most terrible way. What does he see, Father? Who is he talking to? Father, we could not interrupt him; not when he is in such deep prayer."

Malcolm De Laurencin observed the scene for a few more minutes. "Senora Rossini if dinner is ready for the Holy Father I'll make certain he is there in about five minutes. Is that all right?"

De Laurencin tried to smile as he gently urged the cook away from the entrance to the private apartment, closing the door firmly behind him. After taking a deep breath, he moved to the side of the distraught man, whose cries for forgiveness were now punctuated by a seizure like tic which caused him to collapse, falling from the antique oak prie-dieu on to the hard marble floor.

"Malcolm, Malcolm what are you doing here?" De Laurencin had raised the Holy Father's head slightly, but the dead weight of his body made shifting him to an upright position almost impossible.

"Holy Father, if I bring a chair to your side, do you think you could use it to raise yourself?"

"I don't know, Malcolm, I really don't know." Pope Leo raised his eyes to look into Malcolm's. "I can try." He smiled gently. Malcolm repositioned himself slightly replacing the Holy Father's head back on to the marble floor and raising himself to find a chair; it was then that he noticed what seemed to him four deep scratches on the back of the Holy Father's neck near the left shoulder. *'From fingernails,'* he noted mentally.

"Here we are, Holy Father; I'll lift you a bit and if you can get a grasp of this chair, we should be able to get you up!" Minutes later, His Holiness was seated.

"If you'll forgive me, I believe I'll have dinner in my room, this evening. Please tell Senora Rossini not to go through any trouble, just something light will be fine." Malcolm turned on a floor lamp next to the desk and picked up an ancient intercom which connected the Pope with the Vatican kitchen.

"Yes, Senora Rossini, His Holiness will be dining in his apartment this evening. Please have something sent up to him --- something light."

"Your Holiness, would you like me to stay? Are you feeling all right or would you like me to have your personal physician make a visit? "

"I'm all right, Malcolm, really I am; no need for a doctor." Leo's voice was weak and his demeanor quiet.

"Holy Father, I noticed scratches on the back of your neck; they looked deep. Perhaps we should have them looked at. I would hate to see an infection set in."

"Scratches? Where?" Leo reached up with his left had to feel the area of his neck Malcolm had indicated.

"What are these? I don't remember getting scratched!" His left hand was covered with blood. He examined it incredulously.

"Holy Father, perhaps I had better call your doctor. You may need stitches."

"No, Malcolm; I said No!" Malcolm stepped back. "Please, if you could bring me a wet towel; I'll be just fine!" Malcolm complied, bringing two. As he stood by, Senora Rossini knocked and without waiting entered with two other women to set up a tray table and trolley.

"I prepared your favorite Rigatoni with Prosciutto, Holy Father, and after that poached salmon and zucchini; and Paolo made a special tiramisu for you this evening."

Minutes later, at the Pope's insistence, everyone departed.

"Father Malcolm," Giovanna Rossini whispered to him as they headed downstairs to the administrative offices, kitchen, laundry and living quarters of the Memores Domini, who served in the Papal household. "I was asked to tell you that Father Sean O'Reilly called. He just arrived at the Hotel and asked that you call him there in the morning."

"Thank you, Senora. Have a good evening." Malcolm took a deep sigh of relief. Perhaps help was finally on the way.

***

At the insistent chime of his cell phone, Father Sean O'Reilly bolted from his bed and stumbled across the room to a small desk in the Domus Sanctae Marthae (St. Martha's House) in Vatican City. His small two-room suite was on the third floor of the hotel, which had served as the residence of Pope Leo's predecessor, Pope Francis who, in 2013, refused to live in the more luxurious papal apartment. Short on luxury but clean and most of all convenient to those O'Reilly would be meeting in the days ahead, he felt fortunate to have been invited to stay in this auspicious location. It was 3:40 a.m. in Rome, he noted as his bare toes slammed against the battered attaché case on the floor beneath the desk, knocking the travel clock to the floor.

"Hello," he shouted into the phone, "Who? Why yes, Malcolm. Sorry, let me get my thoughts together. It's 3:40... or something like that in the morning. Yes, of course you were right to call me. He's having another 'episode' as we speak. Yes, yes, of course, let me turn on a light and get a pen to write this down. Yes, I'll be there as soon as I can."

Sean O'Reilly lay the phone down on the desk and took a deep breath. He did not need anyone to explain to him what was happening. There was a crisis of major proportion with the Holy Father in his apartment; however, there was absolutely no reason, he could imagine why he had been called in to help.

Chapter 8

Roberto Lombroso slid his rental car into the only available space in the parking lot near the entrance to the Toronto apartment house where Scaramouche was located. He had sent his driver to pick up Monsignor Rosario and, as for the third member of their dinner party, it was best for everyone that he arrive on his own. He had spoken to Lydia earlier to assure her that this trip was strictly business. It would be dinner, a cigar and brandy and then, if he was lucky, he could claim a good night's sleep in his suite in The Four Seasons by midnight. As he locked the rental car door with a click of his key, he was certain he spotted someone loitering near a lamp post fifty feet away. He hurried to the sidewalk and into the building without looking back. It was a Thursday night, not usually one most Toronto restaurateurs would claim to be a good night for business; yet, inside Scaramouche, waiters bustled and Bertrand, the Maitre D', smiled broadly as Lombroso stepped inside.

"Ah, Monsieur, we are so glad to have you with us again. Here, let me take your coat. Your table, number 24 is ready for you. You are the first to arrive, as always." Lombroso followed the diminutive man to a table at the rear of the restaurant, next to a window with a view of the Toronto skyline, but removed from any other guests who might overhear a conversation.

"May I bring you your usual, Sir?" Bertrand made a slight bow.

"No, instead bring me your wine list. I want to order a special bottle or maybe two, this evening. Something for a first course of Oysters and after that a good wine for Duck or Venison as our main course. I'm sure your sommelier will have some suggestions." Lombroso smiled knowing full well, the sommelier would send not just a good wine but one of the most expensive in the cellar.

"Ah, there you are, Robert, quite a wicked night out there. The weather report claims we are in for another blizzard." Lombroso rose to shake hands with Monsignor Rosario who was dressed in civilian clothing for the evening and carrying a shabby, scuffed black attaché case.

"Monsignor, good to see you again; here, why don't you sit next to me? You'll have a good view of the Toronto skyline. And you can place your attaché case, next to the wall."

"Thank you, Robert; I bring you greetings from the Archbishop. I paid him a visit today. I had some time to spare after my plane arrived from Rome and thought I'd see what was happening here."

"And what did you find out?" Lombroso smiled as the sommelier delivered a mammoth wine list. "But before you tell me, let's get a few suggestions from our wine steward. I thought we'd begin with oysters, which I know you like, Monsignor, and which I am hoping our third guest will like; then perhaps something that will go with either the duck or the venison."

"I have an excellent Châteauneuf-du-Pape for the duck or venison and as for the oysters, I would recommend a Vouvray," The sommelier pointed to his suggestions. Lombroso's eyebrows rose as he looked up at the wine steward.

"I'm telling you now, these had better be good," he slammed the leather-covered portfolio and handed it back to the sommelier.

"He knows he has a sucker when I come in," Lombroso smiled. "... and I see our third guest has arrived. "Father Marcus how are you?" Lombroso rose from the table to shake hands with the priest who was dressed in a turtle neck sweater and herringbone wool blazer. "We were just ordering some wine. I hope you'll have a glass with us?"

***

"You know, Lydia you look just like your father." Poulette looked up from the stack of photos, her half glasses perched on her Patrician nose. Dr. Lydia Sindona reached for her wine goblet and took a significant sip from the more than half empty contents.

"I did love him, you know." Poulette's words were almost whispered as she brushed the faded black and white photos.

"I know you did, Poulette," Lydia answered, rising from the stool where she had perched for nearly an hour.

"... but you should know my mother never forgave him for your affair. She punished him even after he could no longer recognize any of us. It was her way; after all, she was the product of a generation of old country Neapolitan wives who understood mistresses existed in marriages, but always with a caveat. If an affair caused public gossip, or anything that could embarrass a wife or her children, well that could be punishable."

"Punishable...in what way?" Poulette looked up truly puzzled.

"Well, punishable in many ways... including death. You are just lucky Mama never came after you." Lydia dropped the empty bottle of Viognier into a small recycling container next to the bar and proceeded to open another.

"Lydia, I have to ask you: Why are you here?" Poulette laid the stack of photos on the cushioned footrest next to her chair.

"Well, Marcus thought you might like company and I needed a place to stay. Is that what you meant?"

Poulette said nothing but the inquisitive expression on her face projected the notion that there was more to her residency in the Granville Barker house than she was saying.

"Poulette, if you think I am here to do you any harm, please forget about that. Marcus and I were classmates. He knew nothing until recently about your affair with my father. Besides, time heals everything, or almost everything. My mother passed away some ten years ago and father about five years before her. My research really gives me little time for planning nefarious acts and certainly you would never be the target."

Lydia did not return to her seat, but stood in front of the gas fired hearth twirling the chilled goblet of wine.

"There's something wrong with me, Lydia. I know there is, but Marcus won't tell me what it is. Will you?"

"My dear Poulette, why does this concern you so?" Lydia deflected the question by walking to Poulette's side where she gave the elderly woman a sisterly hug. "I think what you need is something else to focus on besides your health. The day after tomorrow, a friend of mine will be in town. His name is Roberto Lombroso; perhaps you would like to join us for dinner?"

"Oh, I don't know, Lydia. I ...wouldn't want to be a bother." Poulette looked down at her left hand which had begun to tremble uncontrollably. "I think I'd prefer to stay home and have dinner here."

"Fine, why don't we all have dinner here?" Lydia retorted. "Would you like to talk to Bernadette about the menu or would you like me to do that?" Lydia was smiling, a peculiar response Poulette thought.

"I'll work with Bernadette. I know her limitations in the kitchen. Will your Mr.," Poulette hesitated for a moment not being able to conjure up the name from her memory bank.

"Lombroso, Roberto Lombroso"

"Yes, well, would he mind if we began about 6:30 p.m.?" Poulette's voice was somewhat timid. It had been some time since she had entertained anyone. She hoped that Bernadette Perkins skills were still up to par. It had been even longer since she prepared a meal for a small dinner party on such short notice.

"Poulette, I think that would be wonderful. I'll leave you to it, now. I have some work to do before tomorrow morning. In the meantime, I'll contact Roberto and we'll see each other for dinner day after tomorrow, all right?"

Lydia patted Poulette on the shoulder and headed for the small elevator with wineglass in hand.

"Sleep well," she called back as the doors slid shut.

Poulette's thoughts were clear at that moment. *It was a setup,* she thought. *Lydia had planned all along to invite this Roberto Lombroso person to dinner at the house. Did she really want her to attend, or was she just an inconvenience?*

***

When Lydia arrived in her room, she immediately pulled her cell from the nightstand and speed dialed the first number on it.

"We're on," she said softly. "Yes, I'm almost certain it's here. She was wading through a trunk load of old photos tonight. No, it shouldn't be too hard to find. I'll try to do some searching about before I leave for the lab tomorrow. In fact, I might just go down into the cellar tonight. Yes, yes, I know. I'm always careful. I love you, too." Lydia tossed the cell phone on the chair and slowly opened the door to the corridor. The house was quiet. Both

Bernadette Perkins' room and that of Bertrand Fox, the butler-chauffeur were located in what was once called the servants' wing in days past. Today, it was a section of the house literally set off from the central living quarters by heavy closed doors. Lydia felt quite confident that she could slip undetected from her room to the cellar, if she went immediately. She listened for a moment and then closing the door to her room, crept down the corridor toward the kitchen and pantry. In the corridor, at the far end of the pantry, she found the door to the cellar. It was secured with only a bolt. She slid it back and using a flashlight she had borrowed from the table next to her bed, descended into the cold, moist under croft.

***

"I hardly know what to say," Prior Provincial, the Rev. Austin Cheney was astonished.

"That certainly would be the largest gift the University has ever received and ...."

"It is the least of what I can do for the Order and the University," Roberto Lombroso smiled as he sat back in the comfortable leather chair Austin Cheney reserved for such special guests.

"Well, of course, the answer that you must give is 'yes'!" Lombroso provoked the answer which needed little prompting.

"Now, this would be special graduate school of International Finance in our College of Business which would guarantee on the job training to all of its students, paid training?"

Cheney could scarcely believe his ears.

"Yes, of course. The graduate programs would offer both MBAs and PhDs, the latter being increasingly important today... especially in international finance. The paid student internships would be for at least a semester, perhaps longer; but when these students got their degrees, they would have had meaningful on-the-job experience making them highly desirable to the best firms on Wall Street or frankly any financial market in the world. This would put St. Edmund's on the international map, Father."

"Our Board of Trustees will be meeting in about a week. I really would like you to make the announcement yourself, Mr. Lombroso...."

"Please, Father, it is Roberto or Robert if you prefer."

"Roberto, could you come?" Austin Cheney's eyes were as big as a child's.

"I will make it whenever it is, Father. I pretty much set my own schedule. If you tell me the date, I will have the first part of my installment ready to present to you or your board chairman." Lombroso rose and held out this hand to the still astonished priest.

"....and oh my, our University President, Father Paul Sullivan. In the excitement of the moment, I almost forgot we will have to meet with Father Paul before we can even approach the Board." Austin Cheney felt his excitement overtaking his good judgment. Father Sullivan had to be given the opportunity to hear any of this first.

"Yes, of course, you just tell me when and where," Lombroso answered jovially.

"The earlier the better if we want to meet with the Board next week. Perhaps, tomorrow evening for dinner at the monastery? We have quite a good chef, a Belgian priest. I'll arrange for us to have a table where we can talk."

Roberto Lombroso smiled but did not answer. This presented a conflict of two necessities. Somehow, he had to make both work.

Chapter 9

"It was very nice of Mr. Lombroso to agree to an early dinner," Poulette selected a fragrance from the Venetian glass tray in front of her and sprayed a modest amount on her wrists and behind her ears.

"Lydia, would you go into my closet and get me my jewelry box? It's on the top shelf, right side of the door. I think I'll wear my pearls tonight."

Lydia Sindona switched on the overhead light and gazed around the modest sized room Poulette called a closet, with its sloping ceiling and small window on one side. Poulette had obviously edited her wardrobe, before moving to this third floor apartment. There were few day dresses, even fewer cocktail or evening outfits and only a smattering of off-the-shelf transparent plastic boxes stacked one upon another containing lingerie, sweaters, scarves and other accessory items. From deep behind the sweater box, Lydia spotted a small chest she pulled off the shelf.

"Here it is, Poulette. Would you like me to open it for you?" Lydia turned to see Poulette literally lunge for the chest.

"No!! Stop! That's not the one. Give it to me!" Poulette grabbed the leather covered box and stumbled back into the closet where she stuffed it to the back, behind a container of scarves; she then retrieved another container from a lower shelf and flicked off the closet light.

"This is what I was looking for." Lydia stood speechless as the elderly woman meandered with an unsteady gait back to the stool in front of her vanity table. From a drawer in the vanity she removed a perfectly unremarkable key and opened the book-sized case with a single turn of the lock.

"You see, Lydia, these are three strands of perfectly matched South Sea pearls." Poulette held up the necklace allowing the protective flannel cloth to fall to the floor. "Lucas....your father told me they were the most precious pearls in the world." She turned to Lydia who stood mute. "I don't suppose you like to hear that, do you?" Poulette smiled as she handed the pearls to Lydia. "Would you help me put them on? My fingers don't work the way they once did." Lydia took the pearls from Poulette hands and easily secured them around her neck.

"Don't worry dear. They will be yours." Poulette said nothing more. From the corner of her eye she could see a menacing darkness which had descended over Lydia, an expression that could have been interpreted as frightening.

"Why don't you go downstairs now and prepare for the arrival of your friend, Mr. Lombroso. I'll be down in a few minutes."

Without a comment, Lydia walked to the elevator, the doors of which opened immediately. She had no response, only a curiosity about what Poulette was concealing in the leather covered case. Her foray to search the cellar of the old mansion evening before last had been a total waste of time. It could take years to find anything among the cartons, trunks and stacks of papers and old furniture stored in the area. Roberto would not be happy with her excuse, but he may be intrigued by Lydia's more personal secret box. It made sense. Who would her father Lucas Sindona have entrusted with the most important secret he had but the woman he loved and trusted above all others. Poulette Granville Barker still guarded that secret. Before the elderly woman's mental faculties deteriorated any further, Lydia would have to discover what was in the mysterious box and take it from her.

***

It was an early dinner in Poulette's mind, earlier than she had wanted, but Roberto Lombroso had requested it, with cocktails beginning at 5:30 and dinner served promptly at 6:00 p.m. Lydia had sulked since Lombroso's prompt arrival, consuming two glasses of Chardonnay in rapid succession after which she sank into silence, seating herself away from the other two, while paging through a Granville Barker family photo album that she had plucked from a shelf in the library, where cocktails were being served. When the dinner gong sounded, Poulette immediately seated Roberto Lombroso to her left. It was an undersized circular table that Mrs. Perkins had prepared in front of the fireplace of the elegantly paneled main dining room. Lydia took the only chair positioned at a short distance from the other two.

"I hope you're hungry," Poulette intoned as Bernadette Perkins ladled out bowls of soup from a handsome porcelain tureen. "It's a cream of wild mushroom soup."

"But, I sense something more; something very special in this recipe." Lombroso smiled as he took another whiff from the steamy bowl that had been placed in front of him.

"Well, I add a bit of Madeira wine... and just the merest touch of white truffle oil," Poulette leaned into Lombroso as if sharing a very personal secret. "They are my own additions to the recipe."

"Then, I am delighted you chose to share your secret with me," Lombroso smiled coyly, not oblivious to the playful and flirting allure of his hostess and dinner partner.

"But this isn't the piece de resistance." Poulette's voice was almost seductive. "Do save yourself for something... very special."

"Very special you say, I wonder what that could be?" Lombroso took another sip of the delicate soup.

"It's a standing rib roast, cooked rare. Lydia told me it is a favorite of yours. I hope you will enjoy the way we have prepared it." Poulette glanced at her house guest; Lydia Sindona did not return her gaze but instead continued to spoon her soup in silence.

***

"... and then Prince Charles said, 'It wasn't your fault, old boy. I always win!" Poulette brought her napkin to her lips trying to stifle a chortle. She had not just been been giggling at Roberto Lombroso's stories throughout the dinner, but laughing uproariously.

"Oh, my dear, I don't remember when I have laughed so much. What a very adventuresome life you have led." Poulette looked down at her dinner plate and realized she had scarcely touched the small slice of beef which had been served some time ago.

The antique Kieninger grandfather clock in the library was striking 7:15 p.m. when Bertrand Fox, dressed in a dark server's uniform, moved the silver trolley to Roberto Lombroso's side and rolled back the cover. The fragrant aroma of Rosemary and

Burgundy wine wafted from the standing rib roast that stood in a puddle of au jus. "Poulette, this Prime Rib is incredible; cooked to perfection. I must have another slice." Bertrand Fox proceeded to carve a generous portion from the pink center of the meat and add a dollop of the creamy horseradish sauce from a silver bowl on the trolley. "Yes, I believe I will have more of the Yorkshire pudding, too and of course, another scoop of those mashed potatoes," he instructed.

Lydia Sindona picked away at a rapidly cooling plate of fettuccine, topped with an organic heritage tomato sauce and fresh basil. She was a vegetarian who viewed Lombroso's numerous and diverse appetites with varying degrees of tolerance.

"I'm so pleased you are enjoying everything, Mr. Lombroso. Mrs. Perkins is a fine cook but she gets little chance to show off her skills. My appetite is not what it once was and Lydia...." Poulette did not continue, noting her house guest had barely touched the plate of pasta she had ordered for dinner.

"But I'd bet that Mr. Granville Barker took advantage of both your skills and hers," he said cutting into a particularly succulent slice of the beef.

"He did, of course, but he died quite some time ago, as you may not have been aware. It was all quite sudden. Marcus was still a little boy; it was a terrible shock to all of us." Poulette's voice drifted into a melodic resonance as if she was reliving her memory of the occurrence. "He was such a handsome man, a widower when we met. I was a widow with no children. Friends introduced us and well, we just hit it off, as they said in those days."

Lydia's fleeting look at Lombroso made it obvious his probing of Poulette's past was bearing fruit. While she continued with her story, Roberto reached for the crystal wine decanter and refilled both of their glasses to the rim.

"I wasn't aware that you had been previously married. May I say you are such an attractive...?" He stopped in mid-sentence, interrupted by Poulette who touched his hand and smiled seductively.

"You are a flatterer, Roberto. Yes, I was married... to an Italian banker, Sebastian Calvi. We lived in his family's villa just outside of Milano, a glorious house and, of course we were very much in love. He died quite suddenly in 1982. I met Leon Marcus Granville Barker a year later. He was a widower with a three year old son, Leon Marcus the third. He was somewhat older than I, but I think we were well matched in many ways.

"We married soon after we met and built this beautiful home. My stepson Marcus and I are very close. He is an Edmundite priest and a psychiatrist, you know. I'm certain Lydia told you about him. She knows him very well. They've been friends since childhood; right, Lydia?"

Lydia looked up from her pasta and smiled feebly. Roberto Lombroso continued to cut into the succulent meat on his plate, using the Yorkshire pudding to absorb the herbal-laced gravy.

"You've obviously led a very interesting life, Poulette. Which brings up the topic of your absolutely charming nick-name. How did you get the name Poulette?" Lombroso looked up from his plate, his steak knife in his right hand, his fork in his left, to see a peculiar expression come over Poulette's face.

"Oh, Mr. Lombroso, that may not be a good question for me to answer." She glanced at Lydia whose countenance was frozen as she hovered over the almost untouched Fettuccine.

"No, no, Poulette, tell him; go ahead, tell him!" she stammered.

"My given name is Patricia and that is what I have been called most of my life. As you may have heard from Lydia, her father, Lucas became a dear friend of mine a number of years ago. Poulette means little chicken in French. For whatever reason, he gave me that name and it seemed to stick." The smile on her face only added to the seething emotion that raged beneath Lydia's otherwise calm demeanor. It did not go unnoticed by Poulette or Roberto.

***

It was almost 8:20 p.m. when Chairman of the Board of Trustees, Mark Tobin, University president Father Paul Sullivan and Prior Provincial Father Austin Cheney rose to greet Roberto Lombroso who had hung his dripping wet coat and umbrella on a rack placed outside the dining room.

"I am so sorry not to have been able to join you earlier; but, as I explained to Father Cheney, something important came up that required my attention and then of course, this sudden deluge…. terrible driving weather."

Without being asked, Lombroso took a seat at the center of the oblong table with his back to the rest of the now sparsely populated room.

"We understand, of course," Austin Cheney began. "May I introduce you to our group and again tell you how very generous your offer is." Lombroso did not rise but put his hand out to shake the hands of those seated around him.

"You will join us for coffee and dessert, I hope?" Cheney questioned. "I believe I mentioned to you at our last meeting that our chef, Father Pascal Fouquet is Belgian. Before his ordination, he trained at the Cordon Bleu in Paris. Now, we are fortunate enough to be able enjoy his many talents. I've taken the liberty of asking him to make one of my favorite desserts which he calls O Merveilleux".

The Prior Provincial signaled a young man at the far end of the room who nodded and immediately made his way through two swinging doors to emerge from the kitchen seconds later with a large silver tray filled with frothy pastries and a pot of fragrant coffee. Roberto Lombroso looked down at the extraordinary presentation.

"They look incredible!"

"They're made up of individually baked meringues, spread with fresh red raspberries, topped with whipped crème, and then sprinkled with dark chocolate shavings." a corpulent Austin Cheney smiled broadly at the sight of them.

"Father Fouquet does everything well, but his pastries, well, they are extraordinary." he selected a particularly large and perfectly formed tart for Lombroso.

"I've been telling Father Paul as well as Mark Tobin, who chairs our Board of Trustees, about your very generous offer to create an Institute here at St. Edmund's in our College of Business and needless to say, we are all very excited about the prospect. It was Father Paul's thought that we name the new Institute after you, Mr. Lombroso."

"Oh, no, no…!" Lombroso protested as he scooped up a forkful of crunchy meringue, leaving behind a mustache of whipped crème on his upper lip. "After our last conversation and a meeting with my attorneys, Father, I would prefer, in fact insist, that you not mention a word of this donation to the press or frankly to anyone outside of our group here. As a condition of presenting the gift I will absolutely insist we keep the donor anonymous." Lombroso looked across the table to see the four men stunned. "I'm quite serious: Not a word about who is donating the money for the institute and certainly not my name on the damned building. I take it we understand each other?" His stern facade gradually softened to a smile, a gesture he had perfected in honing a sense of authority that comes only with great wealth and matching power.

"Yes, yes, of course, we understand" Father Paul Sullivan uttered looking furtively around the table for some confirmation from the others.

"Then, if we are all in agreement, my attorneys will draw up the papers. I think you will find them quite standard for a gift of this size in terms of payment schedules. If you have any questions, voice them to the attorneys and we'll do our best to work out any problems." Roberto Lombroso scanned the group for a reaction only to find stunned silence. He took one last forkful of the meringue and whipped cream concoction, dripping some of the juice from the fresh raspberries on the front of his perfectly tailored white shirt. "Well, if there is nothing else, I'll say good night. I have an early flight tomorrow morning. And Father Cheney, please tell your chef, he is indeed an artist."

The table of four rose to their feet when Lombroso stood, each extending his hand to bid their benefactor a good night. Roberto Lombroso hurried out of the dining room alone to retrieve his coat and umbrella unaware of a figure lurking in the shadows of the dimly lit cloister. Clad in a hooded black rain slicker, a figure walked several steps behind the visitor into the deserted rain swept parking area.

***

Roberto Lombroso's black rental, a Ford Focus skidded slightly on the rapidly freezing macadam surface as it stopped for the traffic light at Lancaster Avenue and Spring Mill Rd. Directly behind him, an aged grey Honda skidded as well, missing only slightly the Ford's rear bumper as it came to a stop. Looking into the rear view mirror, Lombroso tried to study the vehicle. The continuing rain blurred the image wiped clear for only a moment between sweeps of the windshield wiper. It could be the same car, he thought; the car that had exited the monastery parking lot only moments earlier and making the same turn on to Spring Mill Road.

"Coincidence," Lombroso said aloud as he flipped the left turn signal just as the light changed, heading East toward Ithan Avenue. He had promised Lydia he'd stop by the house for a nightcap if it wasn't too late. He glanced at the rental car's digital clock on the dashboard. Only 9:30 p.m., she'd be waiting up, he was certain of that. "Damn, another light," he cursed as the traffic light below the church abruptly flashed to red, enabling a parade of St. Edmund's students to saunter slowly across the street to the main campus. A glance through the rear view mirror confirmed that the Honda was stopped directly behind him. Lombroso gunned his engine, making a sharp right on to South Ithan Avenue without using his turn signal; the Honda followed close behind. Lombroso passed the Granville Barker Estate ignoring the 25 mile an hour speed limit and headed to Conestoga Road where he made a sharp right. Directly behind him, the Honda followed. "He is following me," Lombroso said aloud. More stunned than frightened, he took a sudden right at the traffic light on to Sproul Road and headed back to Lancaster Avenue. The nightcap with Lydia would not happen this evening. He would take the blue Route (476) back to Philadelphia and to his suite at the Four Seasons Hotel.

Chapter 10

Vatican City, the Papal Apartment

"... and that's about all, Sean. I didn't rouse him this time. The duration always seems to be about the same, seven to perhaps ten minutes. After that he falls into what seems to be a deep sleep. Sometime, he will wake up after a few minutes; at other times, he appears to be sleeping peacefully." Father Malcolm had opened the door to the Papal apartment only a crack, allowing Father Sean O'Reilly to peek inside. It was a moonless night and the apartment was quite dark except for an ancient looking reading lamp that cast a shadow over the supine form lying in the single bed.

"Malcolm, I'm not certain why I'm here. Our Prior Provincial told me you also summoned Father Marcus Granville Barker. The latter is understandable; after all he's a psychiatrist... but why me?" Father Sean's whisper was intense enough to arouse the interest of a Swiss Guard who turned to study the situation.

"You understand, this is all very confidential. Nothing and I do mean nothing about this matter can ever get out; not now or ever!" Malcolm's voice was intense enough for the Swiss Guard to move several feet closer.

"Let's resume out talk inside the apartment," Malcolm whispered as the two entered and closed the massive door behind them.

"His Holiness asked for you specifically. It was I who asked for Father Granville Barker. Pope Leo remembers your student days here in Rome. You were attending the Pontifical North American College and he was at the Gregorian."

"How many years ago was that, Malcolm? As I recall, we all studied there; you included." Father Sean O'Reilly had moved closer to the Papal bed. Although his breathing was regular, it had a hoarse quality that concerned O'Reilly. "Has he been checked out by his doctor? His breathing sounds like he might have an infection; it's raspy!"

"That's not what I wanted you to see, Sean. 'Holy Father, Holy Father are you awake? Father Sean O'Reilly is here!'"

Leo's eyes opened wide instantly. "You came!" he smiled, trying to right himself to a sitting position.

"Your Holiness, I want Father Sean to see your back. Could you raise your bed clothes?"

"Yes, yes, of course; please take a look at this Sean and tell me what you think," The elderly man lifted the muslin smock to reveal what resembled a tattoo on the left side of his body, inches below the shoulder blades.

Father Sean O'Reilly adjusted the antique reading lamp to get a clearer look at the area.

"Your Holiness, when did you discover these markings?" He gazed at the stains not wanting to touch the skin.

"I have no idea," Leo replied. "It was my internist who saw them during a routine examination a couple of weeks ago and asked if I had gotten a tattoo." He chuckled as he recalled the discovery. "Can you imagine, the Pope with a tattoo?"

Father Sean looked over at Malcolm whose quizzical expression carried a concern not expressed.

"Father Malcolm, might you have a magnifying glass available close by?"

"Malcolm, look in the desk, the center drawer," Pope Leo instructed.

"Yes, here it is." He handed the large philatelist's glass to Sean O'Reilly who promptly adjusted the lamp again and inspected the markings.

"Holy Father," he began, "...these markings are Aramaic. They read, Simon bar Jonah.".

"Those are the words inscribed on the stone where St. Peter's bones were discovered. You found them, Sean, in the Scavi; you discovered the inscription and the bones. But how and why do they appear on my back and how did they get there?"

Father Sean O'Reilly stood up to his full height and handed the magnifying glass back to Malcolm.

"I don't know, Holy Father. But these marks appear to be coming from inside your body to the surface skin. This is not a tattoo. It was not topically applied."

Malcolm helped the Pope to lower his nightdress and ease back into bed again before turning off the lamp. "If there is anything you need, Holy Father, please let me know," Malcolm called as he and Sean O'Reilly walked to the door.

"Yes, Holy Father, please have Malcolm call me; I'll be here instantly," Sean O'Reilly acknowledged.

***

It was 4:45 a.m. before Father Sean O'Reilly's head touched the pillow in his bed again. He would sleep for another four hours before meeting with his colleague Father Marcus Granville Barker, acknowledged scholar and psychiatrist and now a secret adviser on the very peculiar condition of Pope Leo XIV's mysterious eruptions on his back.

Chapter 11

For Father Marcus Granville Barker even the icy cold water he continued to splash across his freshly shaven face could not relieve the jet lag he was feeling this morning. It was already ten past eight and his meeting at the Institute was called for 8:30 a.m. As he patted his face dry, there was a knock at the door.

"Yes, just a moment!" he responded wrapping a bath towel firmly around his waist and pulling back the chain lock from the door.

"Major Salvatore Franco, Swiss Guard to escort you to the Institute, Sir" he announced.

"Yes, of course, I'll be ready in a moment." Marcus slammed the door abruptly on the Guard as he hastened quite literally to speed dress. Within less than five minutes, he reopened the door carrying the well-worn attaché case as well as his coat. Major Salvatore Franco walked close to his side.

"I don't suppose we could stop for a cup of coffee before we leave?" Marcus was hopeful but not expecting a positive reply.

"No, Father; my instructions are to bring you directly to the Institute for your meeting. We are to stop nowhere."

"Of course," Marcus replied slipping into the heavy black woolen overcoat as they walked, while holding tightly to the attaché case.

"Is the IOR far from here?" he asked primarily to make conversation.

"No, Father, you can see the tower over there. It's about a three minute walk." Major Franco nodded with his head in the direction of an undistinguished multi-storied building which literally was a stone's throw from the Domus Sanctae Marthae.

Despite his Swiss Guard escort, Father Marcus Granville Barker was required to go through security, placing his attaché case unopened on the belt while removing his shoes and placing them into the plastic bin with his top coat and suit jacket.

"Father, would you also please remove your belt?" An armed Papal Gendarme requested in English.

"Yes, yes, of course!" Marcus could not ignore the Glock 17 semi-automatic pistol and the 9 mm Parabellum he wore at his side.

Ten minutes later, at exactly 8:30 a.m. Father Marcus Granville Barker entered a small windowless conference room on the sixth floor of the IOR building. Three Cardinals, seated around a small conference table looked up as the door opened and Marcus entered. They did not rise.

"You have the package?" One of them asked as he entered.

"Why, yes; here it is!" Marcus placed the battered case on the table waiting to be asked to sit down.

The most senior of the small group, pulled the case toward him and proceeded to enter two combinations into the two security locks and then with a key from around his neck, turned a lock on the right side of the case. It opened with a snap, its top flung toward Marcus preventing him from seeing its contents.

"Thank you, Father. That will be all. You may go now," he said without looking up.

Marcus stood motionless for a moment. To his left was a wall with a most unusual three dimensional brushed metal sculpture which curved like a wave, away from the partition, dipping down at a most peculiar angle.

While the cardinal had been occupied entering the combination data, Marcus had been studying the design, certain he had detected a silhouette behind the metal waves in the section that protruded at an odd angle. In fact, he was convinced he saw the shadow of someone. The proceedings were being watched, he concluded, by at least one or more likely several persons who did not wish to be identified.

"Father, again, thank you, you may go!" This time the Cardinal's voice was insistent, as he stared at the immobile priest. Marcus took one last glance at the strange wall sculpture and turned to leave. As he pushed hard on the metal lever door handle, he was now certain he heard the rustle of silk coming from the direction of the mysterious piece of art.

It was only 8:40 a.m., an interlude of less than ten minutes. Why had the cardinals insisted he meet them in the board room when they could have easily sent someone to the hotel for the case or ...? It did no good to speculate, he decided. With no Swiss Guard in sight, he headed back in the direction of the hotel. His meeting with Father Sean O'Reilly and Father Malcolm was scheduled for 9:45 a.m., which gave him more than enough time for breakfast with a well-deserved carafe of steamy Italian coffee.

***

"... and then out of the blue, he shouted, 'No, no, not you' whatever that meant. He was looking directly at me. Jess, it was just crazy. I know he's trying to tell me something, but he just can't seem to get it out! It must be terribly frustrating. " Caroline sliced off a minute portion of her cheese and mushroom omelet, then slowly munched away at each ingredient as she recalled her morning visit with Philip. She had joined Jessica for lunch at the Main Line Cricket Club on a brisk Saturday afternoon.

"But, you do think he is getting better." Jessica's crab salad Louis was nearly gone. Not wanting to appear to have rushed through their meal, she began to pick away at what remained of the lettuce leaf base.

"Oh yes, yes, he is better; Bryn Mawr Rehab is doing a terrific job. He is awake, well sort of and he is walking, again sort of; they have this harness contraption that he wears and then pretends to walk on a tread mill. It's really quite fascinating to watch. But, it's this crazy inability to tell me what he is thinking that drives both of us crazy. What do you think he means?"

"Honestly, I have absolutely no idea." Jessica uttered between munches of her lettuce leaf.

"Mrs. Rawlins?"

"Yes?" both women answered in unison to the spunky young table captain who stood before them. "There's a Mr. Watkins on the phone at the front desk for one of you."

"Oh, it's for me," Jessica replied. "It can't be good if he's calling me on a Saturday."

Caroline said nothing but gestured to the waiter who stood some feet away.

"I'll have another Pinot Grigio, Michael, please tell the bartender not to skimp on the portion size this time."

Chapter 12

"... and with Sophomore Bruce Chapman's spectacular 60 yard run, at half time, ladies and gentleman Princeton's Tigers lead the Pennsylvania Quakers 56 to 17!" Jessica heard the roar of the crowd and the competing bands as she pulled into the garage. It was obvious; Alex Rawlins' Tigers and Jed Watkins' Quakers were entertaining "the boys" this sunny Saturday afternoon.

"Hi, Honey, you want something to drink...a Heinekens or a Bud?"

"I'll pop one for you," Jed added pulling an icy can from a large tub Alex had placed on the shiny hardwood floors of their family room. Jessica grimaced but gave a polite "No thank you," to the suggestion.

"Well, you timed your entrance perfectly, Jess. We can have our little meeting and then Alex and I can get back to the important activity of the day... Football," both men shouted in unison.

"Well, until you two are finished with your discussion, I'll make myself unavailable," Alex murmured while clicking off the mammoth 85 inch television screen.

"No, Alex, please stay. There is something I'd like to talk to you about, as well."

Jessica pulled bottle of cold Perrier from the refrigerator and joined the men in the family room.

"Jess, I know it is asking a lot of you after all you've been through this last year, but there is an assignment that calls for the kind of attention you and only you can give to it." Jessica recognized the tone; Jed Watkins, chief of the Philadelphia regional office of the CIA was setting her up for another assignment.

"Let me guess, the president of the United States is calling for me again?" Jessica was highly skeptical, although in the last case, indeed it was the Office of the President that called upon her via Jed.

"No, not the president, this time it's the Pope!"

"Oh come on, Jed, I'm not even Catholic; not Roman anyway. I'm Anglican Catholic; that's Episcopalian. Remember

Henry VIII? Why would the Pope want me? I take it this is another of those international-coop missions where I take orders from some other country's director. I hate those!"

"Well, Jess, let's put it this way, you are experienced in the field; you speak a good Calabrian dialect of Italian, slightly flawed but passable. In addition to that, you fit the final qualification," Jed Watkins paused taking a large swig from the can of Heinekens in his hand.

"And exactly what is that final determining qualification?"

"You are a woman. You'll be working in the Pope's personal service as a member of the Memores Domini, a lay association of men and women who practice poverty, chastity and obedience and who live in an environment of silence and common prayer."

Alex caught the wide grin that was developing across Jed's face.

"You ARE kidding aren't you? Obedience, poverty, silence? This is not an assignment for me. No, no, Jed, you ain't sending me off to a convent; absolutely, positively not!"

"I have no objections, Jed!" Alex was stifling a laugh as he watched his perplexed wife who wasn't certain whether Jed Watkins was jesting or actually telling her about this proposed assignment. "All right, Jed, joke is over with. Now, tell me the truth. What is the assignment? Where is it and when do I leave?"

"This IS the assignment, Jess. You leave Tuesday evening for Italy. You will be at the Vatican for at least four to six weeks as a member of the Pope's personal household staff.

"Now, sit down while I give you a short briefing. When you get to the office on Monday morning, we'll go through the particulars. Alex, I want you to stick around, too. Your clearance is still active and we may be able to use you on this assignment, as well."

Jessica's incredulity was replaced by a serious expression. As a field agent, she had played a number of roles over the years, but none as seemingly dreary as this one.

"This assignment has to do with international money laundering, murder, the Italian Mafia and the Vatican Bank, also known as the Institute for Works of Religion or the IOR. It is one of the most secretive organizations in the world and appears to ignore all the rules other international banks conform to. In fact, most of us would have a hard time recognizing it as a bank at all. Its history goes all the way back to the war years of 1942. It doesn't do anything most of us think of when we think bank. To become a client you must go through a very stringent background check. Once you are accepted, however, don't expect the bank to issue you a checkbook or give you a mortgage or a car loan; you won't find any ATMs around either. What it really is, and, Alex, you probably will understand this better than I do... it is a discreet, off-shore style bank that holds funds for its clients. Il Sole 24 Ore, an Italian financial daily newspaper recently reported that the 8 billion Euros in the bank is invested in currency and bond markets; they're also heavily into gold reserves and most recently, crypto currency." Jed paused for a moment to open another Heinekens.

"Sorry, Jed, what does this have to do with me and an assignment to be a scullery maid or whatever, in the Pope's household?" Jessica was truly befuddled. Alex did not seem to connect the dots either.

"The Pope is going after the bankers. The last Pope tried, but as you know he died very suddenly; I'm not saying anything was amiss, but it was remarkable how suddenly it happened after his announcement. The bank is totally corrupt and this Pope wants to clean it up, once and for all."

"The boys from Sicily won't like that," Alex commented as he leaned against the counter in the kitchen and snatched a potato chip from a bag he'd opened earlier.

"Not Sicily any longer, old man. This new Mafia is based in Calabria and is known as the 'Ndrangheta.' We know that it gathers each year on November 3 high in the mountains in a little church called Santa Maria di Polsi to initiate new members, discuss strategies and pray."

"That's next Thursday," Jessica interrupted.

"Yes, it is, Jess, and you will be in the village on that day visiting with your Calabrian 'cousin' who will brief you on your assignment in the Pope's household. She will be your reference for this position. She also has arranged for you to help her serve the guest-visitors in their meeting places, picking up any conversation or other information that might be valuable. His Holiness will expect you at the Vatican a week from Monday."

Jessica sat silently. She had no comment; not even a question. What could she say?

"You don't have to accept the assignment, Jess, you know that. It really is your decision." Alex put his arm around his wife and gave her an affectionate squeeze.

"Jed will understand if you say no, won't you, Jed?" There was no answer from the Chief.

"Yeah, well, I'll go! It's a dirty job and somebody has to do it, right? But I insist on one thing -- latex gloves. I'm not cleaning anyone's toilet without a good strong pair."

Chapter 13

"You can't just send him home in this condition." Caroline found herself almost shouting. "Look at him! Without those cables on that device holding him up, he can't stand. He certainly can't walk and his speech is almost incoherent!"

"As I told you yesterday, Mrs. Rawlins, we have done all we can for him and it is time for him to go home. Our Social Worker will help you find suitable professional care, if you like; but with or without our help, he must be out of here by tomorrow noon. I have notified our transport service to be ready to move him and his belongings tomorrow. Unless you prefer to do the packing and move him yourself, that is. I've already made arrangements for one of our volunteers to begin getting his things together as we speak."

The Rehabilitation Center's director did not wait for a reply. Instead, he turned, making a hasty retreat from the neuro-therapy gymnasium to a staff only stair case at the end of the corridor.

"Oh, Philip, there has to be another answer." Caroline's words were prayerful and uttered almost silently. They did not go unheard.

***

It was 9:30 a.m. local time when Jessica's C130 military transport plane made a bumpy landing at Camp Darby, a U.S. military fast-response base located on 2500 acres of forested land a few miles north of Livorno.

"Agent Rawlins, Base Commander Lt. Col. Francis Greeley asks that you join him immediately in his office. He is about to conduct a briefing and would like you to attend."

"Of course," Jessica answered adjusting the small canvas bag she was carrying over her shoulder and shuffling down the plane's foldaway metal staircase.

"We have a Jeep waiting over here, Ma'am; hope you don't mind riding in a Jeep." The young American Army Private walked at an energetic clip leaving Jessica to pick up her pace.

"Not at all," she answered recalling the many times in the past she had ridden in vehicles that would make this one look like a luxury sedan.

"First time at Camp Darby?" he inquired opening the door to the two seat vehicle. "It's a very interesting place. We actually have two commanders, one Italian and one American and if you were to ask most military stateside, they'd say they've never heard of the place." He climbed into the driver's seat, turned the key, shifted the clutch and floored the engine.

"In other words, the base is highly classified," Jessica added.

"Yes, Ma'am, highly. We're under the authority of the commander of the 22nd Setaf group of Vincenza. That's the number one U.S. Army base in Southern Europe. We also host a NATO command that is managed by the U.S. Army. We do just about everything here. We're a weapons depot, a maintenance facility and a training facility. You'll also find offices of the 26th Army, Air Force and Pentagon here."

"Just about everything," Jessica repeated wondering exactly why her driver believed she should be pre-briefed on what was quite obviously not for consumption by the average visitor.

"Here we are, Ma'am. You'll find Col. Greeley through those doors and one flight up." The Jeep had stopped in front of an unimposing two story structure with no signage.

"Thank you for the ride and the information." She opened the door herself and slammed it shut.

The Jeep sped off in the direction from which they had just arrived. Jed had told her to pack nothing but toiletries. Everything else would be supplied. By toiletries, he meant a brand-free toothbrush, which was supplied by the Firm, the same with toothpaste, no deodorant nor antiperspirant would be allowed, a comb, again brand free and a bottle of Ibuprofen, packaged in a non-descript generic container. There would be no cosmetics for the next few weeks. Jessica grimaced at the thought of it.

She took a deep breath: The air was fresh with a slight scent of pine. She remembered that Jed had mentioned during his briefing that within the perimeters of the camp there was a large and ancient pine forest which camouflaged silos hidden deep within the earth. What they housed or stored? That he did not include in his briefing.

"Agent Rawlins, right on time, I'm Col. Greeley. Glad to have you with us." He did not offer his hand, but continued with the introductions. "... to my right is Col. Gabriele Vasari; Col. Vasari and I share the running of this place. We'll continue with the introductions and other formalities later, if we have time. Right now, let's get to the point of this briefing. Take the seat right next to Col. Vasari, if you will, please." Greeley's brusque manner was more of a jolt to Jessica's jet lagged body than the hot cup of coffee she craved but was nowhere in sight.

"Agent Rawlins will be with us for only a few hours. We want to make the most of her time here because we can have absolutely no contact once she leaves our boundaries. Her destination, by later this evening, will be the Sanctuary of Santa Maria di Polsi in the heart of the Aspromonte Mountains near San Luca in Calabria." Greeley flashed a large aerial photo of the enclosed mountain sanctuary on to a wall opposite the conference table.

"She'll be staying with SISMI (Italian Military Intelligence) Agent Giovanna Poloni who will be reporting to our Col. Vasari. Agent Poloni has made arrangements for Agent Rawlins to stay with her on the family farm, which quite literally is located on the village border. This, Agent Rawlins will give you a degree of privacy and we believe will be safer for you than any location we might find for you in the village. You will be introduced as a cousin. Agent Poloni will have everything you require in terms of personal supplies and clothing. I understand your Calabrian dialect is sufficient?" Greeley looked directly at Jessica who answered him in Italian. "I hope you will find it passable."

Greeley turned to Vasari who gave a nod, she would be passable.

"You will be arriving literally one day before the start of the annual November assembly of the 'Ndrangheta. This is one of the most important and most secretive criminal consortiums in the world. During this convention, each local boss must give an accounting of the lucrative criminal activities that have occurred under his watch during the past year. He gives this accounting to the capo crimine who is elected each year at the end of the meeting as the "boss of all bosses".

"I should add that this meeting is international. There will be members of the 'ndrine from many countries around the world including Canada, the United States and as far south as Australia," General Vasari clicked the power point to show a large map indicating the locations of various criminal branches of the 'Ndrangheta.

Jessica listened carefully remembering the positions of each 'ndrine she would be meeting, knowing how crucial it would be to completing her assignment in San Luca as well as at the Vatican.

"That about completes the briefing. Col. Vasari and I will meet with you right now, Agent Rawlins, in my office to complete the specific details of your assignment." Greeley stood up, a sign Jessica took to mean,

"... Follow me."

"After you have changed into the clothing in that case, you will walk to the local train station which is about a mile and a half from here. Not a bad walk at all in this weather," Greeley had the uncomfortable habit of not looking directly at the individual he was talking to; in this case, he was pointing to a street map which showed the location of the local train station. Without further comment, he handed it to her.

"How long a ride to Santa Maria di Polsi?" Jessica inquired.

"Oh, about eight hours or perhaps a little longer. The train will make numerous stops and does not go as far as Santa Maria; you will get off in the Villa San Giovanni and walk from there. It is perhaps two miles. The two lane road into the village is in fairly good condition at this time of the year. Agent Poloni or one of her relatives will be on the lookout for you to take you to the farm. Now, you will find your train ticket, money and credentials, I.D. etc. in that piece of luggage over there." Jessica turned to see an ancient leather case, heavily scuffed.

"I'd suggest you buy some food in the station to take with you on the train and definitely something to drink We cannot supply you with anything to eat; as you are aware you should have nothing on your person that would associate you with us and a drink or sandwich might just do that. Good luck, Agent Rawlins. I'll call your boss Jed Watkins to let him know we've connected."

Jessica stood up, picked up the scuffed travel case and left the office. Not so much as a bottle of water or a cup of coffee, she thought to herself. Was it lack of courtesy or truly something to do with security? She doubted the latter; "He's just a thoughtless clod," she thought to herself. "... a truly thoughtless clod." She stopped in front of a ladies room, which neither Greeley nor Vasari had been thoughtful enough to point out. It would make as good a changing room as any.

When she exited, her transformation to Calabrian farm woman would be complete.

Chapter 14

"Well, thank God and you, Alex; Philip actually seems calmer and more settled now that we are at home. If you hadn't suggested using the empty suite of rooms on our third floor for his hospital bed and therapy area, I don't know what..." Caroline's line of conversation was interrupted by one of three nurse/therapists hired to attend to Philip around the clock.

"Excuse me, for interrupting, Mrs. Rawlins, but there is someone on the phone asking for Mr. Philip. I thought you might want to take it."

Alex picked up his coat from a side chair where he had tossed it a few hours earlier, placing the muffler around his neck, preparing to leave. "I should be going, Caroline. You take your call and I'll..."

"No, no Alex, please wait. There is something more...." Caroline's demeanor was less than composed as she accepted Philip's cell phone from the nurse.

"Hello, yes, this is Caroline Rawlins; no, my husband is not available. Can I help you?" Caroline's face turned ashen as she listened to the caller.

"Certainly, Officer; yes, Bertrand Fox was right to have you call us. I'll be there as soon as possible. Yes, I'll bring our cousin, Alex Rawlins. He'll know what to do." Caroline pressed the off button on the screen, ending the call.

"It's Poulette; there's been an accident. I think she hit someone with her car. She's at the Radnor police station."

***

"Please, Mr. Fox, there really is no need to apologize; you did the right thing; I understand. I'm in my car with Caroline Rawlins right now and we're only a few minutes away from the police station. Yes, they have Mrs. Granville Barker there. I'll make certain she gets home safely. Yes, of course, I'll call you just before we leave."

Alex Rawlins clicked off his cell phone and tossed it into the cup holder divider in front seat of his BMW. His cell had been off for most of the afternoon. Supervising Philip's transfer from Bryn Mawr Rehab and arranging for a team of nurse-therapists to take on immediate duty had taken nearly the entire day. Now, Poulette and her auto accident would occupy what was left of it.

"Damn," he cursed aloud to Caroline. "Poulette should never have been driving a car in this weather in the first place. Apparently Mr. Fox had suggested he drive her, but she is so damned stubborn and insisted on driving herself. Now look at what has happened. Poulette not only injured a pedestrian with her car, but the victim is an Edmundite priest from the university."

As he pulled the BMW into a parking space in front of the Radnor Police Station, the tires spun slightly. "What could she have been thinking? Even with all wheel drive, a car could easily have slid into something or someone on Lancaster Avenue's slushy streets."

***

Poulette sat silently and emotionless in interview room number 3, a comfortable space in the recently renovated Police building, off Iven Avenue. It was a small room, but technically equipped with video/recording equipment that could document her every move, every word once the official interview began. In the meantime, she sipped a decent tasting cup of tea, albeit from a tea bag, that was accompanied by a wooden stirrer, a napkin and a cellophane wrapped package of cheese and peanut butter crackers. She had just begun to nibble on one of the cracker snacks when Alex and Caroline walked in, followed by Police Superintendent John Schofield and Detective Beverly Franken. Poulette pushed her chair out in an attempt to stand up and embrace Alex, but, anticipating her move, he wrapped his arms around her shoulders.

"I am so glad you're here," she whispered. "I didn't see him; I swear, I didn't. He just appeared out of nowhere."

"Mrs. Granville Barker, I'm Superintendent John Schofield and this is Detective Beverly Franken. Please keep your seat." Detective Franken closed the door softly.

"We'd like to record our conversation if you have no objections?"

"No, I don't mind; please do," Poulette had anticipated the question. Why should she mind? It was an accident.

"Please, tell us what happened." Schofield's voice was soft and non-confrontational.

"Well, it was a little after 3 o'clock; I was heading home after having a late lunch with a friend at Guillifty's. Believe me, I wasn't driving fast because it was still snowing and Lancaster Avenue had not been plowed. It was very slushy. I was within sight of the St. Edmund's stadium, which is on the right, as you know, when someone darted right out in front of the car. He was walking or running very fast. I swear I didn't see him until I heard the thud and of course put on my brakes. My God, I hope he isn't dead." For the first time Poulette realized, she might have killed the pedestrian.

"No, Mrs. Granville Barker, he isn't dead. He's been injured; he's pretty beat up, but he's a long way from being dead." Schofield's tone was consoling.

"Who is he?" she leaned forward, her well-manicured fingers clasped as if in prayer.

"He's an Edmundite, in fact the Prior Provincial of St. Edmunds, Father Austin Cheney. You may in fact know him. No....? One last question and then I'll let you be on your way," Schofield bent forward.

"Mrs. Granville Barker, what did you have to drink at your lunch?"

Poulette sat straight up in her chair, bit her lip and considered her response carefully. "I had a glass of wine, a Chardonnay," she said softly. "Only one, you can check the receipt in my purse. I paid with a credit card and our waitress attached the order to the receipt."

John Schofield stood up. "We'll be in touch, Mrs. Granville Barker. Alex, her car is being examined by our forensic team right now. As you leave, have the clerk at the desk check her insurance information and give him directions as to what should be done with the car when we have finished with it. If you don't have a tow company in mind, we have a list of legitimate businesses in the area; or you might want to call AAA. It's good to see you again, Alex...in town for a while? And, Caroline, how is Philip doing after his accident?" Caroline gave a shortened version of the many trials Philip had endured and of the ongoing therapy sessions at home

Alex was silent, helping Poulette with her coat. It was the first time he had noticed it, a tremor in her left arm as she raised it to slip into the sleeve. The incidental observation left him deeply troubled.

***

Vatican City, the Papal apartments

"Now, Holy Father, I want you to think back and try to remember when these visions began and if you can remember the first vision." Father Marcus Granville Barker's voice was soothing and calm, almost hypnotic.

"They began when I was still in Seminary, perhaps 25 years of age. I was here at the Vatican. I'd get headaches, terrible migraine headaches. Sometimes, they lasted for days. It was during one of these headaches that the visions began. They are always the same. In these visions, I am not myself. In other words, it is as if I am seeing a scene through someone else's eyes. I may not have one for months and then, they begin again. Sometimes, they repeat themselves, but most often they are continuing. Like a serial.... But I'm afraid..." he paused and said nothing more.

"What are you afraid of, Holy Father?"

"I confess to you, I should never be afraid of death; but in these dreams or visions, I am deathly afraid. I seem to know that I am about to die and in some terrible way!"

Marcus was silent for several seconds. "Holy Father, I think we've talked enough for today. I'd like to visit you daily, if that is possible to talk more. But, right now, I would like to see the markings on your back."

Malcolm helped Pope Leo remove his shirt, and then indicated where the markings appeared. There was no doubt they were present, Marcus observed. They were characters that even he could see were purposeful.

"You will note, Marcus, that these markings do not seem to have been impressed, or carved into the surface area but they seem to rise from below."

Father Marcus Granville Barker grimaced at the painful looking markings.

"When did you first notice these, Holy Father?" he helped the Pope into the shirt he had just removed.

"They began to appear very faintly years ago. Only recently have they seemed 'to bloom' to become more apparent. At one point I was certain they were bleeding and told Malcolm there was blood on the sheets of my bed; but he told me there was no blood; it was so real I cannot believe I was imagining it... and the markings? Father Malcolm says they are in Aramaic... they read Simon bar Jonah; those are the words on the original tomb of St. Peter. Why would they be on my back?"

Neither Marcus nor Malcolm could answer the Holy Father's questions. Both hoped they would be able to find an answer that would satisfy everyone.

Chapter 15

"Then, it's all over, Detective? He dropped the charges; Oh thank God! Yes, and thank you so much for letting me know. When can the car....oh, I see, Mr. Fox knows where to pick it up. Yes, I'll let him know it's available. Again, thank you! I am so relieved."

Poulette clicked off her cell phone and tossed it on the small sofa in the living room of her third floor apartment. It was over with; perhaps now she could forget the whole horrible episode. She wrapped the cashmere pashmina snuggly around her shoulders and picked up the remote to light the gas fireplace. Whether it was an accident or not she blamed herself. How could she not have seen that priest step out in front of her car? Yet, she hadn't. In fact, she could admit to no one that she scarcely remembered anything about that afternoon. Lunch? She went through it again in her mind. Yes, she had driven to Guillifty's to meet Eleanor Thornton to discuss their exhibit in the Flower Show. They had each ordered a glass of white wine and after that, she remembered nothing. It had been a risk telling the police she could prove she hadn't had more than one glass of wine. She couldn't prove it. Truth be told, she could not produce the receipt from lunch. Did Eleanor pay for lunch? She shuttered slightly as she walked to the small wet bar near the ceiling high book case to pour herself a drink. The ice bucket had been filled. A fresh bottle of Johnny Walker Black Label had been placed on the counter. It was almost five o'clock, she noted, as she picked up a small crystal tumbler from the shelf and selected a cube of ice from the bucket. From somewhere distant, she heard a voice scream..."Oh my God!"

Was it she who watched as if in slow motion the crystal tumbler drop from her quivering left hand to shatter into icy slivers across the dark and polished Macassar ebony floor? There was no sound except the voice in her head.

"Poulette?? Poulette, are you all right?" Lydia Sindona, still wearing her coat dashed from the elevator toward the trembling woman who stood above the broken glassware transfixed. Her left hand still trembled, the palsy exaggerated. "I can't make it stop, Lydia. My hand, it won't stop moving."

"There, there Poulette; everything will be fine. Let's sit down over here and you can tell me what happened."

She removed her coat tossing it over a chair. Poulette said nothing but stared into the fire.

"I take it you were making yourself a drink? Why not let me make it for you. Scotch, right, with a splash of water?"

"Thank you, Lydia; that's exactly right. Go light on the water." Poulette grasped her left hand and held it tightly as the trembling diminished.

Lydia handed her the drink and poured one for her. "Now, my dear Poulette, tell me what happened."

Poulette took a small sip of the icy beverage and settled back, not certain exactly how much she could or should say. As she looked at Lydia she felt calmness come over her. Perhaps she could tell her... at least, a little."

***

"But, Lydia, the point was to not leave her alone nor let her drive," Father Marcus Granville Barker stood barefoot in his darkened room at the Domus Sanctae Marthae (St. Martha's House) in Vatican City. "Sorry, I know, I know, you're not her baby sitter and you had to be in Toronto to make your presentation. Look, it's about 2:45 a.m. here, so if I'm not making total sense. Yes, I had a long conversation with Bertrand Fox. He is going to hide the car keys; she is not allowed to drive any longer. If you could, check in on her during the night.... I realize that is an imposition, but .... Then, you understand. Yes, and thank you so much. Yes, we'll talk tomorrow, perhaps a little earlier if you can do that. Right... and thank you again, Lydia, I am counting on you. I may be in Rome a bit longer than I had anticipated."

Marcus clicked off the phone and left it on the bedside table. Lydia should not have left her alone for a night; Bertrand Fox should never have allowed Poulette to drive under any condition, but especially when weather conditions were as dangerous as they had been apparently. He rubbed his eyes and took a deep breath. His alarm was set for 6:00 a.m. He was attending a private Mass with the Holy Father in his private chapel in a few hours. He had to get some sleep.

***

2200 hours (10:00 p.m.) on an unlighted tratturo heading toward the village of Santa Maria di Polsi in Calabria, Italy

In Italy, they are called tratturo; ancient dirt pathways, many of which date back to the days of ancient Rome. Rugged and often rocky, they snake through the mountains, to high green pastures, often winding along streams and through villages. These are the trails formed, over the ages, by the seasonal migration of cattle and sheep. Today, they are used as much by humans who often prefer them to modern paved roads when travelling among the tiny and ancient villages that dot the craggy Aspromonte Mountains of Calabria.

It was on this moonless night that Jessica found herself trekking a tratturo toward the village of Santa Maria di Polsi to meet her contact, SISMI (Italian Military Intelligence) Agent Giovanna Poloni. As to her thoughts, as she followed the trail upward and into the higher altitude, an exact translation would be unprintable. Base Commander Lt. Col. Francis Greeley had totally underestimated or purposely misled her about everything during her short briefing. There had been no food kiosks at the train station near Camp Darby where she expected to purchase sufficient food for her trip. Shops in the area surrounding the station were closed for a siesta that would last long after her train had departed; sandwiches offered for sale on the more than nine hour trip to the final stop at San Giovanni were not only outrageously costly but almost inedible... stale white bread with thinly sliced pungent cheese. The warm bottle of Fanta orange soda available for purchase near the end of the rail trip was all that was keeping her alive now. She was starving, thirsty and very tired; still suffering the effects of jet lag as well as the inevitable exhaustion from walking miles on rugged terrain at high altitude. What was it Greeley had told her? Santa Maria di Polsi would be a short two and a half mile trek from the train station at San Giovanni. He might have added at least several miles to that estimate and mentioned that all of them were up hill. Perhaps the one good thing, she could think of at this point, was the absence of traffic...any traffic. There were no cars, no wagons, no bikes, no cattle, sheep nor horses, absolutely nothing. She stopped momentarily to catch her breath and rest her feet, placing the single piece of luggage she carried in the center of the cattle path to make a seat for herself. How much further, she wondered before someone would come to meet her?

An answer came less than ten minutes after resuming her trek; the sound of a 7092 Kalashnikov automatic rifle pierced the quiet Calabrian night. Simultaneously, an unseen force hurled Jessica and her luggage into a wet and gravelly ditch some five feet below the tratturo. She was thrown with such force, her case opened and the few belongings within, landed with a thud on the top of her head.

Chapter 16

6:50 a.m., the Private Chapel of the Pope, Papal Apartments, Vatican City

A cool moisture permeated the interior of the ancient structure which housed the Vatican apartments. The sun had not risen yet this November morning making the prevalent shadows of those who walked the corridors more sinister than they might be later in the day. The only sound resonating from inside the Cappella Paolina, the Private Chapel of Pope Leo XIV, was that of a raspy respiration. As the Swiss Guard stood aside to admit Father Marcus Granville Barker, almost hidden in the shadows of the chapel and purposefully standing a considerable distance from the pontiff, were Father Malcolm De Laurencin and Father Sean O'Reilly who beckoned to him. Marcus' steps were slow and measured; the leather soles of his shoes ricocheting like canons across the marble floors and walls creating a disturbing dissonance.

The Holy Father seemed unmoved by the intrusion. It was his habit, Malcolm explained, to rise at 5:45 a.m. during the week and come to the chapel almost immediately in preparation for a private Mass at 7:00 a.m. Malcolm, who served as his acolyte at these daily Masses had played witness to this for many months. Today, however, something was amiss. Leo had been in this position of prayer and meditation for more than his usual hour; moving not a muscle. He was kneeling on a 15th century rosewood Prei Deu looking upward at Michelangelo's immense painting of St. Peter's crucifixion; his eyes transfixed on the suffering face of the saint who looked back at him as he was crucified upside down.

"Shall I interrupt him?" Malcolm directed his question to Marcus who motioned the two to step aside while he moved in closer to get a better view of the pontiff. He examined him visually for several seconds. There could be no doubt; the Pontiff was in an altered state of consciousness. Intentionally stepping in front of the Prei Deu, Marcus moved closer to the Pontiff's face, placing himself between the Holy Father and the tortured stare of St. Peter.

"Marcus? Oh, Marcus" Leo's startled face looked up and into that of the psychiatrist. "I have just had the most remarkable experience; I have spoken to St. Peter who wishes me to do something; something that is at Our Savior's request."

***

"Cugina, cugina, please wake up!" Jessica felt the sting of a sharp slap across her left cheek. She gasped and in that moment awakened to the sweet, warm smell of cow dung. In the near darkness she saw a face almost next to her whom she could not identify. "Giovanna?" she whispered, using her right arm to raise herself from the blanket-over-straw bedding where she was lying. A sharp pain radiated up from the elbow to her shoulder sending her back to the mat with an anguished cry. It was either badly bruised or sprained, she surmised. This was not good; she would be off to a bad start.

"No, no, Cugina Gessica, Giovanna is not here. She had to go to work at the Inn. I am her brother Pier Luigi. We have been looking for you since sunset. When you did not appear, I went out with our mule and cart and my dog and we discovered you in a ditch beside the road. You must have fallen. I did my best to get you into the cart; you seem to be hurt."

Jessica maneuvered herself into a sitting position. The only light came from a distant area of the large cattle barn where an oil lantern hung precariously from an iron peg hammered into a beam near her.

"Someone shot at me with what I suspect was more than a high powered hunting rifle." Her Calabrian accent was deliberate and strong. "I was thrown by the blast into that ditch and that is the last I remember until now. How long have I been here?"

"Only a few minutes; Cosimo and I discovered you a very short distance from our farm, less than a kilometer. What time did you leave the station at San Giovanni? It is about 11 p.m., now." Jessica checked her watch, an inexpensive and older Italian model she was certain had been damaged in the fall.

"The train arrived at the station about 6:30 p.m. But Cosimo? Who is Cosimo, your brother?"

"No, Cugina Gessica, he is my dog and a very special dog, too. When I was only three and he was a puppy, he saved me from drowning in the creek. He went into the fast flowing water after me and pulled my shirt with his teeth until my body was safely out of the water and lying on a slender bed of gravel. He then barked until my mother came. We gave him the name of a saint from this area Fratel Cosimo, who saw apparitions of our dear Virgin Mother. Now, he has also saved you."

"Yes, apparently Cosimo and his master saved me, Pier Luigi. You both have saintly gifts!" Jessica sat up to get a better view of the young man she was speaking with. He had dark hair, not unpleasant features and was small, almost stocky in stature. She suspected he was no more than 13 years old. His clothing would have been typical of a local farm worker in the area.

"My clothes, they were in the suitcase," she said, looking around what she assumed was a barn for some sight of her belongings.

"I'm sorry, Cugina, I did not see a suitcase or your clothing. But do not worry about that, Giovanna has clothing you can wear. When she arrives, we will go into the house and she can show you where you will stay. But until then, there is food in the kitchen, if you are hungry."

"Hungry? I am absolutely famished and very thirsty. Let's get something to eat….and if you have a cloth from the kitchen, perhaps a dish towel, I can make myself a sling for this arm." Pier Luigi was already helping her to stand. When at full height, she realized how truly small he was; she suspected no more than 5 feet in height. It had been a miraculous feat for this young boy and his dog to find her and get her into the cart and back to this barn…. another miracle of St. Cosimo indeed.

***

"Alex, it seems we have this discussion once a year at almost this same time; Jessica leaves you for somewhere and returns in the spring. Will you ever tell me where she is and what she is doing?" Caroline was whispering loudly, to her cousin by marriage, as they stood outside Philip's suite in their Rose Lane home. "If you can't trust me after all this time…" She stopped mid-sentence as a therapist rushed from Philip's bedside, demanding with a wide wave of her arm that they come inside instantly. "Mr. Rawlins, please stand up!" she called out as the figure sitting on the side of the bed, using only his right arm raised himself to a standing position. Then slipping a sturdy aluminum therapy cane into his right hand, she ordered him to, "Walk toward your wife." Philip promptly took several steps in the direction of Alex and Caroline.

"Oh, Philip, this is wonderful! In fact, absolutely miraculous. Alex, look! He can stand and walk!" Caroline rushed to her husband to embrace and hold him for several minutes as Alex slowly moved to the therapist who stood arms folded smiling at the reunion.

"It will be all downhill from now on." There was a satisfaction in her observation and a bit of nostalgia as well. "For me, this has been one of the most challenging cases I have taken on. I'll be cutting my time as his Physical Therapist perhaps to 3 ½ hours a day and sending in someone else to work with Mr. Rawlins on his speech and memory. Retraining the brain may take longer than working with his body."

"Do you have a speech/memory therapist in mind or shall I call Bryn Mawr Rehabilitation to ask for recommendations?" Alex was not enthusiastic about having to call the latter considering Philip's hasty, almost irresponsible dismissal from the facility with little notice.

"I do indeed; he's a medical doctor, an Italian resident whose specialty is brain-injured patients. He has had remarkable success with helping those in his care regain memory and use of their speech. His name is Dr. Roberto Succi. He is a colleague of Dr. Lydia Sindona, whom I think you said you knew. She is a research fellow at the University of Pennsylvania and is staying with Mrs. Granville Barker in Villanova. Here is Dr. Succi's cell phone number. If I remember correctly, Dr. Sindona's specialty and research is on recovering memory, which would be the same as Dr. Succi's. Hmm, isn't that a coincidence?" Alex accepted the card. He would call Dr. Succi as soon as he left Caroline and Philip, who now were sitting together on the edge of his bed, both smiling and seemingly conscious of how very much Philip had progressed since his accident.

Chapter 17

The Rev. Paul Sullivan O.S.E., president of St. Edmund's University silently drummed his fingers on the oval-shaped African mahogany board table. This closed meeting of the executive committee had gone on far past the one hour originally projected for this gathering to discuss Roberto Lombroso's exceedingly generous gift to the University. Yet, Mark Tobin, an Estates attorney and chairman of the board of trustees seemed bent on making his point and getting the small gathering to agree to it.

"The Federal government just does not permit so called anonymous gifts to go unreported even to charities. We will not publish the name of the donor to our alumni and students, if that is what he wishes but he cannot ask us to not to reveal it to Uncle Sam! Surely, we're all sophisticated enough to know that's the way the IRS works. They want to know where the money is coming from. What doesn't everyone understand about this rule?"

Edmundite Prior Provincial Father Austin Cheney sighed; his broken left femur, the result of running into Poulette Granville Barker's car, was ensconced in a rigid plaster cast that lay on top of a pillow on an antique footrest.

"Look, Mark, I'm not in the habit of concealing anything from anybody and certainly not from the U.S. government. But Lombroso made it quite clear when he said. 'Here's the money, but I would prefer no one, including Uncle Sam, know it came from me. Capisce?'"

Angus McCauley, the Board of Trustee's Treasurer brandished a check for the first payment, above his head for everyone to see. It had been delivered by messenger several days earlier. "So, gentlemen, what do you suggest I do with this? You will note the name of the bank on which the funds are being drawn?"

Father Paul Sullivan pulled the check from his hand. "It says the Institute for the Works of Religion. So what objection do you have to getting a check from them?"

Angus McCauley took a deep breath before replying. "That's the Vatican Bank, Father. You know... the Vatican Bank!"

Father Paul Sullivan clutched the check. "I'm sorry, what am I missing here?"

"Father, in the last year and a half this Vatican Bank and several of its key executives, including clergy, have made international news when Interpol began an investigation into money laundering by members of international crime syndicates. That's the problem. This could be, what shall I say, dirty money from the Mafia."

"You mean this check for $60 million from Roberto Lombroso could be ill gotten mob money?"

"Exactly, Father," McCauley looked long and hard at Father Sullivan. "Money reaped from murders for hire to international prostitution to God knows what else."

"You think Lombroso is trying to launder some of this money through the University, is that it?"

"In a nutshell, absolutely; frankly, I suggest we contact the FBI on this one. "

"Oh now, Angus," Father Austin Cheney interrupted; I don't know, the FBI? Isn't that a little dramatic? I mean, Mr. Lombroso gave us a gift. For us to turn him over to the FBI because it was a large gift drawn on an account from the Vatican Bank... well, I mean, wouldn't that be jumping to conclusions?"

Mark Tobin pulled the check from the clutched hand of Father Sullivan. "For the moment this check goes into your safe, Father Sullivan, the wall safe behind that painting." Tobin pointed to a large portrait of the Edmundite Founder which loomed over the conference table. "As for, the FBI, I'll agree to have us all consider very seriously whether we should talk to them and then, meet again next Friday to make a decision. Until then, not a word of any of this to anyone, understand?

"Understood," Cheney answered. "Yeah, O.K." McCauley agreed.

"Father Sullivan? Are we all on the same page here?" Tobin looked directly at the University president who was biting his lip and staring at the table. "If you insist," he finally uttered softly. "Father Cheney, will you lead us in an end of meeting prayer for guidance?"

"Lord, lead us in the path of righteousness..." Cheney prayed, hoping in his heart they all would recognize the guidance from above when it came.

"Amen," they atoned.

"Thank you, gentlemen. Until next week, then! Meeting adjourned." Tobin handed the check to Paul Sullivan who rose to accept it, but did not put out his hand to shake that of the Board of Trustees' Chairman.

"Sorry, Paul," Austin Cheney commented as he passed the University president. "It's just the right thing to do under the circumstances. We can't build our business school on money ill gained from crime."

Father Paul Sullivan said nothing as the Executive committee closed the door to his office behind them.

Chapter 18

Poulette took yet another glance across the table at Lydia's gourmet vegetarian plate, as she cut into her own poached salmon with Béarnaise sauce and freshly steamed asparagus spears. For once, she felt actual envy for the vegetarian fare her housemate was obviously enjoying to its maximum.

"It seems our Mrs. Perkins has picked up real speed preparing your vegetarian recipes, Lydia. I think she is a little bored cooking the same old meals for me every day. This must be an exciting change for her."

Poulette was eyeing the nearly finished Butternut Squash Gnocchi, done Mac and Cheese style with an accompanying Persimmon Caprese Salad. Lydia had been gracious enough to share the amuse Bouche, one of six Chevre-stuffed dried dates sprinkled with Pomegranate Molasses and Chili Oil; but there had been no offer to even taste the Gnocchi.

"Poulette, this is just a suggestion, but you really ought to try some of these new recipes. Vegetarian cooking is not only healthful but it can also be very tasty. Would you like me to draw up some recipe suggestions for you to review and if you find something that sounds as if you'd like to try it, Bernadette can make it for both of us? It could be fun." Lydia took another mouthful of the Persimmon Caprese salad. "I hope you'll share the dessert, actually two desserts, I'm trying out tonight: Maple-Lemon Crème Bruleè and a Baked Apple Stuffed with Candied Ginger and Almonds."

Bertrand Fox poured another generous serving of Pouilly Fumè into Poulette's crystal goblet while accepting Lydia's hand signal that she wanted no more.

"Bertrand, please tell Mrs. Perkins that I will try the baked apple for dessert, this evening; but have her bring a bowl of whipped crème for me, on the side." Lydia could see a less than amused shadow cross Poulette's face as she used Bernadette's last name to order the dessert and whipped crème. It was not the first time she had signaled a defiance at a perceived insolence in Lydia's intrusion into her domestic affairs; in this case, perhaps signaling that she would take the menu suggestions to heart, but not necessarily act upon them in the immediate future.

"Poulette, last evening I thought I heard you imply or say that you and my father began your affair before your first husband died; is that true?" Lydia took a deep breath and a sip of the ice water in front of her.

"It was so very long ago, Lydia, what difference does it make?"

"I suppose not much, but I'd just like to know. Was your husband aware? Weren't you afraid he'd find out?"

Poulette didn't answer immediately.

"Lucas, your father and I met in Milan, when he would come on a pretty regular basis to our villa to see my husband. A very short time and I mean days after my first husband died, he came to console me. I suppose you could say there was an immediate spark. He was married to your mother by that time and there was absolutely no way he would ever leave her; so we made a decision and that was to conduct our affair. We both knew what we were getting into and on all levels, I suppose, if you want to judge, you could say that it was wrong. But I regret none of it; absolutely nothing. Lucas and I had a bond throughout our lives that was stronger than anything either of us had with our marriage partners. I'm sorry, Lydia but that is the truth!"

"But, if there was such a so-called bond and you loved my father, how could you possibly have married Cornelius Granville Barker?" There was a definite note of derision in her voice.

"Please don't judge me, Lydia. I'm not here to get your approval or your opinion, only to tell you the truth about our relationship. Why did I marry Cornelius? I did love him; not in the same way that I loved Lucas, but he presented a certain stability that I could never have with your father. Lucas agreed; he said marry him, which is exactly what I did within 18 months of the death of my first husband. Sometime later, when Cornelius, Marcus and I moved to the Main Line and we built this house, I literally ran into your father in Wayne on the street. I swear, it was quite by accident, but it took my breath away and it stirred up all of the raw emotions we both had in Italy. That was when our affair began, again. It continued for thirty some years even after my husband died."

"Was he the love of your life?" Lydia was trying desperately not to condone the relationship which had been so hurtful to her mother."

"I think, I've told you quite enough, for this evening, my dear. Bertrand, please bring me a brandy. I 'd like to sit by the fire for a while before going to bed."

"Would you like some company? I'll happily join you in that drink," Lydia offered.

"No, not tonight, Lydia; I think you should go to your room now. We'll see each other tomorrow. I'm feeling a little fatigued right now." Lydia could see her smile was forced.

There was more in her offer to have that night cap than she dared admit. Roberto absolutely needed the contents of Poulette's jewel box by week's end. Somehow she had to get into Poulette's room while she slept to search her closet for the mysterious box.

Poulette, this night, was obviously not cooperating.

Chapter 19

It was only profound fatigue and an aching right arm that kept Jessica from tearing a chunk from the loaf of hard- crusted Calabrian bread Pier Luigi had set before her.

"Cugina, cugina, Gessica, please let me cut the bread for you," Pier Luigi easily sliced through the hardened crust with a curved knife he had retrieved from his belt. Without asking, he also carved a portion of cheese too large to be eaten without breaking it into smaller portions. Jessica grabbed at the cheese and then the bread. Her hunger had become a primary obsession. It mattered little that the pungent, blue cheese crumbled between her fingers; she greedily stuffed it into her mouth, biting off a chunk of the bread, and then washed down both with a pottery mug filled with red wine. Pier Luigi stood motionless, still holding the wine pitcher he had retrieved from a cabinet across the room. He had re-filled her cup several times with the slightly tart wine the family produced from the Gaglioppo grapes that grew on their mountainside property. With the clay pitcher now empty, the small boy studied his guest, trying to ascertain whether he should offer her something more or show her to her sleeping quarters.

Jessica was silent; her senses dulled by the wine, her fatigue mounting as the moments went by. At the far end of the primitive kitchen she noted a basin set beneath a hand pump.

"Pier Luigi, is there someplace I could wash my face and hands before going to bed?"

"Oh yes, Cugina Giovanna has set up these things in the room where you will be sleeping. There is a basin and a pitcher of water and some clothing, too; if you would like to come with me, I will show you." The maturity of this young Pier Luigi was amazing.

"Pier Luigi, there is one more thing," she hesitated. "… a Baccahaus?" Having seen nothing that resembled a toilet in any of the areas of the house she had visited, she imagined it must be outside.

"It is outside." Pier Luigi directed her to a door at one end of the kitchen which he opened; there, twenty feet from the house on the perimeter of the property was an outhouse.

"In the night, if you are afraid to go outside in the dark, you can use the chamber pot Giovanna has placed beside the bed. In the morning you carry it out to the Baccahaus to empty it."

"Yes, I see; thank you, Pier Luigi."

Without another word, Jessica followed the boy to a small windowless room almost adjoining the kitchen area. Pier Luigi lit a hurricane lamp on a rustic table next to the door and immediately, the entire room was filled with light.

"Your bed should be good for sleeping," he said gesturing to a twin sized wooden platform only inches from the floor. "It has two feather beds to sleep on, both filled recently with fresh goose feathers and the cover on top is filled with sheep's wool. It is sure to keep you warm. Giovanna wants you to feel comfortable."

"It looks absolutely wonderful," Jessica murmured. "... The basin?"

"Oh yes, Cugina Gessica, it is here and the chamber pot is over there, behind the chair." Jessica spotted the container; indeed, it was as described, a pot with a cover set on the floor. She grimaced at the thought of using it.

"Your clothing should be in the cabinet." Jessica turned to see a wooden chest a little over five feet high; the wood matched the paneling of the walls so closely, it became almost indistinguishable in the night light.

"Giovanna may not be home for some time; would you like her to awaken you when she comes in?"

"No, no, Pier Luigi; I will see her in the morning. Thank you again for everything."

Jessica poured a small puddle of water from the pitcher into the bowl on a table near the bed. It was icy cold. She looked around for a bar of soap, but finding none, used her hands to scrub the lingering cheese odor from her hands and with a handful of fresh water from the pitcher, wiped the day's grime from her face. A coarse terry cloth towel lay next to the basin.

Inside the wardrobe, she found a muslin nightgown, and five coarsely woven dresses. Below, six narrow shelves, were several shallow drawers, in which she discovered undergarments, sweaters, head scarves and in one corner of the top drawer, a toothbrush with a tube of locally branded toothpaste. She grabbed both immediately, only to have the toothbrush drop to the bottom of the cabinet floor. As she bent down to find it in the darkened room, she spotted something at the back of the portable closet. It was a shoe, a single woman's black shoe. Carrying it to the lantern Pier Luigi had left behind; she examined the scuffed leather and then looked inside to find the size. There was no doubt this was one of a pair she had packed in her government issued bag earlier in the day; the so-called lost luggage that supposedly had fallen into the ravine when someone attempted to gun her down. Pier Luigi had not been truthful when he told her he had found no luggage with her. She returned the shoe to the back of the cabinet. After brushing her teeth, she finally turned off the lantern and retired to the comfort of the feather bed. Sleep came easily and immediately, but it was dreamless.

***

"This is all you found, Pier Luigi?" Giovanna whispered. "There was nothing more in the luggage?"

"No, it was as I told you, lying open, not far from where Cugina Gessica had fallen. I carried it back here and was examining it when I heard him coming."

"... and, what did you do? Did he see what you were doing?"

"No, Giovanna, I hurried and placed it in the cabinet in her room. When he had gone, I took it out and brought it back out here."

"... and this is all, everything?"

"Yes, Giovanna, it is everything!" Pier Luigi was frightened at the tone of his sister's voice.

"I see only one woman's shoe here. Perhaps, the other is in the ravine; if you lost a shoe, you may have left other items behind. We will go back together in the morning. In the meantime, take this to my room and hide it; do not tell anyone we have it. Do you understand, no one?"

"Yes, Giovanna." Pier Luigi realized his sister was not pleased with him. He had done his best. Had it not been for his dog Cosimo, he might never have found Gessica or her piece of luggage. It was the dog who had discovered the scent that led him to both. He tucked the suitcase into the back of Giovanna's cabinet and then went to his room. In the morning, he would do another search. He and Giovanna with Cosimo would look together.

Chapter 20

Dr. Roberto Succi took no time with small talk. Having arrived at Philip and Caroline's Haverford home twenty minutes early, he neither apologized nor accepted the offer of coffee, but asked to go directly to his patient. Caroline nervously led the way up the broad staircase to the third floor of their brick colonial manor house. Succi followed closely behind, stopping occasionally to take in the surroundings and catch his breath

"Did Albert Lindley Johnson design this house?" He paused on the second landing to admire the finely carved mahogany banister before approaching the last set of stairs.

"How nice it is to hear from someone who knows he was the designer; but, of course the architects Magaziner and Potter came along a few years later when J. Howard Pew, the CEO of Sun Oil, bought the house and they really were responsible for making some pretty impressive and extensive changes. By the time the property came to Philip's family, it was a larger house on a smaller piece of land. We've made few changes over the years.....nothing extensive." Caroline uttered the last few words as they approached Philip's room at one end of the hallway.

"Dr. Succi, we also have a therapy room, fully equipped, on this floor. Philip has his physical therapist coming several days a week; if you would like to...." Caroline's invitation went unheeded as Succi brushed past her, entering the sunny room where Philip, in his hospital bed, lay in a semi-upright position.

"He doesn't speak, Dr. Succi," Caroline began.

"I understood from Dr. Sindona that is why you called me in," Succi's answer took Caroline by surprise, as she stepped to the side of the bed opposite the physician who had begun his examination. Philip seemed barely aware of his presence remaining motionless as Succi peered into his eyes with a pen light and then used his fingers to judge whether Philip could follow their movement.

"Has he spoken at all since his accident?" Succi muttered, not looking up from his patient.

"No, nothing, not a word; sometimes he makes sounds, but not words; he was unconscious when they brought him to the hospital and we thought...." The tremor in Caroline's voice indicated her growing concern. "...but, you can help him, can't you? I mean, he will speak again."

Roberto Succi flicked off the pen light and placed it in the pocket of his well-tailored vest.

"Let's not disturb your husband any further today; perhaps we can speak outside, in the hallway?"

"Oh, yes, of course!" Caroline led the way to a sitting room-kitchenette at the opposite end of the corridor where Philip's former round-the-clock nurses and therapists had micro-waved their meals and taken coffee breaks, during his early days of recovery at home.

"I had one of those Krug machines installed for the medical team. It brews individual cups of whatever you want... coffee or tea? I think there is hot chocolate there, too..."

"Please, Mrs. Rawlins, sit down. Thank you, but I really don't want anything to drink, right now." Caroline took a seat opposite the small sofa where Roberto Succi had planted himself.

"What is it?" Caroline leaned forward. The expression on Succi's face did not bode well for a positive assessment. "Philip will get better, won't he? He's not going to remain in this state forever. He has come so far. You know, he was unconscious... but he can't stay this way. Please tell me you can help him regain ...." For an instant she heard herself pleading. It was almost prayerful; but then Roberto Succi was by reputation, the equivalent of a curative deity

Succi leaned toward her. "The Medical Arts are exactly that. There is a lot of science in what we do, but also a significant amount of creativity which is what often leads to advances in the field. Most neurologists I know, would write Philip off at this point; advise you to keep the physical therapy going to insure his body remains in shape, but as for improving his mental state? Well, most I know, would tell you that any change in his condition would rate as probably a long shot. In other words, no change foreseeable or perhaps even possible. As they say in Philly, 'it ain't gonna happen!'"

Succi looked up at Caroline perhaps expecting her to burst into tears. Her expression, instead, remained controlled and serious.

"But, Mrs. Rawlins, as you know...Dr. Sindona and I have been doing research for the past decade and a half on traumatic cognitive state intervention and we have had some degree of success with the patients under our care."

"Exactly what does that mean?" Caroline's expression had in an instant gone from morose to expectant.

"It means, there is a small possibility, we could regain a more normal state of mind for Philip; however, there is also the possibility, perhaps even the probability, what we do could have no effect, at all, on his condition and ultimately, it could... well, let's just say, it may not work."

"And if it doesn't work?" It had taken Caroline several seconds to ask the question.

"As I indicated, this is research. Philip's sacrifice would..."

"What you really are saying is that he could die, couldn't he?" Caroline's voice rang through the sitting room and out into the corridor.

"Yes, most definitely, it is possible that he could die." Succi's words were as muted as Caroline's had been strident. "But, there is the small possibility that he could regain some if not all sense of his former faculties." Succi looked up and into Caroline's eyes. He knew in that instant that he had her hooked. Like a trout attracted to a feathered fly, she had taken the lure and now all he had to do was to reel her in.

Chapter 21

Father Marcus Granville Barker was under no illusion that the frail and seemingly delusional Pope Leo XIV could be helped without a full medical work up. As he watched the pontiff at prayer and later listened to the recollections of his dreams and visions, the possibility that he was being drugged or poisoned by someone within the household grew more and more conceivable

"Marcus, you know that even the suggestion that a medical profile of the Holy Father is being considered would cause gossip and speculation; something this household could not endure." Father Malcolm De Laurencin's voice was low as the two priests walked slowly through the corridor away from the Holy Father's private quarters. "... and it may not surprise you to know that he has enemies, more than a few, who would like nothing better than to get rid of him by finding him mentally incompetent. Every Pope in the last two hundred years could probably say the same; but with Pope Leo's views, many of which are considered to be too ...what shall I say radical, he is an especially easy target."

"Why exactly did you call me here, Malcolm? You as well as anyone who is close to him can tell he is delusional and growing more so every day. One has to spend only a very short time with him to conclude he is either getting these messages from some spirit, which neither of us deems reasonable, or someone close to him is making certain he takes a toxin which is sending him into these nightmarish states. The ideas that he is coming up with could be and probably are being induced by a person or persons who want him either incapacitated or... worse yet, dead; unless we find a way to analyze what is going on, and do it quickly, Pope Leo may not survive."

Malcolm continued walking several feet further in silence. He wanted to be well out of the hearing range of the Swiss Guard whose ears perked up at the slightest sound of conversation.

"Exactly what are you suggesting Marcus?" Malcolm had grabbed the rosary that hung from the cord around his waist and mumbled his question while looking at the cobbled floor beneath his sandal-ed feet.

"There is no way we can ascertain what he has been given without getting a blood sample and doing some other tests."

Marcus' suggestion startled Malcolm. "That could be very dangerous, not only for the Holy Father but also for us. The slightest hint that he might have health problems ... well, you can imagine the kind of uproar."

Marcus found himself stopping mid-corridor to address Malcolm who had put his fingers to his lips indicating the need for quiet. "What if I could get someone qualified and discreet to do the analysis... right here? That could work."

"But, Marcus, you don't have those qualifications and calling in someone else at this point would only lead to gossip and exactly the kind of speculation we're trying to avoid. Your 'professional' would have to do the testing and the analysis on the premises and in secret. We couldn't risk having anything sent out to a lab. I'm not even certain that we have what it takes to do the testing anywhere on the premises."

"Well, we may soon be able to find out. Here comes the only possible candidate for the position.

"Father Sean O'Reilly, how are you this fine afternoon? Might you be able to join us for a cup of tea or better yet a glass of wine or cold Italian beer? We have a proposition to discuss with you, one you can't possibly refuse."

Marcus' expression was deadly serious; Sean O'Reilly followed the two down the corridor in silence, past two more Swiss guards and into Father Malcolm's small apartment.

Chapter 22

"You'll not find what you're looking for in there, Lydia; I've moved it." Poulette flicked on the lamp next to the chair where she had been sitting, waiting and watching for the arrival of her stealthy visitor. Lydia Sindona appeared to be genuinely startled as she stepped away from the open door of the closet and pressed her body against the wall.`

"You want it for him, Roberto—your charming lover—don't you, my dear? You're not the type to think of anything like this on your own.... even with your heritage. It's just not in you. Now, come along, Lydia, sit down over here and tell me all about it. Exactly what is Roberto looking for and why would you, of all people, agree to find it for him?"

There was a thoughtful pause in Lydia Sindona's response. For an instant, she thought of escaping, making a run for the elevator or the staircase to her room. But then what? What would she do? Where could she go? She still did not have the jewelry box with the pouch that Roberto wanted and needed so desperately. Perhaps she could still find a way to get Poulette to reveal its whereabouts.

"Want a drink?" Poulette had pulled herself up from the chair and was heading for the bar near the fireplace. "I'm having one."

"It's a little late, Poulette, but, thank you; I have to be at the lab quite early tomorrow."

"Nonsense, it's only 9:30. You thought I'd be fast asleep by now, didn't you, dear? The truth is, I can't sleep some nights. I knew you had been looking for something almost since the day you arrived. It was only when I saw your reaction to picking the wrong jewelry box from my closet shelf the other evening that I understood what was going on here. The early dinner invitation to your charming friend; his questions, that evening. I may not be as sharp as I was in my youth, Lydia, but my memory is still relatively intact. You see, my dear, I recognized Roberto immediately and I know what the two of you are after. You can tell him that Poulette will never give it up while she is still alive."

Lydia watched Poulette pour herself a Scotch from the crystal decanter on the bar, the tumbler clutched in her left hand trembling as she poured the amber liquid into it with her right. She added an ice cube from the covered bucket but no water; then, gingerly carried the drink back to her chair.

"Nothing to say? No denials?" She carefully placed the glass on the table next to her chair. "Don't you want to ask me about Roberto? If we met previously? How well I might know him?" The latter question was punctuated with a purr, the implication of which was far from subtle.

"No? Perhaps we should save all of that for another time, then. You look very pale, Lydia. Go back to your room; make your phone call to Roberto and explain to him all that I have told you. He'll understand, I guarantee. He may be surprised, but he will understand."

Lydia Sindona had scarcely moved a muscle since being discovered. Her back remained firmly pressed against the wall; her eyes following Poulette as she maneuvered to and from the bar area. Her words were mesmerizing. Did she know what Roberto was looking for and did she know Roberto before his visit for dinner a few nights earlier?

"I don't know why, but it is very important that Roberto acquires whatever is in that jewelry box, Poulette. If you know him, then you also know that he can be...well, you do know how he can be, I am certain of that. He does not want to be disappointed nor can he tolerate not getting what he wants. You know that he will get the contents of that box in the end. Is it so... so important to you that you keep whatever it is; perhaps even risk your life for it?"

There was no answer from Poulette who simply stared at her house guest. "I'll say good night now and hope you sleep a little, Poulette."

"Good night, dear. You sleep well, too." Poulette's smile was peculiarly poignant, almost fear-provoking. It did not escape Lydia's attention as she pressed the elevator button and headed to her room, two floors below. This night, she would turn the deadbolt lock on the key-less oak door, a precaution she would take from now on.

Chapter 23

"We must hurry, Cugina Gessica, the ceremony is about to begin and we cannot be late!" Jessica followed as best she could; her bruised arm still ached and her blistered feet were cold and painful, the consequence of wearing the ill-fitting shoes Giovanna had provided to replace those 'lost' with her luggage, as well as the pair she had worn the previous night. "These look more appropriate for someone of your station," she had commented as Jessica squeezed into the scuffed, ill-fitting leather footwear, made even more constricting when worn with heavy woolen stockings.

The mountain road to the village of Polsi was steep and rugged. There were no cars this morning, only an occasional cart, pulled by a mule, whose driver barely guided the beast. The thin mountain air was crisp; Jessica could see her breath and noted the moisture that settled on her nose when she stopped for a brief moment. Her body was wrapped in a dress woven from goat hair and flax, over which she wore a woolen shawl that covered her head and shoulders. Her hair was pulled back into a bun at the nape of her neck.

"People in our village are very curious," Giovanna had told her. "They will want to know where you are from. You will tell them that you come from Locri; that your husband was killed. If they ask more, you will lower your head and shake it once or twice. That will imply....." she said no more, looking furtively around as a family of five passed them from behind.

Jessica was certain she understood the implication. The village of Locri was well known to be a stronghold of the 'Ndrangheta. The 'Ndrine, the very basis of the clan system which made up the 'Ndrangheta and maintained a tight hold on the region. Positions within each clan or family were often inherited. Disputes within these families could and did lead to bloody fights; the losers if they did not die, became relegated to minor positions within the 'Ndrine.

"We are going to the statue of Our Lady of Polsi in the square; it is where the 'baptism' will take place," Giovanna whispered. They had reached the edge of the village. It was here the dirt road gave way to cobbled streets and, as Jessica quickly discovered, slippery maneuvering for anyone wearing leather-soled shoes.

"Baptism? What baptism, but I thought....."

Giovanna's menacing expression as she put her finger to her lips, instantly silenced her companion who still looked confused as they headed toward a large crowd of people in the square. As they drew closer, Jessica could see that as many as forty men, ranging in age from 13 to eighty plus, had formed a horse shoe around a statue of the Blessed Virgin, which had been crowned in a ceremony only moments before their arrival with a wreath of fresh flowers. The majority of the men carried rifles on shoulder straps, the leather often as worn as their weathered skin.

"They are getting ready for the 'baptism'." Giovanna whispered. "This is the beginning of the rite where they will welcome a new member into their organization. In a moment the capo società will step out, the initiate will be brought forward and...." Giovanna's whispered explanation was interrupted as rifles were fired into the air and the bells of the Church of our Lady of Polsi rang out in celebration. The time was exactly 8:00 a.m. Jessica watched in fascination as those standing in the horseshoe formation moved in closer to the candidate, whose identification was still hidden from the crowd of observers.

From behind the statue of the Virgin, stepped the capo società who shouted, 'Will the guarantor of the candidate please come forward with him!' A man in his fifties stepped out of the crowd holding the hand of the boy.

Jessica gasped. "Oh, Giovanna, no," she uttered, clutching the arm of her companion who did not acknowledge her reaction. "It is Pier Luigi!" Jessica could scarcely draw a breath as an interrogation began.

The guarantor, as would a Christian Godparent, vouched for the good intentions of the candidate and his desire to enter into the 'family'. The capo in return read to the candidate the honor code he will be expected to observe for the rest of his life; concluding with a series of questions which both the candidate and his guarantor were expected to answer.

"It is now time for the 'baptism' to take place," Giovanna said softly. "It is a blood baptism."

Jessica watched as the capo società retrieved a dagger from a velvet pillow on which it lay. Walking toward the candidate, he took the boy's right hand and drew the sharp blade across his index finger, catching several drops of blood on a prayer card image of St. Michael the Archangel, patron saint of the 'Ndrangheta. Pier Luigi studied his bloody finger and the holy card for a moment and then accepting the card, smiled.

The crowd of observers roared with approval; Pier Luigi was lifted to the shoulders of one of the initiated who had been witness to the baptism and paraded through the streets of Polsi.

"Gessica, you have just witnessed, the creation of a new, giovane d'onore (youth of honor). And now you and I must get to our duties, preparing for the grand meeting of the Crimine. We have only a few hours to do our work. We cannot be seen there, as you know, when the meeting begins."

Jessica, still flabbergasted by what she had observed, followed silently, wrapping the shawl more tightly around her shoulders and keeping her head down. The early morning mist was now a steady, sleety rain. They scurried past the men who were carrying the boy through the village streets, stopping as villagers shook his hands and patted him on his back. Pier Luigi was smiling broadly, enjoying his new found celebrity. He was now a man and one of honor, too.

Chapter 24

The Rev. Austin J, Cheney, Prior Provincial of the Edmundites, perched his cast-bound leg on a stool conveniently placed beneath his desk and simultaneously took a deep, excruciating breath. There was no denying the pain at the point of the break, across the top of the femur; it was intense and no amount of Advil, Aleve, Excedrin or Tylenol had been able relieve it.

His crutches lay within reaching distance should he need them. Most often, that would be seldom. He would remain in this seat as long as possible.

Since his return to work little more than a week earlier, he found even a light schedule exhausting and usually asked an orderly from the Monastery's infirmary to help him back to his room in time for a late lunch. After that, it would be a nap that typically took him into the late afternoon hours, waking in time for the friars' chapel prayers.

On this day, however, he sipped the Arabica coffee Sister Beth had brewed and waited for the call. He was late; which was typical of Father Sean O'Reilly who often lost track of the time when he was involved with a project that held his interest. Austin Cheney could only hope this would not be one of those days when he would forget entirely that he had asked for this reserved time on the Prior Provencal's busy schedule. Taking another sip of the quickly cooling coffee, he glanced out the window to watch the soft swirling snow. It was early in the season for so much snow; too early, he mused, yet, the sight of the flakes clinging to the evergreens and silencing the raucous sound of the University's snow blowers offered a certain benign comfort. He closed his eyes for only a moment almost hypnotically drawn into the wintry scene.

"Father, Father Cheney, your call; the call you've been waiting for. Didn't you hear me on the intercom?" Sister Beth hovered above the priest who realized he must have drifted off. "It's Father O'Reilly calling long distance from the Vatican!" Austin Cheney shifted his slumping frame and reached for the telephone.

In doing so, he also shifted the position of his perched leg causing him to shriek as he lifted the phone to his ear.

"Austin, are you all right?" Sean O'Reilly was alarmed at the greeting from his friend.

"Yes, yes, I just shifted the position of this leg. It is a terrible and painful nuisance more than anything else. Otherwise, patience is what I am trying to learn in this healing process; more patience than I seem to have in me. Now, Sean what is going on over there? I got your e-mail. You told me you could not put anything into writing. Are you on your way back?"

"That's just it, Austin, I'm not. In fact, it may be sometime before I can return. Something has come up which I have been asked not to discuss."

"Well, if you can't discuss it, there must be a good reason. If I can be of any help on this side of the world, let me know."

"As a matter of fact, that is why I am calling you. I need a favor and one that must be done in absolute secrecy; do you think you can do that for me? I wouldn't ask if...."

"Sure, we've known each other a long time, Sean. I know you to be a trustworthy individual. What do you need?"

"I think you will need a paper and pen for this list; it is rather long. One thing more, the delivery has to be very, very special. You personally will send this package to the address I am about to give to you and it will be hand delivered to me after that."

"Sean, whatever you say. Now, what do you need?"

Ten minutes later, Austin Cheney's arthritic fingers still clung to the pen as he continued to scribble items requested by his fellow friar.

"Now, this is very important, Austin; I want the items mailed to this: APO Address: USAG LivornoATTN: Lt. Col. Francis Greeley, Base CommanderUnit 31301, Box 5APO AE 09613. Do you have all of that?" Father Austin Cheney had placed the phone on speaker when he began to scribble the list Sean O'Reilly was dictating.

"Yes, I think I have it all. Let me repeat the items and the address just to make certain." Sean O'Reilly was silent as his friend and superior checked off the precise medical and laboratory items he had requested as well as the mailing address.

"I already have called my new graduate assistant, Angela Coburn on board and she is prepared to work with you in obtaining some of the more difficult items. I've also been in contact with Mary Kennedy, dean of the Nursing College and she too will supply those items which neither you nor Angela may be able to get. This has to be done in total secrecy. No one on campus or within our community must know about this request. Can I count on you, Austin?"

"Well, yes... yes, of course, you can count on me, but why....?"

"Please, don't ask. I promise you, this is...." O'Reilly paused for a moment. "Let's just say that this is extremely important and nothing more. Perhaps, someday I will be able to share more with you, but not now."

"You can rely on me, Sean. I'll get to this immediately." Father Sean O'Reilly said no more. He had hung up the receiver on his end. For a moment, there was only the steady hum of the land line. Father Austin Cheney pushed a button on his aged desk phone to hang up and without using the intercom, shouted for Sister Beth to come in.

"Have Angela Coburn, Father O'Reilly's graduate assistant come to my office as soon as possible. I need to speak to her personally." Sister Beth was about to object, noting what would be an interruption in Cheney's usual nap schedule.

"Nap time is over, Sister Beth. Time to get back to work!" Austin Cheney moved his leg abruptly as he leaned forward in his chair. For the first time since his accident, he did not feel the sharp, nerve wrenching pain.

Chapter 25

"I'm not certain I understand what you're saying, Caroline," Alex Rawlins continued to stir his nearly consumed Bombay martini with three stuffed olives, impaled on a bamboo toothpick. The bar area of the White Dog Café in Wayne was nearly deserted. It was almost 5 p.m. and the office crowd had yet to descend on the chic watering hole. "If you don't trust him, fire him. It's as easy as that!"

"No, it really isn't. If I get rid of him, Philip will have no one. Essentially, his neurologist has said he's done what he can. The therapists at Bryn Mawr Rehab have washed their hands of him and I'm... well, I am all he has, don't you see that?" Caroline reached for a crinkled tissue in her handbag and wiped the tears from her eyes. She had consumed two glasses of wine and the effects were showing. "Listen to me, Alex; you are the only one who understands. Philip is like a zombie, these days. You've seen him. He seems to understand some days and others, nothing... literally, he can stare into space for hours. Occasionally, he will utter something, usually unintelligible. One day, he looked at me and said something like crazy corpse. His speech is so slurred when he does speak, I can't understand him. This doctor, Roberto Succi seems to have the credentials. I looked him up on Google. He studied at several major European universities before coming to the University of Pennsylvania. " Caroline dug deep into her handbag again and pulled out a folded, somewhat crumpled paper with her reading glasses. "Listen to this, Alex '... Dr. Roberto Succi and his team specialize in research relating to patients with disorders of language, number, and social functioning resulting from injury, neuro-degenerative diseases and/or healthy aging. Presently the team is examining bio markers of these conditions, including neuro-imaging, biochemistry, genetics, and pathology. Dr. Succi's specific interest is in using noninvasive brain stimulation as a means of investigating neural function and promoting neuro-plasticity.' Well, what do you think?" Caroline removed her glasses waiting for Alex to respond.

"I think I'll have another martini. Waiter!" Alex motioned to the bartender who nodded at a server who had been polishing glassware. "I'd say, in all honesty, that you have a true professional looking into Philip's condition and that you had better be nice to him or he'll go back to his research and Philip will have no one." Alex consumed all three stuffed olives in one swoop of the toothpick and handed his empty low ball glass to the waiter who had laid the fresh martini in front of him.

"Another Pinot Grigio for Madame?"

"No, I'm just fine, thank you," Caroline covered the half empty wine glass with her hand. "I suppose you're right. He's just, well... a little creepy. I can't put my finger on what I don't like about him... it's just this peculiar feeling."

"Get over it, Caroline; remember this is for Philip. It may be his only chance of regaining a... let's just say some sense of normality."

Alex took a large sip from the fresh Martini in front of him. He hoped Caroline had accepted the positive spin he'd given her on Succi, when in fact, he had his own suspicions about the man as well as Lydia Sindona, for that matter.

He had set up an appointment with Jed Watkins for the following day primarily to check on Jessica but now also to get Jed to give his thoughts on Sindona and Succi. Caroline certainly had done her best to try to provide Philip with the best post trauma medical rehabilitation available in the area, but was Roberto Succi the man to do the job?

"Are you certain you want to drive in this weather, Caroline? I can take you home and you can pick up your car in the morning." Alex drained his glass and signaled to the waiter for the check.

"I'm fine, Alex. The streets look relatively clear of snow. I'll call you to let you know how Philip is doing, when I get home."

"Drive carefully," Alex gave the seated woman a brief kiss on the cheek and signed the credit card statement. Caroline watched him leave through the clear glass door at the entrance, only feet away. She felt very much alone. Why did she distrust Succi so? Something about him made the hair on her neck stand on end.

***

Father Marcus Granville Barker checked his watch before picking up his cell phone. It was just after midnight, Rome time which meant it would be the dinner hour in Villanova, PA where Bertrand Fox would probably be serving dinner to his stepmother Poulette and, if she was in town, his invited houseguest, Dr. Lydia Sindona.

He had missed the previous day's phone call with the butler for good reason; the Holy Father had been in an exceptionally agitated state and had cancelled his weekly Mass and general audience with an influential group of Catholics from Montgomery, Alabama. The group had contributed more than $1,560,000 in Leo's name to Habitat for Humanity.

Malcolm, himself, had become agitated when he realized that the cancellation of such an important Papal meeting, would add to the growing concern and gossip among the papal inner circle about the Pope's recent insular behavior.

"Hello, Mr. Fox?" Marcus shouted into the cell, "...can you hear me?" Marcus had positioned himself close to the only window in his small room hoping for a better cell signal.

"Yes, Mr. Fox, sorry about that but I was not able to get to a phone yesterday. Are you alone and can you talk?" Marcus listened carefully. The reception was about as good as it could ever get under these circumstances. The Vatican was not known for its great cell phone reception. Those who lived within its confines often surmised it was purposeful. What one can't communicate, can better be kept undercover and as Marcus had learned in the few weeks he had been in the Vatican, undercover was an adjective that described most activities.

"Yes, Mr. Fox, I understand. Poulette gave you the box for safe keeping and you are caring for it. No, don't tell me where it is, but perhaps put its location into a note and the note into an envelope to me marked personal. Do you still have the mahogany desk my father used? The one in the butler's pantry? Yes, that's it. Put the envelope into the second drawer... The one where he kept his account records. Yes, and lock it. Should anything untoward happen, I will be able to retrieve the envelope and with good luck, the box.

"… and my stepmother, how is she faring? Yes, I know about Dr. Sindona; she is not there again this evening, nor was she there yesterday, either? Hmmm, how very strange. Did she say when she might return? No, no, thank you, I'll try to call you again tomorrow. Thank you again, Mr. Fox for looking after Poulette." Marcus clicked off the cell phone and plugged it back into a charger on the desk.

He wound the travel alarm on the side table next to his bed, setting the alarm for 5:30 a.m. Pope Leo would expect him the following morning in his private chapel to serve at his early a.m. Mass. It was obvious to everyone in the Papal household that the Holy Father's symptoms were becoming more and more acute.

Although Marcus would have preferred to begin psycho-analysis after a thorough physical workup, that was no longer an option. The items Father O'Reilly had ordered from the United States would not arrive until the following week; sessions with the Holy Father would take place immediately after Mass.

Marcus turned off the goose neck lamp and shook his single pillow in a vain attempt to revive its volume. Outside he could hear the early winter rains pounding the window. The moon had waned; its light barely visible through the ever growing clouds. Marcus pulled the rough linen sheet and single woolen blanket closer to his body. He felt a sudden and pronounced chill; it was one he had encountered before.

Somewhere in his own consciousness he realized he did not want to delve into the Papal psyche. He was truly frightened of what he might discover there.

Chapter 26

Jessica's hands were cold, red and painful, which strangely diminished the pain in her bruised arm. For the previous two hours she had been scrubbing tables, chairs, counters and finally the ancient stone floor of a meeting room in the one-time abbey of the now defunct Sisters of St. Mary Polsi. Armed with buckets of cold water, bars of handmade laundry soap and crude boar's hair brushes the two women had readied this bare bones conference center for a meeting of the Crimine, the international governing body of the 'Ndrangheta.

"Why of all places are they meeting here?" she muttered to Giovanna in a nearly flawless Calabrian dialect. "These are wealthy men; wouldn't they be more comfortable in one of the hotels in the city?"

"Look around, Cugina. Do you see any communication devices? The nuns who lived in this convent for more than 300 years were cloistered. They slept in cells on straw mats, with no heat in the winter. They were awakened every three hours to pray and ate only the most meager of diets. All of this as a sacrificial act dedicated to our Lady of Polsi. When the order died out about two decades ago, the 'Ndrangheta saw it as the perfect place to hold their meetings. You noticed the man with the machine gun outside the abbey? He stands there every day. No one dares to come close and certainly would not be admitted inside. We are the exception. The reason, of course, is that we are women and are doing women's work. Also, I am the sister of Pier Luigi, the newly initiated man of honor. However. you also noticed, that your bucket and scrub brush were checked by the guard?"

"I noticed." Jessica muttered. "I think he thought I had something hidden in this scrub brush. He certainly examined it closely." Jessica pulled her shawl over her hair, grabbed her bucket and brush and proceeded to the entrance. "Where do we go from here?"

Giovanna did not answer, but motioned for her to follow in silence. They walked quickly, passing the guard who had leaned back against the convent's ancient wall to take advantage of the fast fading winter sunlight.

"There is a hunter's blind not far from here. It is well camouflaged. We will climb it now and as the members of the Crimine arrive, we will be able to see them enter the building."

Less than fifty feet from the abbey's entrance, Giovanna turned off on to a rough and dusty foot path that led through fields of tall, swaying wild Farro that clung to their skirts as they moved quickly toward the blind in the growing darkness of the afternoon.

"Hurry, Cugina, it is only a short distance now."

Jessica held her shawl closer to her body. She was tired and hungry. She hoped Giovanna had made some provision for their dinner. Breakfast had been hours earlier.

"It is here, Gessica." She motioned to her companion, pulling down a rope ladder which she encouraged Jessica to climb. "Hurry, hurry, they should be arriving momentarily and we do want to see them."

Jessica climbed the swaying rope as quickly as she dared, maneuvering the bucket as well as her shawl, finally reaching the camouflaged platform some twenty feet above the ground. Giovanna followed quickly after her.

"I thought you might need these," she said passing Jessica a pair of binoculars. "They can be adjusted for the darkness, too. There is a small button on top when you need it.

Jessica grabbed them and directed her gaze to a car travelling at a moderate speed toward the Abbey. It stopped directly in front of the entrance. Both women stared silently at the individuals exiting the vehicle.

"These will be the leaders of the meeting," Giovanna whispered. "The cappo crimine will step out first and after him the maestro di giornata, who is his spokesperson. The latter is the second most powerful member of the organization."

Jessica adjusted the lenses of her binoculars. She realized what she was seeing and did not dare to breathe for the moment. While she could not see the full face of the maestro di Giomata, she most definitely recognized the cappo Crimine who followed him. It was Roberto Lombroso.

The Papal apartment in the Vatican, late afternoon

"Holy father, close your eyes and relax. I want you to take a deep breath, hold it for a few seconds and then slowly exhale; yes, that's exactly right. Now take another deep breath, hold it.... and slowly exhale." Father Marcus Granville Barker sat in a high back chair he had pulled from the Pope's study only moments earlier. His patient, dressed in a simple black cassock lay supine and shoeless in an ancient leather Barcalounger Father Malcolm had retrieved from a nearby Vatican apartment.

"Are you comfortable, Holy Father?" Marcus asked in a soothing voice.

"Yes" The response was soft and slow.

"I want you to set your mind on the dreams you have been having lately. Take a moment to recall those dreams....: Marcus remained silent for several seconds listening to the breathing of his patient.

"You have told me that in your dreams, you are running away from someone or was it several people? They are coming up quickly behind you. Can you tell me how many there are?"

Pope Leo did not answer, but took a deep breath and exhaled slowly. "Look at them carefully, Holy Father. Are there two... or three...more than that?"

"I cannot see their faces. It is dark and I am afraid." Leo's voice trembled as he spoke.

"You need not be afraid, Holy Father; this is a dream you are recalling and you cannot be harmed. Look carefully, who is following you? "

"There are... three of them," he blurted out, a gurgling sound emanating from the back of his throat prompting Marcus to stand up and place his hand on the Pope's throat to check his pulse. Reassured there was no imminent danger to his patient, he resumed his seat in the chair next to the lounger.

"...are the persons chasing you men or women, Holy Father?"

Marcus watched the body language of Leo closely. His previously relaxed body had become rigid; his knees were slightly bent and he clenched his hands to his chest.

"I don't know; but please, you must understand, I am not me they are chasing. I am someone else and I don't know who that is! " The last declaration was thunderous, shouted with such force that the aged pontiff sat straight up in the darkened room, staring ahead while perspiring profusely. "Good Lord, Marcus what is happening to me?" he cried out again looking directly into Granville Barker's eyes. "Perhaps, I am possessed!"

***

The portable ice maker hidden beneath a console on one wall of the office, made a crashing sound as a fresh batch of cubes fell into a nearly empty tray. After pouring himself a dram of Scotch, FBI Regional Bureau Chief Joe Farrell reached into the bin and collected two large cubes.

It was almost 6:30 p.m. in Villanova. A small crew of regular staffers remained in the station office hidden away in an old estate mansion on the grounds of St. Edmund's University. The evening staffers had already arrived and another shift would relieve them at midnight to remain in the office until morning. These round the clock office hours were relatively new. Only a few years earlier, this regional office would have closed for the day at 6:30 p.m. But recent encounters with international terrorists and assorted domestic criminals demanded a strict vigilance 24 hours a day.

Farrell had left word with security guards at the front gate of the mansion to expect his old friend and colleague, CIA Regional Bureau Chief Jed Watkins and Alex Rawlins, a businessman he had met with on several occasions in the past. Jed had given no indication why he needed this meeting nor why Rawlins would be accompanying him. In the past it was because Rawlins' wife Jessica, a CIA operative who worked for Watkins had been in need of some domestic assistance; he suspected this meeting would somehow involve her as well.

"Sir, your guests have arrived," the security guard stationed outside the mansion called out through the intercom.

"Send them right through, please" he responded pushing a button on his desk to admit the two through the front door of the house. "Come right up," he called out as he heard the front door buzzer admit the two. Minutes later they had hung their coats on hooks in the front hall and were on their way to his second floor office.

"You remember Alex Rawlins, don't you, Joe?" Jed Watkins was already helping himself to a drink from the well-known file cabinet drawer. "Scotch, Alex?" he asked as he added a splash of Club soda to the generous portion of whisky.

"Just exactly as you made it for yourself, "Alex answered, taking a seat on the comfortable couch in Joe's sitting area.

"So, I assume this has to do with Jessica, gentlemen? What kind of help can we render to our friends at the Company?"

"Jess is fine; at least we hope she is fine. We haven't contacted her in the field and she has not tried to contact us. This has to do with something or rather someone else, Joe. Alex, will you tell him?"

Alex took a generous drink from his low ball glass and proceeded with a briefing on Cousin Philip Rawlins' nearly fatal car accident and his ensuing treatment, including a new and experimental therapy proposed by a Dr. Roberto Succi.

"Have you ever heard of Dr. Succi?" Alex Rawlins asked.

"No, but I am certain you are going to tell me about him," Farrell answered sitting back and sipping slowly on his drink.

"He claims to be a renowned medical researcher who is continuing his project study at the University of Pennsylvania with Dr. Lydia Sindona. According to what we have been able to find in our files, Roberto Succi was proposed for a Nobel prize for... let me read this to you because it is quite complicated, … 'Succi and his research team discovered that brain-damaged patients or split-brained patients seemed to indicate the presence in the right, so-called 'minor' hemisphere for a considerable capacity for cognitive understanding and the comprehension of language, both written and spoken'.

Joe Farrell said nothing for a moment. "It's good to see you Jed; now, tell me what in the Hell am I doing here with you two bozos at 6:45 on a Wednesday night when I would rather be home watching a basketball game? I'm really sorry, Alex about your cousin and his car accident, but why should I be interested in this Roberto Succi and his research on brains?" Farrell punctuated his sentence with another sip of his Scotch.

"You should be interested, Joe, because what Alex just read to you came from a 1980 document; the real Nobel proposed research scientist Roberto Succi died in 1982 in Milan at the age of 84. He had no children so this would not be his son or even a close relative. The original Succi was an only child, an orphan to boot. The current Roberto Succi is the supposed research partner of Lydia Sindona. Dr. Sindona is the very, very clever and ruthless daughter of a Mafia Chief who also was a medical doctor and who died a number of years ago. There is something not right about all of this, Joe. Alex's cousin, Philip, has gotten himself involved in something nefarious and before it takes his life, I think we could use your help in finding out exactly what is going on with this new version of Roberto Succi. Who is he? Why is he here and what is he trying to do with Philip Rawlins?"

Joe Farrell swirled the remaining ice in his glass. "You guys sure have a way of taking the joy out of what could have been a terrific and entertaining basketball evening. All right, I'm in. Tell me what you need!"

Chapter 27

Checking out the wide variety of special blend teas at one of Rome's most famous tea shops, Father Marcus Granville Barker took one last sniff from several test canisters in front of him.

"... all right, decision made: I'll take the canister of the Blue Lady, the Moroccan Secret and, of course, your suggestion Babington's Special Blend; that should do it." Father Marcus Granville Barker had found himself stumbling through this conversation. His colloquial Italian was lacking some of the most basic phrases. Twenty years ago, as a seminarian at the Pontifical North American College, using the language daily, he spoke like a native. Today, he fought to come up with even the simplest phrases. The elderly sales woman nodded, obviously appreciating his efforts as she hand-picked his selections from a shelf behind her and began to calculate his tab.

"That will be 30 Euros even, Father which includes our special Clergy discount of 15%. Would you like to pay in cash or use a credit card?

"Oh, credit," Marcus presented his Visa card, "... and thank you for the discount! If you could, please gift wrap them into one package?" He smiled; conscious of the elderly woman's flushed face as she retreated to a nearby computer station to register the sale.

Having worked every day since his arrival, almost two weeks earlier, Marcus had taken this Saturday off at the suggestion of Father Malcolm. It was a much needed respite from the intensity of Vatican life with its onerous daily agendas of monitoring Papal meetings and special guest greetings, all of which complicated by the Pope's steadily deteriorating state of mind and his ever more frequent dream episodes.

Father Sean O'Reilly had taken Malcolm's recommendation to heart as well, encouraging Marcus to accompany him to the Santissima Trinità dei Monti, a late Renaissance Catholic church at the top of the Spanish Steps. It was at this site in 1491 that St. Francis of Paola a Calabrian hermit bought a vineyard and obtained permission from Pope Alexander VI to build a monastery.

However, it wasn't until 1502 that Louis XII of France began construction on the late Renaissance titular church and not until seventy years later, in 1585 that it was finally consecrated by Pope Sixtus V. Unfortunately, for international tourists hoping to visit the site today, it is under, what had been described as long-term construction, yet again, covered in tarps and surrounded by scaffolding.

"Don't worry about the scaffolding and the Do Not Enter signs," Father O'Reilly had assured Marcus earlier that day as he bypassed security guards leading the way through the exterior construction and into the nave. "I have Vatican passes for us; ordinarily, no one would be allowed inside because of the restoration."

Indeed, their totally private tour of the premises was an unforeseen treat. As they made their way through the aisles, bordering the nave to the high altar, they stopped several times, to admire the brilliantly colored frescoes, sculptures, immense oil paintings of the saints, and the astounding stained-glass windows, nearly a half millennium old, yet still radiating a dazzling and rich palette of jewel like color that spread like a carpet across the marble floors.

As they were about to exit, Father Sean led the way up the steps to the massive High Altar. where they prayed in the silence. In the shadowy light of this December day in Rome, Marcus was certain, he could sense the Divine presence other worshipers had perceived since earliest times.

With the church tour over, and with Christmas shopping a major item on their "to do" lists the priests parted, selecting Babington's as the most convenient place to meet later in the day.

Now, as Marcus waited for his package, he glanced out of the emporium's large display window hoping to spot Fr. Sean O'Reilly. A heavy drizzling sleet had begun to fall negating any real possibility of recognizing his friend. In the fading light, all that could be seen was a bevy of tourists and Christmas shoppers, seemingly laden with packages, hurrying down the Spanish steps to find shelter in this tea shop, or one of the many nearby cafes and bars.

He checked his watch. It was nearly 4 p.m. If Father O'Reilly was on time, he should make his appearance any minute.

"And, here is your Visa card, Father; please sign right here." Marcus signed with the stylus on the portable credit card recorder.

"Buon Natale!" she said handing him a large shopping bag.

"Si, Buon Natale!" he replied, walking the few feet to the entrance of the emporium to wait inside for Father Sean. Only seconds later, two women with umbrellas covering their heads rushed through the door and directly into Marcus, causing him to drop his package and nearly lose his footing on the wet marble floor in the process.

"So sorry, senor," one of the women apologized in Italian grabbing the now soaked shopping bag from the floor and offering the priest a handkerchief from her handbag for his drenched face..

As Marcus wiped the moisture away, a bolt of recognition caused him to freeze in place. It was the voice; he knew that voice. The woman standing in front of him was Dr. Lydia Sindona.

Chapter 28

"My instructions from Father Marcus were to pack up Dr. Sindona's belongings immediately and take them to the Radnor Hotel." Bertrand Fox placed the last of several pieces of luggage and a single large cardboard carton on the marble floor in the foyer. Poulette watched, not totally comprehending what was happening.

"It's because she left last weekend and hasn't come back, isn't it?" Her voice was soft with a note of melancholy.

"I don't know, Madame. Father Marcus didn't go into detail."

"Mr. Fox, Marcus told me she was to look after me; I told him I didn't need any one, but...."

"I'm sorry, Madame, I'll deliver these to the hotel now and be back in about a half hour." Bertrand Fox wrapped a blue plaid woolen muffler around his neck and pulled on a knit cap. "If you need anything, Mrs. Perkins is in the kitchen preparing dinner."

"Yes, I mean I don't need anything. I'll go back to my apartment." Poulette remained in place watching Bertrand Fox load the luggage into her car before closing the front door and driving off. How did Marcus find out that Lydia Sindona was not in Villanova watching her charge? In fact where had she been for the last five days? She had said nothing to Poulette about travelling; or had she? There had been memory lapses, Poulette was the first to admit and these lapses were becoming more frequent.

"Perhaps, I was to inform Mrs. Perkins and Fox but forgot?" she muttered aloud. "If that is the case, Marcus should know that Lydia has been wrongly accused. Oh dear, it seems so unlike Lydia to pick up and leave without saying goodbye." Poulette toddled toward the elevator where she pushed the button. Fox had left the door to Lydia's room open and the ceiling light on. Perhaps. she would check it once more to make certain nothing was left behind and turn off the light in the process.

She felt a chill upon entering the room. The thermostat had been turned down to 67 degrees. Poulette shivered. Even days after her departure, the scent of Jalaine, Lydia's favorite fragrance permeated the air; the gardenia based perfume seemed to cling to the window hangings and bed spread. Poulette coughed several times, her throat irritated by the scent. She opened the closet door. Fox had done his job. Nothing remained, not even a hanger. There was nothing in the drawers of either side table next to the bed; nor in the desk or chest of drawers.. She entered the bathroom which looked to be in almost pristine condition. It was modest in size and design for a house as large as Poulette's containing a combination shower and bathtub, a commode, sink with a vanity which had several drawers. On the wall, two adjustable cosmetic mirrors, each flat to the wall camouflaged medicine cabinets.

Poulette pulled at the mirror directly in front of her. It opened easily and the cabinet hidden behind appeared to be quite empty. The mirror to her left did not budge as easily on her first try. Poulette pulled at it again with more energy. It flew back; this time, propelling its contents into the sink and across the floor. She bent down to pick up one container and examine its label; it appeared like the others all around her to be a prescription pill bottle, amber colored with a typed label on the front.

There had to be five or six of them. She picked up two that had fallen to the floor beside the commode and another that had landed in front of the vanity. Lining them up on the top of the sink, she examined the labels.

They all had her name on them and had been prescribed by Dr. Roberto Succi. Poulette strained to remember if that name was familiar. It was not. Next, she looked at the dates they had been prescribed. All of them had dates within the last week or two, about the same time Lydia had moved into her home. Poulette quickly grabbed the containers and stuffed them into the pockets of her jacket. She would write-down the names of the drugs on the labels of the bottles and ask Mr. Fox to help her figure out what they were for and where they had come from.

The elevator door opened at her touch. As she headed to the third floor and to her apartment, she examined one bottle under the elevator interior's bright light. The label read carbamazepine. In the lower right corner of the label, its commercial name was Tegretol. The elevator door slid back;

Poulette walked more quickly into the apartment and to the lamp beside her favorite chair where her telephone lay. She picked up the receiver and punched in one of the pre-coded telephone numbers.

"Hello, Rosemont Pharmacy, prescription department, Jack speaking. Can I help you?"

"Yes, Jack, it's Poulette Granville Barker. "

"Oh Hello, Mrs. Granville Barker, what can I do for you today?"

"It seems I have a prescription here for Tegretol? I guess that's how it is pronounced. I've forgotten what it is for and how much I am to take.. Could you look that up for me? "

"Sure, give me a moment." Poulette shook the bottle as she waited. The container had at least twenty-five capsules in it, she estimated.

"I'm sorry, Mr. Granville Barker. That prescription did not come from our pharmacy. At least it is not in our computer under your name."

"Hmmm, you are quite certain about that?"

"Quite certain!"

"Perhaps, it was filled somewhere else. Could you tell me, Jack, what it is prescribed for?"

"Generally, it's prescribed for seizures or mood disorders. But I think you had better call your doctor and talk to him or her before taking any dosage because if you were prescribed this drug and are taking it with several of the others we have on file for you here, well, it really could be quite dangerous, even fatal.. My advice is not to take this drug until you have talked to your physician... Do you understand?"

"Oh yes, Jack, I think I understand quite well and thank you!" Poulette hung up the phone.

"Who is this Dr. Roberto Succi", she said aloud, "and why did these drugs come through Lydia Sindona with my name on them?"

Poulette picked up the phone again and this time pressed a button for an interior call to the kitchen.

"Mrs. Perkins when Mr. Fox returns, please have him see me immediately! Yes, I'm in my apartment, thank you!"

A shudder ran through Poulette. Exactly what was going on? Was Lydia actually trying to kill her? But why? Revenge for an affair with her father that had ended in his death many years ago? That was crazy.

Another thought flashed through her mind. "No!" she answered staunchly to herself; "...even if Lydia and this Succi fellow attempted it, she would not reveal what had been entrusted to her so many years ago... no one, especially Lydia had a right to those secrets."

Chapter 29

"Giovanna, when do we eat? I'm literally starving," Jessica whispered to her companion who was about to deliver another course to the capos who were seated around a long table in a large room down the hall.

"We will eat when they have finished," she whispered lifting the immense metal platter with three portions of Branzino Sotto Sale, whole salt-baked Mediterranean Sea bass. It had been delivered only moments before from the baker in the village who had prepared it and cooked it in his bakery's ancient brick oven. The fragrance was so powerful, Jessica felt momentarily faint.

There were only fifteen of the capos invited to this special conclave. Other attendees of lower rank were assigned to eat in a small tavern in the village. Both locations were well protected by armed guards who were prepared to shoot first without provocation at anyone who might dare to enter their territory.

"Gessica, please pay attention, I need another platter right now of the Vruocculi Ca' Savizzuizza."

Jessica rushed to a preparation area near the kitchen window where she quickly arranged the hot Italian fennel sausage around the edges of a metal platter, adding an immense portion of broccoli rabe mixed with raisins and pignoli to the center.

"This is all that is left of the Vruocculi; if they ask for more, we just don't have it." She grimaced not wanting to consider what might happen if their guests wanted more of this delicacy but they were unable to provide it.

As Giovanna exited, Jessica raced to ready the next course, Risotto con le cozze, a fragrant risotto with fresh mussels, saffron and garden tomatoes. She was ready for Giovanna who had returned looking frazzled.

"The sauce, the sauce for the Branzino; we did not give them the sauce!"

"All right, all right," Jessica hollered back. "I didn't know it came with sauce. It has to be here somewhere, if it was included in the package. In the meantime, here is the risotto!"

Jessica rummaged through the rumpled package from the baker in search of the sauce. She was certain she had removed everything when the two women had unpacked the fish; but for the moment she could not locate anything even resembling a sauce. "Hurry, hurry," Giovanna was motioning. But it was too late; they had made an error and were about to be rebuked for it.

"The Salmoriglio, where is it? We cannot eat the fish without the sauce and the fish is getting colder by the minute!"

Jessica jumped at the stringent voice of the man who stood in the doorway of the makeshift kitchen. His voice was angry and his body language was that of a very intoxicated man.

"You stupid women, have you forgotten the sauce?"

Instinctively, Jessica leaned back, her body pressed against the wide stone ledge that bordered the window.

Her fingers touched a bowl of something. She picked it up and recognized the scent of olive oil, lemon juice, garlic and fresh herbs with red chilies. "No, no, we have not forgotten the sauce; it is here, Senor. I have it right here," she handed the clay bowl with the spoon to Giovanna who without a word ran toward the dining area with their drunken host following behind her.

It was only when Giovanna returned that she had the courage to tell her who had been shouting at them. It was Roberto Lombroso, capo of the 'Ndrangheta the largest and most powerful crime syndicate in the world. Jessica had first noticed him when the two women were observing conference arrivals from the hunter's blind.

Now, seeing him only feet away, she was certain of his identity. She took a deep breath; thank God Lombroso had not recognized her. Their previous and only encounter had occurred only weeks earlier at the Rosalie restaurant in Wayne where she and Lydia Sindona had endured what could only be described as an excruciatingly uncomfortable reunion and Lombroso had escorted the distraught woman from the restaurant.

Jessica knew she had to learn more about his presence at the conference. How she could do this before leaving for the Vatican in two days? She would need a small miracle; perhaps two; the first to get her in proximity of the meeting of the capos and the second, perhaps most difficult of all, keeping to the script and in character. A discovery of her true identity would almost certainly be fatal.

***

"No, Dr. Succi, it would not be convenient for you to come to see my husband, today." Caroline's voice was stringent and hoarse. She was sitting in a chair next to Philip's bed. This was the third call in less than 24 hours from Succi who literally was insisting on coming to see Philip. Caroline had given instructions to their part-time housekeeper to admit no one unless asking first.

"Dr. Succi, please do not call us again. Yes, that's right; I do not want you to treat my husband." Caroline slammed the land line back into its cradle and walked to Philip's bedside. His condition was no better and no worse. His eyes were closed. She could only hope that he was sleeping. His physical therapist would arrive within the hour, which always helped to raise his spirits and she believed, his focus. On a previous visit, she was certain that Philip recognized her after his treatment and tried to speak. She brushed his forehead; it was warm but not feverish. The flu was running rampant on the Main Line, closing schools and small businesses. Posters everywhere advised washing hands frequently and not sharing drinks. She could only hope and pray that it would not hit their houseold.

"Mrs. Rawlins, the physical therapist has arrived. Shall I send him up?"

"Yes, Mrs. Darcy; I think Mr. Rawlins is ready for him."

"Phillip," she called to him, "...your physical therapist is here," stroking his forehead again, he opened his eyes and looked at her. She was certain he understood what she had said.

"Stephen, I think your patient is awake and...." Caroline did not finish her sentence. "You're not Stephen; where is he?"

"Oh, sorry, Mrs. Rawlins. I'm Giancarlo. Stephen has the flu. I'm standing in for him. Now, Mr. Rawlins, shall we get started?"

Chapter 30

University president Father Paul Sullivan sat back in his plush leather chair with his arms folded and his feet crossed. The sleeves of his Edmundite robe were rolled up to reveal a black cashmere sweater beneath, a gift from a generous alum and former student.

Angus McCauley, the Board of Trustees treasurer and Mark Tobin, Board of Trustees chair huddled over the ribbon mahogany conference table in Sullivan's office.

"Now, look Father, I've been working with Lombroso's attorneys for the past two weeks and I think we can find a way to accept the money without having to go through the Vatican Bank."

"It still could be Mafia money, you know," Tobin interjected.

"I guess it could be anything, couldn't it, Mark and that includes a generous donation from Mr. Lombroso who is recognized as an international philanthropist." Tobin sulked.

"As I was saying, Pete Reynolds, Managing Director of Warbeck, Reynolds and Thurmond told us that if we felt more comfortable, Mr. Lombroso would donate the money to his favorite Catholic charity in Canada. They in turn could deposit it in a Canadian bank and the donation to the University could be made via the Catholic Charity in Canada through their bank. Does that make you feel any better, Mark or are you now convinced that our Canadian Catholic brothers are also involved with the Mafia?"

"So let me ask you a question, Angus, why would the Catholic charity in Canada do this for us?"

Father Sullivan had perked up at McCauley's solution.

"Well, Father, apparently Lombroso has been unusually generous with a number of Catholic Canadian groups and they owe him one. He saved a Carmelite group about a year ago. They were going to be thrown out of their convent because it was in such bad repair. He had it repaired and restored and now the Sisters are living comfortably for the first time in about 50 years. "

"Let me get this straight, McCauley, we give this check to Canada to a prescribed charity there; they get the money from the

Vatican bank and then they give it back to us through a Canadian bank? Is that right?"

"Yeah, that's exactly what I said."

"OK, what about Uncle Sam? What do we tell him?"

"Mark, we tell him that we got a donation from our Canadian brothers at this Catholic charity. It's legit and the Canadian government isn't going to interfere; why should they? This is a legitimate deal!"

"I say we go for it, Father!" Angus McCauley looked at Sullivan for an answer.

"Mark, what do you think?"

"I guess it's two against one, so if you guys say OK, I'll tell the board we've accepted this donation from an anonymous donor."

"It's a deal!" Sullivan noted, a broad smile brightening his boyish face. "I've got some good Irish whisky I got as a gift. I think it's time to bring it out and serve it."

"I'm in," Angus answered, "... never said no to good Irish Whisky!"

"All right, I'll have some, too," Mark Tobin agreed. He was the only one in the room that felt a ripple of discomfort at the proposal. The idea had a funny ring to it; one he had heard or read about before, He could not rid himself of the idea that this indeed was money laundering and St. Edmund's was now a party to it.

***

"He has come to me numerous times when I pray before morning Mass. I kneel on the prie dieu and as I look up, it is directly into the face of our beloved St. Peter; his face is redolent with pain as he hangs upside down on his cross. It is then that I hear him. At first, it is soft, almost a whisper as he calls my name, "Leo, Leo..." the Pontiff lying on his narrow bed, his head raised by three pillows spoke in a timbre not his own; one that was tender.

Marcus Granville Barker listened attentively; he had no notebook or recorder. Neither was allowed during these very private sessions with the Holy Father. The door to this private bedroom of the Pope was closed. Father Malcolm stood near the outer door, listening for any movement in the corridor beyond the Papal apartment.

"Holy Father, you said that Peter is in the painting, calling to you from the painting. You are kneeling on the prie dieu facing the painting. After he calls your name, what does he say?" Marcus was probing gently.

"Many things, many things, some which I cannot understand; he has told me numerous times that it does not matter whether I understand or not. I am his brother and he is sharing with me the visions given to him by our Lord Jesus Christ." Somewhat taken aback, Marcus remained silent. The pontiff smiled as if recalling one of the visions. "It was only recently he spoke to me of my death," Marcus sat upright at the statement.

"Go on, Holy Father, what did he say? Did he give you a date?"

"No, no, Marcus, you do not understand at all; it has all happened already. This event, like all others in this life, was a part of the Divine Instant!" Pope Leo XIV punctuated the latter two words with his tone. "My brother Peter has told me about it numerous times, but I am only now beginning to understand." Leo took a long and calming breath and silence set in for several seconds.

"Do you want to try to explain this Divine Instant to me as he did to you?" Marcus probed. "Perhaps, in your words I can try to understand."

"I will, Marcus but not today. Only know that you are and have always been and will be for all time; don't ever forget that and don't worry, it will all work itself out because it already has." He opened his eyes at this comment and then turned away from Marcus Granville Barker to rest on his side. Seconds later his breathing indicated, he was fast asleep.

Marcus did not move from his chair. He wasn't certain what to make of the Pontiff's remarks. His training in medicine and modern psychiatry relied on the reality of test results: MRIs of the brain, blood analyses, CT scans of the body and assorted other methods of determining whether the rantings of this Pope or anyone were a reflection of someone suffering from a brain tumor or schizophrenia. Or, should he consider these visions, as his seminary training might direct, as those of a holy man, perhaps even a saint?

He reached down and pulled a flannel blanket up and over the elderly man's body. It was still early in the afternoon, three o'clock according to his watch but a wintry darkness had already crept across the December sky. He switched on a table lamp in the hallway leading from the pontiff's bed to his bedroom door and had only touched the levered door handle to invite Malcolm back into the room, when the shriek sounded. It was a piercing, wail unlike any Marcus had ever heard.

Malcolm raced to the Holy Father's bedside, where Leo still lay on his side, his back facing them and partially exposed. Emerging, as they stood witness, were the same marks they had seen earlier; only this time they were pushing through the Pope's fragile skin; the Aramaic lettering Simon bar Jonah, the original writing on the tomb of Peter was bursting into a steady flow of deep, rich blood. Marcus gently wiped a corner of the wound and put it to his lips. The blood was real and both Marcus and Malcolm were there to witness its reoccurrence.

Chapter 31

Jessica opened her eyes, slowly turning over and toward the wet tongue that had awakened her. Hovering above her face was Cosimo and above him, the small frame of Pier Luigi who crouched down to greet her.

"What time is it, Pier Luigi? It is still dark outside."

"Yes, Cugina, it is almost 6:30 a.m. Giovanna left about an hour ago to prepare the breakfast for the conference. She has asked that you meet her at the Tavern in the village as soon as you feel ready. She realized how very tired you were last night and wanted you to get some extra sleep."

Jessica rose slightly; the previous day had been exhausting. By the time the two women had cleared the last table at the monastery, washed the dishes, swept the floors and prepared the parcel containing the borrowed serving plates to be picked up by the village baker, Jessica found herself ready to collapse. Discovering Pier Luigi and Cosimo waiting for them with the mule and cart in front of the monastery was the second best thing that had happened to her all day.

The first, was finally getting something to eat after the conference attendees had left the premises; leftover and available to the two were substantial portions of the risotto con le Cozze, a rich risotto with fresh mussels, saffron and tomatoes, and an eggplant salad with garlic mint and hot peppers, over romaine lettuce with cece beans and ricotta cheese. While Giovanna still had room for dessert, the fried sweet ravioli with more ricotta cheese, kumquats and powdered sugar was too rich for Jessica. She chose instead to pour herself a second large portion of the local red wine which she sipped from a heavy glass canning jar she had discovered in the pantry. The slightly raw wine of recent vintage was made from grapes grown only a couple of miles from the monastery, according to Giovanna.

"The vineyard is hundreds of years old. The village continues to keep it going now that the monks are no longer here. We distribute the wine only to those villagers who have participated in the harvest. If you do not work in the vineyards, you do not get to enjoy the wine," she announced proudly. Jessica raised the heavy commercial glass: "To the workers who made this possible!"

"Giovanna left some bread and cheese on the table in the kitchen for your breakfast." Pier Luigi advised her. "Cosimo and I must go into the village now. There will be many things happening today."

Jessica raised herself to full sitting position, and noticed for the first time that the young man she had identified only days ago as barely out of childhood, was carrying a rifle over his shoulder. He was a member of the 'Ndrangheta, now and apparently allowed, if not encouraged to carry the weapon.

"Pier Luigi, if you see Giovanna, please tell her I will be there as soon as I possibly can; I know she needs help!" Jessica stumbled slightly as she rose from the straw bedding set on a platform only inches from the floor.

"Cugina, I will not be seeing her. I will be with the men today, guarding the conference." He smiled as Cosimo led the way out the door and into the early morning darkness.

Jessica cringed slightly at the thought of this small figure securing his position within an international criminal organization that one day would require him to kill or be killed.

She longed for a shower, but could only sponge bathe from the wash bowl and pitcher set inside her room. The water was not even tepid but cold and the soap, undoubtedly home made by Giovanna or one of her neighbors. After drying off with the only small towel available, she looked for her undergarments. She had washed them the previous night and laid them near the drafty window to dry. They were still damp and totally unwearable.

She drew the only fresh items available from a drawer in the small closet cabinet. If last evening's laundered garments were not ready the following morning, she would be in deep trouble. She shuddered at thoughts of the alternatives,

Slipping into fresh undergarments, she could endure wearing the only, less- than- fresh dress she had worn the previous two days. As she pulled on a clean pair of hand knit woolen socks from Giovanna's larder, she spotted the large blister on the bottom of her left foot, where ill-fitting shoes would continue to put pressure on her already damaged and sensitive skin.

"Damn," she cursed knowing that a day of tortuous marathon walks awaited her, which would only add to her pain and misery. But, having no other choice available, she grimaced and forced her feet into the ill-fitting shoes in front of her.

In less than fifteen minutes, Jessica had readied herself for the day and in another ten, she had consumed two hard boiled eggs, several slices of aromatic goat cheese, a mug of strong black tepid coffee and half of a hard, garlic-spiced goat sausage, she had discovered hanging from a hook in the pantry. As she was about to leave the house, a last pang of hunger hit her, driving her to return to the pantry for one more bite from the sausage. She understood quite well that her appetite had not been appeased by the previous evening's enormous but late meal.

By 7:30 a.m., few shops in the village were lighted; but the darkness seemed not to deter a myriad of shoppers who were going about their daily chores in a normal fashion. She passed the bakery where a short line of women and children waited outside the entrance for their turn to purchase a freshly baked loaf of bread. She took a deep breath as she passed them. The fragrance was almost overwhelming.

Next door, with fewer people waiting in line, was the dairy shop. Visible through its open doors, were clear glass door refrigerators filled with milk in glass bottles from local cows and goats. In the window, an array of local cheese were handsomely displayed in straw-lined baskets, tempting passersby.

Jessica hurried by the next shop where carcasses of newly slaughtered goats and venison hung from hooks outside for anyone to inspect. In the cold morning air, Jessica was certain she could smell the still rustic aroma of these animals whose lives had been spent grazing in local fields.

She arrived moments later at the Inn/Taverna where in a short time, the capos and the Crimine would meet with the local Societa Maggiore, the upper house of the local 'Ndrangheta. As she turned a corner to enter through the kitchen door of the Inn, she sensed a dull, but persistent sound... the drone of a motor scooter travelling at great speed and coming up directly behind her.

Despite her intention to step aside, in seconds, she lay on the ground, slightly rattled and surrounded by a crowd, including the scooter's driver, a very young man wearing his rifle across his shoulder, indicating his position as a newly appointed giovane d'onore. In the still dark shadows of the alley near the kitchen entrance, she could see two other figures; a heavy set man whose mighty frame and formidable face she recognized and an aged priest, who hobbled behind him; both, now gazed down at her.

"Senora, are you hurt?" the priest asked gently, motioning for the scooter's rider to help her up.

"No, I... I think I am all right," Jessica replied hesitantly, not certain that she was all right.

"I have seen you before Senora, have I not?" the larger man probed, offering her his hand.

"Si," she replied looking down, not wanting him to get a close look at her face." I helped to serve your dinner last evening. I am here today with my cugina Giovanna Poloni to help again with the luncheon and afterwards to clean up."

"And so you will, Senora; if you feel up to it. Help this poor woman to her feet and into the Inn," the larger man ordered as the crowd scattered and Jessica was literally lifted to a standing position. Hobbling, with the priest at her elbow, she entered the kitchen. Giovanna stood watching the scene in terror and disbelief. Roberto Lombroso had ordered everyone around to take care of "... this dear woman. Do not let her work too hard." He stared at Giovanna who made a slight curtsy, stepping aside as he and an elderly priest, left the room.

Chapter 32

Caroline picked up her cell phone which lay on a desk outside Philip's room; the phone number of Bryn Mawr Rehabilitation was etched into her memory. She pressed the numbers in rapidly and waited, "Yes, yes, hello, Phyllis, this is Caroline Rawlins, Philip's wife. A therapist named Giancarlo is here. He said he is substituting for Stephen who is ill? Is that right?" Before Phyllis could answer the question, Caroline flinched with her phone was thrown to the hard oak floor, her forehead barely missing the leg of the Georgian desk. Giancarlo had sprinted past her, down two flights of stairs, to the kitchen, past Hannah Kennedy the cook and out the service door into the cold December air.

"Call the police, Mrs. Darcy, and now! That man, he's an impostor!" Still dazed, she raised herself to a sitting position. Turning toward Philip's room, she saw him sitting up in bed, one leg over the side of the mattress. He was trying to get up while calling to her. "Caroline, Caroline." His voice was soft, hoarse and his words slow, but she heard him distinctly, "Caroline...." It was the first time he had spoken since his accident. Giancarlo's brusque attack on her had seemingly spurred his return to speech.

"Philip, I'm here; it's all right." She put her arms around him and held him close to her for several minutes. "It's all right." When he looked up, she could see his eyes were wet with tears.

"No, Mr. Fox, we're not going to call the police!" Poulette held two of the amber prescription containers in her hands. The sight of her name typed on each of the labels still sent a shiver up her spine. "These are very strong medications and according to Jack, the pharmacist, should I have taken one of these," she held up the container of Tegretol, "...with everything else prescribed for me, I might have died. He said many of these prescriptions do not mix well with those he has on file for me."

Bertrand Fox examined the prescription containers. "I really think we ought to contact the police, Madame. I also think you ought to let Father Marcus know. The reason Dr. Sindona was here in the first place was to look after your medical needs; to make certain you were safe and cared for. Perhaps, Marcus will have an explanation for all of this. And as for the doctor's name, on the label, Roberto Succi well, I think we can pretty easily find out who he is by calling his office."

"Office, why of course, he must have an office somewhere in the area, Mr. Fox."

"I'll look him up on the internet, Madame. If he has an office, I'll find it and we can deal with it from there.

Now, don't you, worry. I'll take the prescription bottles and store them some place safe." Poulette handed him the bottles she held and reached into her pockets for several additional containers.

"Can I make you a cocktail, Madame? It is after 5 p.m.!" Fox smiled hoping to lighten the mood. Poulette glanced out the window. It was dark outside, very dark.

"No, Mr. Fox. I'll make my own; but thank you. Please tell Mrs. Perkins that I'll be ready for my dinner in about 45 minutes…. And Fox, if you find out anything about that doctor, that Succi fellow, on the internet, call me. I want to know what you find out as soon as you do."

"Don't worry, Madame. I'll call you with any news I have." Fox smiled as the elevator doors slid to a close.

Poulette poured herself a generous tumbler of Scotch over ice with a tiny amount of water from the wet bar, then made her way to the champagne silk settee in front of the fireplace. Fox had turned on the gas flames when he arrived providing a gentle glow and warmth to the room. She sank into the goose down pillows and took a deep breath. Was Lydia really trying to kill her? "No," she said aloud. But, all of these terrible discoveries; Lydia, leaving the house without so much as saying good bye, the mysterious prescription bottles with her name on them…they all had something to do with the terrible secret she had shared with Lucas all those many years ago. She could never reveal what he had told her, because should she, it would be obvious that she was as culpable as he. "No, no," she said aloud again, there absolutely would be no police involvement. She would have to be more vigilant; but she could not and would not involve the police.

Chapter 33

In his role as Regent of the Pontifical Household, Fr. Malcolm De Laurencin acted as chief of staff for the Holy Father, checking even the minutest details to ensure the privacy and personal security for the pontiff. Knowing this, it should have come as no surprise to Marcus to learn that his own schedule had been under scrutiny for the last several weeks.

"I'm not certain what you are asking me, Malcolm? Who did I meet at the Tea shop last Saturday? It was my day off and I did some Christmas shopping at Babington's; as you know Father Sean and I went together. Why is any of this your business? Did you have me followed?"

"I'm sorry, Marcus, but it IS my business. Anyone who is in as close proximity as you are to the Holy Father will be kept under a microscope." Malcolm picked up a report he had on a side table in his apartment just down the corridor from the Holy Father's. "Here, take a look at this. According to this account you were observed with a woman, the woman in this photo, speaking intimately to her. She is...." Malcolm did not finish his sentence.

"... She is Dr. Lydia Sindona, a medical research neurologist whom I had employed to look after my stepmother who is in ill health in Villanova. I was less than pleased to see her with a load of shopping bags barging into a tearoom in Rome when she should have been in Pennsylvania on the Main Line looking after Poulette! Besides, being shocked to see her at the tea shop, she was not alone, there was another woman with her and I was waiting for Father Sean. The other woman had excused herself to use the lavatory and Father Sean had not arrived yet!" Marcus could hear his voice rise and the volume increase.

"As you can see, there is nothing in this photo to indicate another woman being present or Father Sean; just a photo of the two of you talking intimately, head to head... or so it would seem."

"Look, Malcolm, I don't have to make excuses for my behavior. I am here at your request. I have done everything in my power to help out in this very peculiar and unique situation. I am a trained professional and a priest; BUT I also am a responsible stepson for a woman whose mind is growing more frail by the day. I had hoped that Lydia, an old friend from medical school days, could help me out. Apparently, I misjudged her character; she left my stepmother high and dry without letting her know. I have since fired her to ensure she does not return to Poulette's house."

"There are several pages to the report, Marcus. Turn to the next page and perhaps you will understand why we are having this discussion." Marcus turned the page of the legal-sized report. There were two photos at the top of the page and a very detailed printed report, several paragraphs, below describing the contents of the photos.

"These are photos of me: The one on the left was taken just before I came to Rome. It is in a restaurant in Toronto, in Canada." Marcus looked up, slightly puzzled; trepidation mixed with curiosity began to permeate his body.

"Who are you with in this photo, Marcus?" Malcolm asked, pointing to the two men at the dinner table."

"I was invited to dinner by Roberto Lombroso, whom I have known for quite some time; the man on the left who was the other guest is Monsignor Francisco Rosario; why is there a question about these two men?"

"... now, turn the page once more, Marcus." Malcolm instructed. "What do you see in this series of photos?"

Marcus felt his throat becoming dry; he gave a short cough as he studied the grainy black and white photos printed on the paper report. "This one is a photo of me walking into the Institute for Works of Religion or the IOR," Marcus attempted to hand the report back to Malcolm, who had walked to a small console table, which served as a bar in his quarters. "Here, sip this. It's Puni, an Italian version of Scotch; not too bad once you get used to it." Marcus accepted the crystal tumbler and took more than a sip, a swig. "...woof, what is this stuff made from? It's terrible!"

"It should help your throat; you're sounding a bit raspy."

"Yeah, well, O.K... now, back to the photos."

"Marcus, you are carrying a briefcase, the same one Monsignor Rosario is seen carrying into the restaurant in Canada. Is it the same case?"

"Yes, it is. I was asked by the Monsignor to do him a favor; to take the case with me since I was going to the Vatican. I saw nothing wrong with that."

"... And in the next photo?"

"I am walking out of the bank a few minutes later. I delivered the briefcase, as I promised. It took only a few minutes and I was dismissed and sent on my way."

Malcolm said nothing for a few minutes, but merely walked around his quarters.

"Did you open the briefcase to see what was in it?" he finally asked.

"No, of course not; I would not do such a thing."

"But, you were willing to take a case that did not belong to you on a plane, in this day and age, without so much as looking inside or knowing what it carried?"

"Yes, Malcolm, as strange as it sounds, sirens did not go off when Monsignor Rosario asked if I would carry this briefcase to Rome and deliver it to the Institute. As for looking inside, it was locked with a combination lock and even if had I not been an honest guy, I could not have opened it without a combination. Now, what is all of this about? What's going on?" Marcus dropped the report on a coffee table next to the futon style sofa Malcolm had covered with a large Tibetan wall-hanging and waited for an answer.

"I'm not at liberty to discuss anything with you, right now, Marcus. Just be aware that you are under surveillance at all times. It is for your own good as well as that of the Holy Father. We are living in dangerous times and I do not exaggerate"

"Am I interrupting anything?" Sean O'Reilly had knocked and then entered the apartment through the partially open door.

"No, you are just in time," Malcolm announced. "Marcus is trying an Italian Scotch called Puni. Here, let me pour you a shot and tell me what you think." Father Sean O'Reilly looked mildly skeptical.

"I'm more of an Irish Whisky man, myself," he intoned, as he accepted the tumbler. "I have news for the both of you. Our medical supplies will be hand delivered, this weekend. They are coming by way of a personal messenger from Calabria."

"Calabria?" Marcus looked up.

"Calabria," Sean O'Reilly intoned as he took a modest sip of the Puni. His face assumed the most excruciating expression which Malcolm and Marcus appeared to enjoy immensely.

***

It was 12 noon. The sound of the ancient bells in the tower of the Cathedral of Our Lady of Polsi was deafening. They tolled daily on the hour, each hour beginning at 6:00 a.m. and ending at 8:00 p.m., a constant reminder of the sacred, as well as profane obligation, each resident owed to God and his fellow man. Ancient and noble instruments, many believed the bells to have mystical properties which could neutralize a spell or in some cases, enable it.

The bells in the Cathedral of Our Lady of Polsi had not come to the village with the monks in the 19th century, but according to legend, (and supported by the high concentration of copper in the metal composition), arrived hundreds of years earlier, perhaps in the 1st century A.D. from an ancient town called Temesa, known for its copper mines; renamed Nocera Terinese, in modern times, it was located only a few kilometers from Polsi.

At the Polsi Inn/Taverna, where the 'Ndrangheta had arranged to meet for its farewell luncheon, it was an outward sign that the conference was over. This, final morning of the annual 2 1/2 day conference, was considered the most important. It was at this time, the highest ranking capos, representing assigned geographic regions, had delivered their reports to the Capo Crimine and his council of colonels and then presented to the contabile (accountant), the tax, an estimated amount that had been levied at the meeting the previous year.

While delivering the exact amount of the projected levy to the contabile was acceptable; offering more than the estimated amount was preferable and almost always rewarded with a promotion or gift to the capo, which he would share with his 'ndrine or clan.

Unfortunately, the fate of those who turned in a lower amount than had been projected, inevitably were punished with a demotion in rank or even death.

It was in this closed to the public event that the group gathered, utilizing the entire Inn/Taverna including the banquet room and lobby for its farewell luncheon.

When the guests had been seated, the Capo Criminé, Roberto Lombroso entered to take his seat, with his back to the wall, in a chair at the center of a long table in the main dining area. Everyone rose and applauded as he entered; an enthusiastic salute to their capo whom they were certain would reward their fidelity and their levies.

Father Gaetano Gambetta, an aged Dominican priest who would say grace and bless the assemblage, sat in a place of honor on Lombroso's right. The Contabile, his accountant, who was placed on Lombroso's left, rose after the blessing to announce another financially successful year. With praise for Lombroso and congratulations to the assembled capos, he then lifted the massive antique wooden chest, (the valigetta), a symbol of their earnings, above his head for all to see, proclaiming, "... it is filled!"

Wild applause ensued; a band of local musicians entered the room and began to play. "Pour the wine and let the celebration begin," Lombroso announced.

It was not a bash intended to last very long. As was common, most years, attendees would leave immediately after they had eaten; some returning to their villages near Polsi and others to travel to geographic areas as far away as Asia, Africa, South America, North America, the Middle East and of course other countries throughout Europe.

Jessica had rushed to the dining room as soon as the applause broke out, her signal to carry an immense tray laden with a whole roasted Swordfish garnished with fresh lemon and capers, roasted potatoes, squash, mushrooms and broccoli. She would serve only Roberto Lombroso and his table, returning to the kitchen several times for additional trays of food for the 18 capos seated with him. She lowered her eyes as she offered the food, not wanting any one of these capos to remember her face. Each headed a territory, many as large as a state or small country and each was responsible, within the complex structure of the 'Ndrangheta, for a segment of profits from a major crime industry including drug trafficking, human trafficking, money laundering and murder for hire. These were the CEOs of international crime industries, feeling as safe and comfortable in this Inn/Taverna as any legitimate businessman might at a prestigious professional conference taking place somewhere else in the world.

Within minutes, Jessica and Giovanna had served everyone within the main dining room. Other local women, hand-selected by Giovanna had been assigned to the smaller dining areas in the main lobby and bar. Immediately, after the tables had been served, Jessica rushed out to begin clearing while Giovanna prepared platters of local cheeses and fruits and refilled pitchers with the never ending supply of wine from the Ponsi monastery's vineyard.

It was soon after she had served the cheese that Jessica noticed the nausea. Her heart raced; her body temperature was feverish and although she'd had no time to check for bruises, she was certain her earlier run in with the motor bike had left her hip and lower back bruised with noticeable black and blue marks. She took a deep breath and pushed mentally to move forward. The luncheon would soon be over; she could hold out until then.

She had just reached the table of Robert Lombroso when she tripped on the uneven wooden flooring of the ancient Inn, sending a tray filled with platters of such rich and traditional handmade pastries as 'Nzuddha, Cannarìculi, La Cupeta and pitta' nchiusa, flying forward into the lap of a startled Father Gaetano Gambetta. Jessica saw none of it, however. Her head had hit the floor, knocking her unconscious, at the feet of Lombroso.

Chapter 34

His vicious open hand blow struck hard on Lydia Sindona's left cheek knocking her back into the down comforter that covered the king sized bed. This was hardly the reception she had anticipated from Roberto Lombroso whom she had intended to surprise on his birthday with a visit to Rome.

"How many times have I told you never to surprise me, Lydia? You know I hate surprises!" His face was red with a rage she had never encountered before. She cowered, trying to move to the other side of the bed; not knowing what to expect next.

"Secondly, how did you find me? Who told you where I was?" He was now looking down on her, his hand raised yet again, ready to strike. He bent lower to look directly into her eyes, his voice, seething with a rage, but almost whispering.

"I want you to answer my questions; then, I want to you to put on your clothes and get your skinny- assed body out of here; do you understand?"

Lydia moved quickly to the other side of the bed and grabbed a silk robe she had dropped on a nearby chair.

"I...uh, called your assistant Paolo DeLaurentis and told him I wanted to surprise you for your birthday. I thought you'd be pleased to see me. Obviously, I was wrong." Lydia had walked to a nearby closet where she retrieved her dress. A small travel bag rested on a portable luggage rack nearby. "The only thing he told me was that you'd be arriving this afternoon and staying at the Grand Hotel Plaza." She slipped into her pumps, grabbed her coat from another hanger in the closet and picked up her handbag and travel case. "I guess this is goodbye, Roberto." She looked back to see him facing away from her. He said nothing more, as she closed the door to the suite behind her.

It was as she opened a copy of Il Messagerro the next day on board the noon Al Italia flight to Philadelphia that she noticed it. It was not on the front page nor was the headline one which most people would have spotted. "American found dead outside popular men's club". Lydia read the small one column story twice. "Identified by his U.S. passport, the body of Paolo Justino

DeLaurentis, 26 of Gladwyne, PA, was discovered outside the Club Flamingo, just after midnight. The nightspot is popular with tourists for its live music and dancing. The club caters primarily to men."

"He's dead," she said aloud. "That bastard killed him!"

"Were you speaking to me? Did you say something?" the elderly man, sitting on the other side of the business class seat barrier asked.

"No, no, nothing!" she smiled; a chill ran though her body. "Would he now come after her?"

"Hmmm," she thought to herself as she turned to the next page of the newspaper. "I'd never have guessed Paolo was gay."

***

"Please, don't tell me that; he can't be dead!" The bellowing went beyond horrific; it reverberated through the walls of Poulette's third floor apartment, down and into the servants' wing, rousing Bertrand Fox and Bernadette Perkins from their beds.

"Ms. Poulette, Ms. Poulette, everything is all right. You are safe in your home. Everything is all right!" Bernadette Perkins wrapped a cashmere throw around the shivering woman who was still sitting in front of her fireplace, with a now very watery drink on the table beside her.

Bertrand Fox picked up the glass and brought it to his nose. "She may have had a little too much of this," he whispered as Mrs. Perkins continued to comfort the stricken woman.

"It was as if I was right there in Milano again and was being told about Sebastian," she took a breath and began to whimper. "My first husband was Sebastian Calvi, a banker; he went on what was to be a short business trip to London and he never returned. Tonight, I saw it all again, so clearly, how they came very early in the morning, just before dawn, to tell me. They had telephoned, but I did not pick up the phone. At that time in our lives, we did not have servants who lived in. I've never minded being alone and felt perfectly safe.

"It was the pounding on our front door that awakened me. I was surprised, first of all because of the early hour and then frightened by the insistence of whomever was making such a racket. I can see it so clearly, as if...." she hesitated and then went on. "It was very cold and I wrapped my robe around me very tightly. I couldn't find my slippers so I padded down the staircase barefoot. Without thinking to ask who was there, I opened the door." Poulette reached for her glass which Bertrand Fox had taken away and placed on the bar.

After several deep breaths, she continued "There were no soft words; nothing to lead into the fact that he was, first of all, dead. ... and then, of course, there was the shock of hearing the cause of death." She looked up into their faces. "... Oh, you want to know who 'they" were? 'They' were and still are the Polizia Provinciale, a local police force for the region who, without any consideration, just blurted it out. 'Your husband, Sebastian Calvi is dead; he was killed in a terrible auto accident. The car was demolished and the bodies in it, badly burned when it went over a cliff.'"

Bertrand Fox walked to the wet bar and poured a short Johnny Walker Black label into a fresh crystal tumbler and without ice or water, handed it to Poulette Granville Barker. She took a deep sip and sat looking into the flames for several minutes.

"... for so many different reasons, I just could not comprehend that Sebastian would die in that way and that I would never see him again. I am as sure of it today, as I was back in 1982, he did not die in that car; someone murdered him."

"Miss Poulette, that really is no way to talk; you shouldn't worry yourself about things that took place so long ago. You had a wonderful marriage to Mr. Cornelius. He loved you and you loved..." she did not finish her sentence.

"Yes, I did love Cornelius... and Lucas, too ..." she did not continue her sentence but took another sip of the Scotch. Neither Bertrand Fox nor Bernadette Perkins pressed her further.

"Let me help you get dressed for bed," Mrs. Perkins suggested. "There are still a few hours before daylight. Christmas is only a week away, you know. I'll be baking all day and Mr. Fox will be buying the tree. We will make it a happy Christmas, a wonderful holiday season."

Poulette Granville Barker was silent. When she looked up, Mrs. Perkins could see a single tear glistening on her cheek.

Chapter 35

Father Marcus Granville Barker had only arrived in his room minutes earlier. He had participated in the Holy Father's early a.m. Mass in his private chapel and after that returned to the hotel for a quick shower and to put to rest a few personal items on his agenda. It was too early to call Bertrand Fox which left the alternative: Sending him an e-mail message. It was not a form of communication he favored. Not only was it impersonal, but it was, to put it bluntly... too public and too permanent. He preferred a one-on-one conversation which was more and more difficult to accomplish, these days. Bertrand Fox had assured him that Poulette was no better and no worse since Lydia's departure. The recently discovered medications had been stored away so that there was no possibility she could take them, even by accident and most important Fox had put her precious jewel case into their pre-arranged hiding place.

Today's e-mail concerned Christmas. It was only days away and the small items from the Tea shop had been mailed, but Marcus thought it was not enough. He wished he could be home for what could be her last big holidays, but he knew his duties would keep him in Rome for the foreseeable future. The best he could do now was to have Fox purchased several special items for Poulette, something she really wanted, for which he later would reimburse him.

Sending off that e-mail, he headed back to the Vatican apartments. However, only steps away from the hotel, he literally collided with a very agitated Father Malcolm and an equally flustered Father Sean O'Reilly.

"We could do nothing to stop them!" Malcolm whispered loudly. "They just burst in about 10 minutes ago, demanding to see the Holy Father. Sean was there; he can tell you. Neither of us could stop them. They insisted on meeting with him, alone. They won't even let us in!"

"I see, you're saying the door to the Holy Father's bedroom and study is closed?" His tone was inquiring

"Not only closed, Marcus, it's locked. I tried it," Malcolm's voice betrayed his regret. "We tried to call you at the hotel but apparently you had left already and..."

"Stop, Malcolm; let's just cool down for a moment. First of all, who are we talking about? Who came and insisted on seeing the Holy Father?" Marcus' voice was calming. He could see that both priests were over wrought at not being able to protect their charge from someone they interpreted to be possibly 'dangerous'. Marcus led the two to a sitting area to the right of the entrance hall where there were several arm chairs and a sofa. "Exactly, who came in and how many are there?" Marcus asked.

"There are three of them; two are from the Curia and the other is from the Vatican Bank. Cardinal Luca Franconi heads the Apostolic Camera; essentially it is the Vatican's central board of finance in our Administrative system. Cardinal Josef Galleini is the head of the Administration of the Patrimony of the Apostolic See; basically he deals with all of the properties that are owned by the Holy See and administers the funds to keep everything going.

The most powerful Cardinal among them is Cardinal Paolo Torricelli who is at the head of the Vatican Bank or the Institute for Works of Religion."

"In other words, Malcolm, they're all related in some way to the Vatican's resources and its management, is that right?"

"Well, yes and no, Marcus. The Institute, which you call the Bank is legally set up so that assets are not the property of the Holy See, and therefore, it is outside the jurisdiction of the Prefecture for the Economic Affairs of the Holy See. Confusing enough? It's meant to be."

Marcus had stepped away, walking closer to the closed door of the bedroom. "Holy Father," he knocked and called out, "...It's Father Marcus, will you please let me in?" There was no answer.

"Holy Father, are you all right?" The tone of Marcus' voice had changed abruptly. He was now certain something was very wrong. "Malcolm, you must have a key. I want you to open this door immediately!"

"But..." Malcolm hesitated.

"Malcolm, the Holy Father may be in great danger; open the door now or I will try to break it down!" The frightened priest reached inside his robe and pulled out an old fashioned key on a ring. He fitted it into the lock and the door opened immediately.

"My God what is going on here?" he cried out. Marcus followed him quickly with Father Sean O'Reilly immediately behind.

***

Jed Watkins used a plastic stirrer to circle the low ball glass in front of him. He'd ordered the Scotch on the rocks which was heavily diluted with the two now melted ice cubes."

"I'll probably not have the day off, which means eating Christmas dinner, alone unless I accept General Reggie Broadhearst's invitation. With Jessica away, I thought you might like to join us. As you may remember Reggie has a pretty good chef at the safe house and if the weather is bad, well, at least you know you are close enough to get home safely."

Alex raised his hand to signal the waiter. "Another round," he called out. There were few customers in the bar at the General Warren Inn. It was mid-week in December; the roads were icy and the dining room was about to close.

"Would you gentlemen like to be seated now and have the drinks delivered there?" The Maître D diplomatically steered the two into the dining room, off the bar to a table next to the fireplace. There were only two other tables occupied.

"Slow night, I guess," Alex commented as the two sat down.

"That's good for us because I have several things to discuss with you. I didn't want you to have to come into Philly to our office in this weather and I didn't want to have us impose on Joe Farrell again. What I have to tell you is classified, Alex but since you still have your clearance level, I can discuss this with you. The so called "research physician" you wanted us to check out? What was his name?"

"Roberto Succi" Alex answered in a voice that reverberated around the room.

"Well, yes that is the moniker he used. Interesting that he chose a real medical researcher who has been dead for quite some time. We are quite certain we have identified him."

"Your drinks, gentlemen. Here are the menus. Our special this evening is the prime rib, served au jus with mashed potatoes and pureed carrots and green beans. "

"I'm sold," Alex answered, "Make mine medium rare!"

"The same for me and bring us the wine list." Jed Watkins added. "I think we deserve a good bottle to complement the prime rib."

"Now, back to our conversation; who is Roberto Succi?" Alex asked his voice lower than normal.

"His name is Cardinal Rafael Nardoni, a Canadian; he recently was appointed to the board of the Vatican bank. He has contacts with major financial institutions around the world but especially in the United States and Canada. Nardoni travels a lot. He is from an immigrant family that came to the United States in 1939. His family wasn't wealthy, but his father, who started a construction business that grew to be quite a success, had enough money to educate Rafael in Europe, and eventually at the Pontifical North American College in Rome. As you know the latter is a seminary. We could find nothing in his educational background to indicate he has more than a beginner's knowledge of the kind of sophisticated medical research you were talking about. I can't imagine what he was doing suggesting that he could treat your cousin's neurological problems."

Alex said nothing but emptied the glass in front of him. "I think he was planning to kill him," he finally announced. "I'm not certain he won't try again."

Chapter 36

The wooden cart pulled by a single mule lurched as it stopped along the side of the unpaved road. It was very dark. Pier Luigi said nothing but sat silently glancing from time to time at the figure lying on the bench in back of him. He had checked on her occasionally to make certain she was still alive. She had moaned several times during their short ride from the village, but he was quite certain she was still unconscious. He looked at the sky; it was dark, but for the millions of stars that punctuated the moonless night. Cosimo sat beside him, his ears suddenly signaling the approach of someone climbing up from the ravine. "Giovanna?" he whispered. "Giovanna, is that you?" As the rustling sound from the roadside brush grew louder, he could see the silhouettes of two individuals. His sister had not come alone.

"How is she?" Without waiting for an answer, Giovanna climbed into the cart to examine the figure still lying on the rough wooden bench.

"Jessica, can you hear me? Jessica?" She slapped her face sharply, causing the prone figure to wince and moan. "Jessica, wake up! You must wake up now!" Giovanna's voice had risen to a breathless shout. The figure lying on the bench, opened her eyes. "Can you hear me, Jessica?" Giovanna probed. "Jessica, you must wake up. We have got to get you out of here, now. It is too dangerous for you to stay here any longer. Roberto Lombroso wants to send a special guard to take you back to your 'home village'. Since such a village does not exist where the residents would know you, it would make great trouble for all of us. Do you understand?"

"Yes, I can hear you, but it is so dark I have difficulty seeing you. Where are we?" Jessica tried to raise herself, but slumped back to her previous prone position.

"We are on the road to the railway station. Pier Luigi and I will leave you here with Tenente (Lieutenant) Ignasio Neri. He is Colonel Vasari's Aide. You are going back to Camp Darby tonight; do you understand? Ignasio, come here! Meet Jessica!"

Jessica looked up and into the face of a young man dressed in peasant clothing. She noticed his coat was tattered and his cap patched.

"I will tell them you are my mother and you are ill," he explained in Calabrian accented Italian. "We will leave the cart at the station where Pier Luigi will find it and return it to the farm before dawn. Do you understand?" As Jessica looked into his eyes, partially hidden in the shadowy darkness, she could read apprehension. They were in real danger, even more than Giovanna had claimed; or perhaps she was the only one in danger. Either way Ignasio literally was her ticket out of Santa Maria di Polsi and certain execution of herself and Giovanna and Pier Luigi, if she stayed.

"Thank you," she uttered as Giovanna climbed out of the cart. "Thank you for everything!' Pier Luigi looked back only once. He and Cosimo had sprinted ahead and were out of sight in an instant, hidden in the brush of the ravine beside the road.

"Mamma," Ignasio called softly as he took the reins, "I shall have you on the train very soon. It is only about 15 minutes from here to the station. Can you hear me, Mamma?"

"Yes," she answered in her best Calabrian Italian. "I want to get on that train."

***

Father Austin Cheney, Prior Provincial of the Edmundites, sat back in his new ergonomic desk chair, an early Christmas present from a former student who had done very well in a Silicon Valley startup company and who remembered his professor/ mentor each year with an extravagant gift. He had been on this speaker phone call from the Vatican for nearly half an hour, primarily listening and only occasionally being asked to comment. Sr. Elisabeth "Beth" Castelli, his longtime secretary, with notebook in hand, sat opposite taking copious notes on the ensuing conversation.

"Of course, we're delighted that the Cardinal wants to visit us," Fr. Cheney commented, adjusting his boot-bound foot that rested on short kitchen stool beneath his desk. "Yes, Yes, I do understand that he comes at our benefactor's request and I know

Father Paul Sullivan will make every effort to ensure he is received by everyone at the University with appropriate attention."

Sister Beth, who had been sitting stiffly in a position intended to give her an advantage in terms of being able to hear every last word, gave a deep sign as the Papal representative at the other end of the line continued to drone on.

"Be assured, we will accommodate the Cardinal in a suitable fashion. Now, I must ask that we conclude this call. Perhaps, we can speak about the details in the days just before the Cardinal's arrival... which is when exactly?" Sister Beth was listening attentively. No date had been mentioned earlier.

"Next week? Christmas week? Surely you must be joking?" Austin Cheney looked at the speaker box incredulously. "That is six days away. Most of our faculty if not all of them are already gone from the University or will be. Surely his visit can wait until after the holidays,"

Cheney was exasperated. This was a ridiculous request. "Why were we not given more notice and why can this visit not wait a couple of weeks?" Cheney found himself shouting into the tiny hidden speaker phone that looked more like a desk ornament than a communication device.

"Because the Holy Father is asking that you receive him on the dates I have given you!"

The answer prompted a stony silence.

"Well then, we'll look forward to receiving the Cardinal on the date and time specified," Father Austin Cheney responded quietly.

"... and one more thing, the Holy Father asks that he remain anonymous in this matter. You are not to mention nor incur his name; is that clear?"

"Yes, quite clear!"

There were no goodbyes, nor gracious thanks for pushing off a guest with such short notice. Only a sudden absence of speech that left the priest and nun sitting and staring at the desk ornament speaker.

Sister Beth was the first to break the eerie atmosphere. "A cup of tea, Father? Or perhaps a cup of cocoa?"

"No...no, thank you. See if you can get Father Paul Sullivan on the phone right away. We have to get him on board with all of this."

"Ohhh, I don't know if I can, Father; he usually goes away someplace warm for the winter holidays. He may have left."

"Not this year, Sister Beth. If he has left already, find him and bring him back. This year he'll be spending the holidays with me and the Cardinal!

Chapter 37

"Stop, stop this minute! What in God's name are you doing to him?" Father Malcolm had pushed Fathers Marcus and Sean aside as he unlocked the door and the three charged into Pope Leo XIV's bed chamber. With his, bed clothing open at the back and his body nearly hanging off the side of the narrow palate bed, the Pontiff lay on his stomach, his arms and hands dangling from the side and dragging slightly on the fringes of the Persian rug. Cardinal Luca Franconi, head of the Apostolic Camera, the central board of Finance in the Pope's administrative system, stood over him, taking photos of the strange markings with his phone camera. Cardinals Josef Galleini and Paolo Torricelli behind him.

"Stay out of this, Malcolm if you know what's good for you," Cardinal Torricelli, head of the Vatican Bank shouted, his voice muffled as he continued his photography.

"I'll call the guard and they'll arrest you if you don't stop now!" Malcolm screamed back.

"Do that, Malcolm," Cardinal Galleini, head of the Administration of the Patrimony of the Holy See, answered never looking up from the site where Franconi had trained his phone camera.

"No need to call them, Malcolm; they're already here!" Marcus' voice was soft and steady as he and Sean O'Reilly stepped aside leaving the way clear for three Swiss Guard to take charge of the situation.

***

"I don't believe it," Father Sean O'Reilly muttered as the last of the Swiss Guard left the salon outside the Pontiff's bed chamber. "They let them go? What good are these guards if they do nothing in a situation like this one? The pontiff was being taken advantage of. They were, in my opinion, abusing an old, sick man."

Marcus, who had been pacing the small salon area for most of the 45 minutes since the Swiss Guards' entry, was surprisingly not consoling.

"Sean, what did they ask you during your interview?" Marcus probed.

"Not very much. It only lasted a couple of minutes. They wanted to know who I was and what I was doing here. I replied honestly but certainly not in a way that would give them any real information. And what about you?"

"I guess I did about the same thing. They did not seem to be really interested in us. They hardly asked Malcolm anything, right, Malcolm?"

"He was betrayed today and I'm the one who allowed it to happen. It wasn't the Swiss Guards who betrayed him. I should never have allowed those monsters to remain in that room when they locked the door. But..... I was afraid. My God, he could have died because I was afraid to unlock the damned door," Malcolm sank into a leather lounge chair near the door and began to weep. "He is not just the Holy Father but he's my friend and I let him down today. My God, how bad is that?"

"Malcolm, stop looking in the mirror for a moment and think about all of this. We're focusing on the wrong individuals. It is not the three of us we should be blaming but..."

"The trio who invaded Leo's bedroom," Sean O'Reilly answered, as if on cue.

"Exactly!" Marcus answered.

Malcolm wiped his eyes with a crumpled paper tissue he'd found stuffed into his trouser pocket.

"Those Cardinals all have something to do with the Vatican Bank, something important. Leo has been looking into their affairs for the last year since he assumed his position. They are major players internationally and among the most powerful members of the Curia; the Holy Father is not ignorant of their political and financial influence all over the world." Malcolm stopped to wipe his nose.

"... but, why was he taking photos of the Holy Father's back and those markings?" He sniffled for a moment.

"Do you think they know about his...his visions? Perhaps they want to get him out of office?"

"... or perhaps they want him dead!" Marcus interjected. "That would be getting him out of office and out of being able to communicate."

"Changing the subject a little, our supplies should arrive this weekend, I've been told," Sean O'Reilly spoke meekly not comprehending all that had taken place but hoping to change the tenor of the conversation. "As soon as they arrive we can begin the tests; right, Marcus?"

"... yeah, right Sean. I'll do my best; but it has been a long time since medical school and although I am an MD, my focus has been on psychiatry for a while now. I'm more comfortable ordering a battery of tests and having other people perform them and then reporting the results to me."

"...you know I'll do my best to help you with both the gathering of information and the analysis; whatever it takes, Marcus," Sean patted the other priest on his back.

"We forensic anthropologists have a pretty good knowledge of what you medical guys do. We took many of the same classes, remember?"

"So, are you saying, Marcus that you don't have a lot of confidence we can find out the cause of these visions and the terrible markings on Leo's back?" Malcolm interjected.

"I'm not certain what I'm saying; I just hope we can save Leo's life. I'm more and more inclined to think that there is something he has been concealing for a very long time and that something finally is pushing itself through to the surface... quite literally. It may not even be anything he can acknowledge consciously."

"It would have to be a pretty big concealment, I would think, to cause such a strong physical reaction," Sean commented.

"Bigger than any of us can imagine, I'm afraid." Marcus Granville Barker walked to the door of the Pope's bedroom and pushed the half closed door aside. He peered in: The Pope's breathing was normal. He looked peaceful as he slept; but even that was abnormal after such a horrendous ordeal.

Chapter 38

It was at first light the following frosty December morning when a farmer and his son, driving their mule and produce laden wagon to the village, spotted something in the shallow ditch beside the road. A light frost covered the three bodies, evidence they had lain there at least overnight. The boy, using a stick he'd picked up, prodded one of the corpses to turn it over.

His scream was shrill. He knew the face with its eyes wide open.

His father jumped down from the rig. There was no need to touch them further. It was obvious; they were dead: Giovanna Poloni, Pier Luigi Garcea and his dog Cosimo; each, shot dead, with a single bullet to the back of the head.

***

The train to Pisa and Camp Darby rolled along the countryside in almost total silence. The few passengers who had boarded it at Villa San Giovanni near Polsi had left Jessica and Tenente Ignasio Neri alone in the car. Jessica's body lay slumped against the window. Her shawl was wrapped around her shoulders, yet she seemed to shiver occasionally. He felt her forehead. There was no doubt, she had a fever. The train screeched as it stopped at a small station. It was already three thirty in the morning. Neri wondered what passengers would embark at such a late hour; or perhaps it was an early hour for someone going to a morning meeting or event. The door at the end of the car slid open. It was a priest, an older man, who wore a heavy jacket over his clerical collar and what Neri believed was a suit.

"May I sit here?" he asked without waiting for an answer. "Quite a chill in the air out there. I wouldn't be surprised if we had snow." Neri noticed his accent. It was Calabrian, but not a perfect dialect. He examined his face, perhaps hoping to find a clue as to where he might have come from. He was older, in his late fifties or sixties, grey haired and balding, with a round face and small silver framed oval glasses. He unwrapped the muffler from around his neck revealing an even more prominent double chin than Neri had imagined when he first saw him.

"Your mother? Is she ill?" he asked as he folded the muffler and placed it beside him on the seat.

"Yes, she isn't well. She seems to have developed a fever." Ignasio Neri put his arm around Jessica, affectionately wrapping the shawl even more tightly around her shoulders.

"She has not been on a farm, by any chance has she? Perhaps a farm in this area?" The priest looked more closely at Jessica whose eyes were closed. Her breathing was steady but they both noted a raspiness as she exhaled.

"Yes, we have been with relatives on a farm not far from here. Why do you ask?"

"Perhaps you have not heard; there is an epidemic of swine flu in this area. The National Health Service (Servizio Sanitario Nazioanale) has issued a bulletin warning individuals who have been on a farm during the last few weeks to get vaccinated. Your mother may already have the flu; it will be important for her to go to a clinic. And you, my son, you must get a vaccination to prevent it."

Ignasio Neri answered only, "... yes, Father and thank you, Father." It was obvious, the woman in his care was very sick. Ignasio did not want to engage in any conversation with this man, priest or not. He turned his head to the window; it was still very dark but he could see the lights of a small station ahead.

"Ahh, this is my stop, my son. Do take your mother to a clinic immediately, "he added as he rose from his seat. "She needs immediate care." He slipped into his coat, grabbed the muffler and left the car at the station. Ignasio checked his watch again. They should arrive in Pisa in another ten minutes. There would be a car to meet them and then, they had only a ten minute drive to the base. He would take Jessica to the Base Health Facilities immediately. He only hoped he would not be too late.

**

"Mr. Fox, you've chosen well!" Poulette applauded softly as Bertrand Fox added the angel atop the 8 foot Scots Pine.

"And I have brought some sherry, hot buttered rum, a pot of your favorite Constant Comment tea and freshly baked sugar cookies and scones, still warm from the oven." Mrs. Perkins placed the elaborate silver tray on a table near the tree which Mr. Fox had set up in one corner of the library.

"How long has it been, Mrs. Perkins that we've been sharing these holidays?" Poulette selected a mug of hot buttered rum and a sugar cookie from the tray.

"Oh, it's been a long time, Mrs. G, a very long time. I began with you when my husband Orfeo was your first husband, Sebastian Calvi's driver in Milano.

"But of course, how could I forget... and you let me prattle on and on about Sebastian and never said a word.

"Yes, now I recall; you were both so young and he... Orfeo died the same night that...." Poulette stared at the tree, her silence lasting for several seconds.

"I'm sorry, ma'am, I didn't mean to make you recall all of that. It was a long time ago and really, there is no need for you to think about it at all." Bernadette Perkins offered a cup of tea to Bertrand Fox who hovered near the tree not wanting to become involved in the conversation.

"But, Mrs. Perkins, there are things I want to remember and now, I can't seem to grasp them. They're like wispy thoughts." She looked up at Bernadette Perkins. "... Wispy thoughts, do you know what I mean? They are there and then... they disappear. Sometimes in my dreams I can recall everything, but when I open my eyes...". Poulette sipped the hot buttered rum and sat back in the lounge chair across from the tree.

"Thank you both for everything. I think I'd like to be alone, now. Mr. Fox, please turn on some lovely Christmas music. I'll just sit here and enjoy your work. Thank you, Mrs. Perkins, for this delicious repast."

"Will you be having dinner in your apartment at the usual time?" Mrs. Perkins picked up the tea tray but left the scones, jelly and sugar cookies behind.

"Yes, about 7:30 p.m. would be fine." Bertrand Fox noticed that Poulette had closed her eyes. He lifted the mug from her hand, placing it beside her on the table and arranged a cashmere throw to cover her knees. Perhaps if she would sleep for a short time she might remember what she had repressed so successfully for these many years.

Chapter 39

"No, no, no, Marcus, you don't understand. When you talk about a vision, it is as if..." the Holy Father paused for a moment and looked directly into the eyes of the psychiatrist. "It is as if you think I'm mad," He put down the pen he had been using to write notes for his Christmas Eve homily. "Listen, I can understand how at times, what I tell you must seem abnormal to many people. But, you are a psychiatrist. You should understand that my dreams are dreams. I understand the difference between dreams and reality. I have no idea what they mean or why I am having them. Yes, they are becoming more frequent and more frightening. I fear...." He paused again, as if to select the right words, "...what I fear is that when they end, I will as well. But, if that is God's will, then, so be it."

"Holy Father, I'm not here to judge you, you know that. However, I am hoping to understand exactly what is happening inside your head. You and I both know that the markings on your back, those raised Aramaic letters, are quite extraordinary. Obviously, since they appear on your back, they must be the result of something within you that quite literally is fighting its way to the surface to be recognized. " Marcus was still in eye contact with the Pope.

"Then, you think I am holding something back, is that it?" Leo placed the pen on the desk and pushed his chair back.

"Yes, Holy Father; I think there is something very, very important locked inside of you that you know, in your heart, must be told and yet, cannot bring yourself to recognize what it is. Now, shall we try again to talk about your dream last night?"

Leo walked to his cot where he lay down and closed his eyes. Marcus merely turned his chair, allowing the pontiff a semblance of privacy even in this least private of psychological acts.

"It seems that immediately, as I enter into the dream, I am running and it is still very dark; only, I know that the... the ones who are chasing me, are so close that soon I will be caught. I am afraid, very afraid that they will kill me."

"Can you identify any of them?" Marcus asks softly.

"No, no but I literally can feel their presence. They seem to want something that I have and..."

""Do you have it, Holy Father?" Marcus has stopped taking notes and was watching the Pope as his face winced and it appeared that he was re-living the dream.

"I'm not sure; I tell them I don't have it, but they say I do. I am running, running and the water is closer and closer and I see the staircase going up the river bank." Leo's voice grew gravelly and his breathing sounded raspy and unsteady. Marcus lifted his wrist to check his pulse; it was racing.

"Malcolm, Malcolm, please come here, right away!' he called out.

Pope Leo opened his eyes and pushed his body into a semi raised position. "They're going to kill me; that's it. They are going to kill me!"

Malcolm hurried to the bedside lowering the pontiff's head on to a large overstuffed down pillow. "Rest, Holy Father," he said gently pulling a sheet and light blanket over the pontiff's body.

Marcus led the way out of the bedroom and closed the door behind them.

"I got a call," Malcolm said softly. "The order that we placed should arrive this weekend. I hope it will not be too late."

"I hope not either," Marcus whispered.

***

It was blatantly obvious that University president Father Paul Sullivan was not happy. He had only just arrived at the Kukio estate of St. Edmund's University alum, Ambassador Josh Campbell on the island of Kona in Hawaii when he picked up the call to return immediately to the University. Now, as he sat in the nearly empty monastery refectory awaiting Prior Provincial Father Austin Cheney, he found himself thinking the most unholy thoughts about the order's PP and wondering exactly what Cheney might have done had he not returned.

"Sorry to keep you waiting, Paul," Father Austin Cheney made his way to the table slowly and with effort. His leg had not healed completely and he was required to use a three pronged cane for support. Sullivan stood up.

"What's this all about?" his question was churlish and from the expression he wore, Cheney was certain he could interpret his mood.

"Listen, Paul, I know how much you relish your holidays and especially Christmas in Hawaii, but, I'm afraid this has to come first." He sat down, landing with a thud on the hard molded plastic chair that served the few who required breakfast during these holidays when most residents were away.

"The truth is that I got no notice. The Cardinal called the day before yesterday and said we could expect our visitor today. There was no negotiating. Whatever, this unnamed representative has to say is top secret; but again the Cardinal did not ask if or when he might come, instead he literally ordered the two of us to be here to greet him.

"So, this is serious; you have absolutely no idea what is going on here?" Sullivan's tone had softened, even if his mood had not.

"Frankly, I was looking forward to a few days of peace... not in Hawaii but just being able to rest and relax in my quarters. This has rather taken the glimmer off that dream and put it so to speak on the back burner. I've made arrangements for our guest, whoever he is, to stay right here in the Monastery. The guest apartment is Spartan but sufficient.

"I take it then, that we won't be inviting him out for dinner?" Sullivan's question held the promise of at least a good meal at one of the Main Line's top rated restaurants.

"No, I'm quite certain that would not be acceptable. We'll have dinner right here in the refectory. I think we may be the only ones here, in fact. It is a perfect place for the kind of privacy that seems to be needed."

"Austin, you said you have no knowledge of why he is coming and exactly who he is. This wouldn't have anything to do with our ... our gift, would it?" Paul Sullivan's voice was almost a whisper as he said the last few words. The gift, what a peculiar philosophical concept it had become. He remembered the late French philosopher, Jacques Derrida who had lectured several times at St. Edmund's on the topic of the gift and when a gift is not a gift.

Father Austin Cheney did not have a chance to answer. Walking toward them through the refectory entrance, was a clean shaven man in his mid-forties wearing a hooded parka and rolling a single piece of luggage behind him.

"Father Cheney, my name is Jacques Dumont. I believe you have been expecting me?"

Chapter 40

Caroline walked Alex through the three-story foyer to the front entrance of their house in Haverford. A large Norse Pine wreath with a red bow hung inside the front door, while garlands of holly bedecked the chandeliers. "Your house looks lovely; Caroline, very festive." Alex tucked his muffler into the front of his coat and removed his gloves from his coat pocket.

"This year especially, I know Philip would want us to decorate. I...." she stopped in front of the door, her hand on the brass lever lock. "I have to ask you, Alex; what do you think? Does he seem any better to you?" Alex considered the question carefully before answering. He understood he must choose his words carefully; Caroline's, as well as Philip's state of mind depended upon it.

"Honestly, yes, I can see some improvement. He seems cognizant of my being present. I noticed that with his new therapist, he is more engaged. Less vague, if you know what I mean; but, you're the one who should notice the improvement."

"I do see progress. Then again, I am looking for it. After the disaster with those two bogus doctors, I really had been at wit's end to find someone reliable. This therapist, Dr. Craig Halaby came with not only the right medical credentials, but several letters of recommendation from people I trust. Believe me, I know it will take time."

"You both have plenty of that, Caroline. I'll come back tomorrow, if that's convenient. I'll call you before just to check if you two are up for company," As Alex opened the front door, a gust of wind carried its icy sting across his face. It was going to be another long, cold winter, he feared.

Caroline shut the door and locked it. She had told their small staff to take the day off, leaving her alone with Philip. She climbed the broad staircase to the third floor. Although it was only mid-afternoon, darkness was already setting in. A bleakness penetrated the house. At the top of the staircase, she walked directly to Philip's room. It was empty.

"Philip, would you like something to eat?" she called out walking into the lounge, which was dark and empty.

"Philip, where are you?" Her voice was frantic as she headed down the staircase to their second floor Master bedroom suite. "Darling, are you in here?" The door to their bedroom was closed. She specifically remembered leaving it open when she left earlier.

"Philip? Darling, are you all right?" She thrust the door open.

"Oh my God, Philip! What have you done?"

Caroline walked slowly toward her husband. Her vanity was in disarray; drawers open, cosmetics scattered about. Philip stood beside it; his pajama top unbuttoned to the waist. He had opened tube after tube of lipstick and smashed the waxy colors across his skin. His face was smeared with slashes of pink and orange and scarlet; his chest a palette of reds and violets. His hands smeared with color. What remained of his destruction lay at his feet, color smeared across the oak flooring and tubes crushed beneath his feet

It was only when she moved in closer to the scene that she saw it. Written in large childlike scrawl on the wall behind him was a message: *Let me out! Help me! Please! Out! Out! Out*!

***

Jessica let the hot spray of the shower wash over her face and body. Her hair, still frothy from its second shampoo, released days of grime that created rivulets of grey suds as they made their way to the drain. Part one of her assignment was over. She had made it safely out of Polsi and the hands of the 'Ndrangheta and back to Camp Darby and the Base Commander's private office shower....

Her stay in the base hospital had been brief. She was given an IV of saline solution and an antidote to reverse the effects of the drug she had been given by Giovanna, which effectively mimicked a serious infectious fever, and she felt no worse for it. Her back still ached from her run in with the motor bike, but a couple of ibuprofen would take care of that. As she toweled dry, she inspected the clothing her minders had left for her to wear.

"This certainly is no fashion mission" she said aloud. The peasant dress, shawl and ill-fitting shoes she had worn in Polsi had been replaced by an equally drab ill-fitting grey wool flannel dress, black cotton stockings and comfortable black tie Oxfords. She hung her hospital gown on a hook in the dressing room and with still wet hair combed back and secured into a bun, she left to meet Lt. Colonel Francis Greeley, the Base Commander in his office adjoining this private lavatory and shower.

"Come in, come in, Jessica; feeling better now?" Jessica was surprised at his ebullient greeting. When she had last encountered him, his rudeness and lack of concern for her well-being had been astounding. She still had not forgotten the lack of direction as well as the incorrect information given to her as she went to find the train station, get food and make her way to Giovanna in Polsi.

"It has been quite a time, Sir. Seems like I've been away for a year not ten days."

"You remember, Colonel Gabriele Vasari, my colleague?"

"Congratulations, Agent Rawlins, you did a fine job in Polsi, I understand."

"Well, that is very kind of you. But, thanks really should go to Agent Giovanna Poloni and her little brother Pier Luigi. They were immensely helpful." Jessica smiled, but noted neither Vasari nor Greeley replied. Finally, Colonel Vasari whose mood had in that instant turned very sober said. "I'm sorry, Mrs. Rawlins, but they didn't make it. Their bodies with that of the dog were found beside the road. They had been shot execution style."

"Oh, My God, no!" Her words were barely audible. She sat down on the nearest chair and took a deep breath.

"Are you all right?" Greeley inquired after a few seconds. "Can I get you a glass of water?"

"Yes, I'm fine," she replied, "… and yes, I'd appreciate a glass of water. Giovanna was very professional. I can only think that it was…."

She stopped in mid-sentence recalling her last day at the restaurant in Polsi. It was at the farewell luncheon where she had fainted, falling at the feet of the elderly priest. Could that fall somehow have caused their deaths? If Roberto Lombroso discovered she was not a relative of Giovanna... if she was not a widow who lived in a nearby village? It was speculation on her part, but if that was the case, she might still be in danger.

"I thought we'd have lunch here in my office so that we can get through the de-briefing with the least fuss. I've invited your escort, Colonel Vasari's, Tenente (Lt.) Ignasio Neri to join us." Greeley handed her a glass of water with ice. It was the first time she had seen ice in what seemed like an eternity. "Lieutenant Neri told us that on your train trip, you were approached by someone dressed like a priest. Do you remember any of that, Jessica?"

"No, nothing." Jessica took another sip of the iced water.

"He seemed to come directly to your car and we suspect he was checking on you. We doubt he was a priest at all, but probably someone from the 'Ndrangheta. I'm fairly certain that they want you out of the picture, too."

"They want me dead." Jessica's voice was unemotional.

"Yes, and we'll give you to them, dead... figuratively speaking, you understand."

"Well, that's comforting."

"We've planted a story in the Italian Associated Press reporting that the National Health Service has put out a notice to residents and travelers declaring a health emergency. Anyone who has been in or will be travelling to Calabria should be aware that there is an epidemic of Swine Flu and should be vaccinated before travelling. It will be reported that a woman, who recently visited Polsi has died from the disease. That woman, of course, will be you."

"Will it work?" Jessica was skeptical.

"I don't know. If it doesn't, you will find out soon enough." Colonel Greeley's mood had changed in that instant. His ebullience, replaced by a seriousness Jessica knew to be genuine. She had seen Roberto Lombroso in his element. She could identify him and if he did not think she was dead already, he certainly would come after her and make her so.

"You know you can always leave at this point... go home. No one would think any the less of you for it; you've already given us some very valuable intelligence. I'm certainly OK with calling Jed Watkins, if you decide you want to..."

"Stop, I'm not throwing in the towel. It wouldn't do me any good anyway. If Lombroso can find me on a night train in Calabria, he certainly can find me on the Main Line in Pennsylvania. I'm going ahead with the assignment." Jessica heard herself. Her voice sounded confident, but within, she felt a pang of apprehensiveness. Roberto Lombroso would not be fooled by the Swine Fever story for long and he would not let her live while he was still alive.

"I've ordered us a good bottle of Calabrian wine to go with our lunch," Greeley announced as a trolley made its way through the Colonel's office door laden with both hot and cold specialties of the region.

"This is to celebrate your safe return to us from Polsi and your continuing assignment in Rome."

Jessica could only smile as she watched Greeley pull the cork from the wine bottle and Gabriele Vasari gather the glasses for a toast.

Chapter 41

Caroline had begun to sob again. "... but Alex, I don't want him hospitalized. Look at him; they'll just pump him full of drugs to keep him quiet and then put him into one of those rooms with padded walls and…. You know, that really will kill him!"

Alex had phoned Philip's psychiatrist asking him to return immediately when he saw his catatonic cousin looking totally unhinged. As his psychiatrist observed, Philip sat mutely in front of the vanity where Caroline had discovered him smashing tubes of her lipsticks into his chest and then using one to write his strange message on the wall. But now, he was silent; He neither moved nor spoke. His seeming recovery, she believed, had been set back perhaps triggered by something she had said or done. Unfortunately, she had no idea what that trigger might have been.

"Mr. Rawlins, I'm Aurelian Gibbons, your cousin's psychiatrist. This so called 'set back', your words, I should add, Mrs. Rawlins... with the lipsticks, have you any idea what might have set him off? He seemed quite placid when I left here earlier."

"He really has been improving, Dr. Gibbons, it wasn't an illusion. In less than an hour after you left, I found him like this, in our bedroom, where he was doing these things. I can't understand …." Caroline began to whimper again, reaching for a tissue from the box Aurelian Gibbons had handed her.

"Just before his accident, Mrs. Rawlins, you told me that he had been visiting someone. You also said something about lipstick involved there. Can you remember what that was all about?"

"Why, yes, of course. It was on the day of the accident: I was coming back from an appointment. It was about four o'clock in the afternoon. I was just pulling into the driveway of our house, when I saw that Philip was leaving. He rolled down his window and said something about going to visit a client, Poulette Granville Barker who seemed to be putting her house on the market and removing it every other week. I don't remember which one she was doing on that day. Anyway, he said the meeting with her shouldn't take long. Later, of course, I learned that he could not have been going to see her because she was in the hospital. Apparently, he saw something or witnessed something when he arrived at her residence that sent him dashing from the house and into his car. He drove out of her driveway, without a seat belt, at top speed and right into rush hour traffic on North Ithan Avenue; that's when he was broadsided. The doctors in the emergency room at Bryn Mawr Hospital said he had lipstick on his face, beneath the blood, that is. He was a mess. I think the implication was that he had been... well, you know, having an affair. I don't believe that, of course; but I don't know how to explain the lipstick either and the fact that he had lied about seeing Poulette."

"Mrs. Rawlins, I believe your husband is trying to tell you something; in fact, while this may not look like a sign of progress in recovering his memory, I believe it is the first major break we've had. He is remembering. He knows what he saw; it is inside his head, which is why he wrote that message on the wall and it definitely has something to do with lipstick... and what he witnessed that day."

Caroline noted a slight smile on Gibbons' face.

"Then, it could be a breakthrough, you think?" Alex added.

"Definitely, Mr. Rawlins, definitely; and you both should know, I will not suggest that he be hospitalized. I've given him an injection to sedate him. He should be quite comfortable for the next 24 hours. I'll ask my nurse to stay with him until you can hire someone from the agency. He should have 24 hour monitoring for the time being. Be reassured, we can expect more progress in the future. Round the clock nursing probably will be necessary for only a few days, but until then, call the service. I'll be back tomorrow morning."

Gibbons handed her a business card on which he wrote the name of the nursing agency, followed by his private telephone number.

"If something occurs and you want to reach me, call this number. It will cut out the 'middle man', our service operator." Caroline smiled for the first time all day. "I'll walk you to the door."

Alex shook hands with Aurelian Gibbons and proceeded to the third floor where Philip had been taken only moments earlier. A brawny male nurse, with the help of an aide had carried Philip up the staircase on a gurney to his room. His face was now clean, free from the lipstick he had wildly applied; but his chest, still carried diluted remnants of the slashes of color.

"Philip," Alex called to him softly. "Philip, everything is going to be all right. You are safe here... safe to remember."

There was no response. Philip was in a deep sleep.

***

"He's not going to be able to do it, is he? The Pontiff absolutely has to be functioning normally for the Presentation of the Christmas Greetings to the Roman Curia, Marcus; it's on the calendar for the day after tomorrow and right now, he certainly doesn't appear to be ready for prime time." Malcolm had been seated in front of his computer for the last 45 minutes reviewing the heavy pre-Christmas agenda of the Pontiff. In addition to his daily duties, the Holiday season brought extra responsibilities, including visitors from abroad, many of them VIPs from other countries who would be accompanied by international press photographers. "It's the last gathering of the year for the Curia and after what we saw going on in Leo's bedroom, you can imagine what Cardinal Franconi, the head of the Apostolic Camera and Cardinal Galleini, who administers the Patrimony have planned; they absolutely want Leo out. I hate to ask, Marcus but is there anything medically you could give him that might make him appear... well, more normal for that meeting?"

Malcolm had noted, that recently the Holy Father had bowed out of meetings with important guests at the last minute leaving the responsibilities to his Secretary of State, an elderly Spanish Franciscan Cardinal, Pablo Gomez, whose temperament was totally unsuited to conversing with dignitaries, kissing babies and engaging in idle conversation with visiting clergy, all while photographers snapped pictures for the world's press outlets. Unfortunately, it seemed, Cardinal Gomez would have to be available for every public function going forward. Malcolm would explain that the Holy Father had the flu.

"You know, I can't medicate him without a physical exam, which at minimum has to include a blood test. I also want to do a brain scan. While the Holy Father's conversations are unusual by most standards, a couple hundred years ago, a Pope who talked to a saint might be considered for sainthood himself."

"Then, he hasn't stopped with the conversations?" Malcolm's concern was heightened.

"No, he hasn't; he continues to perceive this voice, which he believes is St. Peter. He literally looks forward to hearing from him as he prays before Mass each morning; he believes the saint is amplifying this philosophy of the Divine Instant which obviously Leo has concocted but which he now believes is a revelation. Today, Leo told me that Peter is telling him this 'secret' at Jesus' request."

"Marcus, I beg you, please don't tell anyone else about this last remark... ever," Malcolm voice was almost a whisper. "The Curia would have a field day with that bit; they'd have him carried out of here in an instant and transported to some far away retreat where no one could ever get to him." Malcolm's nervous energy was increasingly evident. He walked to an under- counter refrigerator in the corner of his office and pulled out a bottle of orange Fanta, flipping the cap off with his fingers and drinking half the bottle in a single gulp.

"This Divine Instant stuff, he hasn't written any of this down anywhere has he?" Malcolm's voice was increasingly apprehensive.

"I have no idea, Malcolm. I could ask him, but you and I both know, if he has, what could we do about it?"

Marcus was watching Malcolm closely; peculiar behavior often instigates equally peculiar behavior, a response which seemed to be going viral at the Vatican these days.

"Malcolm, you told me that the supplies I'd ordered would be here any day; where are they or when can I expect them? If I could do a few physical tests on the Holy Father and Sean could work with me to analyze these tests, we might be able to at least control some of Leo's more unusual behavior."

"Your order should be here tomorrow at the latest. I'll let you know if there is any change in the arrival time. It is being transported by an individual who is scheduled to arrive here at the residence sometime in late morning." Malcolm's voice was tinged with annoyance; he was obviously frustrated and tired at their seeming inability to take the lead in propping up the Holy Father.

"Thanks, Malcolm, now, back to the meeting with the Curia: The Holy Father did mention, a few days ago, that he has been preparing something in writing to present to them for this year-end meeting. Have you any idea what these presentations usually contain? Would they be religious highlights? Statements of Faith ...anything like that?"

"What it contains really depends on the current Pope. The idea, as interpreted by Popes in the past, has been to write a Christmas letter which he reads to the Curia. It can be light or it can be fairly heavy. One of our previous Popes made it his habit of praising the Curia for their past year's hard work, then followed it with heavy chastisement. I have no idea what Leo might be planning. It is no secret, relationships, with his brother Cardinals have been on a downward spiral, lately. If the elections were held today, he would never be elected. As for what he's planning to say to the Curia, I have no idea. I guess, I'm no longer in the loop." Malcolm was pensive for a moment, gulping down the rest of the orange Fanta and tossing the empty bottle into a waste basket. "But, I do think you and I had better talk more about this Divine Instant philosophy he is getting from St. Peter. I'm not afraid, but apprehensive that he might decide to make it the main topic of Christmas message."

Marcus did not answer. If Malcolm knew everything Leo had told him, he might be even more fearful of the Curia's reaction to the topic.

Chapter 42

"Where's the Holy Father?"

Marcus awakened with a jolt, opening his eyes to see Malcolm standing above him in the Pope's private chapel. "I don't know, Malcolm; we've pretty much been talking all night. I guess I fell asleep here.

"What time is it anyway?" His entire body ached as he tried to sit up straight. The high-backed wooden chair he had pulled up next to the Pope's prie dieu had done little to accommodate the six foot three inch frame of his healthy but aging body.

"It's 6:20 a.m.; the Holy Father should be here any minute for Mass."

"Well, it was about 10:45 p.m. when I finally finished unpacking the items delivered by the courier. They're all stored in your office, Malcolm, under lock and key; and we did receive everything we asked for. I was on my way back to the hotel when the Holy Father called out to me from his apartment door. He was on his way to the chapel for his nightly prayers and he asked if I would join him." Marcus sat up, rubbing his eyes and stroking his chin, both of which verified a night spent with little sleep and no time to shower or shave.

"We prayed, of course and at one point, I noticed that the Holy Father had gone into what I would call a trance state." Marcus was now standing and stretching. It was obvious he was in pain, a result of keeping his body contorted in the hard, straight-back chair for several hours.

"Was he talking to St. Peter again?" Malcolm pulled up another vintage chair from several that lined the inner wall.

"No," Marcus answered crisply, choosing his words carefully. "It is no longer a two-way conversation. He now becomes Peter and is speaking in his voice." Marcus stated this last comment in a near whisper. "... and yes, it most definitely represents a progression of the disorder."

"What does St. Peter say?" Malcolm's demeanor reflected an amazement and curiosity at what he was about to hear.

"It's this increased focus on the Divine Instant, Malcolm. In the voice of St. Peter he tells me that at the instant of creation, God in one breath created "all for all time". There is no progressing universe which we hear about from our astro-physicists. We are not being hurled through space and time. It was and is at the same time. All that will ever be and ever was came about in that one breath of the Creator in that Divine Instant. The beginning, the now and the end were all in that same instant. What we experience is that divine instant in our lives if we have Faith. He tried over and over to explain how man has not yet been able to comprehend this. Jesus spoke of it numerous times, he said but the apostles, being plain men, did not have a mindset to accept it. Essentially, what I have been able to grasp from what he is saying is that we are and have always been since the time of creation. We perceive ourselves to be alive and live our lives within that context."

"I'm not certain what religious context that is and whether it aligns with the precepts of our Roman Catholic Faith, are you?" Malcolm did not answer immediately; instead he began to pace around the small chapel speaking as he strolled.

"I'm not a theologian, Malcolm, and I certainly am not qualified to interpret doctrine. But, if this is what the Holy Father believes is being revealed to him and to the world, it is profound and he seems to comprehend all of that; but does it mean anything in the context of his mental health? Are these just the thoughts of someone suffering from a mental aberration?"

"It means an enormous breakthrough in our understanding of the Divine, Malcolm!" The voice of Pope Leo XIV resounded in an abnormally vigorous voice. He had entered the chapel silently.

"It will be the final expression of my flawed life; one which I have tried so very hard to...." Leo did not finish his sentence but moved to his prie dieu to kneel again in front of the painting of St. Peter on the cross, the saint's face only a few feet from Leo's.

"Oh, Peter, you said they would not understand and they do not But, you also say that my words will bring many closer to our Lord Jesus. How can that be when I am such a failure?"

Leo began to weep, his tears staining the fresh white cassock.

"I think the Holy Father needs some rest. Let's take him back to his apartment. I'll watch over him, Marcus. You go back and get some rest. I have a terrible feeling we'll be needing your time even more in the coming days."

Marcus lifted the praying pontiff to his feet, guiding him by the elbow back to his apartment.

***

"I have a letter of reference from Monsignor Giacomo Morosini at Our Lady of Polsi who tells me that you are a widow from the village of Locri." Maria Scopoletti, mistress of the Memores Domini looked up and into Gessica's eyes. "How long have you been a widow?"

"A little more than a year," she answered lowering her eyes. "Was he ill for long?" Scopoletti pressed the poorly dressed woman sitting across from her.

"No, Madame, he was not ill, at all, he was...." she did not complete the sentence.

"I see, and Monsignor says in his letter that you are very thorough in your cleaning and also very dependable." She looked up again to see Gessica's head still lowered.

"You understand that if you are to work in the Holy Father's household, you will be asked to join our association, the Memores Domini. We are not a religious order, but we do practice obedience, poverty and chastity and we live, here at the Vatican where we also observe a regimen of silence and common prayer. Your wages will not be high, but they will include a private room, your meals and clothing, all of which have been donated to our association. If we make you an offer and you accept the position, you will report directly to me. I will assign you to whatever duties I believe are best suited to your talents. Is all of that understood?" Maria Scopoletti's voice was crisp and less than welcoming.

"I take it you can read and write?" Scopoletti reached for a computer typed page on her desk. "Do you by any chance know how to use a computer?"

Gessica looked up. "Yes I can read and write and no I cannot use a computer. I have never been taught to do so." Her voice reflected the rustic Calabrian accent of Locri. "In our village and also for the short time while I was in Polsi, I worked in scullery and did cleaning for the Monsignor in his residence and at the church." Gessica lowered her head again and said nothing.

"I'll call Father Malcolm. He may or may not be able to see you immediately. If he cannot, I will take you to one of our visitor rooms where you can wait." Maria Scopoletti punched in several numbers on the old fashioned land line on her desk.

"Yes, Father, the candidate has arrived. Can you see her now or...thank you, I'll bring her to you immediately."

"Please take your luggage with you, Gessica. If Father Malcolm accepts you, I will take you to your room. If he does not, he will have someone show you out."

Gessica picked up the badly worn leather case she had been carrying. Another piece of luggage had been left at a drop point before she entered the Vaticanus ager, the Vatican territory. It had been that piece, loaded with equipment and supplies that Father Dr. Marcus Granville Barker and Father Sean O'Reilly had been waiting for so eagerly.

Gessica followed behind Maria Scopoletti who walked at a brisk clip across the serpentine corridor of the lower level of the Vatican's living quarters and up several flights of marble stairs to the floor that held the Pontiff's private quarters as well as Father Malcolm's office and private quarters.

When the two women finally emerged in front of the Regent of the Pontifical Household's office, Gessica found herself quite breathless.

"Father Malcolm will be looking for someone with energy, stamina; do you understand? May I suggest that you exhibit some strength?" Her words were crisp and it was obvious to Gessica that Maria Scopoletti would prefer she not return after the interview.

"Please come in, Senora Scopoletti, and you must be....."

"Gessica, Gessica Scolon Morosini; yes, Father Malcolm; the Monsignor is my uncle. My husband, Francesco Scolon died only a short time after we were married; so on the advice of my family, I have gone back to using my maiden name."

Maria Scopoletti's look of surprise brought a certain delight to Gessica as well as Father Malcolm

"You did not tell me that," she murmured.

Gessica said nothing but accepted the offer to enter the office and sit down with Father Malcolm who shut the door soundly behind him... and Maria Scopoletti.

Chapter 43

"Mrs. Perkins.... Mrs. Perkins!!" Poulette Granville Barker bellowed as she sat in front of her vanity table with every drawer open. "Mrs. Perkins!" She called out again, this time with urgency, hoping to be heard above the drone of the vacuum cleaner which hovered near the entrance to her bedroom.

"Were you calling me?" Bernadette Perkins turned off the machine as she appeared at the open door.

"My special collection of lipsticks, I can't find them. You know the ones I mean... the old ones...with the jewel studded caps?" Bernadette Perkins said nothing but listened as Poulette deftly described the collection, waving her hands about. "They are works of art; they have real gem stones and are made from 18 karat gold!"

"I'm sorry, Ms. Poulette, I haven't seen them in years. You've always had them tucked away. I don't think I ever knew where you kept them." The housekeeper could see the distress that had hi-jacketed Poulette Granville Barker's once youthful face and body. Her beautiful, wrinkle free complexion was fading fast and the despair of losing her memory was evident in her eyes. She had not brushed her once well-coiffed hair. It's fine texture was matted in places exposing her scalp and it others, spiked as if electrified, increasing the effect of madness that surrounded the elderly woman like an aura.

"I keep trying to recall when I last laid eyes on them. They were so special. I was a young girl when I got the first. I had just moved to the Main Line with my husband, Cornelius and his son Marcus. Lucas was such a thoughtful man, so generous. Cornelius traveled a lot; but then you know that Mrs. Perkins because..." Poulette did not finish her sentence.

Do you remember, Lucas always brought me presents from wherever he went? He knew how lonely I was and how often Cornelius had to be away." Poulette's face brightened as she began to recall those times.

"In the beginning, they were small, just tokens, really ... and then, he discovered something I really treasured...those magnificent cases with beautiful lipsticks inside. One of my favorites was from Cartier, with a heart made of rubies encrusted in a golden case... and the case that resembled an ancient Roman gold coin with an Emperor's face embossed in gold." Poulette's words were slow and well chosen. She seemed to be visualizing the gifts as she spoke. "I could not have lost them; I must have put them someplace to protect them and now... oh, Mrs. Perkins, why can I not remember where I put those beautiful cases?" Her speech had softened to be nearly inaudible.

"... No, no...They're not misplaced...She stole them. I know she took them!" Poulette's voice had risen in volume and pitch.

"Who are you talking about, Ms. Poulette?" Bernadette Perkins dropped the vacuum cleaner handle and calmly walked to the troubled woman, who stared into the vanity mirror, apparently recalling an event in the not too distant past.

"Mrs. Perkins, it has to be her... Lydia Sindona. I found her on several occasions looking for things in my closet and also in the drawers of this vanity table. Yes, I'm certain of it. She knew all about the lipsticks and that they were gifts to me from her father. Call the police; I want to report her, now. We'll get those cases back. She has no right to them!"

"But how can you be certain Dr. Sindona took them, Ms. Poulette?"

"Because, she knows about our secret, the one I swore to Lucas I would keep forever; she will never get her hands on any of them. I swear to that!" Poulette was speaking softly but in an almost breathless tone. Suddenly, she stopped; silently, she attempted to push her body upright from the chair; trying, it seemed, to stand up. She gasped, her legs, unable to hold her slender frame, gave way. It was a frightening and profound scene, a sign of serious deteriorating mental and physical capacity that Bernadette Perkins had not seen before.

"Mr. Fox! Mr. Fox, please come to Ms. Poulette's quarters, now!" Bernadette Perkins shouted through an intercom next to the vanity.

Poulette had fallen to the floor. Her breathing was irregular and her skin color pale.

"Mr. Fox, call 911 for an ambulance right now!!"

It was late on a Saturday morning for Marcus, nearly 10:00 a.m. Accustomed to rising at about 5:30 o'clock to accompany the Pontiff at Mass, he had taken a well-earned day off, on the orders of Father Malcolm. Since the arrival of the medical testing equipment early in the week, he and Sean O'Reilly had been burning the Midnight oil analyzing blood samples, measuring the Pontiff's oxygen intake and with a new handheld Brainscope, developed for battlefield use by the military, scanning the Pope's brain for noticeable damage which might call for a CT scan or MRI at some later date. All of the data they obtained had been transferred for expert analysis to Marcus' medical colleagues in the United States; and all via his smart phone.

According to the calendar, Christmas was only days away, but outside the Villa Santa Marta, Marcus Granville Barker's Hotel in Vatican City, there was no sign the festive day would be white. The badly lit, simply furnished boarding house where a past Pope had made his residence and where Marcus and Father Sean O'Reilly were now residing, reflected the gray skies, harsh wind and stinging sheets of rain that had all but emptied the landscape of the expected hoard of last minute holiday shoppers.

Reflecting the gloom of his environment, Marcus sipped his coffee and munched on the last of what was now a very hard, cold and dry roll, retrieved from a nearly empty basket on the cafeteria style breakfast bar. His IPad lay in front of him, revealing a barrage of news and e-mails he had not read in several days.

"Do you want some company, or would you prefer your solitude?" Father Sean O'Reilly stood across from him, carrying a tray laden with what Marcus was quite certain were freshly scrambled eggs, crisp bacon, rye toast… and hot, brewed American coffee.

"No, I do not want to be alone and where in Hell did you get that breakfast? All I could scavenge this morning from the buffet were these!" He held up the remnant of the crusty, stale breakfast roll. "No butter, of course, just margarine and a couple of pods of grape jelly."

"You just have to know the right people, that's all. I've made friends with Sister Mary Finbarr, who heads the kitchen; she took my order last night, asked me when I wanted my eggs and…

well, here we are. By the way, she keeps a can of Folgers in her cupboard for 'special' guests and the strawberry preserves are from a Monastery up north."

O'Reilly smiled mischievously as he lowered his tray and placed the steaming plate of scrambled eggs, bacon, buttered rye toast with a generous portion of strawberry preserves in a bowl, orange juice and American coffee with a small pitcher of crème provocatively in front of Marcus.

"Her name is Sister Mary Finbarr?" Marcus keyed in the name on his IPad without looking up.

"You should also know that Sister and her fellow nuns like a nice bottle of dry Sherry every now and then." Sean O'Reilly's impish expression had grown into a wide smile by now.

"I'll remember that, too," Marcus said, keying in 'dry sherry' as a bribe for the nuns.

"What do you hear from home?" Father O'Reilly asked while taking a large bite from the rye toast now lathered in preserves.

"Nothing good, I'm afraid. Still waiting for Pope Leo's test results to come back. I should get some answer by today. They told me 48 hours.

I got a rather disturbing phone call from Bertrand Fox, last night, about my step-mother." Marcus looked up.

"Is she all right?" Sean O' Reilly asked picking up the bacon with his fingers and crunching noisily on the fragrant breakfast meat.

"She had a 'spell' as he described it. She fainted at her Vanity table. Thank Heavens Mrs. Perkins was with her at the time. Apparently, Poulette was looking for her jeweled lipstick collection, which she believes is missing. She is convinced someone stole it." Marcus stopped to take a sip of the now cold Espresso, but put it down after a small sip of the bitter cold brew.

"You don't think Sister might have another cup of coffee... real American coffee somewhere back in the kitchen, do you?" He whispered his request to Sean O'Reilly who was relishing every mouthful of his meal.

"I do indeed. Just to the left of the door to the kitchen is the American Coffee King Coffee maker. Sister Finbarr left it there should I want another cup." Without a word, Marcus shot toward the kitchen door. Moments later he returned with a mugged filled with a steaming cup of Folger's.

"Thank you, Sister Finbarr, and thank you, Sean, for sharing your secret. Now, where were we? Poulette: The attending doctor in the Emergency Room at Bryn Mawr Hospital did not believe she needed to be admitted. He said to keep an eye on her; gave her a prescription to calm her down and sent her home."

"Is this a reflection of her disease progressing or something else?" Sean O'Reilly had finished his eggs and bacon and now was launching into his second piece of toast with an additional dollop of strawberry preserves.

"I think it's both, Sean. But there is some paranoia in all of this, too. She was telling Mrs. Perkins that she believes that Dr. Lydia Sindona, who was staying with her for a while; quite a short time really, had stolen the jeweled cases. That, of course, I believe is ridiculous."

"Lydia Sindona?" Sean O'Reilly dabbed a smear of preserves from his bottom lip as he asked the question.

"Yes, you remember her. We had tea with her and a friend at Babington's only a couple of weeks ago. She was my former classmate at Harvard Medical School who was doing research at the University of Pennsylvania. I had asked her to look after Poulette and for that she would have free housing and meals at Poulette's house. Of course, we know how that ended; you and I ran into her after a shopping spree here in Rome when she should have been watching my stepmother."

"Then, I guess you haven't heard or read about it," O'Reilly did not look up as he poured a dab of crème into his coffee mug.

"Heard what?"

"It was front page in the Philadelphia Inquirer several days ago: Lydia Sindona was found dead in her car in a parking lot in Wayne. Apparently, she had gone to dinner at the White Dog Café with a friend. She and the friend left the restaurant at the same time; but Lydia never made it to wherever she was staying. Someone shot her in the back of the head!"

Marcus looked up with a start. "When did you say this happened?"

"I didn't; but, it had to be four or five days ago. I thought I had mentioned it to you, apparently not. All that I know is...." Father Sean O'Reilly stopped mid-sentence; outside the large window next to their table, running through the rain and wind toward the Villa Maria, was Father Malcolm.

"Marcus, Sean the Holy Father is missing from his quarters. I've checked everywhere. "

"How could he go missing with all of the protection he has around him? Has he seen anyone; talked to anyone in the last few hours? My God, we left him at 11 p.m. last night!" Marcus' voice had an incredulous tone that might have been interpreted as mocking.

"I know how this sounds," Malcolm was apologizing. "I've spoken to the Swiss Guards and they have an all points out on him; but you know how he is. If he wanted to get out of here, he could. He knows all of the little secret passages."

Malcolm looked exhausted.

"How long has he been gone, do you know?" Sean O'Reilly had risen from his chair and was headed toward a large commercial waste container and tray stand where he would leave his tray and dirty dishes.

"I don't know exactly. He did not show up for chapel at 4:30 a.m. I checked his room and suspect he left sometime between midnight and four."

"Let's get our coats and we're with you," Marcus rose from the table, closed his IPad and picked up his tray.

"I only hope he was wearing something protective. It's very cold and raw out there!" Malcolm's body shivered as he spoke. He was wet to the bone and the cafeteria, like the rest of the hotel was only minimally heated.

"The Holy Father must not be outside. I pray to God, he hasn't been wandering around in this rain."

Chapter 44

University president, Father Paul Sullivan huddled over his drink in the sitting room of Prior Provincial Father Austin Cheney's modest apartment on the top floor of the Friary. It was five o'clock on this drab afternoon; an ominous darkness had settled over the campus which added nothing to the sour mood Sullivan had been experiencing since his command return from Hawaii the day before.

The apartment was warmer and cozier than the large refectory where they would have dinner later, as well as more conducive to the confidential discussion he anticipated with the Vatican's representative, Jacques Dumont. Neither he nor Father Cheney knew anything about this man. Was he clergy or layman? Exactly what was his position with the Vatican Bank and, to Paul Sullivan, the most important question: why was this meeting so necessary and so confidential that he had to fly back from the warm and sunny sands of Kukio?

"A drink?" Paul Sullivan inquired as he noticed Dumont on the other side of the open door to the corridor. "Oui... oh yes," he answered with a heavy French accent Sullivan had failed to detect when they first met earlier.

"You don't, by any chance, have Lillet, do you?"

Paul Sullivan looked up as he stood in front of Cheney's makeshift bar.

"I'm afraid not. Father Austin seems to be a whisky man. He has several brands of Irish Whisky, some Scotch, Gin, Vermouth... and oh, yes, a full bottle of real Russian Vodka."

"That will do; a Vodka, no ice, please" Dumont had wandered to the window which faced westward across the lushly landscaped University campus. "Your campus is very beautiful; so many trees. I see no one about. I take it your students are on holiday?" he turned to face Sullivan.

"Yes, they don't return until mid-January," Sullivan answered as he handed the low ball glass with the Vodka, no ice to his visitor. "As for our landscaping, until recently we were an official arboretum which means, we gave tours to outside groups to show them our 1,500 trees and 254 species of plant life...but with budget cuts...." Paul Sullivan did not continue his sentence.

"Father Cheney should be with us shortly. Would you like to sit down? Perhaps we can go through your reason or reasons for being here?"

Dumont smiled. "I think it is preferable to wait," He sipped the Russian liquor and returned to the window.

"How many students are there at St. Edmund's?" Paul Sullivan tried to pick-up any inflection in Dumont's voice that might give him a clue as to what this guy was all about.

"Oh, approximately 6500 undergrads and a total of 10,000 if you include the Law School and the grad students."

"That is quite a large student population, at least by our European standards." Dumont turned to look directly at Sullivan, who found himself gazing at the floor. It was obvious, Dumont too was analyzing him.

"Oh, Paul, I'm glad to see you made Monsieur Dumont and yourself drinks. Sorry, to have kept you, but I had several things that had to be attended to before I could give my full attention to anything we might discuss."

"Can I get you a drink, Austin?" Paul Sullivan asked.

"No thanks, Paul. I'll just pour myself an Irish Whisky and be ready to join the two of you. We might find this area with the couch, chairs and coffee table a comfortable place to talk." Cheney turned on another floor lamp, which gave a pleasant glow to the room.

"Monsieur Dumont, I'll come right out with it, why did you come?" Cheney plopped himself in what Paul Sullivan assumed was his favorite chair. His foot which was still covered in a soft cast, came to rest on a short stool near the chair. Jacques Dumont selected a seat on the sofa directly across from Cheney. Paul Sullivan chose a chair to Cheney's right.

"I know you are wondering who I am and why I am here. First off, I am not clergy, I am a banker —a cop, in your terminology. I was hired by the Holy See, a few years ago, under the direction of your previous Pope, when it became apparent that the international markets were beginning to investigate some irregularities in the Vatican Banking system." Jacques Dumont stopped to take a small sip of his vodka before continuing.

"You're talking about money laundering, aren't you?" Paul Sullivan's ears had perked up and his hands suddenly felt moist from nervous perspiration.

"Yes, Father, that's exactly what I'm talking about. I had a rather difficult time in the beginning. Many of the people I interviewed were… shall we say reluctant to talk to me; but in the last year or so, things have become considerably easier."

"Well, that is good to hear, "Austin Cheney smiled at the visitor. "But what possibly can we do to help you? I mean, money laundering and St. Edmund's?"

Jacques Dumont was silent for several seconds. "Gentlemen, we have to be totally honest with each other or…." He did not continue with what Austin Cheney was certain sounded like a threat.

"… I am here as an official representative of the Pontiff who has set me the task of looking into St. Edmund's involvement with one of the world's most notorious crime bosses and money launderers, Roberto Lombroso."

Paul Sullivan's face blanched at the sound of Lombroso's name. He clutched his glass, his fingers turning white as he rested its bottom on his knee, which was now trembling.

"We know you have been in contact with Mr. Lombroso several times, the last only a few weeks ago. We also know, that you are planning to receive a rather large amount of money from Canada, via the Vatican bank branch there. Isn't that correct, Father Sullivan?"

"Yes, but…."

"… let me finish the sentence for you, 'you never suspected that this money was being laundered; is that correct?"

Paul Sullivan's embarrassment, anger and frustration seemed to mount beneath his portly frame.

"I'm not even certain I understand what money laundering really is," he finally muttered.

"Well, to explain it simply: A friend, let's say Roberto Lombroso, decides to launder a lot of money. First of all, he creates a 'charity' in Canada. We can call it RL Associates, a firm that collects money to give away. People from all over the world donate to his charities. Let's call these donors the Calabrian Mafia. This firm is headed by Roberto Lombroso. Now, all the 'donations" he collects are put into branches of the Vatican Bank for safe keeping. But he, Lombroso needs to get that money out of the bank to spend it. So, he creates charitable "projects"...one of those is to St. Edmund's University for a business school internship with a building or whatever. He does not want his name on the building; in fact, he doesn't even want his name on a check; so this time, he uses his charity in Canada, conveniently run by the Catholic Church with the Vatican bank (his institution of choice), which allows him to make his donations incognito."

"But... but.... We would still get the business school internship program and the building, so why would that be a crime?" Paul Sullivan could see his dreams of a super modern legacy program slowly slipping away into the winter night.

"Had this project gone forward, this is what would have happened: Once the plans were drawn up and approved with your initials on them, Mr. Lombroso's associates would be the ones to come forward and would be totally involved in the project. They would take over everything from the architecture of the building to the provider of brick and mortar and even to hiring the workmen too. That is called "funding" or "funneling" the project, a way of providing laundered money for his cohorts here. Lombroso brings in the money via a charity, they, the project people over bill by 200% or more and the money he has collected via his criminal activities all of over the world, are distributed to other criminals the world over. As you know, Mr. Lombroso has the reputation for being very, very generous."

"I've actually seen this wonderful orphanage in Southern Italy that he built. It is, just outside of Naples. It was in one of the worst areas of the city. He is known to be one of the most generous benefactors in the Catholic Church," Austin Cheney added ruefully. "So, you are telling us that we cannot accept the money, is that right?" Austin Cheney's voice had become very quiet.

"Ultimately, no, you cannot keep it; but I, let's say we will work up a plan for you to go through with this little drama and you will help us to catch a very big fish in the criminal world."

"We must cooperate, is that what you're saying?" Paul Sullivan asked.

"Exactly! We're asking you to do so and hoping you will cooperate!"

"But... but isn't that dangerous for us and.... for the University? Will it harm the reputation of the school?" Sullivan's face had become very pale. His hands still clutched the glass holding his untouched drink.

"We will try our very best not to do anything to harm the reputation of St. Edmund's ... and may I add, not to harm anyone in this room, either."

***

Jessica no longer dreamed of snuggling with Alex in their cozy, comforter-covered bed in Berwyn, on Philadelphia's Main Line. She had adapted almost fully to being Gessica Morosini, a Calabrian widow and now servant in the very private household of the Pontiff, Leo XIV.

By the time she was able to complete her assigned duties this first full day on the job, take her turn at a tepid shower in a shared bathroom and fall into bed in the small basement room assigned to her by Maria Scopoletti, mistress of the Memores Domini, it was close to midnight; it was no wonder, she fell into a deep sleep almost instantly.

Her small windowless bedroom was totally dark, which was why for a moment, she could not be certain that she had even heard it; a hard thump against the outer wall next to her headboard. Had she heard something or was she dreaming? She closed her eyes again only to be awakened again moments later; this time by an anguished moan. The tile floor was icy cold as she searched with her feet to find her shoes.

"Ahhhh..." she heard again. It was a moan, the cry of someone or something that was wounded or badly injured.

The lamp next to her bed had been fitted with a single low wattage light bulb which was not sufficient for reading, but gave enough illumination to move about the room safely and allow her to find the robe provided by the mistress. Sufficiently clothed, she pulled back the bolt on the door and looked out into the dimly lit corridor.

"Ahhhh, oooh…" The elderly man lay on his side, his face almost touching the wall. He wore leather slippers and a white nightshirt visible beneath an ivory colored muslin robe.

Jessica bent down to try to turn him over. "Are you hurt?" she asked in a Calabrian dialect.

His expression as he looked up into her face was one of shock. "Who are you?" He shouted.

"Gessica Morosini," she answered immediately, frightened by the tone of his voice and the startled expression in his eyes. "I am a member of the Memores Domini and who are you?"

When he did not answer, but instead turned to look toward the wall again, she noticed the back of his robe; there was a large blood stain on it. He quite obviously was bleeding and it was enough to permeate the fabric of the robe.

"… Are you hurt?" she asked, staring at the stain. "Did someone hurt you?"

He looked up again and tried to stand. "I must go; I must leave now. Please help me up. I lost my footing…they are expecting me."

"What is your name and who is expecting you?" Jessica asked quietly. "Do you work here in the household? Are you Memores Domini too?"

"No, no Memores Domini… I have to go and go quickly. Now, help me up, please." His voice had grown stronger. As Jessica helped him to his feet, she noticed he also had a bruise on the side of his head.

"I really think we should call someone from the house hold. I think you need to see a doctor. That bruise…"

"No!" he shouted vehemently, "I said no doctor. I am leaving now." He brushed her aside and continued along the dimly lit corridor that led to….; that was the question. Where did it lead? He had staggered ahead about 40 feet, when Jessica made her decision.

Whoever he was, he needed medical attention and she could not, would not let him go by himself into the darkness to "meet someone". The latter, she feared was a figment of the old man's imagination and ... she also had to see if she could help him whether he wanted help or not.

The marble tile felt like ice beneath her feet. She had no stockings to shield her from the cold which penetrated the soles of her work shoes like tiny needles. The old man, she had noted had no stockings either. A priest or monk, she suspected, who lived somewhere in the complex and having escaped his quarters, unattended had wandered out into the maze of passages that go above and beneath the Vatican.

She had no watch, but heard the muffled bells of a church strike 2:00 a.m. The old man had gained speed, moving through the passage faster than she could keep up. The ceiling seemed to become lower, she noted and the illumination dimmer.

They were travelling downward, of that she was certain. She also sensed a slightly musty smell and a humid feel to the air.

Was her body temperature rising as she moved along, or was she actually feeling warmer? She began to run, seeing the old man turn a corner ... and in that moment, she lost him. Everything ahead of her lay in total darkness.

"Hello," she called out in accented Italian. "Are you still there? I'm only trying to help you. Please let me know where you are?"

In the distance she saw a light flicker, indicating that he must be ahead and had found a light switch. She ran toward the light. As she came closer, she saw a door cut into the rocky wall that now lay open; its heavy metal structure indicated it was protecting something.

On the rough rocky wall next to the open door, she saw it, a high tech, hand print security mechanism. Whoever she was chasing had a security clearance.

She entered, slowly. Her eyes had become accustomed to the darkness. What was this place? On each side there were structures, buildings, ancient looking ruins. There were passages leading into the darkness on three sides. There also were metal posts and chain barriers with signs which needed no translation.

They featured skulls and cross bones that read *Danger, Do Not Enter* in black and red lettering. Where was the injured man she had been chasing?

"Hello," she cried out again, peering into the darkness of each passage hoping to see or hear something. And then she heard it, what sounded like a pop, but what she immediately recognized as something more...a pistol firing...with a silencer!

Chapter 45

"Bartender, I'll have what he's having only make mine a double," Jed Watkins took the stool next to Alex's in the bar at the Main Line Cricket Club. "Make that another one for me, too," Alex shook the hand of the Regional CIA chief who seemed to appear at the most unexpected times, in the most unanticipated places.

"You're not a member, so I assume I'm picking up the tab for this, right?" Alex smiled and returned to his seat not far from one of the club's super-sized TV screens where the Philadelphia Flyers were scoring heavily against Toronto's Maple Leafs.

"This is as safe a place to talk as any, Alex. The noise level here would drown out anyone trying to record our conversation."

"... put it on my tab. He's my guest," Alex shouted to the bartender who was ready to prepare a separate tab.

"So, what's on your mind?" Alex took a rather large sip of the Johnny Walker Black label in his low ball glass.

"It's about Jessica. I know I told you I'd try to get her home as fast as possible, but that doesn't look as if it going to happen any time soon." Jed was watching Alex for a reaction which didn't seem to be coming. "I had even hoped it might be for New Year's Eve but…."

"Forget it, Jed. I've gotten to the point where it really doesn't matter, anymore. In the last few years since Jess has gone back to work for the Firm, she's been away more than she has been at home. Every time she comes back, her health has been more precarious. Now, it is affecting our marriage." Alex did not look up from his drink. "I'm planning to ask Jess for a divorce when she comes back, whenever that may be. It's pretty obvious to me that she considers her job more important than our marriage."

"Now, Alex don't be too…" Alex gave Jed's arm a rough push away from his shoulder causing several club members standing near the bar to stare at the scene. "I think it's the liquor talking, my friend. You really don't mean that." Jed's voice was almost a whisper. He was calm hoping to instill the same in Alex who quite obviously had been drinking for quite some time.

"Look, Jed, she doesn't need the money; she can go anywhere in the world she wants with or without me. She has a beautiful home, loving relatives and friends. What in the Hell is she doing travelling all over the world getting herself into trouble with people who could kill her? The only conclusion I can come to is that I'm not exciting enough for her. Our life is not exiting enough for her. The only time in recent years when I thought we were really…. what can I say… in sync with each other was when I took that assignment in the Middle East for the Firm and was nearly killed in the process. That, she understood and could relate to." Alex's voice has risen in volume.

"Alex, she does love you. There are very, very few agents anywhere that have the abilities Jessica has. She is smart, pretty and has language abilities. Her Calabrian dialect is…"

"Yeah, I know all of that, Jed. Sorry, I should have never brought it up. When do you think I might see her again?" Alex's head was bent over his drink. He had turned it slightly to look at Jed. His eyes were filled with tears.

"Sorry, old man. I've heard Philip's health is on the up side. I'm sure you're feeling better about that?"

"Yeah, sure; every little bit of good news helps. Frankly, these last few months have not been, shall I say, good for the psyche. What is really a concern is that there seems to be no progress on any of the things that have happened to Philip. What happened to him in that house? Why did someone try to kill him? I should add, kill him again and again after they missed killing him the first time?"

"I can't answer that, Alex. It's not my area of expertise. The local authorities are investigating that." Jed looked straight ahead as he spoke and took a long drink of his Scotch.

"Well, you and I both know they are not making any progress; none at all. Frankly, it's way out of their league, in my humble opinion. Now, what did you really come to see me about? I'm sure it wasn't to tell me that Jess wasn't going to be home to light the Christmas tree."

"You're right, it wasn't! I'm issuing a mandatory dinner invitation for Christmas Eve at General Reggie Broadhearst's residence. You never got back to us on the first invitation; this one is a must attend. We'll pick you up at 6:30 p.m. at your house. Bring an overnight bag." Jed finished up his drink in a single gulp and got up to leave. "And you had better make this one the last, old boy! Can I give you a lift home?"

"No, Jed thanks! I'll be leaving in a few minutes anyway, after I finish this drink." Jed put out his hand, but Alexis did not return the gesture. When the CIA Director was out of sight, Alex raised his glass and called out. "Make it another, my good man!"

***

In near darkness, Jessica struggled to move forward; she had abandoned the dusty trail she had been following, crossed the chain barrier with the "Do Not Enter" sign into territory that was without question treacherous. Her hands traced the craggily hewn rocks of the 1st century Pagan tombs that lay behind her. In the dim light of a lantern that burned ahead, not far from her present location, she could see at least twenty-five or more of the elegantly constructed mausoleums that lined the passage, reminiscent of homes in a modern day suburban neighborhood.

It was the ground beneath her that posed the greatest danger, with crevasses of unknown depth that ran the length of the alleyway, meandering like a river sometimes almost abutting the tombs. She stepped cautiously, clinging to the craggy stone facades, her back to the tombs, advancing slowly toward the area where she had heard the gunshot.

She was certain the old man, the priest she had been following, was involved, somehow. Was he dead or was he the shooter? She had not seen a pistol when she discovered him in the corridor, moaning after his fall. When she helped him to stand, she had noted that he was wearing night clothes, which left little room to conceal a weapon, especially a gun with a sizable silencer. But, the back of his nightshirt was stained with what could only be blood

The light from the lantern grew brighter. She must be near the area where the shooting had occurred. The ground became more level. The fissure in the earth had narrowed and moved into a dark area to her right. She could now walk with added speed and the certainty she would not fall into a crack in the earth.

"Ahhh," The moan was coming from someone not far away. Her pace increased. "Hello, hello!" she cried out in a Calabrian dialect. "Where are you? There was no answer, only the whimper she had heard previously. She hurried down the passageway toward the lantern light. Standing nearly under it was the old man. At his feet, the bloody corpse of Cardinal Paolo Torricelli, the head of the Vatican Bank or the Institute for Works of Religion, whose photo she had seen only days earlier in the briefing with Colonel Greeley and General Vasari. In his hand, a Beretta 93R with a silencer, a handgun with the capability of a single fire or a three round burst.

"Father, Father," Jessica cried out instinctively. "... Are you all right?"

"No, no I'm not," he answered, leaning forward and lowering the Beretta so that it merely dangled in his hand. Jessica grabbed the gun from the old man's hand. "I didn't do it," he said. There was someone else. I came here to meet Cardinal Torricelli but... but when I came forward, Cardinal Nardoni raised this gun. He was going to shoot me. It was then that I caught my foot in this...this crack in the earth and I tripped, lunging toward the shooter. Nardoni, he shot him and dropped the gun." The priest began to weep. "It should have been me. I killed Torricelli with my clumsiness. He, he...."

"Father, I'll take the gun," Jessica, immediately secured the decocking safety mechanism on the stock, withdrew a wad of tissues from her robe pocket and wrapped the barrel of the Beretta in the tissue. "We have to get you back to your room. I'll find someone who can take care of this. Where are you staying? Do you remember?"

"Why, yes, in the Papal apartments; I'm... I'm Pope Leo the XIV."

Chapter 46

Alex removed his Tingley overshoes as he entered the foyer of Philip and Caroline's Haverford home. It was still several days before Christmas; the snowy landscape shimmered in the late morning sun. The only noise: the sound of snow blowers, carving pathways through the drifts that had accumulated overnight.

"How is he?" Alex removed his muffler and coat and handed it to Simmons, Philip and Caroline's new house manager as he followed Caroline up the broad staircase to the third floor.

"Well, I think he's better. He's been working with the new speech therapist for two days now and ... listen for yourself."

"How....how...how..." Philip sat at the edge of the hospital bed in his third floor room, his legs hanging over the edge of the bed; soft leather slippers on his bare feet.

"Doug... Mr. Harrison, this is our cousin, Alex. He's come to see how Philip is faring today?" Caroline smiled at the sandy haired man whose lean physique and stubby facial hair could not disguise his youth.

"Oh...how do you do, sir?" Harrison rose from a chair where he sat next to the bed. "I believe we've made progress; not a lot, but it is progress. Mr. Rawlins appears ready to try to communicate. We had a reversal, as you know, recently, but he seems to have gotten over that and now, we are on the right track again. He repeats the same word over and over again...'How'. Does that mean anything to you?"

"No, not really; although he may just be asking how he was injured? Could it be as simple as that?" Alex came closer to his cousin who physically looked normal in appearance.

"It could be; but he seems insistent when....." Harrison did not finish his sentence.

"Howwww...howwww," Philip cried out again, his voice pleading as he looked straight at Alex.

Before he could say anything else, Philip grabbed at Alex and buried his head into his cousin's chest weeping copiously.

"I think we'd better call it a day, Mrs. Rawlins. He is obviously very tired and with that we have frustration, as well.

We'll keep working at this and... well, perhaps in the not too distant future, we'll have him talking again." Douglas Harrison gently eased Philip away from his cousin and helped his client lie back in his bed. He removed the slippers and gently placed the sheet and light blanket over his body. In only a few short minutes, Philip was asleep.

"It can be very frustrating for a patient who knows what he wants to say, but can't put the words together for someone to understand. It really is a matter of the brain healing. He has made great progress, but he is not there just yet." Harrison explained as he grabbed his jacket from a nearby sofa. "If you want me to come by tomorrow I'll be happy to do so; but I will be away after that with family out near Shanksville for the holidays."

"Yes, yes, of course; do come tomorrow and then let me know when you return." Caroline had already started down the staircase with Alex following behind the therapist.

"See you tomorrow," she called out as Harrison trudged to his car at the end of the driveway.

"Well, what do you think?" Caroline closed the door and flipped the security lock.

"About Harrison or about Philip?" Alex wandered toward the kitchen hoping for a cup of coffee before he would hit the road.

"Both, really."

"Harrison looks capable... young, but capable, I guess. As for Philip, progress? He is trying to communicate something. Before you hired this therapist, didn't you say he was calling out 'Purr...? Purr....; now it is how, how.' As Harrison said, the brain has to heal and it will do that at its own pace. We can't hurry the healing." Alex headed for the coffee pot; at its side lay a tray holding several Christmas mugs and a platter of Christmas cookies. "You wouldn't have any milk, would you?" Alex had grabbed a mug and was pouring a nearly full cup of coffee.

"Better yet, I have a creamer... chocolate peppermint, for the holidays." Caroline retrieved the container from the fridge and was ready to pour a dollop when Alex gave her the high sign."... no thanks...I think I'll drink it black."

"Suit yourself; you don't know what you're missing!" Caroline had grabbed another mug from the tray and was about to pour the coffee when they both heard the sound.

"Howww ... howww," came the jolting, primitive bellows, one after the other, emanating from the third floor bedroom.

"Howww, howww!" Alex passed Caroline on the staircase, bounding into the bedroom. Philip stood near the door, his face flushed with exasperation. From an end table, next to the sofa where Caroline had been seated earlier lay the Philadelphia Inquirer, Philip had grabbed a section of the newspaper and was holding it in front of his chest, like a banner.

"Howww," he cried out again. "Howww!"

Alex stared at him and then at the paper. "It's the Real Estate section" he shouted to Caroline who had rushed in behind him.

"Philip, are you trying to say House? House?"

"Howww, howww!" Philip cried again, dropping the newspaper and wrapping his arms around Alex. "Howww, howww."

"You're trying to tell us something about a house, aren't you?" Philip was sobbing and nodding his head. "We understand, Philip. You are remembering." Caroline embraced the sobbing man and with Alex's assistance helped him back into his bed.

"What is he trying to say, Alex? What house? "

"Poulette's!" Alex's voice was decisive. "It has to be Poulette's! Something terrible happened in that house and Philip found out about it."

***

Prior Provincial, Father Austin Cheney scooped another portion of Yankee pot roast from the communal pottery crock on to his plate. The aroma was enticing; an exotic blend of herbs, seasoning, morsels of prime boneless beef amidst an abundant mélange of root vegetables, all mingling in a dark, rich wine gravy.

Noting his own glass was nearly empty, he first refreshed Jacques Dumont's empty goblet with a newly arrived bottle of Beau Joubert Cabernet Sauvignon 2007 that had been breathing on a sideboard for the past 20 minutes and then refilled Paul Sullivan's glass and finally, his own.

Father Paul seemed hardly to notice. He had helped himself to a second and then a third helping of the stew and now was using a freshly-baked Buttermilk biscuit to sop up the last of the gravy on his refectory plate.

"In Grindewald, Switzerland where I grew up, my mother would make something like this with lamb instead of beef and, of course, fresh, wild, mountain mushrooms. It was always one of my favorite meals." Jacques Dumont smiled as he gently dabbed his lips with the starched crisp linen napkin. "The biscuits, of course, were not part of it. She would serve crusty bread; sometimes a day old. But, it worked well with the extra gravy." His smile was soft. Paul Sullivan was certain the wine was having its effect.

They were alone in the dining room of the refectory. What small staff had remained to serve them this evening was behind the swinging doors at the far end of the hall. Father Cheney had advised them he would ring a buzzer under his foot if they needed anything additional. Except for the additional bottle of wine, they had not.

"And so, Mr. Dumont,..." Father Cheney began.

"Please, Fathers, call me Jacques. I know that is the custom in this country...."

"All right, Jacques, where do we go from here? What do we do?" Austin Cheney found himself speaking softly despite the absence of anyone in the vicinity.

"It is very easy; you do nothing. We do all the work. You will be receiving a bank transfer in the New Year. I suspect it will be in the first week after the holidays. It will be from Canada. Do not worry a bit about it. Accept it as you might have had I not come to visit you. I am certain if you have not already been contacted, you will be very soon, by Roberto Lombroso's architect, builders etc. Cooperate to the fullest with them."

"But...what will happen if they begin to build? If they actually start to do some work?" For the first time Paul Sullivan seemed to comprehend the serious nature of their relationship with Lombroso.

"You do absolutely nothing, Father. That is very important for you to understand... absolutely, positively nothing. After this evening, you will not see me again. If... and I emphasize if, I need to contact the University, I will do so through Father Cheney. You, Father Paul, must stay totally out of this. If you, in any way, let on that something is 'amiss', it could be... well, quite serious." Paul Sullivan picked up his wine glass and emptied it.

"I know you're uncomfortable, Paul. But, he's right; we're not experienced in any of this. If we try to help, it could get us and the University into greater trouble than we are in, already."

Dumont checked his watch. "I have someone picking me up outside in about five minutes. I thank you both for the opportunity to talk about this and rely on your discretion for keeping it totally confidential."

"Yes, yes, of course...but, Jacques, you haven't had coffee and dessert," Austin Cheney seemed more than surprised at his guest's sudden leave. He had prepared a room for him at the monastery.

"No, but thank you; it is better that I go tonight. It will be safer for you. I believe you left my coat and bag in the corridor?" Dumont had pushed back his chair and risen; Sullivan and Cheney followed suit.

"We'll walk you to the door," Cheney followed the visitor, who already was several paces ahead of them, grabbing his coat from the rack that stood near the entrance to the building and picking up his single piece of luggage. Austin Cheney, lifted the antique latch from the heavy oak door to see a black sedan idling only feet away. The windshield wipers steadily moved across the windshield brushing the wet, flaky snow from the glass.

"I thank you both for your hospitality. We probably will not see each other again." He gave a brief wave, draped the dark cashmere muffler across his mouth and entered the back seat of the car.

Paul Sullivan checked his watch. "It's 9:00 p.m. exactly. The S.O.B. had it timed perfectly. How did he know ...?"

"...what time we would finish dinner? That we'd planned to have him stay the night? I'm sure, Paul he thought this whole thing out and besides, we're pretty predictable. Let's go back and have some dessert and to top off that dinner, I have some twenty-five year old cognac and a couple of cigars I got as Christmas gifts. We'll celebrate a bit early."

It was the first time all day Austin Cheney had seen Paul Sullivan smile. Neither of them knew what the future held, but both suspected it would not be good, whatever happened."

***

Only minutes later, and less than 100 feet from where Jessica had discovered Pope Leo XIV standing with the Beretta in his hand, and Cardinal Paolo Torricelli quite dead, she found herself climbing a 27 foot extension ladder hidden inside one of the ancient mausoleums. It was obvious Leo knew the location well; he led the way directly to the tomb, squeezed through a narrow opening in the side wall and went immediately to an area, out of view, where the aluminum extension ladder had been maneuvered into position and began to climb upward. Jessica had followed close behind. The rough-hewn passageway was narrow, dusty and dark.

Leo exhibited an amazing new-found energy; when she had seen him, only a short time earlier, he was moaning, as he lay on the cold flooring outside her room. She had speculated that he was an old priest, perhaps one with dementia, who had escaped his secured residence. Now, he seemed to outpace her as he moved swiftly through this rocky tower to where? The shift in energy puzzled her. Where did this new found strength come from?

Leo stopped, almost stepping on Jessica's clenched fingers. Although she was not in a position to see what he was doing, she could hear him pushing aside what sounded like a stone cover. Within moments, there was light and a wisp of incense-scented air. Were they emerging into the Basilica?

The Pontiff pushed the marble lid aside and was out, seating himself on the edge of the opening for a moment while he caught his breath.

"Can you make it only a few steps more, my dear?" he called down to her. "I am not able to pull you through, but I can call someone if you need help." Jessica popped her head through the gap to discover they had emerged into what looked like a chapel. The Pontiff, whose claim to weakness seemed incongruous at this point, had pushed aside a sizable square of marble tile which now was abutting the back of a prie dieu.

Jessica looked up and directly into the mesmerizing eyes of a dying St. Peter, whose agony was captured in an immense painting only feet from her. In that instant, she seemed to identify with the horrifying agony he was experiencing, as his body was crucified upside-down.

"What is this place?" Jessica pulled herself up and sat, for an instant, with her feet dangling into the cavernous hole, before sliding the marble covering to its nearly invisible position on the floor.

"This is the pontiff's chapel; my personal quarters are located right through that door." Leo was already walking toward an indistinguishable panel in a less than well-lighted part of the small room. He pushed it aside.

"My God, Holy Father, you're back! Where have you been?" Father Malcolm De Laurencin, Regent of the Pontifical Household, Father Marcus Granville Barker and Father Sean O'Reilly rushed to the elderly man to virtually pull him inside. Jessica followed unnoticed.

"We were ready to search the streets. How did you get past the Swiss Guard?"

"I'm not certain, Malcolm, but I shot someone... Cardinal Torricelli; and I'm quite certain he's dead."

"You what, Holy Father?" Malcolm's faced blanched in the eerie light of the early winter morning.

"It was an accident!" Jessica had moved from the shadows of the Papal chapel into the sitting room and now stood next to Leo. "Here's the gun; I put the safety on. It was Cardinal Torricelli who was trying to shoot the Pontiff. When Pope Leo got his foot caught in a fissure in the Scavi...."

"The Scavi, Holy Father, what in blazes were you doing down there?!" Malcolm's voice betrayed his greatest fears that Leo XIV's mental state had deteriorated to such an extent that he no longer was capable of making rational decisions. If Torricelli recognized this, it meant that Leo was now the direct target of the Curia, most specifically those Cardinals related to the financial dealings of the Vatican Bank. They wanted him dead and soon!

"Malcolm, I don't know how I got to the Scavi. I don't even know why I was going there. The point is this woman helped me to get back here." Leo sauntered to the window to look out.

"What time is it?"

"9:15 a.m., Holy Father," Marcus answered.

"I've been gone a long time," He turned to look at Marcus. "The last thing I remember was saying my night prayers in the chapel. That was about 11 p.m. "

"I found him wandering outside my room in the Memores Domini under-croft, He had fallen and was not ..." Jessica did not continue.

"I think you had better go now, Senora. I am certain you will be missed by Maria Scopoletti. Please do not mention any of this to her." Father Malcolm grabbed Jessica's right elbow and ushered her out of the room and into the hallway outside the apartment.

"Not a word of this, do you understand me. Nothing to anyone!" Malcolm's voice was stern.

"As to where you have been, I will verify that you were asked to come up and clean the Papal chapel after an unfortunate health mishap by the Holy Father. Do you understand?"

"Very well, but what do you want me to do with the Beretta?"

"Keep it hidden in your quarters!"

It was obvious, Jessica concluded that this man had no idea what he was asking her to do. Her very tiny room, the size of a closet, had only the most meager of locks on the door. Should the nosy Maria Scopoletti decide to search it, there would be almost no doubt she would find the gun easily. There was no place for one's belongings, only a meager wooden cabinet for hanging what few pieces of clothing she had. The so called chest of drawers had three drawers with almost nothing in them; and then there was her bed, a thin mattress on top of old fashioned, squeaky springs. The Beretta was not a small pistol. "I'll do the best I can, Father" she whispered.

".... Ahh yes, there you are, Senora Gessica. Father, she has not been about her duties this morning! She is several hours late!"

Maria Scopoletti's eyes narrowed to a slit as she paused in front of the priest and her charge.

"Yes, I know Senora; she has been on duty, at my request for several hours now, working in the Papal chapel. The Holy Father became ill when he was praying and unfortunately vomited on the chapel floor. I called upon Senora Morosini to clean it up."

"You should have called upon me and I would have assigned someone else. She does not know the rules of the Memores Domini yet, Father, but I do. We must earn our way to work directly in the presence of the Holy Father. You cannot...."

"Cannot? Cannot what, Senora Scopoletti? You seem to forget that I...I am the Regent of the Pontifical Household. Your staff and you... report to me. I am advising you that as of now, Senora Morosini does not report to you, but directly to me. I will assign her duties as I see fit and as of now, she works here in the Papal apartment area. Is that clear? Do you understand?"

"Only too well, Father; only too well!" There was no disguising the rage that shook the very sinews of Maria Scopoletti's body. She seethed, her lips curling menacingly, her hands clenched as she turned to leave.

"Oh, and Senora Scopoletti, I am arranging for Senora Morosini to move to this floor. We have an unused servant's room at the end of this hall. There will be no need for you to deal with her, except during mealtimes. Is that understood?"

Maria Scopoletti had paused at the last order, but did not turn to face Father Malcolm, instead, she skittered to the end of the hall and quickly descended the staircase to her office, several floors below.

Chapter 47

Marcus was clearly shaken as he left the Pontiff's private apartment. He checked his watch: It was 4:00 p.m. already The Holy Father was sleeping soundly and it was time to have a serious discussion with Malcolm and Sean about the repercussions of Leo continuing on as Pope, in his precarious mental state.

"What took you so long?" Malcolm looked up from his place in front of the weathered oak cabinet that served as his bar. The door had not been closed; it was obvious Marcus had been expected. "Scotch?" he offered, handing a low ball glass to the psychiatrist, with no splash of water and no ice.

"Is Sean around? I think it's best for all of us to hear and to discuss this together," Marcus took a deep drink of the amber liquor nearly emptying the glass.

"I'll call him. He decided to rest in his apartment, until needed. As he reminded me, this is his day off, and yours, too for that matter."

"Yeah, sure, thanks, some day off." Malcolm's apartment looked dismal in the growing darkness of the winter day. Marcus switched on two floor lamps to lighten the premises but the sullen mood prevailed.

Malcolm hung up the receiver of the ancient internal Vatican dial phone on his desk.

"He's on his way and asks that you pour him an Irish whiskey." Malcolm reached down to the bottom shelf of the cabinet and pulled out a half full bottle of Jamison's which he handed to Marcus.

"Sean is the only one I know who drinks the stuff. It was never opened until he arrived."

"Rest assured, it will be gone by the time we leave,"

Marcus grinned as he poured two fingers of the whiskey into Sean O'Reilly's favorite Irish cut crystal tumbler.

"Now, that's what I call service," the forensic anthro-pologist exclaimed as he made his entrance and reached for the glass. "I take it you have something to report, Marcus?'

"Shut the door, please. Sean; we have a serious problem to discuss; one that goes beyond anything I've ever been asked to deal with, in either my professional practice or as a priest and unfortunately, it is one that has implications for the church world-wide now and possibly into the far future. If it is not handled well, it can and will have repercussions no one would want to see happen. Calamitous repercussions to the church worldwide!"

***

Jessica wrapped her shawl tightly over her head and around her shoulders. The Roman wind was strong and piercing. She had only to step a few feet out of the Vatican City gate to make a cell phone call, but she realized the danger of ever present surveillance cameras and strolled further down one of the side streets to find a place to make her weekly report to Jed Watkins in his Philadelphia office.

After she had made her call, she would deposit the phone in a public trash bin, one that was scheduled to be picked up by a "private" hauling service in exactly 20 minutes. She walked hurriedly down the ancient passageway; a light mist had begun to fall, covering the streets in what would soon form an icy sheet.

She walked several steps further and stopped almost directly in front of an awning-entrance with a hand-painted sign above it. A wooden staircase with a rustic hand rail led down into the Dolce Maniera Pastry Shop.

"Senora?" the elderly man behind the tall pastry cabinet asked.

"Si, un saccottino al cioccolato," Her voice was soft with a touch of raspiness, a cold was beginning to add to her already miserable physical condition. "...and a cappuccino, please."

She paid for the order with coins and a bill from what she carried in the pocket of her dress.

Minutes later, she carried the coffee and pastry to a small table some distance from the counter. The shop was empty. The shopkeeper had already returned to a comfortable arm chair several feet from the counter near a portable electric heater where he had been watching a talent show on a small television.

Jessica punched in a number and waited for an answer. "Jed?" Her voice was almost a whisper. "I'm not certain how long I can keep this up. Our man was almost killed today. He is the target, as we expected; but there is something else behind all of this, which I believe will come to a head very soon. Yes, I'm... well... let's say, almost fine. Please tell Alex I, I love him. Sorry about not being home for Christmas, again. Yes, next week, same time."

She clicked off the phone. Took one more, long sip of the warm cappuccino and picked up the sack with the pastry in it. As she exited the shop, she glanced around her. The streets were virtually empty. Every shop except the pastry had been closed for the weekend.

The temperature had dropped noticeably since she had left the Vatican Palace. It was sleeting; the wind beating an icy rain against her face. She tossed the phone, as directed, into the trash container about a block from the shop and headed directly at a fast pace to the Swiss Guards station at the entrance gate to Vatican City. She was feeling extremely exhausted. It had been a long and demanding day physically and although it was still early in the evening, all she wanted was quiet time to herself; time to take a long hot shower and then climb into what would probably be a very uncomfortable bed. At this point she could care less about comfort.

The good news: she had nothing on her assignment sheet until the following morning. She could only hope there would be no surprises again this night!

As she identified herself and walked through the Swiss Guards' gate, the figure of a man who had been following her, waited at a distance and then, minutes later, he too made his way into Vatican City by the same gate.

***

Bertrand Fox fumbled in the darkness to find the well-worn leather slippers he had placed beside his bed, only an hour earlier. A most peculiar noise had awakened him and for the last five minutes he had waited, wavering between the thought that a nest of squirrels might be scampering within the walls of the old mansion or the possibility that an intruder had invaded the residence and may be robbing the house.

It was a strange sound, a swooshing noise that seemed to emanate from the wall which separated his bedchamber from an unoccupied room next door. Although a somewhat cloudy night, the moon shone through the window with enough light to see his robe lying across the back of a nearby chair. He slipped into it quickly and hurried toward the door.

The noise continued as he opened it and crept toward the room next door. It was a rustling sound, like papers being shuffled or moved. He opened the door quickly.

"Mrs. Perkins what are you doing?" The housekeeper stood up abruptly, nearly overturning a goose neck desk lamp that had been moved to the file cabinet and was now illuminating the area where she stood. In her arms, a mass of papers, balanced precariously.

"This was Mr. Granville-Barker's private office. You know, it is out of bounds to us. Nothing in here is to be disturbed." Bernadette Perkins said nothing for the moment. She stared straight ahead and then dropped the cumbersome load on to the floor, where they spread themselves across the hard oak flooring.

"I... I don't know what I'm doing here. I...I must be dreaming." Her eyes were pleading as she took Bertrand Fox's hand and allowed herself to be led from the office and into the corridor.

"This room is always locked, Mrs. Perkins. How and where did you get the key?" Bertrand Fox was certain that he was the only one in the household, on Marcus' order, to have a key to this locked space.

"But I.... I don't have a key. It must not have been locked. Please, let me go back to my room; I'm not feeling myself! Let me go!" Bernadette Perkins removed her arm abruptly from Fox's clutch and headed to her room at the end of the dimly lit hallway. He heard her enter her room and the door close behind her.

As he turned back, he focused his attention on a small file cabinet tucked under one corner of Cornelius Granville Barker's stately desk. He felt for it, checked to find the lock still in place, unlocked the drawer and reached for a pouch tucked into a back corner of the file drawer. It was intact.

Bernadette Perkins was not sleep walking. He was certain of that. She knew exactly what she was looking for; she just did not know the exact location of where it had been hidden.

The papers she had dropped to the floor were old legal files, real estate filings, all of them more than 20 years old. She had even moved the desk lamp to get a better view.

He returned the pouch to its hiding place in the drawer and locked it again. The goose neck lamp still lay on the floor. After placing it back on top of the desk, he turned off the light.

"Oh no, Bernadette" he said aloud. "You cannot get mixed up in all of this."

***

Jed Watkins had watched the weather forecast all day and finally determined this was not a night to travel from the CIA regional headquarters office in Center Philadelphia to his home on the Main Line. Temperatures had been dropping since early afternoon and now as evening approached, a fierce wind was blowing through the city's sky scraper-lined streets, creating a snow squall that lowered visibility to almost zero.

It was 9:30 p.m. but the office still bustled with activity. As he had done so many nights in the past, Watkins reserved an overnight cell in the Company dormitory located one floor above. It wasn't the most luxurious accommodations, but it was adequate with a foam – mattress Queen-size bed, a shower stall and a commode. What more could one ask?

In the meantime, he would make himself as comfortable as one could in his 45th floor office. He sank his less than perfect frame into one corner of the well-worn leather sofa across from his desk; propped his loafer-clad feet on the coffee table in front of him and grabbed a Scotch, neat, that had been placed within easy reach of his right hand.

Next to his drink, still in its brown paper bag was dinner: His favorite sandwich, a Reuben, made up of 1/2 corned beef, 1/2 pastrami, Swiss cheese, sauerkraut, and Russian dressing, grilled between slices of seeded rye bread, from the Hershel's East Side Deli on Arch Street.

"Sir, the report from Agent Rawlins has just been delivered." Jed Watkins assistant, Elizabeth Wolcott did not wait for an answer on the intercom, but knocked and entered a moment later.

"Hefty," Wolcott remarked as she handed the highly classified document to Watkins. "It always amazes me how a field agent can manage to get so much information into a report while talking on a cell phone about...inane things like family matters."

"She doesn't consider her remarks to be inane either, Wolcott. She makes good use of any contact she has with us."

"I... I didn't mean that in a derogatory sense. She obviously is an expert at calculating how much time it will take to get her encrypted message to us during her call, I guess that's the only time to send a personal message; and, Sir, what happens to the phone after she is through talking?" Wolcott stood holding the door lever, prepared to exit.

"The innards, the workings of the cell quite literally dissolve. Anyone trying to retrieve anything from that phone would find it useless."

As Watkins sat back again, he reached for the sandwich, took a large bite and washed it all down with a swig of Scotch. It would be a long night. He had an Intel briefing with his Italian Counterpart at 8:00 a.m. But before that, he would call his friend Joe Farrell at the FBI and the two of them, together, in the Situation Room would contact the head of Homeland Security for a debriefing and after that the White House. Agent Jessica Rawlins was about to reveal one of the most tightly held secrets in the world; one that would bring a bevy of violent international criminals to public attention but one that would, most assuredly, also damage the credibility of an ancient sacred and respected institution.

Chapter 48

Marcus wasn't certain whether he actually heard his cell phone ring or whether it was part of his dream. "Oh no!" he finally shouted as the buzzing continued; he reached for the phone on the table beside his bed.

"Yes, what it is?" he mumbled, trying not to open his eyes. "Oh Christ, not again! Malcolm, where in Hell are the Swiss Guards when he goes out? Aren't they supposed to be minding him?" Marcus sat up in bed and reached for the bedside light switch. Instead, he turned on the bright overhead ceiling light which caused him to squint. He rapidly readjusted the electronic bedside control to light only the lamp on his desk.

"You realize, that we have to get Sean in on this escapade if the Pontiff has gone down into the Scavi again; Sean is our expert. He was with the Holy Father on many exploratory trips, years ago and literally knows every centimeter of the property. Yes, yes I'll call him and let's say we meet in ... 20 minutes at the outside entrance. Do you have a key? A code? Better yet!"

Marcus clicked off and reached for the house phone. Father Sean O'Reilly would be none too cheerful at this hour and who could blame him? Working with Pope Leo had not been so much a spiritual experience as a baby sitting job.

As Leo's Psychiatrist, even before receiving confirmation from tests sent back to the United States, he had been confident his diagnosis was correct.

Leo XIV had anaplastic oligodendroglioma, a brain cancer, with a prognosis of only weeks to live. The Pontiff knew what was happening to him and in these last days, was trying his best to "make things right", as he confided to Marcus. "I want to settle what I did not complete; atone for what I have done in the past, in the time I have before I meet my Creator." Leo had looked him straight in the eye when he said this, but then surprised Marcus when he said, "Oh, no, I certainly do not want to make my confession to you. It's not that I don't want to confess my sins, but...." He hesitated for a moment and then turned to look directly into Marcus' eyes. "... in doing so, you would be bound to keep what I tell you a secret. That I cannot allow. What I have done, what others have done and I have participated in knowingly, willingly...well, these are things that need to be made public. You look shocked, my dear man. Please, this is, perhaps the most important thing I will do in my life... or what is left of it. Can you understand?"

Marcus remembered the conversation so clearly that while recalling it, he was lost in thought and had not heard the cell phone ring again.

"Yes, what is it?" Malcolm's voice was trembling at the other end of the line. "Oh my God! Yes, I understand. Who is it?" Marcus looked into the mirror above his bathroom sink. His face was bleeding. He had nicked himself several times while shaving. "Cardinal Rafael Nardoni? He's a Canadian who recently was appointed to the board of the Vatican bank. Where was he found?" Marcus could see his face in the mirror drain of color. Now, there were two dead Cardinals in two days. Was Leo on a killing spree? The Pope admitted he had accidentally shot Torricelli with the gun that Nardoni had intended to use on the Cardinal.

Torricelli's body, as far as anyone knew, still lay undiscovered and unreported on the floor of the Scavi. Now, Cardinal Nardoni was found with a dagger in his back by a Swiss Guard just outside the Papal Chapel. "Have you any idea how long he has been there or what he might have been doing there?"

"Well, when I left Leo, he was in bed and I thought asleep." Marcus looked out the bathroom window at the darkness of the early morning. The sun would not rise for at least four hours.

"Malcolm, I think we should be with the Holy Father when he speaks to the Swiss Guards; that is if and when we can find him. For now, try to hold them off."

Marcus clicked off again and this time, turned on the shower for an instant mental 'wake me up'. He was feeling physically and mentally fatigued and no wonder; in the last four days he had less than 14 hours of sleep... total. That wasn't enough for anyone to be sharp and present mentally, especially when a clear head and rational thought process was necessary. Hopefully, Sean O'Reilly could add to what Marcus might miss. As he toweled himself off, he reached for a heavy Shetland wool sweater and a muffler, both gifts from Poulette on a former Christmas. That day, that year and that Main Line house seemed very, very far away right now.

***

"Mark, what in Hell are you talking about? It's Christmas Eve. Yes, I know where Paul Sullivan is; he's here, why do you ask?" Austin Cheney has just celebrated 7:30 a.m. Mass in the priests' chapel and was on his way to the refectory when his cell phone rang. "No, perhaps Paul knows something that I don't, but ... all right, all right, calm down. Why don't you come by in half an hour? Yes, we'll have a cup of coffee in the Refectory and get this straightened out." Cheney clicked off on that call and immediately speed dialed Paul Sullivan who picked up. "Paul, don't kill the messenger, but Mark Tobin is mad as a wet hen. He just called and is on his way over. I told him to come to the Refectory. Of course, I know it is Christmas Eve."

Austin Cheney could hear the sound track of White Christmas on Broadway blaring in the background. "Yeah, I'm pretty certain it has something to do with our visitor yesterday. Right, see you there." Cheney clicked off the phone and slipped it into his trouser pocket. This was not how Austin Cheney had pictured spending his holiday. He was more than certain; in fact, he was positive, that Jacques Dumont had initiated whatever scenario he had talked about the previous day. What at one time had seemed like the gift of a lifetime from Roberto Lombroso, now appeared to be a huge mistake in judgment that could affect the University's existence. Jacques Dumont, in saying nothing about his Agency's plans, had left everything to the imagination, including fear. Father Cheney's cell rang again. "Yes? Tell him I'll be right there."

Mark Tobin had arrived, 25 minutes early. For a man not noted for his punctuality, this was a sign of great urgency. As he walked through the Plexiglas covered cloister to the Refectory, he again thought of Jacques Dumont's warning. "You are to say nothing nor do anything. Everything from now on is in our hands. Do you understand?" Austin Cheney had thought he did at the time; but now, he was not so certain.

***

Joe Farrell and Jed Watkins stood in front of the large screen in the Situation Room. "Yes, Sir, everything has been verified. It's exactly as she has reported it to be. Our analysts concur, that the ramifications of making any of this public would be catastrophic," Watkins continued. "I've been trying to reach her all night but I've had no response. She could be dead already."

"Then, you do understand, that we would hate to lose her or any agent, but ..."

Director of Central Intelligence William Burns interrupted. "I have been in contact with Interpol; they are standing by, ready to go in if we give the OK. If they do, you know we cannot guarantee our agent's safety! "

Jed Watkins nodded. The President of the United States sat somberly at the head of a conference table. Beside him, FBI Director Christopher A. Wray stood facing the camera.

"It's Christmas Eve, gentlemen. The Pope is scheduled to celebrate a Midnight Mass in a few hours. I suggest we get this over with... " Christopher Wray would not finish his sentence before Jed Watkins emergency phone began to vibrate and he pulled it from the pocket in his suit jacket.

"What is it?" Wray asked.

"I'm not certain, Sir. This is coming from the NSA, which is reporting on our dedicated line that they've detected an explosion or tremors near or at St. Peters Basilica in the Vatican. It emanated from the area where the archaeological excavation, the Roman Necropolis or the Scavi is located.

Chapter 49

"Mr. Fox, Mr. Fox, come here this instant! Where are you?" In the growing darkness of the late December afternoon, Poulette's panic was evident. She shouted again through the intercom. There was no answer.

"I'm afraid Mr. Fox has gone out, Ms. Poulette. Can I get something for you?" Bernadette Peters appeared in the open door of the elevator which had glided open silently.

"Yes, it's freezing in here. I feel very cold. Would you light the fireplace, please and then get me a cup of tea, with a little something to go with it … to ward off the chill?" Bernadette Peters picked up the remote control for the gas fireplace that lay on a table next to Poulette's chair and handed it to her. "Here you are; you can do it yourself. The top button is for a low flame, the middle button is for a full fire. To turn it off, just push the bottom button."

Poulette held the control for a moment, staring at it and then handed it back to the housekeeper. "No, I can't; please, do it for me!" Bernadette Peters saw the fear and confusion in her mistress's eyes. "Yes, of course." She pushed the center control and a full flame burst thorough the lava logs, immediately adding light and warmth to the room.

"I'll make you that pot of tea, now. I believe we still have a half tin of your favorite, Chinese Darjeeling oolong, would you like that?"

Poulette nodded, staring into the flames. "When will Marcus be coming home, Mrs. Peters? He has been away for such a long time." Poulette's voice was weary and frail.

"He's not been away that long, really, Ms. Poulette. In fact, only about eight weeks. Father Marcus is a very important man, if the Holy Father wants him at the Vatican. If he cannot be with you for Christmas, you know he must be doing something significant. But, he sent you all those wonderful presents which we'll be opening, very soon. He is thinking about you." Bernadette Peters had placed a glass pitcher of water in the microwave in Poulette's mini-kitchen. It was seldom used. Poulette had given up preparing anything for herself and rarely came down for dinner in the dining room. On most days, she took long naps and during her waking hours gazed silently from her bedside window at the snow crested woods that surrounded her property.

When she heard the bling from the timer, Bernadette Peters poured the hot water into a Chinese porcelain pot to which she had already added a tablespoon of the rare muscatel scented leaves. While the tea was steeping, she picked up a nearly empty bottle of Cherry Herring from the bar and emptied it into a miniature snifter.

"Here you are, Ms. Poulette, this should make you feel a little warmer. Have you decided what you might like for dinner and when?" Although her question was gentle, Poulette's reply was not. "I have no idea what I want for dinner nor when I want it... if at all. I'll let you know when I'm ready."

Bernadette Peters nodded.

"All right; I'll be downstairs if you need me." Poulette took a large sip of the Cherry Herring and watched the elevator door close. She wanted to see and talk to Bertrand Fox. She wanted him to show her where he had hidden her precious package. She knew it had to be Fox who took it from her hiding place. She trusted him. He would always be the one she could rely on. That was no longer the case with Bernadette Peters. The tea was perfect...soothing. She took another taste of the Cherry Herring and deposited the empty snifter on the table. Her eyes closed. She was asleep.

***

There was, at first, a shuddering of everything around her and seconds later a vibration of tremendous force, followed, a few seconds after that, by what she would recall was a furious explosion somewhere below. It shook the spiral staircase in the narrow tunnel she had been following, causing Jessica to lose her foothold for a moment and fall two steps, landing on her hands and knees. To raise her body, she grabbed for the ancient metal railing on her left with both hands, pulling out a large section from the stone wall that had held it in place for centuries. It now lay precariously in the middle of the staircase preventing her from using it as an escape.

A cloud of dust rose from below, making it difficult to breathe or see anything. A fine grit had settled on her face and nose. She stopped for a moment to wipe her face with the single tissue she had in her coat pocket. The air smelled fetid, stale. An emergency light gave off a red glow somewhere in the distance. She coughed, to rid her throat of the fine dust that she had inhaled and now was making it difficult to breathe or speak. "Holy Father, Holy Father can you hear me? Please answer me if you can!" There was no reply.

Only minutes earlier, after sending her encoded report to Jed and tossing the burner phone into a public trash bin, Jessica had been on her way to the new room Malcolm had assigned to her, located only feet away from the Papal Apartment. It was as she passed the Pope's private chapel that she noticed the door ajar; she stopped, knocked and hearing no reply stepped inside to see if the Holy Father was feeling all right. The Swiss Guards were nowhere in sight.

Inside the Papal chapel, there had been no sign of Leo. As she neared the ancient altar, she spotted a marble wall panel that had been pushed aside to expose a narrow metal staircase which spiraled down, into what Jessica assumed, was yet another entrance to the Scavi where Leo seemed intent on going, these days.

Now, as she made her way through the rubble, she could see the dim but flickering glow of a lamp; the narrow passageway, she had been following, came to an abrupt end in front of her, splitting itself into a Y shape with two stone paved paths to follow. The one, leading to the right, was filled with debris from the still unrestored ancient architecture of the necropolis. The other, with the flickering lantern in the distance was adjacent to a reconstructed modern wall. On the wall, a modern marker, covered in Plexiglas indicated where ancient graffiti carved into the stone had been recovered. It read Simon bar Jonah.

It was only feet away from the marker that Pope Leo XIV lay face down in the near darkness, bleeding and moaning. Jessica rushed to his side and tried to turn him over. He resisted, crying and clutching a stained white linen cloth pouch.

"Holy Father can you hear me?" She asked again. There was no answer for several moments. "Holy Father, are you awake?" Leo slowly opened his eyes. His forehead had a jagged gash close to his left eye which produced a trickle of blood that oozed down his cheek. Jessica was not certain if he had been injured by the falling debris or had hit his head when he fell.

"Can you speak?" she asked.

"Yes," he answered mostly mouthing the words.

"Hand me your pouch," she suggested, " and I'll help you to get out of here. You definitely need medical attention." As she reached for the linen bag, he shouted "No!" and drew it even closer to his chest.

"You cannot touch these! They are sacred. These are the true bones of our dear St. Peter; I was trying to return them." Jessica recognized the strange look in Leo's eyes. He was obviously quite mad.

"You don't understand, but listen to me. I stole them from the excavation almost 55 years ago. I placed them in this bag and have kept them all these years in a drawer with my belongings. But I am dying; you must understand how important it is that I put them back where they belong...." The elderly man began to weep. "You must help me... please."

"What bones are in that sacred grave now are the remains of someone else...someone, far from saintly. Please, whoever you are... please, help me to get these back. It is only over there, the place that they belong; very near, but you also must promise that no one will ever learn about this. No one, no one!"

Jessica had no time to reply. In what felt like an instant in eternity, the silence of the Scavi exploded; the ground rumbled and the walls of the ancient monuments shattered, sending shards of stucco like missiles to puncture virtually everything that lay in its path.

***

A pale and exhausted Jed Watkins stood mesmerized before the giant screen in the situation room of regional CIA headquarters in Philadelphia. He had not slept the entire night and now, in an instant, had witnessed what he was certain was the demise of one of his agents, Jessica Rawlins. It was 12:30 a.m.

Christmas Eve in Rome. Thirty minutes earlier, The Swiss Guards and Interpol had sent several of their agents into the ancient necropolis in search of the Holy Father, Father Malcolm De Laurencin, Regent of the Pontifical Household and presumably Jessica who could not be found in her quarters.

Now, in what was in all probability an act of terrorism committed by 'Ndrangheta, the ancient burial grounds, presumably lay in rubble with those same Swiss Guards, Interpol agents, Pope Leo XIV, Father Malcolm and Agent Jessica Rawlins, all buried beneath.

"Sir, there's a visual report coming in now from Interpol in Rome that I think you ought to see," Agent Lauren Henry sat at one side of the situation room communication desk. "Put it up there," Jed Watkins responded, his voice raspy. He stepped forward to get as close to the screen as possible. Major General Reginald Broadhearst was already front and center.

"Jesus Christ, what is that?" Broadhearst whispered as the Interpol camera focused on an immense pile of debris surrounded by a massive cloud of dust.

"Interpol says it is, or was the main or papal altar in St. Peter's Basilica, Sir," Lauren Henry's voice was soft in disbelief. "There appears to have been a massive explosion; one caused, we suspect, by a terrorist wearing a vest embedded with an explosive device. It was either on a timer or set off when the wearer approached the main altar."

Watkins and Broadhearst stepped closer to the wall-sized screen to view the destruction. Directly in front of them they saw what had been the baldachin or canopy over the Papal Altar. Designed by the esteemed 17th century sculptor and architect Gian Lorenzo Bernini, it had collapsed. Its massive columns broken and scattered like common debris atop the sanctuary, crushing the altar and presumably what lay beneath the altar as well, marring and damaging the sculptural ensemble, on both sides of the altar. It was often referred to as the most magnificent work of the renowned Bernini, who was; perhaps best known, for his symbolic Chair of Saint Peter which was nowhere to be seen.

"Sir, I have Interpol's Secretary General, Jurgen Stock on screen four, from Paris." Watkins and Broadhearst turned to look to the other side of the room where a grim man faced the two.

"We are doing everything we can to ascertain whether there are any signs of life coming from the Scavi," he announced without any introduction. "Thank you for recommending the MIT WI-FI X-ray vision technology to us several months ago. By pure chance, both of the MIT scientists instrumental in creating the technology are in Rome currently attending an international conference; they are scheduled to present their new Emerald wireless technology tomorrow. We already have someone picking them up at their hotel and we'll take them directly to the area with their equipment; perhaps we can find your agent and the Pope."

"The equipment can do that... even underground?" Broadhearst asked.

"Yes, General, if this technology does what we believe it can do, it will show us where and in what position a person is lying or sitting or whatever. Emerald also can read a person's heart rate and respiration. We should easily be able to determine if the individuals are alive and based upon the condition of the rest of the structure, how much time we might have to remove them from the rubble."

"Go to it, Mr. Stock, and thank you for personally debriefing us." Jed Watkins watched as the Interpol Secretary General's image faded from the screen.

"... and so we wait," Jed said softly walking toward the exit.

"Sir, one more thing," Agent Henry announced." Alex Rawlins has arrived, as you requested and he is waiting in your office." Broadhearst got the door. "Are you planning to tell him, Jed or should I?"

Jed Watkins was silent for several seconds. "I'll do it; but please come with me for support. I think he'll take it pretty hard."

Chapter 50

He had a ringing in his ears and his eyes felt the grit of dust which made it very hard to breathe, but Father Sean O'Reilly was alive and perhaps the first to acknowledge consciousness.

"Marcus, Malcolm where are you and are you all right?" The blast had come as they neared the body of Cardinal Paolo Torricelli which still lay on the pavement in the Scavi where Pope Leo had left him a day earlier. There was no response. In the near darkness, he could see the dim light from an emergency lamp that flickered somewhere along the paved path they had been following.

O'Reilly tried to rise, but realized his legs were buried beneath the contents of a sack of construction sand that continued to pour from a rip in its burlap side. His back rested against the remains of a reconstructed Roman tomb, the ancient bricks once again shaken from their walls. He tried to kneel, brushing the sand from his legs, but felt an immediate pain He was injured, but not enough to curtail what had to be an immediate search for his companions. "Marcus... Malcolm? Do you hear me? Please call out if you do!" Again, there was silence.

It was Jessica who heard the call. She had covered the body of the elderly Pontiff with her own when the explosion came and in a near miracle, the two were still alive. She raised herself slightly and called back again. "I am here with the Holy Father. He has been injured but is still alive. Where are you?"

Sean O'Reilly could hear her quite distinctly. "I can't be far from you because I can hear you quite well. Can you describe anything around you? I know this area very well."

"Yes, we, quite literally, are leaning against the wall that leads to St. Peter's tomb; in fact, I believe we are only a few feet from the tomb, if it still exists. The passage seems to have collapsed only a few feet from where we are."

"You... you are speaking English. Who are you?" Leo had tried to turn himself over and was looking up at Jessica. "You are not Memores Domini, are you?"

"Please don't be afraid, Holy Father. I am only here to help you and hopefully get you to safety." Leo recoiled, defensively raising one hand as she attempted to brush the sandy grit from around his throat.

"We must try to get you out of here; can you stand?" Jessica had reverted to Calabrian Italian hoping the dialect would be more comforting to the elderly man.

"No, I don't think so; but I don't know. I must get St. Peter back. I must do that, now!" He grasped the linen sack even closer to his body and turned away from her. Even in the near darkness she could see his tears.

Sean O'Reilly's eyes were gradually becoming accustomed to the lack of light. Making certain not to hit his head on the still solid roof above him, he squatted to exit the tomb. Almost directly in front of the doorway, lay Malcolm, his head crushed by a large rock that now covered it. To his side, was Marcus, unconscious but breathing. "Marcus, Marcus," he called to him, kneeling down to try to move his body to a more comfortable position. "Marcus, wake up!" Sean O'Reilly gave his cheek a not-so-gentle smack, which caused the priest-psychiatrist to open his eyes in near shock.

"What's going on?" he asked trying to raise himself. "We're in the Scavi, Marcus. We came here to find Pope Leo; do you remember?"

"Yeah, I think I do. Where's Malcolm?" Sean O'Reilly turned his head in the direction of the body. "His head was crushed by a large rock that must have been dislodged during the explosion."

"Hello, hello, are you coming for us?" Jessica shouted from a direction that seemed only a few yards in front of them.

"Yes, I'll be there in a minute. I'm helping another colleague. Is Pope Leo still all right?"

Jessica looked down on the elderly man. She noted that his breathing had changed; it was shallow with short breaths.

"No, he is not all right. I have his head in my lap." Tears, uninvited, began to flow down her cheeks. It was apparent, as she looked around, that she, like the Pontiff, might end her days in this ancient cemetery.

It was obvious, as well, to Sean O'Reilly that Marcus could not be asked to rise. He had a head injury, which could only be made worse by moving around too much. He left his colleague, as he had found him, lying outside the mausoleum near the body of Malcolm.

"I am near the wall now; please say something so that I can follow your voice," he called out to Jessica.

"We are right here; you have almost reached us... and yes, you have found us!"

It was a grizzly scene. Father Sean O'Reilly felt nauseated. What Jessica had surmised were only tears, were in fact rivulets of blood oozing from a wound and mixing with tears above her left eye. Pope Leo's appeared lifeless; he could see no respiration, his lower body crushed beneath an ancient block of stone. O'Reilly was certain, he was in fact quite dead.

***

Mark Tobin found himself breathless. His pallor was grey. The sixty-two year old retired Wall Street Banker - CEO was on the verge of a panic attack. Unshaven and wearing the same clothing he'd been seen in several days earlier, he stood in the doorway of the empty Refectory taking two puffs from an asthma inhaler.

University president Father Paul Sullivan waited a moment and then seated himself directly across from the Board of Trustees chairman, hoping to calm the nearly hysterical man. "Mark, Father Austin is getting us some fresh coffee. Until he gets back, take a deep breath and tell me what in the world is going on with you?"

"Paul, my signature, your signature, not one of our passwords... nothing is valid any longer at the bank. Do you understand what I am saying? Nothing works any longer! We can't pay our bills; we can't deposit checks... nothing! The bank officers at Main Line Trust won't even talk to me. They won't take my calls.... What in the Hell is going on?" Tobin banged his fist on the table to punctuate his sentence and looked Sullivan directly in the eye.

"Paul, for whatever reason, you have chosen to make me the scape goat and I don't even know why? I've worked my butt off for this institution for more than 40 years and brought in millions to the endowment of this f---ing school. For God's sake before you wreck a man's life and reputation, you could at least tell him why; I'm now ... God, what am I?"

Austin Cheney took a chair next to the weeping man, placing a tray with the decanter of coffee, mugs, creamer, sweetener, stirrers and a plate of cookies directly in front of Mark Tobin's slouched figure.

"We couldn't tell you because we didn't know about it... well, not exactly what you are describing, at any rate," Paul Sullivan spoke in a near whisper much to the disapproval of Father Cheney who scowled and shook his head as he pulled out the chair and sat down.

"Look, Mark," Paul Sullivan began,"... you have a right to be angry and yes embarrassed. I was the one at the Board meeting who pushed through accepting Roberto Lombroso's so-called gift to us. Blame me, if you want to. I guess there were plenty of signals along the way that the money coming to us was not exactly .... Kosher? But, I wanted it enough to look the other way, not to care and yes, I guess I probably coerced the Board into accepting it."

Tobin looked up. "You son of a bitch, what are you talking about? Not exactly kosher? You told me that the money was coming to us from a branch in Canada of the Institute of the Works of Religion, the formal name for the Vatican Bank. You said that it was through the Vatican that Roberto Lombroso did his international banking and that he used these different branches around the world to ... to do his good work." Tobin's eyes were red from lack of sleep and now, what looked to Paul Sullivan like a strong indication of Tobin's rising blood pressure.

"Mark, Mark, please settle down. Here, let me pour you some coffee and I'll tell you what I know." Austin Cheney placed the filled cup in front of Tobin, who added three sugars and a splash of creamer.

"Yes, I agree we were naive as Paul said in accepting Lombroso's all too generous gift. The only personal reward for either of us would be a legacy, I guess. The St. Edmund's Business School would suddenly be on the map internationally, which would certainly be feathers in all of our caps. Lombroso has a reputation for being a generous, charitable man. Neither of us still understands exactly how he acquired all that money, but we can imagine it was through purveying the same old vices, sex, drugs and murder. If there is any good news to all of this, it is that we are cooperating with the authorities and as soon as all of this gets cleared up... well, we and the University are in the clear."

"Oh my God! You both really are innocents, aren't you! Take a look at this. It arrived late yesterday ... hand delivered. Yes, read it aloud Paul." Mark Tobin pulled a rumpled envelope from his pants pocket and handed it to Sullivan who opened it immediately.

"It's from the Office of the U.S. State Department's International Narcotics Control Strategy. It informs us via you, Mark that at midnight last night this Office has seized all funds in the St. Edmund's University accounts linked to the Vatican bank over suspicions that all of our funding was involved in money laundering... Holy Shit!" Paul Sullivan's voice was almost inaudible. "So much for the promise of that SOB Jacques Dumont."

"So, now you understand what I am saying. There is no money available any longer for St. Edmund's. Uncle Sam has taken all of it; not just the portion given to us by Roberto Lombroso!"

***

"Caroline, and good morning to you, too. Yes, I'll try to get there later today, but I can't promise!" Alex stood under the watchful eye of Jed Watkins in his "controlled communication" office area.

"Yes, I do understand, but.... of course, and Merry Christmas to you, too." Alex Rawlins clicked off the cell phone he was using and shoved it into his blazer jacket.

"Sorry, Jed. It's Christmas Eve and Caroline phoned to say that Philip has been asking to see me...but that will have to wait: I take it you have information about Jess? Is she on her way home?"

Jed Watkins did not answer immediately. "I'm going to have to ask you to hand me your phone, Alex. You know the rules around here. No civilian cells in this office. I'll return it to you... later. Come on over here and sit down. Can I get you something to drink? Coffee? Juice? Scotch?"

"Hey, it's nine in the morning, Jed, I think that calls for coffee and anything else you may have around here to eat. I didn't have dinner last night."

Watkins poured the coffee from a full carafe and handed it to Alex.

"You want anything in it? Sugar, sweetener, creamer? I'll see if we can locate some real food to go with it that coffee and not just cookies. Ms. Wolcott?" he shouted through the office intercom.

"Yes, sir," she replied by entering the office immediately. "Do we have anything to eat out there? Anything suitable for breakfast?"

"Yes, sir, we have some Stollen, that's a German coffee cake and I think there is some left over baked ham from yesterday's Christmas luncheon. It should be in the refrigerator if the night shift has not consumed it all. Let me take a look and I'll bring back supplies."

"So, Jed, when is my bride returning?" Alex sat back on the comfortable couch and crossed his legs. "… Unless, of course, you want me to meet her at some swank Swiss resort as you did the last time?"

Jed poured himself a cup of coffee, slowly added two sugars and a splash of creamer. "She may not be coming back, Alex." His voice, calm in its demeanor, slashed the ambiance of the moment like a scythe. There was no response from Alex who sat stunned, almost unable to breathe.

"Is she dead?" His voice was a whisper.

"We honestly don't know, but we are working very hard to find out."

"I suppose you can't tell me where she is or anything about what happened to her?"

"You know, I can't. Suffice it to say we are doing everything in our power to …to bring her home. You have to trust us on that."

"Jed, I'm…I'm speechless. You have to save her…. Can you at least tell me that you know where she is and there is a plan to get her out of wherever?"

Jed Watkins leaned forward; his chair, almost directly across from Alex Rawlins, was made of a soft leather, stuffed with a squishy foam that made a whoosh sound as he sat forward.

"We know where she is and we are working very hard to make certain she comes back. Now, you can stay here in my office or even better, I can have someone drive you back to your house to wait for an update or to your cousin Philip's house to spend time with him. There is nothing, your presence here can add to the situation. Your clearance is not high enough to get you into the situation room and ...."

"Ahhh..., Ms. Wolcott, what have you on that tray? Alex, I think this should satisfy your hunger. Boiled eggs, baked ham, orange juice ... and what is that, Ms. Wolcott?"

"It's called Kringle, Sir... Danish Christmas cake."

Alex did not look up to see the elaborate breakfast tray that had been delivered to him. His head bent, he felt the tears, pouring from his eyes. Only days earlier he had talked to Jed about filing for a divorce from Jess; now, he knew he had never meant it. All he wanted was her safe return, which may not be possible.

Chapter 51

Bernadette Perkins was frightened. Standing in the doorway of the small office was Bertrand Fox who had discovered her on her knees, using a letter opener, trying to pry open the bottom drawer of a file cabinet hidden beneath the late Cornelius Granville Barker's desk.

"I trust you have an explanation for this, Bernadette?" Bertrand Fox was still wearing a puffy outer coat covered with a quickly melting layer of snow. "This office was locked. I have the only key. Exactly how did you get in and what are you doing?" He removed a woolen muffler from around his neck and held it menacingly in his right hand as he moved closer to the woman.

"It was Ms. Poulette who wanted me to look for her lipstick cases. She wonders every day if they were stolen by Dr. Sindona. I know they weren't. I know that you took them away but what I don't know is why? Why, would you deny this old woman those things she treasures so much?"

Bernadette Perkins struggled to her feet. "If you have hidden them, then you must take them to her. She's dying. You know that, Mr. Fox. Don't let her go without at least holding those small memories one last time."

"... and you, Mrs. Perkins, what other than Ms. Poulette's dying wish is your interest in all of this?"

"Nothing, you have to believe me; what could it possibly be? Absolutely nothing!" Bernadette Perkins saw what was coming. Bertrand Fox now held the muffler stretched out in front of him, holding it with both hands. He slowly moved toward her. "Mr. Fox, what is wrong with you? I've never done anything to...." Bernadette Perkins did not finish her sentence. Bertrand Fox had wrapped the muffler around her throat and was quite literally squeezing the life from her. In only moments her lifeless body slipped to the floor. Without a moment's hesitation, he picked her up and carried her to the car still parked in the Porte Cochere. He wrapped the still warm form in a clear plastic trash bag and loaded her into the trunk. Ten minutes later, he dropped the corpse just inside the gates of St. David's Church cemetery. It was now snowing heavily. It could be weeks before her body would be found.

***

"... and when he woke up yesterday, he could actually put words together into a sentence." Caroline placed the mug of coffee in front of Alex who sat in her kitchen. "His new therapist doesn't credit himself but just says it was a matter of time. The brain had to heal and it is now in a mode which should help Philip return to a 'somewhat normal' way of expressing himself. Would you like some milk or sweetener with your ...?" She did not complete her sentence before Alex answered.

"No, nothing except the coffee, Caroline. I... I have something to tell you. It's about Jess; she's ... in a bit of... there has been an ..."

"What are you talking about?" Caroline placed a small carton of half and half on the kitchen counter and grabbed an already full mug of coffee for herself.

"I'm not really certain myself; suffice it to say that she..." Alex hesitated, knowing that he was sworn to secrecy about Jess, where she was and what she was doing.

"Caroline, I can't tell you anything more than that Jess is in a lot of danger. Don't... don't ask." He looked up and into Caroline's eyes.

In truth, he looked terrible. She had never seen him so slovenly. His eyes were bloodshot; his face with at least a day's growth of beard and his hair tousled. This was an Alex she had never seen before and she was having a difficult time dealing with it. It was Alex she could always come to for help, for advice. Now, he seemed distant, detached. Whatever was on his mind, he had internalized it to the extent that he was near a breaking point.

"Alex, did you hear anything I just said about Philip?" Her voice was soft but to the point.

"Sorry, Caroline... something about Philip improving and that he is healing. I'm very tired. I've ...." He stopped mid-sentence and took a gulp of the coffee in front of him. "It's hot," he quickly added a generous splash of the half and half from the carton.

"I'm not pushing you to tell me about Jess and whatever she is doing, but I take it from the little you have said that she is in some kind of terrible trouble or danger. Is it really that bad?"

"Yes, it's that bad. She... she may not be coming back and there is nothing I can do to help her."

"Jessica? No, no... Did... they... get... her, too?" Philip stood in the doorway to the kitchen wearing his pajamas as well as a robe.

Alex turned abruptly to look at his cousin. It was the first time in months that Philip's words had been more than babble; more than sounds. This, quite obviously was what Caroline had been trying to explain.

"My God, Philip, You are talking!" he said rising from the counter chair to help his cousin to the seat next to him.

"What did you mean, did they get Jessica, too? Did someone try to attack you?"

" Yessss, the Houseman." Philip was drawing out his words which were being expressed very slowly. Alex tried not to rush him or show impatience.

"I think we should not push this," Caroline's voice was firm as she looked directly at Alex.

"No, Caroline I want to tell him," Philip sat his large frame on one of the counter stools and spoke directly to Alex. "It was Poulette's houseman, Fox. He was stealing from her. He wants to kill her and .... meeee."

"You can't mean that, darling. Bertrand Fox has been with Poulette for .... for at least 50 years, maybe longer. He moved with her from Europe. I think this accident you had may have given you ... well, let's say, bad dreams, delusions. I am sure Mr., Fox did not..."

"No, Caroline, he did try to kill me. Believe me... he did!" Philip's face was crimson. Caroline looked at Alex and then at her husband. It was obvious his blood pressure had risen to what looked like a dangerous level.

"Philip, I believe you. Now, let's get you back to bed." Alex tried to help his cousin stand. "It's true, Alex; it's true," Philip muttered as he allowed himself to be led to the adult-sized but antique food service elevator built into one wall of the kitchen; it would take Philip to his bedroom on the third floor.

Once, tucked into his bed, it took only moments for Philip to fall into a deep sleep. Both Caroline and Alex watched from the doorway to his room for a few minutes and then proceeded down the spiraling staircase.

"You don't really believe that lovely gentleman Mr. Fox would attack anyone, do you, Alex?"

"No, not really. I think Philip's still healing brain is playing tricks on him. I am sure if you ask his therapist he'll tell you hallucinations are quite common for this kind of traumatic injury..." Alex glanced out the window. "My God, it's snowing again. Caroline, if you wouldn't mind, may I take a short rest in one of your guest bedrooms? I'm feeling more than a little tired ...."

"Of course, second door on your right at the top of the staircase. You even have your own bath. Rest as long as you want. It's Christmas Eve, the staff is off and there's nothing to be done but have a restful day. I might take a nap myself."

"Thanks!" Alex felt an extreme fatigue as he made his way back up the now well-travelled staircase. This was more than normal physical exhaustion. Although the utterances from Philip had been unsettling, he doubted there was any real merit in them. Philip was indeed having delusions. As he entered the guest room, he closed the door, removed his shoes and launched his still clothed body onto the bed. He pulled the quilt up and over himself and immediately fell into a deep dreamless sleep.

***

Roberto Lombroso sat quietly looking out to sea from the third floor terrace of his baglio, a glass of gently aged Barolo in his hand. It was a mild day, with a slight breeze. The giant sphere of a winter sun splattered the ancient stone walls with hues of scarlet as it slowly slipped into the late afternoon horizon. He had arrived by hydrofoil from Palermo only an hour earlier. It was a last minute decision to come to the island; one that made his immediate staff apprehensive but an act that he believed, would keep him safe and perhaps even alive. On this isolated and ancient sliver of land in the Tyrrhenian Sea, he could relax and enjoy the modest pleasures of local, simple cuisine accompanied by wines from his own ancient vineyards that grew on the mountainous terrain behind his baglio.

There were few people anywhere in the world who knew of this remote island and even fewer who had knowledge of this house built into the craggy Marettimo massif. It was his haven, remote and discreet; a piece of land where one could truly hide in the secluded Egadi Islands.

Those on Marettimo who knew of this house and the identity of its inhabitant, were year round residents whose ancestors long ago had pledged their lives to keeping the resident and his location a secret. For an 'Ndrangheta capo, this was the safest place on earth.

"Oh, Mr. Roberto, I am so glad to see you. Everything is prepared for you exactly as you asked for it. I did not buy anything special for tonight so it will be a regular dinner of grilled fish and pasta. I promise to get you something special for tomorrow if you just tell me what you want." The elderly woman glowed. Her affection for Roberto Lombroso had a patina of maternal pride. She had known this man for many years; first on his visits to the island as a young man to guard his chief and recently as the head capo himself, which in her eyes, made him the most important man in the world.

"... and so, Angelina, how is your daughter?" Lombroso's question was sincere and softly asked. He could see the esteem emanating from the woman who had carried out a tray of steamed crayfish and a pitcher of wine to refill his glass.

"She now has six children," she replied placing the tray on a convenient table for him. "Four of them are boys, the oldest 10 and two beautiful girls, ages 3 and 1. She is very busy as you can imagine, but she will bring freshly baked bread tomorrow morning. She bakes very early in the morning so that you can have it right from the oven for your breakfast."

"Please tell... what is her name?"

"It is Carolina, her name is Carolina."

"... how much I appreciate that?"

"...oh, but she does this with pleasure.... and Mr. Roberto, I have also prepared your private room. Nothing has been touched.

It is exactly as you left it, but I did use the mop on the floors and dusted." She smiled accommodatingly.

"I'm certain, it will be fine. One thing more, I have a guest arriving; actually two guests arriving tomorrow close to noon. They may be staying for several days. If you could please ready two rooms. I think the cottage at the end of the property might be best for them. It has two bedrooms and it will give me the privacy, I need."

"Very well. Mr. Roberto. Now, enjoy the sunset. It is exceptionally beautiful tonight."

Roberto Lombroso watched the woman leave and then made his way to the room she referred to as "private". It was his communication headquarters, fitted with the latest in dark web encoding equipment. He could easily communicate with anyone anywhere in the world without ever being detected. He would use the time he had before dinner to check on several things; most importantly, the situation at the Vatican. Had it gone off as he planned? He smiled as he thought of the event.

"It must have been quite a blast," he said aloud. "Yes, a real blast!"

Chapter 52

Jessica wasn't certain how long she had been entombed in the badly damaged Scavi. She felt a level of claustrophobia, not encountered before. It was very dark. She could sit up, but there was scarcely room above her to do more. The heavy rocks that enclosed the area were within an arm's reach, above her head. It was truly a miracle she had not been crushed. Her head ached from the lack of oxygen, and the air was thick with a fine dust that made her eyes feel gritty and her lungs gasp.

Father Marcus Granville Barker and Father Sean O'Reilly lay close by. They had been caught in the explosion, less than thirty feet away and after discovering Malcolm's head crushed, had crawled through the rubble to her aid and that of the Holy Father.

"He's dead, you know," she told them cradling his head in her lap. "Will we be able to get out of here?"

"I'm not certain," Marcus answered truthfully. And then it came, the voices of their rescuers, who called down to the party through loud speakers.

"Can you move?" They were asked.

"Minimally," Marcus answered.

"Wave your arms if you can!" Marcus waved as best he could with so little overhead room.

"There seems to be an opening behind you," one of the responders called back.

It was Jessica who suggested to the rescue team that there would be an opening in the Papal Chapel to the Scavi; the same one she had used to gain entrance.

"Is the Holy Father with you?" a responder called down.

"Yes, he is" Jessica answered. She did not indicate that he was no longer alive.

The body of the deceased Pope Leo had grown quite rigid. She had taken the ivory linen bag containing the bones from him and tucked it protectively in the oversized pocket of her garment.

"We will have you out of there very soon," came the last message.

It wasn't very soon. When the rescue team finally made its way to the threesome, Jessica clung protectively to the old man's figure in her lap. She cared for him, she realized. Yet, she hardly knew him. Reluctantly, she allowed Pope Leo XIV to be taken from her as the rescuers readied her for safe passage through the expanded crawl space they had created. There, she was strapped into a half-back harness device to protect her cervical cord and lifted by pulley into the papal chapel. It was only as she was within a sight line of the opening that she remembered. Leo had told her that he knew how it would end. "I will die here," he had whispered. "I saw it in a vision. Peter told me so!"

***

Bertrand Fox had ignored both his cell phone and the house phone which had been ringing sporadically for more than 30 minutes. He was quite certain one call would be from Marcus, calling his step mother on Christmas Eve from Rome. The other, caller on the house phone, would be Poulette who needed something. She always needed something. Sitting in the office of the late Cornelius Granville Barker since dropping off the body of Bernadette Perkins at St. David's cemetery, he was preparing to inspect the pouch. It certainly was insignificant looking. On first glance no one would expect this worn piece of suede, the size of a sandwich bag, to be anything more than a receptacle for cheap costume jewelry. Yet, he knew, however shabby the exterior, the contents were priceless. So valuable were they that, Roberto Lombroso, Dr. Lydia Sindona and Poulette Granville Barker all considered the contents precious enough to kill or die for.

He had closed the door to the office when he unlocked it and entered. After removing the suede pouch from Cornelius Granville Barker's desk drawer, he placed it with the tools of his trade on a small table away from a window. Although there was little chance to no chance of an outside visitor on Christmas Eve, but he wanted to ensure there would be no interruption. He withdrew white cotton gloves from a drawer, a microscope, a jeweler's eye piece, pincers, a gem scale and a computer tablet. It was quite dark outside which made the goose neck lamp, with its 100 watt bulb, all the more important.

He reached into the pouch and removed the lipstick cases. It was he who had discovered these gaudy objects that Poulette had stored for many years in her vanity drawer. On the day of the fainting spell that had sent her to to Bryn Mawr Hospital by ambulance, he had gone to her quarters just to make certain everything was properly in its place, What he found instead was the open pouch. He had only begun to examine its contents; removing the jeweled metal covers to reveal the lipsticks themselves, when the real estate man, Philip Rawlins had walked right in, to see him, quite literally, with his hands on the goods. Rawlins had claimed he had an appointment with Poulette who had told him to come directly to her apartment via the elevator. What was it that Rawlins had shouted at him?

"My God, you are stealing from her, aren't you? Where is Poulette? What are you doing with her jewelry?" Then he tried to grab the jeweled cases from my hands. What could I do? Bertrand Fox smiled at the thought of it. "Before I punched the bastard sending him flying down the staircase and out the front door. I smeared the blasted lipstick from one of the tubes all around his mouth. Between the blood and the lipstick Rawlins looked like a clown!"

Chapter 53

The only thing Jessica could remember of the event was a sharp blow to her forehead just as the litter used to rescue her was hoisted through the opening in the Papal chapel. Moments later, she found herself looking into the eyes of the crucified St. Peter, his tortured body, being stretched to its limits, upside down. This was the Caravaggio painting that literally seemed to speak to Pope Leo during his daily prayers. But now, as she looked into those eyes she felt herself quite literally sinking, free falling into unconsciousness; not one of blissful peace but instead of tumult and rage. She clutched at her chest, gasping for air. It was the first time she felt the palm-sized chunk of basalt that had struck her head and now lay beneath her hand.

Behind her rescue litter lay the shattered remains of the relic. It had been unearthed from the holy of holies in a pagan temple in the ancient Canaanite city of Hatzor, in what is today northern Israel.

A treasured gift from an Israeli Ambassador to the Pope, it had been sanctified and placed in a niche near the old staircase entrance to the Scavi. The piece had for decades remained unnoticed in the shadows of this private chapel, It was far from sumptuous in its full form; a less than twelve inch by fourteen inch basalt altar, used by pagan priests for burning incense. The piece she clutched was quite identifiable, the unscathed carved symbol of the storm god Baal, the circle with a cross in the center.

It was a quick pick up. Without ceremony or checking the identity of the patient, two men collected the litter, maneuvering it down two staircases and through the back hallways and tunnels of the private quarters and finally into the rear of a waiting van. With doors secured and headlights off, the passenger and her minders sped away into the darkening night.

***

It was dark when Alex opened his eyes. He had heard the knock on the door several times but was disoriented, not knowing exactly where he was.

"Alex. Alex, you have a phone call on our land line. The caller says it's important! Alex, are you awake?"

"Caroline, yes, yes. I'm awake now. I'll be right there." His phone, where was his cell? Alex checked his trouser pockets and then remembered, Jed had taken it and in his rush to get out of the office, he had not remembered to claim it again. This had to be the reason for this highly unusual unsecured land line call from Jed.

"Hello, Jed? Yeah, I thought it had to be you. You have my cell. What's up? Sure, I'm ready to go now. He's at the back door? Sure, I'll be right out!"

Caroline stood in the shadows not far from the hallway phone which rested on an 18th century rosewood console.

"I have to go, Caroline. Sorry, I can't spend Christmas Eve with you and Philip but..."

"I take it there is news about Jessica?" Alex did not answer but grabbed his coat, wrapping his muffler around his neck as he hurried to the kitchen and through the door leading to the porte cochere where his car with a driver waited. "I'll call you later." Caroline stood silently shivering as a blast of wind swirled around her. In a moment, the car was out of sight.

She closed the door and turned on the kitchen light. The house was silent. Philip must still be resting. She would check on him later. He was getting better, she thought. This time it wasn't just wishful thinking. He was truly better, remembering more and more about that terrible day and the accident.

He would improve if he could verbalize, talk about it. All of the doctors had agreed on that point. Perhaps it would be a new beginning for them. She walked to the wine fridge and pulled out a bottle of champagne. After all, it was Christmas Eve. If not now, when? She would take out their fine crystal flutes, open a tin of paté de fois gras and they would celebrate...to a new beginning.

***

"You missed the turnoff," Alex called to the driver. "We are going back to the office, aren't we?"

"No, Sir, my instructions are to bring you directly to General Broadhearst's house which is about seven miles from here."

"Oh, yes, of course, I remember the invitation."

Alex had just turned to look out the window when he shouted to the driver, "Stop! Stop right here, please!" He unbuckled his seat belt and threw open the door open and began running toward a car stalled in a snow bank only a few feet in front of him.

His driver was right behind him. "Mr. Rawlins, what's going on? Why did we stop?"

"This car, it belongs to my cousin Philip Rawlins. He seems to be driving it, or he was until he ended up in this snow bank. He's not well. As you can see, he's... he's not dressed to be outside. He should be in bed, in fact."

Alex pulled open the driver's door. Inside, he saw Philip, eyes wide open, staring through the windshield. The motor was running and his foot was on the pedal, ready to accelerate.

"Philip, Stop. Please stop, Philip!"

Alex grabbed at the door handle and pulled it open. It wasn't locked; it should have been automatically locked.

"Philip, I'm going to turn off the engine; do you understand?" Philip looked up for the first time acknowledging his presence.

"No, Philip, don't get out of the car yet. You only have slippers on. Where were you going? It's snowing and I'm certain Caroline doesn't know you've gone out."

Philip stared at him. "Why, I'm going to rescue Poulette. He's going to kill her." Philip spoke in a monotone voice but quite coherently.

"Who is going to kill Poulette?" Alex asked, his driver standing right behind him.

"Bertrand Fox. He is going to kill her. He steals from her."

"Yes, yes, let's take my car, instead and go over to investigate." Alex ordered the driver to pull his car next to Philip's and transfer him to the back seat. "What do you want to do about this, sir?"

"First, I'll call his wife who will be worried sick about his disappearance. Next we'll go to Poulette's house which is only about a mile from here on South Ithan Avenue to check on her. I suspect this story is some fantasy of his. And then, you will take me to General Broadhearst's house and after that return my dear cousin to his house."

"... and his car, Mr. Rawlins? It will be towed away."

"Perhaps, we can get a little help from the Radnor police with that. Now, if I might borrow your cell, I'd like to call his wife."

Philip's silence was far from comforting. His face now wore a determined grimace. Alex looked down at his cousin's feet. He had stepped into the snow as the car transfer took place and now his slippers and his bare feet were wet and presumably very cold; yet, he seemed unaware.

"On second thought, I think we just might have to get Philip back home before we continue." Alex punched in Caroline's number. Philip needed immediate attention. Poulette and the General would have to wait.

***

"Amazing," The conservatively attired Frenchman in his mid-forties leaned against the marble balustrade. It extended out and overlooked a one hundred foot drop to the sea. A rush of monumentally high waves crashed against the boulders below, creating a violent froth of white foam that propelled a fine spray of azure blue water to the terrace.

He wore no tie. Instead, an open collared, long sleeved shirt of pale blue Egyptian cotton. Its French cuffs closed with discreet gold links that peeked provocatively from the perfectly tailored sleeves of his cashmere suit. The temperature at 10:30 a.m. had already climbed into the mid-70s F; the breeze barely noticeable.

"In fact, it's almost hypnotic!" He pressed against the balustrade, leaning more closely into the magic of the moment and took a deep breath

"What is amazing?"

Roberto Lombroso cut into the second of a large home-made boar sausage which lay beside a puddle of egg yolk that remained on his breakfast plate.

"The sun, Sir; the sun reflecting on the water below and the waves crashing against the boulders beneath the terrace. You probably have one of the best views in the world."

"I do, Jacques, and you are one of the few to be invited to see it." Lombroso looked up; his face showing a mixture of amusement and tolerance at the reaction of his house guest.

"Where is your colleague? Sleeping in?"

"No, sir, he'll be here very soon. Something he ate last night didn't agree with him. He'll be here when you are ready for us."

"I'm ready now, Jacques. I don't want to keep you two here on Christmas day. So, I've arranged to have a boat take you back to the main land when we've finished with our business. The Monsignor can see a doctor there if he is not better by then."

"Yes, sir. I'll call him now on his cell and get him down here." Jacques Dumont turned his back on Lombroso and walked toward the edge of the terrace. This was a command performance.

"Monsignor Rosario, Mr. Lombroso is ready to meet with us now. Yes, immediately, on the terrace and then, be prepared to leave." Dumont pushed the cell back into his trouser pocket.

"He's on his way, sir."

Lombroso did not answer but swabbed the remaining egg yolk on his breakfast plate with a slab of hard crusted bread, supplied only hours earlier by Angelina's daughter.

"Ahhh, there you are, Lucrezio. Jacques tells me you are feeling a little under the weather, this morning." Lombroso rose to shake the hand of the Monsignor who had served him for more than 20 years.

"It is good to see you again, Roberto. Yes, I seem to have picked up a bug; perhaps it was from the shell fish I had last night." Rosario's face was pale; his eyes watery.

"You don't look so well, my friend. Please sit here at the table with me. Perhaps I can get you something. Tea? Juice?"

"No, please do not trouble yourself. I'll be just fine. "

"All right then, Jacques, let's hear what you've been able to do to make certain our organization is protected."

Jacques Dumont picked up a leather brief case he had placed next to the table near Lombroso and removed an I-Pad for his presentation. "I have scrubbed the Institute for the Works of Religion's records of any reference of you or our projects. There is not a trace."

"You're quite certain of that, Jacques. I'd hate to find out later that you'd missed something."

"Roberto, I know he speaks the truth. I have examined everything. There is no mention of you or any of our organizations anywhere." Monsignor Rosario interrupted.

"... and the investments, where have you...?" Lombroso did not finish the sentence.

"We have relocated some cash and bitcoin, of course in Switzerland at several friendly institutions. It is always available in any amount you may need. In addition, we also have converted some cash assets into investments in fine art such as paintings, which are also stored in bank vaults in Switzerland. We have diamond mines and gold mines in Africa, wind energy producing power plants in Asia, the United States, Italy, Australia and Scandinavia and we've made some major investments in the Seychelles which should increase in value substantially very quickly. The distribution circuit is clean and clear and nothing can be directed back to you or our groups directly... but you have immediate access to it."

Lombroso smiled and patted Monsignor Rosario on the back. You have been a good and loyal friend," he said. Thank you!"

Jacques Dumont watched as Roberto Lombroso stood and opened his arms to hug the elderly Rosario. "You look very tired, Lucrezio. Perhaps you should take a little vacation during this Christmas holiday?"

"I think I just need to get some rest, Roberto. I am not feeling like myself." Rosario looked up into the eyes of his patron. He looked fragile.

"I have arranged for a boat to take you back to a port in Sicily. A car is waiting for you. There is a lovely resort there called The Etna. It is only semi opened at this time of the year. If you both want to take a few days to relax and recover, then please do so; you will be my guests."

Jacques Dumont smiled. "That is very, very generous of you, Sir. Thank you! It sounds wonderful and, sir, here is the I-Pad with the presentation on it. You can read it in detail after we leave."

"Good work deserves a reward. If you feel confident that I am protected, you do deserve something special. I take it this is the only copy of the presentation?"

"Absolutely, sir. You have the sole copy."

"Oh, Roberto. You are like my son. Take care of yourself and thank you from an old man who is feeling his age today."

"Get your luggage, Lucrezio and Jacques. The car will meet you at your villa. And again, thank you and Merry Christmas."

Roberto Lombroso raised his coffee cup in a silent salute to them.

His guests would be at the dock and departing in less than 15 minutes.

He felt a twinge of regret for finalizing the departure of the elderly Monsignor who had been a faithful aide for many years; but, no sympathy for Dumont. The two would not be spending a restful Christmas week at Etna, but instead both would find an eternal rest a few miles out, beneath the same azure waters Dumont had admired from his terrace.

Chapter 54

Jessica opened her eyes with a start. The jolt of the Boeing C-40 military transport plane hitting an air pocket caused her gurney to rise slightly off the floor of the aircraft. For a moment, she was unsure of where she was. Her head throbbed; her left eye was covered. She reached up to feel gauze extending across her forehead and the top of her head. She looked to her left, moving her head very slowly. She was in the middle of the right side of the aircraft. There were at least four litters in front of hers and the same number on the other side. She guessed the plane held about 20 patients. But why was she here and, how did she get here and where was she going?

"Hello... hello, is anyone here?" As she called out, she noted how very dry her mouth felt. She craved water. Her voice sounded unnatural too; rough, raspy.

"Ah, Mrs. Rawlins you are with us, again. We were wondering when you would awaken." Jessica looked up and into the eyes of a young Naval Hospital Corpsman in his early 30s. "No, no, stay where you are. I cannot let you sit up, but I can get you something to drink and if you are hungry, perhaps some broth or juice."

"First of all, where am I? Who are you? And where are we going? And secondly, yes. I need water desperately! I am absolutely parched."

"I'll be back with your water in a moment and then, I can begin to answer some of your questions."

Jessica tried to look around, but the bandage covering her left eye made seeing objects on the left very difficult. The transport had no windows, but LED red lighting on the ceiling of the plane gave her some ability to see what was around her. The sound of the engines were louder than in most commercial aircraft She knew from previous journeys on transport aircraft that everything would be minimal from toilet facilities to food offerings. It was only then that she realized she was wearing a catheter which would make visits to the minimal lavatories unnecessary; she also became aware of an IV drip inserted in her right shoulder.

".. and so, here you are. All I can give you are ice chips. You're not allowed to sit up, but these should alleviate your thirst if you let them melt on your tongue." Jessica grabbed at the small paper cup with the chips in it. The cool taste of the ice was an immediate relief to her thirsting lips and throat.

"Please, what is your name and...?"

The Naval Hospital Corpsman First Class bent down to be at her eye level. "I'm Marine Sgt. Harold Reagan and you are wondering how you got here. Well, you were rescued from an explosion at the Vatican in Rome. Somewhere and sometime during that rescue, your head was hit with a chunk of the rubble which gave you a concussion and injured your left eye. As to where you are now? On your way to Landstuhl Regional Medical Center which is about five miles south of Ramstein Air Base in Germany."

"... and the others? I see there are other patients on this flight?"

"Yes, well, I can't discuss their conditions, Mrs. Rawlins. Privacy rules, you now. But I can tell you that they, too are on their way to Germany." Jessica could read the intonation in his voice, that these patients were seriously injured, perhaps even very seriously. She wondered exactly who they were and why they were on a military transport.

"Now, Mrs. Rawlins, our orders are to offer you chicken broth and of course a cup of cherry gelatin. Would you like that now?" The corpsman stood up. Jessica imagined him to be more than six feet tall.

"I'll take anything you have. I'm feeling really hungry."

When he had stepped away, she realized she could not remember when she had eaten last; in fact, she could remember little of the previous day. She took another small taste of the crushed ice and studied the two litters immediately in front of her. Both were occupied by men, she was certain. They appeared to be sleeping. In the near darkness she could see that they too had IVs attached to their arms.

What was this explosion the sergeant had mentioned? Were these men rescued from it, too?

"Chicken consommé, Mrs. Rawlins. I can raise your pillow just a little so that it will be easier to sip." Jessica felt the back of her gurney being rolled up by hand, several inches. It would be just enough to get a better view of exactly who was travelling with her to Germany.

***

"I can't stay, Caroline. I'm... "Alex did not elaborate but helped Philip into a chair and wrapped his own coat more firmly around his body. It was a dramatic gesture intended to show her that no amount of coercing would encourage him to stay.

"But, there is no one else that I can call on, Alex. You know, it's ... "

"I'm truly sorry, Caroline, but I really must go." Philip stared ahead seemingly not comprehending where he was or what was going on around him. His feet were now blue from the cold; his leather slippers soaked from stepping in the icy slush. Caroline knew she had to get him into bed and somehow change his current clothing into something that would restore warmth.

"Caroline, look, I'll help you get him upstairs but I can't stay," Alex noted the tears in her eyes as they walked Philip into the kitchen elevator that would take him to the third floor.

"Please, Alex; I really can't do this by myself."

Fifteen minutes later, Philip was back in his bed wearing woolen socks and flannel pajamas and Alex was rushing down the front staircase grabbing his coat from a chair and putting it on as he made his way to the kitchen.

"Alex, you have to believe me I had no idea Philip had left the house and certainly no idea that he had taken the keys to my car."

"I know, Caroline, but I am very late already and my appointment is... important. Look, call one of the nursing services and ask them to send you a male nurse right now. You look exhausted and it's obvious you cannot be here alone. I'll call you later to see how you are. In the meantime, make certain the security system is turned on. If he tries to leave again, the alarm will alert you. Alex wrapped the woolen muffler around his neck as he exited the kitchen door where his car and driver were waiting. "Lock the door and turn on the alarm, now!" he called out as the car sped away.

General Broadhearst's invitation had requested that he arrive at his home 90 minutes earlier. He hoped his host would be understanding when he explained the reason for his tardiness.

***

There could be no doubt; the man lying atop the pale jade Chinese silk rug was dead. The 19th century brass harlequin table lamp with its green, leaded glass shade rested in jagged splinters on the temple of this one-time butler and from his head flowed a stream of bright red blood.

Poulette stood aghast at what she had done for only a moment and then stepped gingerly, bending slightly to get a better look at the body.

"Yes," she said aloud, "... you are quite dead." The jeweled lipstick cases lay strewn across the desk; several had been disassembled. Next to one, lay a mound of small rubies and sapphire that had once studded the outer case. A portable jeweler's lamp still shone brightly on the remains of her collection. "Oh, Mr. Fox, this didn't have to happen. I trusted you. You knew what these lipsticks meant to me. They were all... literally the only things I had from Lucas." Her hands trembled; she reached forward to touch the cases, but then realized her fingers were not agile enough to pick them up. She could never reassemble what he had taken apart. How could he have done this and why? As she turned away, the heel of her satin slipper stepped firmly upon something solid. It was Bertrand Fox's left hand; clutched between his thumb and index finger was a small object. Steadying herself on the edge of the desk with her left hand, she bent over gingerly to retrieve the item. What was it? Cardboard, less than ½ inch long and 1/4 inch wide and covered in... not blood but... lipstick? She stood up a gingerly to study the object, holding it under the jeweler's lamp. It was then she recognized it. It was microfiche. But, had it been hidden in her lipstick case? She assumed that was where it had come from. She placed it on the desk, turned off the lamp and slowly walked toward the door closing it behind her. Somewhere in another part of the house, she could hear the land line ringing. No one was picking up. "Oh where was Bernadette Perkins when she needed her?" The telephone continued to ring as she entered the front hall. She picked up the receiver of an extension that lay on a console table. "Hello? Hello? Anyone there? Marcus, Marcus is it you? I can't hear you, dear. Is anyone there? Marcus?"

There was no answer just a click. She replaced the receiver. The line was as dead as Bertrand Fox and the precious memories his destructive acts had taken with him.

Chapter 55

"... but if I only have a slight concussion, why can't you release me? Can I at least speak to my husband?" Jessica could feel the bandage over the left side of her eye. There was no pain, merely the feeling of the adhesive pulling, which irritated her skin.

"Mrs. Rawlins, in terms of your medical condition, I'd allow you to go home today; but I am not in charge of your release. You still have to go through a debriefing. When that has been accomplished, well I'll be back to sign those papers for you." The American doctor smiled. He had a gentle bedside manner and she understood why she had to be debriefed, but it had been so long since she had spoken to Alex; so long since she had been back home in Berwyn, on the Main Line, that her patience in process was quickly evaporating.

She watched the physician leave the room and close the door behind him. She looked at the clock on the wall. It was 9:05 a.m. The sun was only now beginning its climb into the late December horizon, peeking through a curtain of heavy dark grey clouds that typified the weather at Landstuhl military Hospital and nearby Ramstein Air Force Base in Germany. She surmised that Christmas Day had come and gone. She remembered only some of the chaos of Christmas Eve at the Vatican; her discovery of Pope Leo in the Scavi, the sudden explosion... and the linen sack which Leo told her contained the bones of St. Peter. She had taken the simple bag from Leo after he died and placed it in the deep pocket of her dress. The sack? Was it still in her dress pocket? My God, she thought where are those bones?

She threw back the sheet and light flannel blanket covering her and tried to get out of bed. As she stepped on the cold linoleum tile floor, her knees began to give way and she found herself falling forward toward the only chair in the room. It was that damned concussion, she murmured. It had given her a sudden case of vertigo. She struggled to right herself on the chair but stumbled over one of its legs. Taking a deep breath, she ordered her body to right itself and move toward the closet. If they had not discovered it, the bones still should be in the pocket of the garment. The locker-sized patient closet was portable and positioned against the outer wall next to the door. She pulled at the locker door handle. The dress was there, hanging on a hook with the shoes she had been wearing on the floor. She reached into the pocket of the dress, hoping to find the linen bag still intact.

It was gone. They had taken Pope Leo's precious treasure, which she had tried to protect. Where had they taken what remained of St. Peter?

***

"The important thing, Alex, is that she is alive." Four star General Reggie Broadhearst handed his guest a Johnny Walker Black Label, with a splash of soda, almost immediately upon entering the room. "Don't worry about the delay. I've advised our chef and he is used to working around delayed dinner schedules." Jed Watkins had arrived only minutes before Alex; he too was late but armed with the good news that Jessica had been rescued from the Scavi and was alive and on her way to Germany.

"You'll be able to talk to her sometime tomorrow, Alex, or the next day; she still has to be debriefed. General Broadhearst and I will be in on that debriefing with a few Washington politicos involved as well." Jed sipped his drink slowly and reached for a handful of mixed nuts from a large, cut crystal bowl, on a table near the fireplace.

Alex' hand brushed the ten foot white pine Christmas tree with its array of tiny white lights, antique ornaments and a garland of silver that wrapped it from its base to the porcelain angel on top.

"It's hard to remember when Jess and I spent our last Christmas together. She always seems to be on assignment at this time of the year." Jed looked at General Broadhearst before speaking. "If you want this to be her last assignment, then I promise it will be, Alex. She has done a splendid job, one that we could not ask of any other agent. She literally had all of the necessary qualifications."

"But at what cost, Jed?" Alex took another deep drink from the low ball glass.

"Our marriage is not exactly in tip top shape. Jess is pretty banged up as you said. She is not dead; but she is … what would you say? Wounded psychologically and physically?"

"This isn't a James Bond movie, Alex. Our agents do not go into the field and announce who they are and drink vodka martinis. Jessica speaks a top grade Calabrian dialect of Italian; she was willing to go into the field to scrub floors, and infiltrate a dangerous inner circle of international criminals. Literally, there was no one else who could do what she did. She, we believe, will help the U.S. government put a lot of really bad people behind bars. "

"Look, Jed, I know the drill. It's all for God and Country."

"In this case, it really was. She was working inside the Vatican!"

Alex looked astounded. "What?"

"Exactly what I said, she was working for the Pope in the Vatican."

"Holy crap!" Alex dropped into a large leather club chair next to the fireplace.

"That means… oh no, tell me that she wasn't in that explosion they've been reporting on the news. Something about a bomb exploding in St. Peter's Basilica at the High Altar? That is how Jessica got injured? "

"She's alive, Alex. She has a slight concussion as well as a few cuts and bruises. She's already in Germany at Landstuhl Military Hospital. We'll set up a camera and you'll be able to see for yourself, probably sometime tomorrow."

"But the Pope… no one has said what happened to the Holy Father? Was he injured?" Alex's voice had taken on new strength and a higher pitch.

"He's dead, Alex; the Vatican will announce that sometime tomorrow, I believe. Jessica was with him, when he died." Jed's voice had become softer. He could tell by the expression on Alex' face, that he was only now beginning to absorb the weight of the information he had been given.

"This is why she must be debriefed before you can speak to her. Even then, do not ask her anything about this, do you understand? She will have only certain things she will be able to tell you. The rest... well, the rest will be classified far above your security classification... and perhaps even mine."

"Dinner is served, sir," General Broadhearst's personal aide had entered the room surreptitiously just as Jed had completed his comments.

"I hope you are hungry, Alex. We are having a rather special Christmas feast with roasted Christmas Goose or a Beef Prime Rib roast." Broadhearst put his arm across Alex's shoulder. "The news is all good, my boy, all good for you, tonight!"

Alex's mood had lightened and with it the memory of Philip's urgent plea to check in on Poulette and her well-being. As they entered the dining room, a large trolley rolled into the room from the kitchen. On both sides of the heated silver trays, lay the presentations: Crispy skinned, roasted goose basted with melted butter in a brandy syrup with lingon berries on the side, as well as a chestnut and orange stuffing, and a Cumberland sauce of red oranges.

On the other tray, a medium rare prime rib roast with its own horseradish sauce. Mashed potatoes, green beans and acorn squash.

"I'll have both," Alex announced. The sight of the magnificent dinner had reduced the urgency of even placing a call to Edencroft to a mere suggestion. "It's Christmas Eve," he thought to himself. "She'll be fine with Mrs. Perkins and Mr. Fox tending to her needs. I'll call her tomorrow."

Chapter 56

"… but, as I told you yesterday, Doctor Williams, I really don't have anything else to share. You've got everything, I can remember." The room was dimly lit by a single overhead lamp in the ceiling. Jessica suspected the lamp also concealed a video camera. All high security debriefings were recorded, as a matter of policy. Still, she was conscious of the camera being on her as she lay in a leather recliner, a blanket covering her legs and a pillow beneath her head. This was their third session or was it their fourth? She had recounted the story of her mission, as she remembered it; how she met Pope Leo on his way to the Scavi; the dead Cardinals, the explosion…but she realized there were parts of her narration that either did not make sense or had been changed. Was it that her injury had caused memory loss? Had her memory or memories been altered in some way, replaced by induced memory? She drew a deep breath and exhaled quickly. This was crazy thinking; any more pondering about altered memories and the medics would surely send her to a sanitarium.

Dr. Simon Williams, sensed something was occurring as he observed his patient's growing circumspection, her uneasiness. He was well aware of Jessica's discomfort in regard to his youthful appearance. He was short and sinewy, with sandy red hair, pale skin, freckles and clear blue eyes. As a board-certified practicing psychiatrist, he was well into his thirties; yet his physical appearance, could, for some including Jessica, be interpreted as a lack of experience.

"When can I leave here, Dr. Williams? I want to see my husband."

"I may be able to arrange that; I've requested a Skype call with him in our secure communication room; it could take place as early as this afternoon. How would you like that?"

"I'd rather be going home, Dr. Williams."

"Yes, you've said that several times. For now, let's go back to talk about something that occurred on the night you were injured; this second time you encountered Pope Leo was not in the

Papal Chapel. You reportedly saw a dead body lying the corridor near the apartment and recognized it...."

"No..." Jessica interrupted, "I didn't tell you I saw a dead body in the corridor near the Papal apartment."

"I believe you did, Jessica. We have it on tape. You said you recognized the individual. It was one of the Cardinals who had visited the Holy Father only a few days earlier; a member of his 'inner circle' is how you described him. Do you remember seeing that body on the floor and stepping around it and walking back into the chapel to see that His Holiness had taken another one of his covert exits, using a hidden entrance in the chapel to the Scavi?"

"Where are the bones?' Jessica's voice was abrupt. She looked directly into the lamp above her. "Who took the linen bag from my pocket? Those bones are ...very important!"

Simon Williams walked to the lounger where Jessica was now sitting upright. "Those bones are what you all are after, isn't it? You want me to talk about those bones?"

"Jessica, what bones are you referring to?" Williams's voice was soft and un-challenging. He pressed his hand gently against her shoulder and she lay back down again.

"The Holy Father entrusted them to me; they meant everything to him. Now they have been lost or stolen."

Williams pushed a buzzer next to the lounger and immediately two aides entered.

"Mrs. Rawlins is ready to go back to her room. We'll be arranging a Skype call for her this afternoon to speak to her husband. In the meantime, I'm writing a prescription for a low dose anxiety reliever. Here, make certain she receives her first dose ASAP and then once every six hours." Williams tore a sheet from his prescription pad and handed it to the medic.

The moment the room was cleared, he picked up a secure phone on his desk.

"She remembered the bones; yes, she said they were very important to him, referring I am sure to Leo and she said that he had entrusted them to her. Yes, I understand. I'll continue to push further on that one. Yes, she's resting now."

***

"... Following the five alarm blaze in Radnor that has left Edencroft a virtual shell, investigators will be combing the wreckage of this notable Tudor estate on Ithan Avenue for signs of arson. The owner, Patricia Granville Barker, age 78, is said to have survived the inferno but was taken to Bryn Mawr Hospital for treatment of smoke inhalation and observation. Mrs. Granville Barker is the widow of well-known Main Line philanthropist and international banker Cornelius Granville Barker. Prior to their marriage, he was tapped by President Kennedy to be his personal envoy to the Holy See, a position he held until the president's assassination and which helped the U.S. State Department form a diplomatic platform for a future, more comprehensive relationship. Edencroft has been the site of many diplomatic, social and philanthropic events since that time."

Caroline Rawlins watched the image of local ABC TV News anchor, Jim Gardner fade, as she flicked off the channel's 11:00 p.m. local news. Poor Poulette, she had survived an inferno but at what cost? There had been no mention of Mrs. Perkins nor of her long time butler, Bertrand Fox. Had both perished in the fire? How could it have started?

She turned off the lights in the family room and slowly made her way up the grand staircase to her second floor bedroom. She climbed the additional flight of stairs to kiss Philip good night. His nurse was keeping watch in the corridor outside his room, reading a book, which he laid aside as Caroline approached.

"Mr. Rawlins is sleeping soundly. I administered a light sedative, after speaking to his doctor, when I came on duty. He should sleep through the night. However, if he awakens and tries to take a walk somewhere, he won't get far. I'll stop him." Caroline shook his hand as the Grandfather clock at the foot of the staircase struck midnight!

"Thank you," she said as she turned away. "... and Merry Christmas!"

"Merry Christmas, Mrs. Rawlins!"

***

Father Sean O'Reilly cut into the finely sliced salmon carpaccio with the lemon parsley sauce and raised his fork to his lips. "This has to be the finest smoked salmon I've even had," he garbled ignoring every rule of etiquette regarding speaking with one's mouth full of food.

"That's because it's not smoked. It's Gravlax, Sean; very popular in Northern countries like Germany and Scandinavia." The two priests had been seated at a table near the windows, on the second floor of Kafer's in Munich.

"See, I told you I knew of this terrific restaurant. As long as we have the evening free before our flight, we might as well take in one of the really fine restaurants in the city."

Father Sean was already slicing into another large portion of Gravlax and only slightly paying any attention to his dinner companion.

"Yes, I'm glad we have the evening free. Yes, I'm even more pleased we are not returning to the U.S. in one of those transporter planes and finally, I cannot tell you how happy I will be to get back to St. Edmund's with its snowy, cold, damp Main Line climate."

"Then, you really are feeling all right? The concussion still has to be dealt with at home; you do realize that, don't you?"

"Yes, Marcus, I realize that; but ...." The priest stopped in mid-sentence continuing to chew the rather large piece of salmon he had cut from the filet on his plate and using the time in between to butter a hard roll he had taken from a bread basket between the two priests.

"If you don't mind, I'd like to talk about Pope Leo before we get back to the United States. This may be the only time we have to talk about this privately. I realize that once we are ... what shall I say... on home turf, it probably will mean total silence on the subject. What are your thoughts on talking about him?"

"We, meaning Leo and I, had some deep conversations, philosophical talks about difficult topics. None of them were under seal of the confession. He actually said he did not want to confess, but he wanted me to know what he was thinking ... what he had done and that he was truly sorry. He also knew who I was."

"You mean, as a psychiatrist? He put a big burden on you, didn't he? Was that fair? I mean, you and I know what he did, but how important is it that the rest of the world knows?"

"I'm not certain anyone should know, Sean. The fact that Pope Leo murdered someone, someone important, in fact someone that I am indirectly related to...well, that is significant to me. But, it was a long time ago. Leo was not the same person who committed that crime. He truly had repented, I believe. "

"It was a pretty terrible murder, too, Marcus. It was planned, well planned and well-orchestrated. I remember when it was in all the papers... around the world. Leo and the other paid thugs literally chased their victim along the river bank and to the bridge, where they held him down, put bricks in his pocket and then put a noose around his neck. Leo said he was bleating like a lamb, aware of what was happening to him and begging for mercy. He knew he was about to die and in a terrible way. Every time Leo talked about the incident, he said it reminded him of Christ, in the Garden at Gethsemane, being taken away and that same night beaten, scourged and....." Sean O'Reilly took a large sip of wine from the heavy red glass goblet which had been filled to the brim with Gewürztraminer.

"Leo, paid a large price for that night. He relived it over and over and over again. The bones he was retrieving in the Scavi the night he died? He believed they belonged to his victim, Sebastian Calvi."

"Sean, I'm not certain you know who Sebastian Calvi was. He was my stepmother Poulette's first husband; he reportedly was killed in a car accident. Instead, some other fool ended up in the car. In those days forensics was not what it is today and the badly burned body wearing Calvi's clothing was what convinced the police it was Calvi. Poulette had no idea. In fact, has no idea I am sure that the unidentified man hanging from the bridge in Rome was, in fact, her beloved Sebastian. Leo said they had mutilated his face with acid and burned his fingers so that there would be no fingerprints. The authorities buried the victim in a pauper's grave in Italy, while the ashes of some unknown chap lay is in a Swiss cemetery with a headstone that reads Sebastian Calvi, beloved husband." Pope Leo on one occasion claimed that he had rescued Sebastian's bones from that pauper's grave; but who knows what he did with them, and whether indeed he really recovered them.

Marcus Granville Barker cut into his Presssack, a Bavarian headcheese accompanied by a mound of sweet red cabbage salad and Cornichons, tiny, tart pickles.

"I wasn't aware of any of that, Marcus. I assume you won't say anything to Poulette about what you've learned?"

Marcus did not answer for several seconds. "You know, Sean, my inclination was to tell her. But, now I'm not certain if that would be a right decision. She isn't well, we both know that, but she has plenty of support around her. Her butler, Bertrand Fox for example has been with her since Switzerland as has Bernadette Perkins. In fact, I think I remember Mrs. Perkins losing someone in that terrible car crash and perhaps Mr. Fox lost a son around that time, as well. I know they always have been very protective of Poulette."

"Marcus, it's obvious you're very protective of Poulette, too but... how can I put this, there has been for many years, and I suppose there still is, talk about her relationship with ...." Sean O'Reilly did not finish his sentence.

"You mean with Dr. Lucas Sindona, the surgeon. Yes, yes, he was married; yes, they had a rather torrid affair. It was after my father died. Dad and Poulette's marriage had been very successful; but... he was dead. She was still beautiful, relatively young and lonely and Lucas saw the opportunity to..."

"To take advantage of her?" Sean was looking down at his nearly empty plate of salmon, He did not want to see Marcus openly deflect or defend Poulette's behavior or outright lie about the affair.

"She knew it was wrong. Lydia told me, the affair had hurt her mother terribly, but for whatever reason, Poulette has never said anything to me about the whole episode. It lasted quite a while, until his untimely death. He was very generous to her, that I do know."

"There's a lot more to the Leo episodes, Sean. I'm not certain whether I think he was a devil or a saint. Some of his 'revelations' which he believed came from St. Peter, were really quite remarkable....sophisticated."

"He was well educated. He was also a scholar as both of us can attest to."

"But, Sean, it was more than that. In any previous century, he'd have been proclaimed a saint. Whether these revelations were anything more than the ravings of a mad man, well, I'm not the one to ask, I guess."

"...Ah, and here comes our waiter, ready to take these empty plates away and replace them with our main courses; let's see, Sean, you're having the..."

"Venison with plums and buttered noodles!" The waiter removed the cover from the fragrant plate and placed it in front of the priest.

".. and for me, the wild pheasant in a brandied cherry sauce with fresh herbed spätzle." Marcus smiled as the cover was removed from his platter.

"We have plenty to give thanks for, Sean. Most of all surviving a situation which should have sent us both back home in caskets."

"I know, Marcus I know. Let us pray...."

Chapter 57

"Thanks, Wesley," The Regional FBI director, Joe Farrell accepted a foam coffee cup from one of the few agents on duty, during the holidays. The office, located in a 19th Century mansion, on the grounds of St. Edmund's University, required a minimal staff be on duty 24 hours a day; but those who had vacation time or leave coming, were allowed to take it and in an emergency, should they be needed, be on call.

The latter did not seem to be of concern this day, December 27th. It was 10:45 a.m. All was calm and all was bright, out of doors. The sun was shining brightly, melting any snow left on the roadways and sidewalks.

"Sir, these are from my wife. She thought you might enjoy some of her special Cherry strudel." Wesley smiled as he presented a tin container lined with aluminum foil holding several layers of the rich and fragrant fruit pastry.

"How thoughtful of her. Please give her my thanks. They look delicious."

"… and Agent Farrell, Mr. Mark Tobin has arrived; he's in the waiting room. As you know, he's the chairman of the Board of Trustees of the University. Father Austin Cheney, the Prior Provincial of the Edmundites and Father Paul Sullivan, the University president are walking over from the monastery. They should be here momentarily. After they called yesterday to request this emergency meeting, I created a briefing folder for you; it's on your desk. Should I send Mr. Tobin in right now or would you prefer to have him wait?"

"Let him wait until his colleagues arrive. I'll look over that brief and I have to make a call before I meet with them; close the door behind you, please."

Joe Farrell picked up the secure line on his desk and pushed the button for Jed Watkins.

Watkins answered immediately and in as few words as possible revealed some information that had not been on the 24 hour cable news broadcasts about the explosion at St. Peter's in the Vatican. "No, it was not ISIS; yes, it was a subversive, intentional explosion. Yes, we should get together as soon as possible." Jed volunteered to come to Joe Farrell's office.

"I'm in my car, now; I can be there in... let's see...about a quarter of an hour, Joe."

"Great, and the Johnny Walker Black Label is waiting." Farrell hung up the phone and reached for the folder. It was amazing, with all the modern electronic equipment at their disposal, most agents preferred to read paper reports. The information may be stored on line – encrypted, but to read it on line was not comfortable.

Joe Farrell turned to the last page. "Jacques Dumont?" he said aloud and closed the folder. "Wesley, send in Mr. Tobin, even if the priests haven't arrived yet. "

"Yes sir."

Mark Tobin's appearance was unexpected. Joe Farrell had encountered the fifty-ish plus executive on numerous occasions, at civic and university functions. Under most circumstances, he would arrive looking well groomed, wearing a well-tailored, pin-striped custom-made suit, with an elegantly cut shirt and a smartly patterned silk necktie, and with well-shined brogues on his feet. On most occasions he also would be wearing a subtle fragrance from the Christian Dior for men collection.

Today, judging from his appearance, he could well have been a drunk who'd just awakened from a weekend bender.

"Coffee, Mark?" Joe Farrell offered as the chairman of the board took a seat across the desk from his host.

"Make it black with two sugars," he answered. Farrell handed him a St. Edmund's mug with a wooden stirrer and two packs of sugar.

"Well, I understand you have had a little trouble at the University over the Christmas holiday, Mark. What seems to be the trouble?" Farrell offered the tin of strudel to Tobin who waved it away with a grimace.

"We have trouble all right and it is all because of one of your agents, Jacques Dumont. He's frozen our University accounts --- all of them because of some sting you guys are operating."

"Mr. Farrell, Fathers Sullivan and Cheney have arrived. Shall I send them in?" Wesley's voice over the intercom interrupted Tobin's mini tirade.

"Yes, Wesley, thank you!"

"Father Cheney, Father Sullivan. Now that you've arrived, let's convene over there. It's a lot more comfortable sitting on a sofa and upholstered chairs than around this desk. There's a coffee bar on top of the fridge and I'll add this tin of homemade cherry strudel, compliments of Wesley Wells, one of our new agents."

Mark Tobin heaved a sigh as he rose from his chair and settled into a place on the sofa. Neither priest sat next to him. Paul Sullivan rolled the chair on casters that Tobin had been sitting on to the conversation circle.

"As Mark had begun to tell me... something about Jacques Dumont?"

"Well, he seems to have literally done something to our bank accounts which does not allow us to get into our accounts.

"We can't even pay the light bill at the monastery," Paul Sullivan sputtered. "... nor the salaries"

"Literally everything... every dime is frozen." Austin Cheney added. "... and it is all the fault of your Agent Jacques Dumont. He said to leave everything in his hands and we did... and now what? What do we do? We need that money to run our university!"

Joe Farrell sipped his coffee slowly and sat back as if contemplating his answer. "I'm truly sorry to tell you this, gentlemen, but Jacques Dumont is not our agent. He does not work for the FBI. He hasn't been with us for ... let me see... at least a decade, perhaps longer."

"My God, then who is he working for and why did he shut us down...and how in Hell can we rectify it?" Tobin's face was now crimson. His appearance indicated he was one note short of a stroke or heart attack.

"Here, Mark, take a sip of this." Farrell had risen quickly, walked to the bar to pick up a small crystal tumbler and to pour two fingers of Scotch into the glass. "Drink it, now! You look like you're ready to collapse."

Tobin threw back the drink.

"Agent Farrell, Mr. Watkins has arrived. Shall I send him in?" the voice on the intercom sputtered.

"Please, Wesley."

Tobin's color had returned to normal, but the sight of the slovenly executive, slumped in one corner of the sofa was not one to instill confidence into an observer.

"Gentlemen, Jed is a friend of the Bureau. I thought he might be able to add something to this conversation.

"Jed, they were just telling me that Jacques Dumont has frozen all and I do mean all of the university's accounts. They can't get into their bank accounts to even pay the electric bill. On top of that, Jacques claimed he was an FBI agent."

The expression of amusement on Jed Watkin's face was stunning. Father Cheney and Sullivan stared at him in disbelief while Mark Tobin hovered on the brink of hysteria.

"Jacques Dumont is dead. I just learned about this. It happened about 24 hours ago. Apparently the small motor boat he was travelling in over the holidays, exploded a few miles off the southeastern coast of Sicily. All on board were killed."

"Dead? Dead! What are we going to do?" Mark Tobin's reaction to the news of Dumont's death put him into a state of hysteria again.

"Relax, relax, Mark, and you too, Fathers. Your money is safe. First of all, Dumont was not with the FBI. He was at one time working with the Vatican bank to trace criminal activity. Unfortunately, he turned to the dark side when he was tempted once too often. Our security systems have been tracking Dumont's activity since he apparently left you and began trying to transfer money from the University funds. While it may look easy for crooks to do this in the movies, we Feds do have a few cards up our sleeves. We put flags on the accounts. Before you leave here today, I'll give you some codes to punch into your systems and everything will be restored... nothing lost and nothing gained. Is that all right with you? Anything else?"

"Thank You, God!" Austin Cheney stood up to embrace both Joe Farrell and Jed Watkins. Mark Tobin began to weep, hanging his head low and almost collapsing on to the floor in front of him.

"Mark, does that work for you?" Tobin looked up.

"Sure as Hell does! Pour me another Scotch, please... a triple this time!"

***

Jessica sat reluctantly in her wheel chair on her way to the strategic communications center set up in a building that adjoined the hospital proper. Although, the transparent skywalk connecting the two buildings would have allowed her to see something of the campus surrounding the healthcare center where she was housed, security measures mandated a canvas curtain cover the entire area, making her passage seem more like a trip through a giant tent.

"Exactly where is this communications center?" she asked when she and her male nurse finally reached an elevator at the end of a second skyway?

"Not far from here, ma'am." Jessica had noted that no one except the doctors attending her were allowed to speak about anything, even if that something was as insignificant, in her mind as to how far it was to a center where she finally would have the promised Skype call to Alex.

"We're here, Mrs. Rawlins." Her attendant pushed a security code into a panel next to the entrance and added his thumb print on a pad. The immense double doors flung inward as he pushed Jessica forward.

"... and here we are!"

The room was in semi-darkness which she had anticipated. As she moved toward the screen at the front, she noticed three men with their backs turned toward her. One, she recognized as her youthful, red-haired Dr. Simon Williams, who had arranged the Skype call; another man wearing a military uniform she knew as three-star Air Force General, Perry Burckhardt who commanded the intelligence unit at Ramstein Air Base. He had visited with her upon her arrival from Italy; and there was a third man whom she did not recognize until...

"Alex?" she cried out" Alex is that you? Are you really here?" She threw the lap blanket to the floor and rushed into his arms. "You came for me. You came for me," she whispered. I wasn't sure you'd even want me back."

She kissed him again and then again. When she opened her eyes, she felt the tears on her cheeks and noticed that he too was weeping.

"Well, Mrs. Rawlins, I thought this might be better medicine for you than a Skype call. Was I right?" Dr. Williams face knew the answer

"You betcha'," Jessica's voice was a whisper. "You betcha'!" She could not remember when she had felt as happy as she did at that moment.

"We've arranged a private dinner just for the two of you in the small conference room on the other side of this wall," Dr. Williams explained. General Burckhardt will pick you up a little later, Alex, and take you to the Officers' quarters, about a mile from here. There's a nice comfortable room waiting for you there. Your luggage has been sent on ahead. So, if you follow me, please --- you in your wheelchair, please, Mrs. Rawlins, we'll show you to a very fine and private dining room, where you can get reacquainted."

Chapter 58

"I'm sorry, Marcus, but we were advised not to inform you about your stepmother until ... well, until you were back safely with us." Prior Provincial Father Austin Cheney sat back in his large faux leather wing chair, an easy place from which to view Father Dr. Marcus Granville Barker who had aged considerably during his time in the Vatican.

"The good news is that she is alive and unscathed from the fire. The not so good news is that her disease has progressed and her physician acknowledges she probably does not have much longer. You'll see her later today at Bryn Mawr Hospital."

"... and the house? Was it burned to the ground?" Marcus' voice was very low, a near whisper.

"It was heavily damaged. Remarkably, your father's study, which had a safe room construction survived; but the rest of the house has been... almost totally burned. The fire inspector says he believes their tests will indicate arson." Austin Cheney knew the latter would be greatly disturbing to Marcus.

"Then someone was trying to kill Poulette; is that what you're saying?"

"Honestly, Marcus, I think you should talk to the Fire Chief yourself. He can give you direct and correct information. The house has been left almost untouched since the fire. The body of the butler – what was his name? "

"Bertrand Fox, a fine gentleman. I am sorry he perished." Marcus looked up and noted a strange expression in Cheney's eyes.

"Well, eh... there is some inconsistency there, too. He did not die from the fire or smoke inhalation. As I noted the room, which, apparently was fire proofed was left relatively unscathed by the flames. However, and I probably should not even be telling you this, but your Bertrand Fox died from a brain bleed. He'd been hit on the head by something heavy which caused an aneurysm."

"And what about Bernadette Perkins, the housekeeper and cook? Did she also die in the fire?" Marcus appeared honestly shocked by the news of Fox's death.

"There has been no sign of Mrs. Perkins, I'm afraid. The police have an all-points bulletin out for her. She may have been able to escape whatever took place in the house the evening of the blaze or...."

"You think or the police think, she may have been involved in some way with the fire?" Marcus' face had changed. His expression had gone from grief to incredulity.

"Father, these people, Mr. Fox and Mrs. Perkins, they are literally life-long companions and servants of Poulette. She brought them with her from Europe. They were among the first people I met, as a child, when she married my father Cornelius Granville Barker. Mrs. Perkins would never harm a fly and certainly not..."

Marcus did not finish his sentence. Sr. Elisabeth "Beth" Castelli, the Provincial's long time secretary, interrupted with a knock as she opened the door to his office.

"Father?" she motioned to him. Austin Cheney rose slowly. His leg had never properly healed and the cold weather only made his prevalent pain worse.

"Father, I'm sorry to interrupt, but there is someone on the phone from the Vatican. He needs to speak with you immediately." The Prior Provincial closed the office door behind him and walked to a phone on Sister Beth's desk.

"Hello, Father Cheney here," Sister Beth stood at a distance watching the expression on his face. When the Vatican called, it was never good news.

"Yes, of course I understand. He just arrived today. Tomorrow, will be fine. We'll expect you at... 3:00 p.m. Will your ... ah Cardinals... be staying with us at the Monastery? Fine, we'll have two rooms set up for them." Cheney waved at Sister Beth who already had her pad and pen at the ready and was taking notes. "Their names are Cardinal Luca Franconi and Cardinal Josef Galleini? Yes, we'll have someone to meet their flight. I'll put Sister Beth on the phone now and she'll take all the details."

Father Austin Cheney limped back into his office visibly shaken by the call.

"That was one of the secretaries of the Curia calling. Two members of the Curia are flying in tomorrow to meet with us. Yes, Marcus you and me!"

"But why and who are they?" Marcus' expression wasn't hard to read. He was both concerned and frightened.

"One of them is Cardinal Luca Franconi who heads the Apostolic Camera, the central board of finance in the Pope's administrative system and the other Cardinal Josef Galleini, who heads the Administration of the Patrimony of the Holy See. Do you know either one of them?"

Marcus was silent for a noticeable interval.

"Marcus, do you know either or both of them?" Austin Cheney asked again.

"Yes, Father, I know them... both of them."

"Have you any idea why they feel it necessary to come here to speak to us... to both of us?"

"No, not really, but I have a terrible hunch!"

***

"A little more wine?" Alex held the half-filled bottle of Konig's Assmannshauser Hollenberg Spatburgunder Spätlese Trocken in the familiar presentation of a wine steward.

"I'm tempted, but would my doctors allow it?" Jessica realized her healing was incomplete. Her eyes blurred at times when she was tired and her head still ached. A normal reaction according to the physicians who examined her daily.

"They didn't say one way or another, but I imagine you would be the best judge of that," Alex poured the fine German red wine into his empty goblet.

"Alex, what was it you said earlier about Poulette's house burning down? Is she all right?" Jessica poured, the sparkling contents of a bottle of Gerolsteiner mineral water, into her empty glass.

"How much have you heard?"

"Not too much; you do know Marcus was at the Vatican the same time as I was. Neither of us spoke during that time nor really very much since we arrived here. I recognized him, of course, but in my so called working clothes, he probably had no idea who I was; in fact, I hope he didn't. That was the idea; I was working incognito. If he knew who I was it would have blown my 'cover',"

"Well, the fire was suspicious. The house burned very quickly. The fire officials reported it was not an electrical fire. Poulette did get out safely, but her butler died and Mrs. Perkins is still unaccounted for. Poulette was placed in the hospital for observation and I suppose until Marcus gets back to the Main Line, she is safest there. Even after he gets home, one wonders what he'll do about the situation. She cannot live alone; that is pretty apparent. But, it would kill her, I'm sure to be put into some home."

"Wasn't she living with someone? A friend of Marcus from Med school?"

"She was, Dr. Lydia Sindona. Somewhere along the line, Lydia left the house and I read in the Inquirer that her body was found in her car in the parking lot of the White Dog Café in Wayne. And yes, her death is being ruled suspicious."

Jessica squeezed a bit of lemon from the fresh fruit that lay on a small plate near the sparkling water.

Alex could see that Jessica's energy was fading. "I think we should get you back to your room," Alex motioned Jessica to keep her seat, while he went after the wheel chair parked in one corner of the room.

"You are staying, aren't you? I mean, you're not going back without me, are you? " Her eyes were pleading.

"You know I'll be here as long as you are. We'll go home together. I 'll be with you as long as it takes to make that journey."

***

"Yes, we've met," Cardinal Luca Franconi, head of the Apostolic Camera, the central board of finance in the Pope's administrative system and Cardinal Josef Galleini, chair of the Administration of the Patrimony of the Holy See joined Father Marcus Granville Barker and Fathers Sean O'Reilly and Austin Cheney at a large conference table in the room adjoining Cheney's office.

"Can I offer you gentlemen anything? We have soft drinks, mineral water..." Cheney motioned to a tray which had been set up on a side table by Sister Beth who also had arranged a tray of pastries prepared by the Monastery's chef.

Luca Franconi picked up a bottle of Ferrarelle water and poured it into a glass next to the tray.

"It was very kind of you all to receive us on such short notice and I believe you understand the importance of why we are here." Josef Galleini wasted no time in starting the conversation. He waved his hand at Franconi indicating he wanted neither the water nor the pastries.

"We will be celebrating a Requiem Mass for Pope Leo in a few days and after an appropriate period of official mourning, the Curia will assemble to discuss who will be the next Pontiff."

Father Sean O'Reilly had plucked a cream puff from the tray before he sat down and found this a convenient moment to bite into the creamy delight. Galleini paused to stare at O'Reilly before going on.

"After that, of course, the College of Cardinals will assemble for discernment and eventually, the new Pontiff will be voted upon. In addition to naming a new pontiff, we have learned that there already is discussion about initiating proceedings to canonize Leo. Father Marcus and Father Sean, I am certain you realize what a challenge to the church this could present if...."

"If what?" Austin Cheney sat back in his chair, his expression, one of curiosity and fear. "Exactly what are we talking about here and why should Father Sean and Father Marcus be involved with something that on the surface has nothing at all to do with them nor with me?"

"Let me be honest with you, Father Cheney. You are here because your two Edmundite priests are involved in something.... incidents that are so staggering in some ways and so... incredible in others, that they must be discussed privately and considered highly confidential. Even in your role as Prior Provincial, I am under no obligation to invite you to listen to our interrogation of your two priests. But, I have chosen to do so if...if, you swear to be silent. There will be no questions from you; you are to take nothing from the exchanges in this room, out of this room or talk about the subject matter with anyone. If you do, it could be very dangerous for you. Do you understand?"

Austin Cheney was livid. The veins in his temples protruded as neither Marcus nor Sean had seen them before. "That sounds like a threat, your Eminence!" Cheney said with mock dread.

"You can consider it what you will; I guarantee you will not live to see another day if you do not abide by these rules." Galleini kept eye contact with the Prior Provincial. Austin Cheney sat back in his chair and took a deep breath which sounded to Marcus more like a sigh of resignation.

"Father Marcus, you are aware that we have seen the markings on the Pontiff's body. Could you tell us about them? Remember we have photographs taken while you were present."

Marcus sat upright, moving closer to the table. "Well, I witnessed them for the first time just after I arrived on site in the Vatican apartment. Pope Leo had awakened from an afternoon nap and was in terrible pain. Both Father Sean, Father Malcolm and I were present when I examined the Pontiff's back."

"What did you find?"

"I found Aramaic lettering which translated would read Simon bar Jonah, the original inscription on the tomb of St. Peter in the Scavi. It was bursting through the skin on his back and beginning to bleed."

"You are certain it was blood?"

"Yes, Eminence, I have a medical degree I know blood when I see it."

Sean O'Reilly winced at his friend's arrogance.

".. And how do you know that this was first of all Aramaic and secondly that it was inscribed on the tomb of Peter?"

"Many years ago, when I was studying at the North American College I worked as an intern on the Scavi dig. It was during those years that I came into contact with the man who one day would be Pope Leo. He was a graduate student at the Pontifical Gregorian University and was involved in the excavation of the Necropolis and the eventual discovery of St. Peter's tomb."

Cardinal Luca Franconi who had been silent until this moment broke into the conversation. "Is it because of these markings that Father Malcolm called you to the Pontiff's bedside?"

Marcus was silent for several seconds, his mind racing. "There is medical privilege you know. As a medical doctor I do not have to reveal information about my patient or his condition."

"No, you are quite right, you do not; but may I remind you that the patient is dead, quite dead. He held some very dark secrets that we must uncover and very soon. I ask you as a priest and as a physician to understand that we are not trying to destroy the reputation or the memory of Pope Leo; in fact, quite to the contrary. But, we must and I emphasize must find out the truth." Franconi did not look away, but kept his gaze on Marcus."

"Pope Leo revealed to me that he was having dreams, very violent and vivid dreams that haunted his sleep. In these dreams he was a young man who was being chased. His attackers were advancing on him. He stumbled at one point and had trouble getting up again. He stumbled again and...." Marcus paused and looked down at the table.

"...and what, Father Marcus?" Franconi asked, his voice probing.

"He... he eventually was caught and ... and hanged from a bridge while his tormentors ..." Marcus could not finish the sentence.

The room's silence was broken by a knock at the door. Austin Cheney rose to discover why his 'Do Not Disturb' order to Sister Beth was being ignored.

"Please tell Father Marcus that Bryn Mawr Hospital is on the line. His stepmother has gone into a semi-coma. She is calling for him. They are suggesting he come immediately and bring with him his sick kit to administer the Last Rites."

Father Marcus Granville Barker had heard everything; he rose from the table without a word. A deluge of guilt overwhelmed him. He had planned to visit Poulette as soon as he could after last evening's arrival, but this sudden visit with these Cardinals had intruded on that plan and now... now, he may never get to tell her how much she had meant to him. Tears welled up in his eyes as he rose and headed toward the door.

"Father, we're not finished by a long shot. We'll continue this discussion later today" Galleini called after him.

Marcus did not look back. The woman who had been the only maternal figure in his memory as small child was dying and he may not be able to let her know how he felt about her. She had shaped his life, encouraged him, and loved him like her own blood.

"I'm coming with you, Marcus" Sean O'Reilly was gathering up his coat as Marcus put his on in Austin Cheney's outer office.

"Marcus, you go to Poulette. I'll get everything you need to administer the Sacraments and meet you there. Go, just go!"

Marcus nodded "Thank you, Sean."

***

Twenty minutes later, Father Marcus Granville Barker was standing beside Poulette who lay quietly in a private room on the 3rd floor of Bryn Mawr Hospital; her head was raised slightly, her eyes closed. She appeared to be sleeping, but Marcus knew better. She may already have lapsed into an irreversible coma and he might never be able to tell her how important she was to him, to his father ... to everyone.

Chapter 59

"Do you feel well enough to go through this debriefing, Mrs. Rawlins?" Jessica sat alone in front of a giant screen in a special CIA situation room at Ramstein Air Base less than a mile from her hospital at Landstuhl Medical Center. Jed Watkins, CIA chief John Brennan and several members of the President's Intelligence Advisory Board (PIAB) looked at her from a conference room in Langley.

"Yes, I'll be fine," Jessica voice was markedly resilient, which was noted by the two physicians sitting in on the interview.

"Should you begin to sense fatigue, physically or mentally, during our discussion and you wish to rest or have a drink of water, even stop the session, let us know and we will take a time out. Is that understood?"

"Yes, perfectly." Jessica reached for a bottle of mineral water on the table beside her and poured it into a plastic glass.

"I want to take you back to the time you spent in ... what was the name of the village?"

"Santa Maria di Polsi in Calabria," Jessica voice was softer now.

"Why were you given the assignment to go there and what did you understand that assignment to be?"

"I speak a very special Calabrian dialect fluently which the Company thought might be of value on this assignment. On a special date, each year, N'drangheta chiefs from all over the world meet in a small Calabrian mountain village to initiate new members and give an accounting of their 'business' during the previous year. They also present to the chief a purse filled with gold or money. If there is less money in the purse than was promised the previous year, there is a penance; but, if there is more in the purse than was previously promised, a reward would be given." Jessica reached for the glass of water again.

"And who are the N'drangheta?"

""They are the most powerful criminal organization in the world. They exist in all parts of the world, but their corporate meeting takes place annually in Santa Maria di Polsi."

"Were you present during any of these meetings, Agent Rawlins?"

"Yes, I was."

"... and how is it that if you were there, and no one spotted or identified you?"

"I was working as a char woman and introduced as a relative of one of the villagers, a widow from another nearby town. I scrubbed floors and did other scullery work and lived with a host family on a farm just outside the village."

"Tell us, from the beginning, what you did in Polsi and what and who you saw. If you grow tired, again, just signal me and we will stop and resume later. Is that all right with you?"

"Yes," Jessica answered, her story flowing as freely as she remembered experiencing it. She described her host family in Polsi as Giovanna and Pier Luigi Garcea and their dog Cosimo; how she observed members of N'drangheta's international, meeting in an abandoned monastery the night before the official meeting began. The shocking blood ritual initiation of young Pier Luigi into the N'drangheta crime family in the city square, before the statue of Our Lady of Polsi. The accidental encounter in the kitchen of the abandoned monastery and later at the farewell luncheon in a village eatery with Roberto Lombroso, N'drangheta's chief of chiefs. Finally, the parade of international and high level Vatican clergy who attended and participated in the N'drangheta conference.

At the end of the two hour debriefing, Jessica found her voice almost inaudible and her throat parched and scratchy.

"I think we all have had enough for today, Agent Rawlins. We'll resume tomorrow. Thank you!"

Jessica sat alone in front of the screen for what seemed like an eternity. There was so much more to tell; the worst was yet to come. How could she go through a virtual reliving of the deaths of the Garcea family, Pope Leo and Cardinal Torricelli? She could still see the soft eyes and gentle face of Leo as she held him, dying in her lap, his lower body crushed by the wall of stone that had fallen on him. He had begged her to take the precious package he carried and rebury it at the site from which the bones of St. Peter had been taken. But she could not do that now, because she no longer had them. Who had taken them? She felt a commitment to bring them back to their intended burial ground?"

She wheeled herself through the automatic doors of the situation room and into the corridor near an exit to an outside parking lot.

"Oh, Mrs. Rawlins, there you are. Your transportation is here to take you back to the hospital."

Jessica looked up, startled at who she saw. Dressed in the green scrubs of a nurse from the Landstuhl Medical Center was Senora Maria Scopoletti, supervisor of the Vatican's Memores Dominil. There could be no doubt any longer, she most definitely had ties to the Calabrian N'drangheta.

Chapter 60

"Marcus? Marcus?" Poulette opened her eyes scarcely believing what she was seeing. The Rev. Doctor Marcus Granville Barker, O.S. E. (Order of St. Edmund) quite obviously sleeping while sitting in a chair next to her bed in Bryn Mawr Hospital.

"My God, Poulette you're awake!" Marcus jumped to his feet and stared into Poulette eyes.

"You've come back, my dear boy."

"Poulette, you've come back. We did not think... I mean, I was almost certain..."

"...that I was dead or dying? Well, they're right, I am, but I'm not there, yet. I had to see you. I am so very glad you came back." Tears welled up in the elderly woman's steely blue eyes. Squeezing Marcus' hand even harder she tried to sit up, but could not muster the strength.

"You must listen to me. They have burned down the house, looking for it. It might have been destroyed in the blaze, but there is a chance it was not and you must find it, Marcus; it is so very, very important." Her eyes were wide with urgency as she stared into his.

"What is it that you think, they want?" he whispered not understanding exactly what she was talking about."

"It's the micro-fiche. It has been stored for many years in the lipsticks, my beautiful jeweled lipsticks. But Mr. Fox took them. He found them and was pulling the microfiche from the tubes. When I saw what he was doing I...."

"Ahhh, Mrs. Granville Barker, you are awake. How nice it is to see you with your eyes open." A male nurse pushed through the door with a mobile blood pressure tester, electronic thermometer and an electronic tablet on which to register her readings.

"You must be her son," he said smiling at Marcus who relinquished his place allowing the nurse to minister to her.

"She had us quite concerned, you know. She inhaled quite a lot of smoke before the fire department discovered her and were able to administer oxygen," Marcus watched as he squeezed the blood pressure ball and noted her reading.

"Are you hungry? I can offer you some Jello, chicken broth, crackers, cranberry juice or all of the above."

"Oh, I don't know," she answered honestly not able to make a decision.

"Then, I will order the whole lot for you." He nodded as he took her pulse followed by a temperature reading, using a forehead thermometer.

"Good," he concluded as he made notes on the tablet. "You will have your tray in about a half hour!" Smiling again, he left the room.

"Poulette, Mr. Fox was your friend. I thought he was mine, as well, looking after you all of these years. You told me yourself that you brought him from Switzerland because you could trust him," Marcus voice was low as he resumed his position in the chair and pulled it closer to the bed so that he could speak in a very low voice.

"I believed that to be the case, Marcus, but... he fooled me. I discovered him in Cornelius' office. He had unlocked your father's secret drawer in his desk. It was still open. He had seated himself at a little table, across from the desk, and was examining the gems encrusted on the lipstick covers with a jeweler's glass. Then I saw what he had on the table. He had removed all of the lipsticks from their tubes. I knew at that moment exactly what he was doing. I grabbed the desk lamp and I struck him on his head with it as hard as I could. He just fell over, collapsed on his back; his eyes were wide open. I knew immediately that he was dead. But, you can see, I was defending myself; he was going to kill me. Instinctively, I picked up the lamp to put it back on the desk and that was when I spotted the micro fiche on the floor. I didn't know what to do at that moment; I was in a panic so I put it back on the little table with the jeweled covers beside it. Marcus, you must go immediately to find the other cases and the microfiche. They... they... hold all the secrets that I promised Lucas I would protect."

"Poulette, I... I have not been to the house yet. I just arrived. I wanted to see you first, but...I don't know if I'll even be allowed to go inside. I understand it has been burned to the ground. There may be nothing left but a shell."

"Marcus, Marcus you must do this for me. I cannot tell you how important it is. This micro fiche, it...it has a list of names that Lucas had compiled as insurance. It included the names of... his colleagues, all of them."

"What are you talking about, Poulette? I thought my father gave you those lipstick cases? You always told me they were important to you because he would bring them back from his business trips. They were really from Lucas? While you were still married to my father? When he was alive?"

"I loved your father very much, Marcus. He knew it and I knew it. I had known Lucas before, in Switzerland. When he suddenly turned up on the Main Line, in Wayne, one day, well I had no intention...."

Marcus said nothing. His mind was racing. He was feeling the betrayal for his father who had been dead many years, as had Lucas.

"Poulette, what kind of secrets are in those lipstick cases that could make them so important?" Marcus' voice had turned from loving to questioning. "If I am going to risk my life by going into a burned-out building that may collapse on me, I think I ought to know why I am doing it." He looked intently at Poulette, whose demeanor was now one of fear,

"They contain the names of individuals in an international cartel, a criminal cartel. There are bank account numbers; and there are reports of ...." "Of what, Poulette?" Marcus' voice was now demanding. "...of, of individuals assassinated and by whom. Lucas called the list his insurance policy. He said that either he or someone close to him might come to retrieve it from me one day. Of course, that day never came.... until now. Please Marcus, you must get them back for me!"

***

Alex struck quickly. First kicking the medic in the kidneys as she attempted to push Jessica's wheelchair into the waiting van and then by applying pressure to her carotid sinus as she attempted to attack him. In the next instant she lay at his feet and Jessica was standing beside him.

"Do you know her?" he grabbed the unconscious woman by the scruff of her neck and pulled the cell phone from his pocket.

"Security, I need some help out here," he screamed into the phone. Instantly, two military police darted from the building to take charge of the still unconscious woman.

"Are you all right?" one of the guards asked Jessica who had seated herself again the wheelchair.

"Alex, I know her. Her name is ..." Jessica stopped in mid-sentence. "I think I had better talk to Jed again. Would you take me back into the building to the Sit. room?"

"Mrs. Rawlins wishes to return to the Situation Room; could you alert the appropriate military staff member? This is very important."

"Yes, sir, right away."

Minutes later, Jessica found herself in front of the same screen she had left only forty minutes earlier. Her security guard had left the room, as was protocol, with the request that she notify him as she had earlier when she was ready to leave the room by pressing the alert button on the table.

"Jed, I'm telling you, Maria Scopoletti is alive and here in Germany. Alex just knocked her out as she was trying to kidnap me."

"Jessica, don't get excited. We'll do some investigating. immediately and find out what is going on. The remains of the suicide bomber in the crypt below the High Altar at St. Peter's were pretty much scorched flesh, unrecognizable. We are waiting for the results from the DNA tests which would give us some possible clues as to who set off the bomb; but those tests take time and the results have not come back yet. Whoever she was, our suicide bomber was dressed to look like Maria. She even wore the cross of the Memores Domini around her neck. We know that the bomber used a Dead Man's switch which makes it ever more likely that it was the cross itself. If she had her hand clasped around the cross, when she released it, the explosives would have gone off. "

"Jed, if Alex had not come along, looking for me, I'd have been carted off somewhere by Maria. I'm not feeling very confident when something like this can occur at a U.S. Airforce Base as supposedly secure as Ramstein."

"Well, Jess, now that we have her in custody, perhaps we can get more information from her. The first thing will be to find out who she had doing her handiwork and the second how, she managed to get out of Rome, into Germany and on to our ultra-secure Air Force base without anyone discovering her; in addition, what happened to the medic assigned to pick you up? He or she obviously has been incapacitated or killed, that I can assure you."

"I think that when it comes to the poor medic," Jessica's voice was soft. "...Maria and her thugs play for keeps. With her in charge, I certainly was not supposed to survive...."

Jessica was not able to complete her response. The sound of the first explosion was deafening. The situation room, a fortified bomb shelter, made of high density steel, shuddered as another two explosions, one after the other, threatened to cut off transmission between Jed and his agent.

"What happened, Jess?" Jed's words were calm and neutral, but expression on his face was as fearful as what she imagined her own to be.

"I don't know, Jed. I think we can assume, Ramstein's supposedly secure Global security intelligence section has been infiltrated. I have to sign off now and try to find Alex. This room is safe from almost every kind of explosive device; but outside the door. I'm not certain what I'll find. I'll get back to you when I can."

The security button used to summons an escort from the Situation room failed, which was no surprise. Jessica used the "iris" ID next to the door to slide it back and open. It had automatically locked when the first explosion occurred.

Outside the situation room, the lobby was dark and littered with a jumble of concrete. The exit to the outside was completely blocked by large chunks of building material; and there was no sign of Alex. Jessica called to him. As she stepped further away from the situation room, a cloud of dust, an after-shock from the explosion engulfed her body causing her to cough violently.

"Jess? Jess? Can you hear me? I'm...I'm over here."

"Keep talking, Alex. I hear you, but I can't see you yet."

"I'm over here... keep walking."

"It's OK, Alex... I think I'm right above you and can get you out of there!" Jessica picked her way through a small pile of debris, far less than what she had walked through outside the situation room.

"Alex, keep talking and if you can move an arm or leg... yes, that's it. I see exactly where you are, now."

In the near darkness, she lifted a heavy metallic gilt picture frame with the damaged canvas of an oil painting that had fallen from the wall above and now lay on top of Alex. The canvas, like a tented blanket, had, in all likely hood, saved his life.

"Are you all right? Anything broken?" Jessica held out her hand, which Alex grabbed to maneuver his way out from under the massive painting."

"I'm alive," he said looking around. "... and I can't quite believe it. I was certain I would die when I was thrown to the ground and something landed on top of me. "

"That something was a painting of a saint!" Jessica mumbled as she noticed the signature on the canvas.

'What are you talking about?' Alex used his hand to dust off his heavily coated clothing. "You were quite literally saved by a painting of St. John of Nepomuk. Look here, it's on this little brass plate. St. John of Nepomuk, by Ignaz Stern. He is not only the patron saint of this part of Germany, but also the patron saint of intelligence officers. He was martyred in about 1393 when he refused to reveal the secrets of the confessional to the King. In fact, he told the King to go spin a flax when he, a priest was asked to reveal the Queen's confession. Her husband suspected her of infidelity. Nepomuk said no way and so the King killed him. Now, he has saved you."

"My, you certainly know a lot about saints these days, Missy." It was the first time Alex had smiled since he and Jessica had dined the previous evening. Jessica looked at the damaged painting. She could see quite clearly through the debris, the extraordinary eyes of the martyred patron saint. He indeed had made contact with Alex to save him and for that she was very thankful.

***

"These visions, Father O'Reilly, did Leo really believe he was in communication with St. Peter?" Sean O'Reilly took a sip from the water bottle in front of him, disregarding the glass that sat beside it.

"I'd have to say, yes. Marcus may have another opinion; but in my mind, it was all very real to him. He talked about this Divine Instant numerous times. How he must bring it to the attention of his brother Cardinals." Father Sean O'Reilly slipped in a glance at his watch as he replaced the bottle of Whole Foods brand water. It was nearing 7:00 p.m. and pangs of hunger were indeed being felt

"You've mentioned this before as has Marcus," Cardinal Luca Franconi, head of the Apostolic Camera, the central board of finance in the Vatican looked down at a small pad in front of him, scanning his notes.

"This Divine Instant meant exactly, what?" the Cardinal looked up.

"Well, Eminence, as I said before and as Marcus explained it is really quite simple. As St. John reports in Revelation, "In the Beginning was The Word. That was the Divine Instant when everything was created; absolutely everything. Every age was created; every human, every animal, every planet, every Universe. What we see is not a 'rolling out' of history but history as it was created in that Divine Instant. When our astronomers look back into the creation, they can see exactly what St. Peter was revealing to him. We were and are in that "instant". What we believe is the living out of our lives is indeed what is, was and ever shall be, according to St. Peter as told through Leo."

"Frankly, it sounds like Presbyterian-Calvinistic philosophy to me, what think you, Joe?" Franconi was addressing Cardinal Josef Galleini, chair of the Administration of the Patrimony of the Holy See. Galleini had been resting his eyes for the last several seconds and the sound of his name jolted him from his near somnambulism.

"Well, not really; although, it probably comes close. I think most people would ask how creating people with the intention of damning them could be the mark of a loving God?"

"No, no, I am not explaining it correctly, if that is what you are thinking. It is this: In that single second of creation, everything was there instantly, all of history... everything was created and the decisions which we believe we are making now were actually in that instant. We only perceive what occurred in that Instant it to be now. The fact is, that we already have played everything out in that instant of creation and what we are experiencing now IS in that instant. When we finally die in this second, we will come to see and understand it more clearly. Our free will is and always has been a part of who we are as intended by our Creator. In God's mind, he gave it to us and saw in that Instant how we would use it. It definitely is not ... what I think you believe... streaming consciousness or a river of time? It is and was and always has been and will be the Divine Instant."

Father Sean O'Reilly found himself exhausted after that explanation and not seeing the kind of understanding and response he had hoped to elicit.

"Well, yes, all right, all that is very interesting, why would St. Peter give this information to Pope Leo? Did Leo consider himself to be a saint, as well: Did he ever consider that these messages could be coming from Satan and not St. Peter?"

"I... I think... he believed them to be real; his past, the things he had done. The nightmares, all of them were a part of this. He believed for some time that because of his past that he was doomed to Hell. He thought that he did not deserve God's love ... and that was why St. Peter's message to him became an obsession. St. Peter was saying to him 'I see you as saved because you are repenting now'. When the understanding of both St. Peter and Leo as he eventually understood it, was that God saw this redemption in that Divine Instant but it was only recognized by Leo after he had repented for his ... his ... past."

The last few words of Father Sean O'Reilly's explanation were close to a whisper. He thought after he had said them that perhaps he had revealed too much. It was Marcus who was the psychiatrist. He was just along for the ride. However, having Marcus occupied with Poulette, he had been stuck with these two interrogators.

Father Austin Cheney sat to one side of the table, not participating but listening carefully to everything said by O'Reilly and the Cardinals.

"Gentlemen, it is nearly 7:30 p.m. The Refectory formally closes in half an hour. If we could adjourn for now and get something to eat, I think it would help all of us." He attempted a smile, but it was forced. The two visitors checked their watches.

"Yes, yes forgive us. We certainly should have something to eat. That was a kind suggestion." Luca Franconi rose, closing the small notebook with the attached pen and placing it into the pocket of his black wool cassock.

Austin Cheney continued in his role as host. "We have an exceptionally fine chef who has prepared cacio e pepe, which for you and me, Father Sean, can be translated as homemade pasta tossed with finely grated Pecorino Romano cheese, butter, heavy cream and coarsely ground black pepper. That is just to begin with..." Father Austin Cheney's smile and lively recounting of the dinner menu could not hide his fear that Fathers Marcus Granville Barker and Sean O'Reilly had gone too far in describing the thoughts and admissions of the late Pope Leo XIV. It had not gone unnoticed by either Father Cheney or the two cardinals that both priests had alluded to something very dark in Pope Leo's past. Whatever 'that' was would have to come out, but should it and what would be the effect, not only on these Cardinals, but on the church as a whole? It was for this reason, that Austin Cheney had sent Father Sean ahead to order drinks for all, wine for the dinner table and placement of that table as far away from stray residents or staff as possible, in the nearly empty monastery. Having almost everyone away for the holidays had indeed become a blessing.

Chapter 61

"Sorry, Father, you can't get in." Marcus Granville Barker had been shaking the chain and lock that kept the gates to Edencroft closed, but they stayed steadfastly in place.

"My name is Joe Farrell," he opened his wallet to show the priest his FBI identification badge. "We called the hospital and when we heard you had left, I suspected you might come here."

Marcus turned to acknowledge the director. "Yes, my stepmother wanted to see if there was anything left of my father's office. It was a safe room and supposedly fire resistant if not fireproof; but from what I can see, everything is pretty much gone... quite literally, burned to the ground."

"Well, not quite everything. Your father's study was indeed fireproof. We have recovered some things, some very interesting things that we would like to talk to you about. Could you come with me, right now?"

"Where to?" Marcus was curious about what had been found and where this FBI Bureau chief might be taking him.

"We're going to our regional office, which is on the campus of St. Edmund's University. I think you'll find it quite convenient to get back to your quarters at the Monastery after our talk. Will you come now?"

"Yes, yes, of course, I'll follow you. My car is right there at the curb. One question, my mother's housekeeper, Bernadette Perkins, was she found in the fire?"

"Let's talk about it at my office. We're in the old Drummond mansion; you know where that is don't you?"

"Yes, yes of course. I'll follow you." Marcus slid into the driver's seat. He looked back one more time to see what he was certain was smoke still rising from the long dead embers. The scene was ghostly, made more so by a brisk wind and the increasingly heavy snow that had begun to fall. As he drove away from Edencroft, the once grand manor house that had been his childhood home, he stepped on the accelerator, following closely behind Joe Farrell. At the last marker on the property, he felt a deep sadness. His father was dead for many years. His stepmother would probably not live much beyond the winter and now, the house he had called home for so many years was totally destroyed. What, he thought, from all of that destruction, could the FBI's Joe Farrell have possibly recovered?

Fewer than ten minutes later, the two were sitting on the sofa in Farrell's office and the Regional Director was pouring Marcus a large glass of Glenmorangie Single Malt Scotch, no ice, no water.

As the Director settled into a leather chair not far from Marcus' place on the sofa, the intercom interrupted.

"Sorry sir, it's Jed Watkins on the secure phone. Will you take it or do you want to call him back?"

"I'll take it out there," Farrell answered.

When Farrell had closed the door securely behind him, he picked up the secure phone. "He's here now, Jed. Just arrived, in fact. Of course, I understand. Come on over. Where are you now? Perfect, we'll see you in five." Farrell hung up the receiver. It was going to be a very long night.

***

"Well, I think that is about it, Mrs. Rawlins. We'll have you and your husband out of here today and on a plane back to the States." Jessica almost leapt from the exam table where she now had been given a clean bill of health, following the explosion.

"... and what about Alex?" Her voice was hesitant. He seemed to her to have come through this latest disaster with only a few scratches and bruises, but an MRI had shown that he had suffered a mild concussion and often plane travel would not be permitted for someone with a head injury.

"All things considered, I think he will be able to go with you. His concussion was mild. There were no signs of a bleed, which would have mandated he stay on with us for a while. All in all, the two of you should thank your lucky stars. You both could have been killed; literally buried under tons of concrete."

Jessica took a deep breath. She could still taste the dust from the explosion. It was miraculous that Alex had been saved by the painting of a saint, the immense canvas of which literally fell on top of him. It had sheltered his body from debris that might have buried him.

"Are we travelling commercial or...?" Her voice was hopeful.

"You'll be flying on a government transport. We can't risk letting you on a commercial flight under the circumstances." His expression conveyed a security concern which she knew was a part of the decision to send her home.

"I have to ask this, "Jessica's voice was almost a whisper. "Is it assumed that my being here was the reason that the ... the explosion occurred? Did I cause it?"

"I don't think we have had enough time to analyze what actually happened and be able to make such an assumption; that will take considerable time. As for why you are flying on a government transport and not commercially, let's just say it is largely based upon economics. We have to send a group of military from Ramstein Air Base back to New York and having them land in Philadelphia is not only cheaper for Uncle Sam, but less conspicuous as well."

Jessica was silent. There was always a reason, or two or three, for the decisions that were made on her behalf by Uncle Sam. She was only glad that both she and Alex would be returning together. It was time to get back home.

"Now, Mrs. Rawlins, if you are dressed, I personally will escort you to our in-house Situation Room. It's only one story up in this medical facility. You are scheduled to attend a meeting there in about ten minutes and my orders are to get you there on time."

Lt. Col. Alvin Sousa, M.D., the facilities' medical director had been attending to her personally. She had paid no attention to his name tag until now; but when he turned to sign his name electronically on the tablet where he was reporting her condition, she became cognizant of who he was.

"I appreciate the care and attention you have given me while I have been here. I know I can speak for Alex as well. Thank you!"

"We care for our own. Now, if you're ready, let's go." He opened the door for her.

"It would be better if you were in the wheelchair, Mrs. Rawlins. You may be going home but as long as you are meandering through our halls, we are responsible for your good health. Translate that to mean: you have to be in the chair with someone pushing you until you leave here. Is that understood?" Jessica nodded meekly. For some reason, she took this order to mean she wasn't as well as she had rationalized. "Administrative rules, should you fall or slip...."

A short elevator ride to the third floor of the medical building and Jessica found herself again in front of another secure conference room. "Now, if you'll stand up, Mrs. Rawlins and just put your eye...."

"Yes, I know, I know the drill." She did not allow Sousa to finish his sentence. The door slid open and she was wheeled inside.

"I'll leave you here. Just ring when you're ready to leave and someone will come to escort you back. This time, we'll show you a photo of specifically who that escort will be. No surprises, I guarantee." Jessica smiled as Sousa left her. She was again in front of a large screen with no one else in sight. Moments later, Jed Watkins and Joe Farrell appeared on the big screen. With them a surprise figure, Father Dr. Marcus Granville Barker.

***

"Your husband's ability to speak clearly has improved immensely, Mrs. Rawlins. He seems to be more engaged than he was when we started and ...." Douglas Harrison, Philip Rawlins most recent speech therapist stepped outside into the hallway to give a final message to Caroline. "... He still insists someone painted him with lipstick on the night of his accident. I'm not certain whether this is an aberration or..."

Caroline walked further down the corridor to avoid any chance of Philip hearing their conversation. "I'm not certain either, Douglas. He seems bent on going to the house and I..."

"Well, Mrs. Rawlins, there is no house; you do know that, don't you?" Harrison interrupted. "It burned down. I think it was on Christmas Eve. The butler was found dead and the housekeeper is still missing. It was in all the newspapers and on TV news. The fire may have been arson." Harrison did not go further in his quick description of the Edencroft disaster. He could see that Caroline Rawlins was terribly disturbed by the news. "No, I, I had not heard; I've not been paying attention to the news lately." She looked toward Philip's room. "Well, Mrs. Rawlins, I'll be off. My thought is that we can begin to adjust your husband's schedule so that I do not have to be here every day. Perhaps, three times a week? How would that suit you?"

"I believe the answer is how would that suit my husband's needs going forward? If you believe that he has made enough progress, then, of course. I just want to get him back to normal, again."

"Then, your assignment, Mrs. Rawlins will be to engage him in conversation as much as possible. Get him to open up about the night of the accident. I think he will feel relieved to get whatever he is trying to say out into the open."

"I'll do that Mr. Harrison. When will we see you again?" Douglas Harrison opened his I-phone. I have 4 p.m. on Friday open. How would that suit your schedule?"

"Sounds fine to me. We'll see you then."

"Talk to him... as much as you can. Get him to respond." Douglas Harrison smiled as he wrapped the Burberry cashmere muffler around his neck and left by way of the front door. Caroline stood staring after him for several seconds before she closed it. A fire had destroyed Edencroft and she had not even been aware of it. What was happening to her, not to be engaged in what must have been a major news event on the Main Line? Philip had been trying to tell her that he wanted to prevent a disaster at that house; somehow he sensed something malevolent was about to occur. Although he had pleaded with Alex to go to Edencroft, neither he nor she had bothered to call the police nor fire station to request that someone do a safety check on Poulette and her staff. Harrison had made no mention of Poulette. Did she survive the flames? Caroline suddenly felt nauseated. The burden of blame lay heavily on her.

She climbed the staircase to the third floor. It was dark and Philip's room was silent. "Are you awake?" Caroline called from the doorway.

"Yes," he answered.

"Do you feel like talking?" She slowly entered the room.

"Yes," he answered again in an almost automaton response.

"Phillip, about Edencroft and the night of your accident. Can you remember enough to tell me about it?" She looked at the man in the bed. He had made tremendous progress, but he still seemed so fragile.

"Perhaps, darling you can tell me some of what you remember? About the lipstick. How did you get that lipstick on your face?"

"Bernadette Perkins called me, asking that I come over immediately. Poulette, she said, was not making any sense and Bertrand Fox was nowhere to be found. I told her to call 911 but she said, No, Ms. Poulette wouldn't like that. I insisted on the call to 911, but told her I would come right over to persuade Poulette to go to the Bryn Mawr Hospital Emergency. When I arrived, Poulette and Mrs. Perkins were already gone, but I came upon Bertrand Fox rummaging around in the room that had once been her late husband's office. Drawers to file cabinets were open; the door of a wall safe had been smashed in an attempt to open it. The room looked as if it was being or had recently been burglarized. Everything was amiss and then I spotted Mr. Fox; he was on his knees in back of the antique desk that had belonged to Cornelius Granville Barker, obviously stealing these beautiful jeweled lipstick cases from jewelry boxes that belonged to Poulette. He had opened up several pouches and was ... I don't know, examining or doing something to them. He had some kind of pick and a jeweler's lens in his eye. He saw me as I was coming out of the elevator. I guess I was shocked to see him coming after me with this rage on his face and what looked like a pick in his hand. He chased me down the staircase; I tripped on the last step but not before he landed on me, punching me with his fist and smearing my face with one of the lipstick tubes. I'm not sure why he did that, but I ran out of the house and got into the car and ...."

"... and what Philip?"

"He called me Lucas, over and over and said, 'Lucas, you son of a bitch, I'll get you for this. I'll kill you. You set me up!"

"Caroline, Fox is going to kill Poulette. I know that is what he intends to do. We have to warn her."

Philip fell back on his pillow, breathless. He was gasping for breath; emotionally exhausted, by the realization of what he had seen and now understood. Caroline stood immobile not certain whether to believe her husband or add it to the list of illusions he had suffered in the weeks after his accident. Bertrand Fox had been Poulette's most ardent butler and caretaker.

"I am telling you, Fox will kill her, Caroline. We have to help her. She is in terrible danger."

Caroline remained silent. She stroked her husband's forehead. He would sleep now. He finally was able to reassemble his thoughts and memories enough to tell her what he believed had happened the terrible night of the accident. But how much of what he said could she believe? How much was the product of a damaged mind? She straightened the blanket and sheet that covered him. It must have been an exhausting day for him, with his speech therapy session and now this so called story of Bertrand Fox and the jeweled lipstick cases. Caroline smiled to herself. It was a fanciful tale but as Harrison said, he had made great progress in the last few days. Adding this colorful tale could be nothing but good news to his healthcare team. He was finally getting back to normal. When he felt better, she could adjust his fanciful version of the accident with the truth.

She made her way through the house to the kitchen, where she opened the double door refrigerator to reach for a bottle of open wine from the door. Six wine goblets lay on the open shelf next to the fridge. She pulled the cork from the half-filled bottle and poured herself a large drink. It was a Vouvray...a gentle, fragrant and soothing wine. "No," she said to herself, "not Bertrand Fox. Philip has to be mixed up. He loves Poulette. Never Mr. Fox."

Was Poulette still alive? Had Edencroft really been completely destroyed in the blaze? Was it arson?

She still had a few days without staff, who were on their holiday break. She would use this time to probe more deeply into Philip's memory of that afternoon.

Chapter 62

"Then you know Agent Rawlins, Father Marcus?" Jed Watkins watched the expression of the priest whose eyes were bloodshot and whose face was drawn from fatigue.

"Know is a difficult and complicated way to describe our relationship. Jessica married into one of the oldest and best regarded Main Line families. I play squash and handball and sometime court tennis at the Main Line Cricket Club with Philip Rawlins, her cousin-in- law. That said, I have to admit when she showed up at the Vatican, as a member of the Memores Domini, I did not recognize her as anyone other than someone to scrub the floors and empty the waste bins." Father Marcus Granville Barker held up his glass for a refill. It was going to be a long night, better be relaxed enough to get through it.

"So, when your stepmother hired Bertrand Fox and Bernadette Perkins, you..."

"Hey, stop there, Mr. Farrell; she brought these servants with her into the marriage to my father. They were with her in Switzerland. From what I have always been told, they were part of the entourage she had when she was married previously." Marcus took a long swig of the Scotch from his recently refilled glass.

"... and she was first married to Sebastian Calvi? Is that it?" Jed Watkins interjected.

"Yes, to Sebastian Calvi who was... killed in an automobile crash or so I believed until very recently." Marcus' body sat crouched at the edge of the arm chair he had occupied since arriving. He repeatedly looked at the floor instead of his interrogators. Was it fatigue or was he hiding something? Watkins wondered.

Joe Farrell grabbed a handful of nuts and tossed a small portion into his mouth.

"Let's talk about Lucas Sindona and your relationship with him and his daughter Lydia."

"Lucas... Lucas was a very talented Main Line surgeon and a friend of Poulette. He died a number of years ago. I went to Harvard Medical School with his daughter, Lydia. When I found out that she was coming to Philadelphia to do research at the University of Pennsylvania, I offered her a place to stay at Edencroft with the provision that she look after Poulette... make certain she was all right. Poulette had Mr. Fox and Mrs. Perkins to care for her, but because she... she also suffers from a neurological disease, which is fatal. She needs to be watched closely by someone with medical experience, especially neurological experience. If she keeps up with her medication, she can extend her life, but nothing at this point will save it."

Jed Watkins looked up to see tears forming in Marcus' eyes. He offered him a tissue from a box on the table between them.

"We understood there was, shall we say a more intimate relationship between Poulette and Dr. Sindona; was Lucas her lover?"

Marcus looked up. "Oh God, does this really have anything to do with my stepmother and her marriage to my father? Do you really have to delve into such ... such trivia?"

"Father... Father," Jed Watkins interjected, "I'm sorry if this is difficult for you, but this is extremely important for us. Did Poulette and Dr. Lucas Sindona have a consensual and intimate relationship? "

"Yes, Poulette admitted that they did."

"Did that relationship exist from the time that she was in Switzerland?"

"Yes, it did."

"Did Lucas kill Sebastian Calvi for Poulette's sake?"

"Oh my God, No!!" Marcus looked up horrified. "As she explained it, both of them were married. When Calvi was killed in the automobile accident, she was very lonely and continued the affair with Sindona, who was practicing medicine in Switzerland at that time. Sindona did not believe in divorce. He considered himself to be a very good Catholic and never would have left his marriage. He did not offer to marry Poulette and even gave a blessing to her engagement to my father, a year or so later. She told me she did not see Lucas again until a chance meeting in Wayne sometime later; it was after we had moved to Edencroft. They met quite by accident; literally on the street in front of Aux

Petits Delices. He told her, he had decided it was time to set up his practice in the United States and ...." Marcus stopped. "... and, I guess, she decided to resume the affair they previously had. That affair lasted through the death of my father, almost ten years later. Lucas died a year or two after that."

"The jeweled lipstick cases... 18 karat gold with real stone garnishments: Where did they come from?" Joe Farrell was looking at an I Pad with notes he had taken earlier. He scrolled occasionally as if comparing answers.

"I always believed they came from my father, Cornelius Granville Barker. Poulette led me to believe they were 'little gifts from his travels'. I learned only recently that they were really from Lucas. He told her they carried some great secrets and that she must guard them with her life. I thought they were only sentimental treasures; but, very valuable because of their physical worth. In fact, I was the one who told Bertrand Fox, whom I trusted, where Poulette kept them hidden and asked him to conceal the pouch in my father's desk in his old study; which is where they were discovered after the fire, I believe."

"Director, the pizzas are here!" The intercom announcement came as a welcome relief to Marcus who found himself sweating profusely.

"Yes, please bring them in... and bring a pile of paper napkins with you!" Joe Farrell's shouted through the small speaker.

When the agent on duty had closed the door and Jed Watkins had opened the three boxes of fragrant pies, placing them on the conference table not far from the sitting area, Joe Farrell continued the questions.

"Father, these bones Leo was protecting in a linen bag, the one he handed to Agent Rawlins, what can you tell us about them?"

"Pope Leo believed them to be the bones of St. Peter which were discovered when he, Leo was a young priest and working on the archaeological dig under St. Peter's. It is a Roman necropolis which we call the Scavi today. Leo said that he had stolen the bones early on from the dig, when he was working there as a graduate student and seminarian. Sometime, not long after, he said he replaced them with the bones of.... of ... someone he had killed. I believe those bones to have been Sebastian Calvi's remains. On the day of the explosion, he said that he was trying to return the Saint's bones but, before he could do that… well, he died."

***

"Please don't tell me I'm looking well!" Jessica jested as she sat in front of the large screen in the Landstuhl Hospital Situation Room.

"Jess, you DO look surprisingly well" Jed Watkins countered. "I guess you don't need that vacation in Switzerland that the Firm offered."

"I need a vacation, but I'd rather spend it on the Main Line, Jed."

"In that case, let's get you home as fast as possible. I think you've already been notified that we have you and Alex on the transport leaving Ramstein, this evening. You'll be back home tomorrow. In the meantime, let me introduce a few people to you. I think you know Joe Farrell,"

"Yes and if I am not suffering from delusions I think I also see Father Marcus Granville Barker sitting in the chair to the side. Is that you, Marcus?"

"It is, Mrs. Rawlins. Nice to see you out of that Memores Domini uniform you have been wearing."

"Jess, Joe has a few questions for you and … well, I suppose I'll let him get started. We need to have you debriefed before you get back. There are, shall we say, insights that you may be able to give which will help us along in the process of discovering what is valid and what is not." Jed had been pacing in front of the FBI screen and now sat down.

"With my track record of finding trouble wherever I go, I think you might be better interviewing me now because God knows if we'll ever make it home. Two episodes in one day is a lot, even for me and either or both of today's incidents could have been fatal."

Jessica's tone and mood had gone South without question. Her face was completely serious.

"We honesty have no idea how Maria Scopoletti was able to infiltrate the compound and how she was able to find you, is of even more concern. Sorry about that." Jed looked directly into the camera to make his point.

"Jessica, do you remember seeing her when you were in Polsi? We have reports that she was working in the same restaurant where you were doing scullery." Jed was reviewing information on his I Pad. It was apparent that he had a report of some sort in front of him.

"The truth is, Jed. I don't know. It is perfectly possible. As you know I was the guest of Giovanna Poloni and her brother Pier Luigi. Both of them were killed.... Murdered the night I left for Rome."

"We know that, Jess, and we believe that Maria was responsible for those murders. She comes from one of the nearby towns and we have information leading us to believe that she was in Polsi when you were there and was working in some capacity at the restaurant in Polsi as well as at the inn ..."

"You mean the deserted monastery, outside of town that was used for the pre-meeting of the chieftains?" Jessica interrupted.

"Yes, the deserted monastery... do you remember her from there?"

"Well, as I told you and Director Burns the last time we spoke yesterday or the day before, I don't remember seeing her there, but that does not mean that she wasn't. If she was serving tables, considered a privilege in that society, well, I certainly would not have bumped into her. The only bumping into anyone I did was on the final day of the meeting, when I was asked to serve Roberto Lombroso's table, in the dining hall, by Lombroso himself. He quite literally had picked me up after I had been run down by a biker. I was dressed for the scullery, but Giovanna cleaned me up a bit. Gave me a fresh apron and out I went with a tray in hands. Of course, as you know I tripped and fell, spilling the tray near the chair of one of the priests. Just another incident that would have been memorable to anyone who might have thought I was not who I claimed to be. I met Maria when I checked into the Vatican to work as a member of the Memores Domini where she was my boss. Thank heavens I was rescued by Father Malcolm, otherwise she would have killed me before I even started."

"Maria, we have learned is the blood sister of an N'drangheta crime boss, as is her nephew. Her appearance in Polsi was not so much to scrub floors and serve meals, it was to weed out intruders such as yourself." Jed added. "So, she is still on the loose, I take it, since you made no mention of finding her?"

"She is still on the loose, but we'll get her, you know that."

"I do hope it is before we board the transport, I'd hate to meet her on the flight. We do not need Maria Scopoletti as a flight attendant."

"On to something else, Jess, the bone bag? The linen bag? "

"Did you find it, Jed? It is very important. It was taken from my dress pocket. Pope Leo told me it contained the bones of St. Peter himself. The bones must go back to their burial site. He had taken them from there many years ago, when they were first discovered." Jessica's eyes were tearing up as she remembered the gentle face of Leo who was dying in her lap, his fragile body crushed by the heavy stones which lay across his lower body. "Jess, we... uh, we have the bag."

"Thank God, those bones are treasured relics. Imagine, St. Peter ..."

"Stop, Jess... you know what the term bones means in underworld parlance don't you? "

"Of course, but, I'm not certain what you mean, Jed." Jessica looked through the screen into Jed's eyes, trying to interpret what he was asking of her.

"Jessica, Joe Farrell here. Have you ever heard the expression 'making one's bones? It is something that the Mafia requires of its incoming members. The term 'made' man means someone who has made his bones."

Jessica said nothing, continuing to stare into the screen at the two men standing in front of her and the priest sitting in a chair to one side.

"Of course, I've heard the term. Who hasn't? If you've seen The Godfather, you know what it means. But what has that got to do with anything? How does this relate to Pope Leo and St. Peter's bones?"

"Jess, we have examined the contents of that bag. We are doing an analysis on the contents as we speak. At this point, what was in the bag were not the bones of a saint but primary evidence of numerous murders committed by the N'drangheta over the years. The term bones in this sense means "bona fides", to establish one's credibility. This bag was filled with information about major crime figures. It was Leo's insurance against any harm ever coming to himself."

"No, no you can't mean that. He was such a kind and innocent man, a truly holy man." Jessica appeared to be abnormally troubled by the revelation.

"I'm certain he was in later years, but in his youth, he...."

"He was what? You've told me so much already, might as well tell me the rest."

"He murdered Poulette's first husband, Sebastian Calvi, a banker whose primary client was the Vatican Bank. Calvi was the original Vatican Banker. Involved with rather unsavory business deals and dealings, from what we have been able to uncover. He was among the first to successfully 'launder money' for the Vatican in the modern sense. Leo, after kidnapping him from a limousine, the driver of which had been paid to stop the limo, literally chased Calvi like an animal until he collapsed. Then, in true mafia fashion, Leo and his accomplices stuffed his pockets with bricks and hanged him from a bridge. His face and fingerprints, were marred with acid so as to be unrecognizable. Some other poor chump was burned in the so called auto accident and buried with honor in a Swiss cemetery. Poulette has always believed her husband died in the auto accident.

"Leo, probably suffering from remorse over the many crimes he had committed, at some point, decided to become a priest. He studied at the prestigious Pontifical Gregorian University the Gregoriana in Rome under the Jesuits and of course, you know the rest. He rose through the ranks to Cardinal and was elected Pope."

"Oh no. Jed, this WAS a holy man. He, he believed he was getting messages from St. Peter. Important messages."

Father Marcus Granville Barker interrupted. "Jessica, Pope Leo suffered terribly in his later years from guilt. His past, I believe caused not only his visions, but also the terrible bloody eruptions on his back, the Aramaic letters scratched on the wall next to

Peter's tomb, Simon bar Jonah or Simon, son of Jonah. What he was concealing, holding back from the world, was a guilt so deep, his soul was crying out to be heard. He could not control it, only deal with the terrible visions that haunted him over many years."

"What you are saying is that he was a murderer? Leo was a common criminal?"

"At one time, Jess. We have recovered one big haul of micro fiche dating from the days of Calvi's demise... all of it in that little bag of bones you retrieved from the dying Leo.

"...and from Father Marcus, we also have another haul of micro fiche found in Poulette's lipstick cases... jeweled 18 karat lipstick cases."

"What in the world are those all about?" Jessica looked totally confused.

"They contained microfiche with some very specific information, including names, of crimes committed by an array of international crime syndicate members, many of whom are still alive. This information was collected by Dr. Lucas Sindona, who of course knew Leo as an up and coming killer in Switzerland. Sindona, as a physician became very wealthy over the years tending to members of crime families, as well as Sebastian Calvi, the Vatican's favorite banker and his beautiful wife Poulette."

"Did I hear you right...The Dr. Lucas Sindona?" Jessica voice rose an octave at the latter.

"Yes, it seems he was aware of the assassination of Poulette's first husband because he had befriended them. It seems he befriended Poulette in a more salacious way. Later, when Calvi died or was murdered, and although he was quite married, he increased his friendship with the widow and he provided her with among many other things, a collection of exquisite 18 karat jeweled lipstick cases, asking her to guard them carefully until sometime in the future. She knew they were valuable, for more than their perceived beauty, but she probably had no idea exactly what Lucas Sindona was really up to.

"Poulette's butler, Bertrand Fox had been a connected man, who over the years became concerned that he might be implicated in whatever secrets Lucas Sindona had entrusted to Poulette. Things became exceptionally dicey for him when Lydia showed up and seemed to be trying to find the "gifts" to Poulette from her father. Fox wasn't certain exactly what kind of gifts Lucas had used to hide his secrets, but he knew Poulette kept her special treasures locked away at first in a drawer of her vanity and later on a shelf in her closet. When Marcus asked Fox to take charge of those 'treasures,' fearing that Lydia Sindona might be after them, Mr. Fox saw it as an opportunity to delve into the gifts and find out for himself how he might preserve whatever information could be utilized to his best benefit and destroy what might be …."

Jed stopped mid-sentence. "Jess, we will have to continue this when you get back. I believe we have incoming information about Bernadette Perkins, Poulette's long time housekeeper. Her body has just been discovered in a snow bank at St. David's cemetery.

***

Father Marcus Granville Barker had grabbed the last slice of cold pizza from the box as he was leaving Joe Farrell's Villanova-based FBI office.

"I'll be at the Monastery, if you need to speak to me further." Marcus did not shake hands with Jed or Joe, but nodded instead. His eyes were deeply shadowed, showing the emotional pressure and grinding fatigue he was enduring. Farrell hoped he would not have to call the priest again.

When the inner office door closed, Joe Farrell poured himself another drink and refilled Jed Watkins' as well.

"We know where Lombroso is. That hideout of his isn't really a secret. Interpol has been watching his movements via satellite for the last few weeks…." Watkins stopped in mid-sentence. "…getting to him and having Interpol serve him so that he can be taken into custody, well that is another matter. That island, its people are very clannish in the most elementary sense. His house is impenetrable. No one gets to him and I do mean no one, unless he has asked to see them."

"So, what do you intend to do?" Farrell sat down again and grabbed another handful of mixed nuts from the wooden bowl on the table.

"Wait, patience can be a great virtue. We want this guy alive. He has information that can be very valuable. Killing him would solve nothing and would not help to add to our information about the 'Ndrangheta."

"In other words, you are calling off the hunt?" Farrell asked.

"For the time being. He'll be back in the nited States one of these days. He'll also be in Canada. His position hasn't changed.

"What about the Vatican Bank and those..." Farrell did not finish his sentence.

"Those involved are already being taken care of. The Church is an amazing institution.... Very ancient rituals as well as beliefs with often archaic, but effective means of getting rid of people." Watkins had a smidgen of a smile on his face.

"I know, Joe, don't ask. Repenting for one's sins can sometimes be brutal. I'm sure the governing Cardinals will make certain that appropriate penance is prescribed for those who have erred and want to meet their maker free of sin."

***

It was 10:45 p.m. according to the chiming grandfather clock in the foyer of the Monastery. Father Marcus Granville Barker walked quickly and took the staircase to his quarters on the third floor. The corridor was dark, but the sound of voices could be heard coming from the suite located almost directly across from his.

"Father, you're back. How is your dear mother?" The inquiry was coming from Cardinal Luca Franconi, head of the Apostolic Camera whose large frame had found a chair that suited his portly figure.

"Yes, please do come in and have a night cap with us, Father," Austin Cheney agreed rising from his place on the sofa and tending to his guest by dropping two ice cubes into a crystal a tumbler and filling the glass to the brim with Scotch. "Paul has already bowed out. This entire episode has been pretty stressful for him; this isn't typical University President activity."

"Thanks," Marcus answered as he accepted the badly needed drink and dropped his trench coat on a chair near the door.

"Well, she's awake, but the prognoses remains the same. I'd probably have to say that she has a very short time with us. The most recent MRI which was done a couple of days ago indicates the disease has progressed; there is nothing medically I nor anyone else can do to slow it at this point." Marcus spoke in a monotone, his face drained of color.

"Have you been at the hospital all this time?" Cardinal Franconi asked pouring himself another Scotch from the now nearly empty bottle.

"No, no, the FBI invited me to visit them to... to relate... my experiences in Italy."

Marcus' voice was soft but the pauses in his speech were noted by everyone present.

"What did they want to know, my dear boy?" Cardinal Franconi appeared concerned.

"They wanted me to sit in on a meeting with someone else, someone who had been in the Vatican at the same time Sean and I were there. In fact, someone who was there when his Holiness died."

"... and what did you tell them?" Cardinal Franconi sat back in his chair.

"The truth; I told them everything I could."

Franconi took another sip from his glass. "We can do this in private, if you prefer, Father Marcus, but we too have questions which need answers. Shall we continue this discussion in your quarters, or....?"

"No, stop, Eminence, I'm happy to discuss anything you wish among all of you. I have nothing to hide."

"Son, I am certain there is a good explanation for this but, I have failed to come up with one," Cardinal Josef Galleini, chair of the Administration of the Patrimony of the Holy See who had been sitting silently in the near darkness of the Provincial's small suite. Now, he sat forward. His face stern in the shadow of the single bulb floor lamp that lit the area near his chair. His voice, foreboding in its quiet insistence on getting an answer.

"This past autumn on your way to the Vatican, you made a stop in Toronto, Canada where you had dinner with Roberto Lombroso and Monsignor Auguste Rosario, aide de camp to Cardinal Torricelli, head of the Vatican Bank."

"Yes, sir I did, at Scaramouche."

"You arrived empty handed but were seen leaving the restaurant with an attaché case; this case, you delivered to a committee in the Vatican when you arrived."

"Yes, Eminence, I did that, as well."

"And have you any idea of what you were delivering in that case or why?"

"No sir, again I was asked to do it and I did it. Monsignor Rosario has been a friend of mine as well as a mentor for many years. As you must know, I was assigned to work in the Toronto Diocese for a little over six years. Monsignor had been my superior during that time. Monsignor Rosario told me he had heard that I was going on a long term assignment to the Holy See and wondered if I would do him a favor and deliver the case personally to one of the cardinals. Of course I said yes. I had no reason to ask any questions about the contents of the case. I wasn't stealing anything. And, of course I never would have considered opening it." He paused for several seconds. "I did not open the case, Cardinal."

"... and when you arrived at the Vatican, you delivered the case; then, what happened?" Lucas Franconi's voice raised its volume above the soft spoked Galleini.

"I brought it into a conference room as I was directed. There were a lot of ... well not a lot, but perhaps eight or nine Cardinals sitting around a table. I did not recognize the Cardinal who sat at the head of the table. It might have been Torricelli. He opened the case while I was in the room. The top of the open case was toward me so that I would have no way of seeing what was inside. He then said I should leave... I was dismissed. Essentially, he made it clear that he wanted me out of there and promptly. "

"That's it? Nothing more you can add to all of that?" Galleini asked.

Marcus was thoughtful. "Only, that I sensed someone watching the entire scene; it was as if, I intuited a hidden bystander viewing all of this from behind this great modern style screen on the wall. I thought I heard the rustle of silk as well."

The room was totally silent for several minutes. Outside the tower bells from St. Edmund's church on campus tolled 11:00

p.m. Marcus Granville Barker had the peculiar feeling they tolled for him.

Chapter 63

Police Lt. Melinda Reynolds lifted the sheet from the corpse lying on the gurney. "Have you called Dr. Hayes Whitfield, the coroner? He may want to have the body picked up immediately." Melinda Reynolds hated weekend duty. It was a Friday night and she knew no one would be available, including the very social Hayes Whitfield, who had the cell phone number of every available widow on the Main Line. Police Sergeant Todd Freedman had an inkling where he might be found and had already called an unlisted very private number that only a few privileged individuals were privy to have.

"Dr. Whitfield? Yes, this is Sergeant Todd Freedman from the Radnor police... yes sir, it is important. We have located and retrieved the body of Bernadette Perkins. Yes, sir, Perkins was the housekeeper at Edencroft. We could not locate her after the fire. Yes, sir, unfortunately, she is very dead and... and Lt. Melinda Reynolds who is on duty this evening asked that I tell you, she is frozen stiff, sir. Yes, like a side of beef. No sir, I was not being irreverent... only that she really is frozen solid. Yes, I understand you're at dinner. Our question, sir is what to do with her? We can take her to Wally Stuard at the funeral home, but... do you want her to stay.... Damn, he hung up on me." Freedman put the phone back into his pocket. "I'll call Wally Stuard. Let him decide whether she should be thawed out or not."

Postlude

Patricia "Poulette" Granville-Barker's funeral was a major social event on the Main Line. She died in early March, after spending nearly three weeks in a semi-conscious state and finally lapsing into a coma and succumbing five days later. Marcus had kept a personal vigil until the end, often sleeping in a chair or on the sofa in the small but elegantly appointed room at Bryn Mawr Terrace. Poulette had made her peace with God, confessing to Father Sean O'Reilly during one of his visits. However, it was to Marcus, the special privilege of administering the Last Rites was given. He was certain he felt her hand squeeze his as he gave her a final kiss goodbye on her cheek at the end of the Sacrament.

Now, ten days later, extended family and friends gathered at The Anglican-Catholic (Episcopal) Church of St, Michael the Archangel and presented their invitations to the ushers at the closed service. There was only a single pew on the right side of the aisle assigned to Poulette's immediate family which might have included only Marcus had he not invited his Edmundite family of Roman Catholic priests, Father Sean O'Reilly, Father Paul Sullivan and Father Austin Cheney to attend.

The appearance of the Catholic priests did not go unnoticed by the assembly of matrons representing a long line of genealogical societies, who sat opposite the clergy, in pews that carried modest but highly visible placards with their societies' crests and names on them. Poulette had been a member of all of them: The Mayflower Society, Daughters of the American Revolution, Colonial Dames, Daughters of The Cincinnati, U.S. Daughters of 1812 and others, totaling six rows of pews to the left of the center aisle.

Jessica and Alex arrived with Philip and Caroline. It was Philip's first outing since his accident and although he used a hand carved walking stick with a silver handle to maneuver his now slender physique, his gait was strong and his speech surprisingly clear. On his way to a seat, he stopped so often to speak to so many people, the usher escorting the family, finally had to insist, they take their seats.

Jessica had not fully recovered. Her complexion was pale; she appeared to be tired, almost listless. Alex still bore the remnants of cuts and bruises on his face and hands caused by the explosion.

The family had only been seated a few moments when Marcus left his pew to approach Jessica.

"Thank you for coming." His smile was authentic and infectious. Jessica found herself smiling back. "I don't know if I'll have a chance to speak with you later at the Cricket Club reception, but I wanted to thank you for everything." He paused for several seconds and reached for her hand."... And I DO mean everything. You probably read in the papers that Pope Leo is being considered for an early canonization. There already have been two reports of miracles, both involving children, cured of nervous disorders. In light of these cures, our new Pope Gregory XVI, Cardinal Josef Galleini, who was chair of the Administration of the Patrimony of the Holy See, has decided to hasten the process. Perhaps to wipe away the rather scurrilous media reports that have come along after his passing. Our new Holy Father wishes to invite you and your husband to the canonization. It would be a thank you for the service you provided during the dark and final days of Pope Leo's life."

Jessica took a deep breath and placed her hand on Marcus arm. "Alex and I wouldn't miss it. I understand that Maria Scopoletti has been located in Argentina and Interpol has her in custody; but the bones, St. Peter's real bones, were they ever recovered?" Jessica's voice was a whisper. She looked up and into Marcus' eyes.

"They were never gone, Jessica, They had never been removed."

"But... I thought," Jessica countered.

"I know, some things will have to remain a mystery. I don't know if in his last days Leo really comprehended what he was doing and if in some muddled way he interposed his wishes and hopes with a certain brand of reality which only he understood."

There was no more to be said. Wally Stuard was standing behind Marcus, a signal that the procession of the casket was about to begin. The organ began its prelude: Henry Purcell's Music for the funeral of Queen Mary. Jessica turned for a moment to see the fully seated church. It was majestic music that suited Poulette, she thought.

The procession moved slowly; in Jessica's eyes almost in slow motion. Marcus, his face somber, his head bent, strode to one side of the polished mahogany coffin, a spray of pink and white roses lay atop the white silk brocade pall. Behind the casket, Marcus marched, followed by the Episcopal Bishop of Pennsylvania. Robert Benjamin Wickham, two retired bishops and the Rector of St. Michael the Archangel, Father Louis Morgan Stratham. Poulette would be pleased, she imagined. It was the very vision of how she would want to bid her farewell, elegant but far from understated, with just that touch of dissonance.

"Oh Poulette, how you will be missed!"

~~~~~~~~~

Meet our author
Barbara K. Clement

There are few women anywhere, who have experienced a life and career(s) as exciting and challenging as has the author of the *Main Liners Mysteries Series,* Barbara K. Clement. Growing up in the Mid-West where she attended the University of Minnesota, completing her degree-studies in 3 years, she continued on for a fourth academic year to work as the only undergraduate research assistant to the renowned psychologist, Dr. Stanley Schacter who was completing his oft quoted study on *The Effects of Emotional Manipulation upon Industrial Productivity.*

Upon graduation, she began her professional life as an Intelligence Officer for the U.S. Government and went on to become a syndicated columnist for the *Newhouse National News Service and the Chicago Sun Times/ Daily News Wire Service,* working directly for publishing scion, Sam Newhouse. Her lively fashion/lifestyle column appeared in more than 150 Newspapers throughout the United States. She also served as a Foreign Correspondent for two years covering European news for the wire services from a home in Amsterdam and the Conde Nast Offices in the Palais de Bourbon in Paris. Moving back to New York, she went on to join Leslie Fay Inc., a multi-faceted fashion company as its Corporate Vice President. During her time as a Newhouse columnist she had interviewed Mrs. Estee Lauder, founder of the prestigious cosmetic firm; Mrs. Lauder, was impressed and hired Barbara to work for Estee Lauder International, as Vice President for Estee Lauder International Public Relations, responsible for communication with the press et al in more than 150 countries, including numerous clients, still behind the Iron Curtain, where Lauder cosmetics were being sold.

Eventually, she was persuaded to move to the *Philadelphia Main Line,* with and by her husband, Charles F. Clement 3rd, whose family's roots dated back to the Revolution and where she took on the position of Asst. V. P., Public Affairs for the celebrated Villanova University.

She retired from Villanova, located in Villanova, PA. a little over a decade ago to begin a new career writing novels. *Visions* is the 6th installment in the highly successful *Main Liners Mysteries* series which delves into secretive associations of even the most privileged in this historic environ outside of Philadelphia. It is here that family roots still rule and many, many enigmas are being hidden in the dark realms of the heart and conscience.

www.ingramcontent.com/pod-product-compliance
Lightning Source LLC
Chambersburg PA
CBHW070052030726
47506CB00002B/434